RACHEL L. SCHADE

EMPIRE OF DRAGONS

CURSED EMPIRE 1

RACHEL L. SCHADE

EMPIRE OF DRAGONS

CURSED EMPIRE 1

DRAGON SHADOW
PUBLISHING

Cover & map design by MoorBooks Design

Interior design created with Canva

ISBN 978-1-7364856-0-6

www.rachelschadeauthor.com

OTHER BOOKS BY RACHEL L. SCHADE

Silent Kingdom Series

Silent Kingdom (Book 1)

Forsaken Kingdom (Book 2)

Broken Kingdom (Book 3)

*For anyone who fights battles the world never sees.
You're strong. You're brave. You're not alone. You'll make it.*

PRONUNCIATION GUIDE

People

Lo'laeni (LO-lane-ee)
Nolanhou (No-LAWN-hu)
Jaliana (JAY-lee-ahn-uh)
Kovi (KOH-vee)
Ettonou (ETT-uh-new)
Caesiem (KAY-see-um)
Pauni'a (PAWN-ee-uh)
O'emia (OH-em-ee-uh)
Wilvhe (WILL-vay)
Mio'e (MEE-oh-ay)
Naina (NAYN-uh)
Karye (KAR-yay)
Yaelti (YAYL-tee)
Leanai (Lee-AN-i)
Marukio (Muh-ROO-kee-oh)

Locations

Alrenor (Al-REN-or),
Alrenian (Al-REN-ee-uhn)
Forwyth (For-WITH),
Forwyn (For-WIN)
Teramyl (TARE-uh-mill),
Teramese (TARE-uh-meez)
Inalgoth (I-NEEL-goth)

Other

Ryke (RY-kee)
Elhani (Ell-HAN-ee)
Nesrelle (NEZ-rell)
Vylae (Vill-AY)
Kowra (KOW-ruh)
Hilvoku (Hill-VOH-ku)
Ahnla (ON-luh)

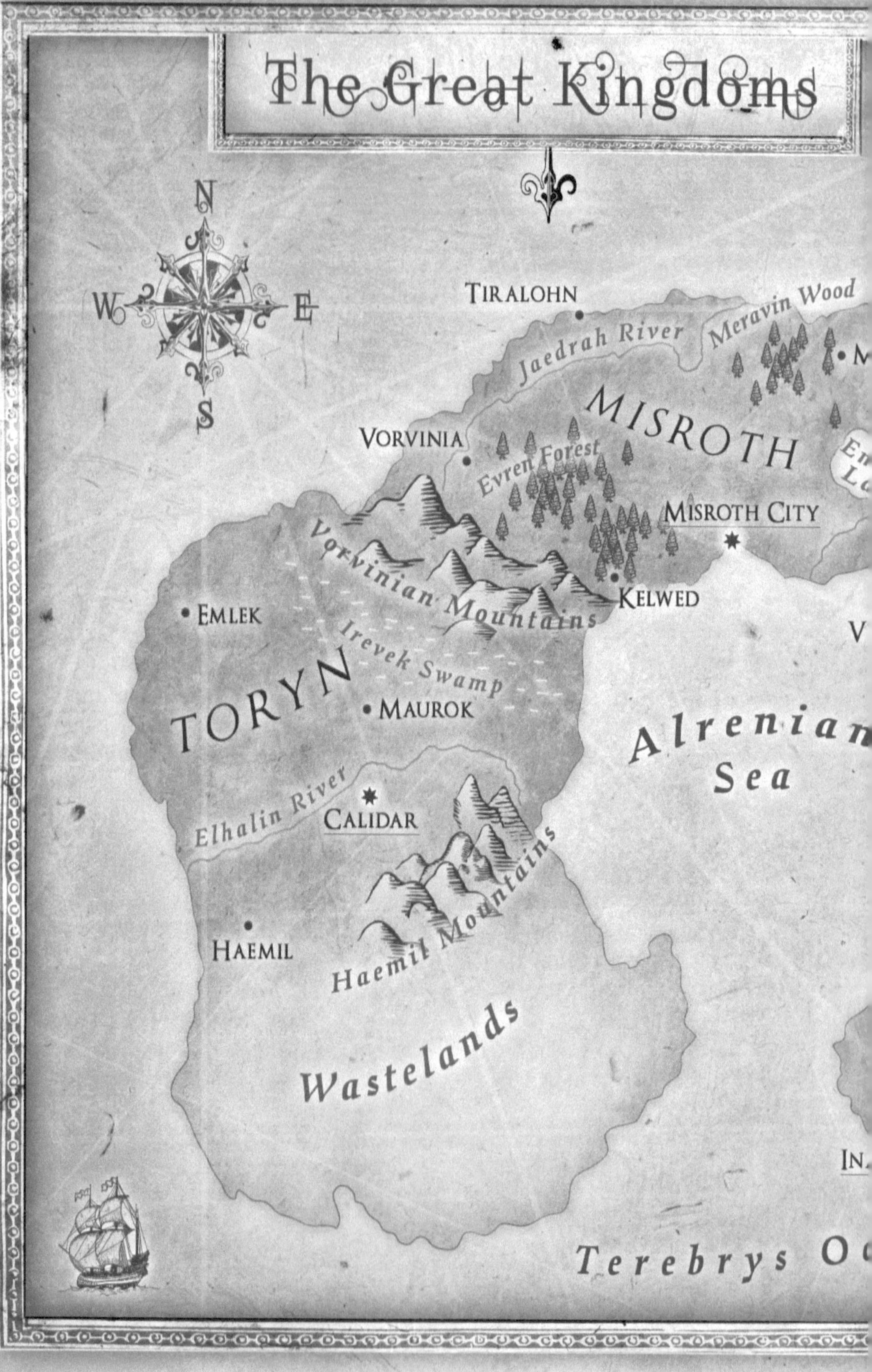

The Great Kingdoms
N
W
E
S
TIRALOHN
Jaedrah River
Meravin Wood
VORVINIA
MISROTH
Evren Forest
MISROTH CITY
EMLEK
Vorvinian Mountains
KELWED
Irevek Swamp
TORYN
MAUROK
Alrenian
Sea
Elhalin River
CALIDAR
Haemil Mountains
HAEMIL
Wastelands
Terebrys Oc

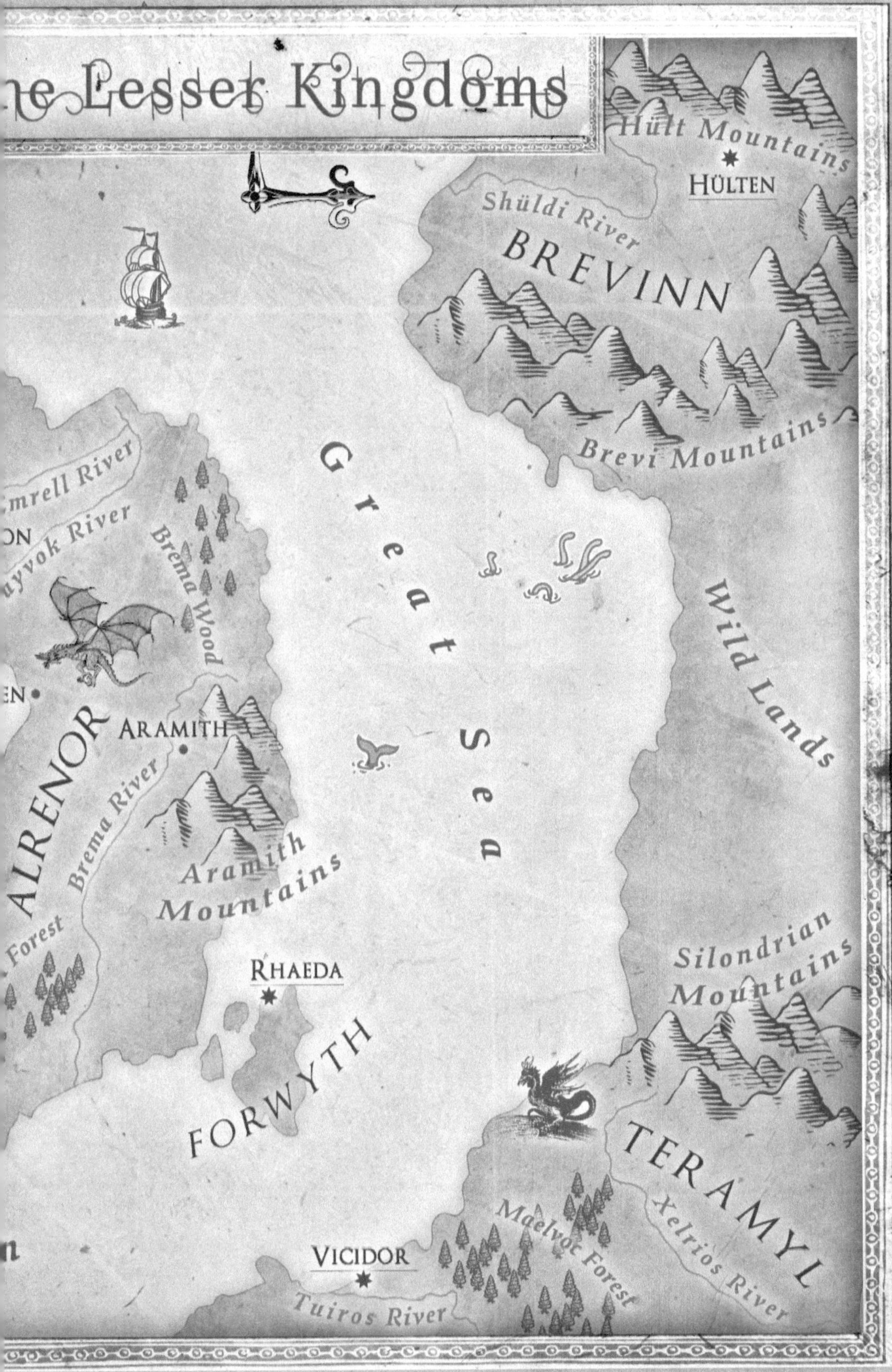

The Lesser Kingdoms
Hült Mountains
HÜLTEN
Shüldi River
BREVINN
Brevi Mountains
Emrell River
Tayvok River
Brema Wood
Great Sea
Wild Lands
ALRENOR
ARAMITH
Brema River
Aramith Mountains
Forest
Silondrian Mountains
RHAEDA
FORWYTH
TERAMYL
Xelrios River
VICIDOR
Maelvor Forest
Tuiros River

PROLOGUE

Jaliana of Alrenor, Daughter of Empress Karye

BEFORE I WAS OLD ENOUGH to ride the dragons or imagine a world without her in it, Mother would tell me stories about our magnificent creatures. They were such a source of honor and pride for the Alrenian people that my mother happily obliged, even when I requested a story at an inconvenient time. It didn't matter when it was or where we were, not in those early days. She always had time for our dragon stories. For me.

In the mornings, when she spent hours at the arena watching her Dragon Keepers train and perform before mounting her own dragon, I'd be beside her. She'd laugh when my mouth dropped open in awe as a dragon dove off the nearby cliff's edge and swooped low over the glistening city far below. As if we shared a secret, she'd nudge me and brush a strand of hair as golden as hers behind my ear.

During the day, I took walks with her throughout the palace grounds or sat with her at court. Each night, she'd tuck me into my bed with a lullaby, kissing my forehead tenderly. "Sweet dreams, my strong and fearless one," she'd say, always with the same adoring smile on her lips. And throughout it all, no matter what we were doing, I was always asking for her stories.

The stories varied somewhat. Sometimes Mother told me about a great Alrenian conquest with a dragon, other times she related the origin of the dragons entering Alrenor, and still others she explained how the first Dragon Keepers came into being. But some aspects of our story ritual always stayed the same.

"Tell me a dragon story," I'd whisper, whether I was watching a dragon soar overhead or plucking a flower in the gardens or struggling to keep my eyes open as I snuggled under my covers.

Mother's eyes would shine, delighted that I loved the beasts as much as she did. "The dragons first came across the Great Sea from Teramyl," she began, "where they live wild and free. A greedy Teramese merchant thought he could convince the Alrenian Emperor Vilrev to give up a large portion of his treasure or some land for a pair of dragon eggs.

"But the merchant knew little of dragons, which went untamed in Teramyl, often attacking its people and burning its cities. He miscalculated, and not long before he docked in Alrenor, the eggs hatched.

"The dragons were male and female, one with pure gold scales as bright as the Alrenian sun, and the other with scales every color imaginable, glistening in the light like a rainbow. At first, they were small and almost harmless, living off rats aboard the ship and scraps of jerky the sailors fed them.

"Of course, young dragons grow swiftly, and by the time the merchant went before the emperor, the dragons had wingspans as long as a man is tall. They were much more dangerous then, and the merchant, both terrified for his safety and afraid of losing them, had his sailors chain the animals. They guided them like dogs on leashes before the emperor."

"But that was worse," I interrupted. I almost always did when Mother told this particular tale, because it led to one of the best parts of the story.

"Yes," my mother would respond with a nod. "The dragons snapped and snarled, severely burning one man and almost tearing off the arm of another. When the merchant bowed before Emperor Vilrev, those of his men who hadn't fled were quaking in fear."

"And dragons can smell fear," I said with my mother. We always quoted that part together, no matter whatever else varied about the tale she told, because there was always some mention of this in every single dragon story.

"Their fear only fueled the dragons' hunger, because when a young dragon is growing, it is always hungry. Always restless. Smoke curled from their noses as Emperor Vilrev and his court looked on in fascination. The dragons tugged at their chains and studied the people about them hungrily.

"'Why have these beautiful beasts been chained and dragged before me like slaves?' Emperor Vilrev demanded of the merchant.

"Thinking himself clever and smooth, the merchant said, 'These creatures are beautiful, but powerful and dangerous. I did not want to risk Your Imperial Highness's safety.'

"He'd hardly finished his words when he was devoured in a burst of fire. Both dragons had tired of their chains. They'd yanked until they'd broken free, and the first thing they did was destroy their unfit master, who had never appreciated them and had never been their equal in power or grace."

This was where my favorite part came in.

"The merchant's men fled screaming in terror, leaving the merchant himself to burn to ash in the throne room. Emperor Vilrev and his Alrenian court, however, were unintimidated. Vilrev strode toward the dragons and subdued them. In him, they found someone powerful enough to control them. Someone they could follow."

"Did he use the scent of the vylae plant to calm them?" I often asked, even though I'd heard the story many times and knew the answer. Our storytelling had a rhythm, almost like a dance, one that I dared never break.

"This was before the Alrenians knew that vylae could be anything other than a deadly poison," Mother answered. "Vilrev was a great man, fearless and fierce enough to tame dragons even without the help of the vylae's power to calm them. Some say he had a gift with animals—perhaps he did. The stories are old now, so who can say for sure?"

Then she grinned at me, and I always grinned back. "But what we can know for certain is that those two dragons became the first royal Alrenian dragons, living within the Dragon Keep. They started a line of dragons that remains strong to this day, one that is tied to the empire's strength."

We always said the final part together too, because it was a well-known saying often quoted throughout the palace.

"Whoever controls Alrenor's dragons, controls Alrenor."

CHAPTER ONE

Lo'laeni Nolanhou

BY NOW, I WAS USED to the anger flowing through me, hot and heady, like a shot of Naina's whiskey when I was sick. My veins lit with fire and every one of my muscles thrummed with adrenaline. As familiar as it was, it never lost its thrill, the way it filled me with strength and focus in a way nothing else did.

The pounding in my ears was my only rallying cry as I slammed my fist into the arrogant young man's face. Blood spurting from his nose, he snarled and lunged for me, but I ducked away. In the same motion, I swung the heel of my sandal into the back of his knee, and he collapsed to the cobblestones in a grunting heap.

"*Filkni kowra!*" he shouted, his Alrenian curse garbled by his swollen nose.

Smirking, I considered hurling some insults back at him in my own language, knowing he would have never stooped to sully his refined Alrenian mind with learning the Forwyn tongue. But my smarting knuckles, decorated with his blood, were satisfying enough, and I couldn't risk lingering. No matter this man's crimes, he would have more allies in these streets, and I refused to be caught.

Slipping from the shadows of the alley, I was gone before he could stagger to his feet and pursue me. My heart calmed to a peaceful rhythm as I clutched the torn strand of braided ribbons the man had ripped from around my neck. Unshed tears burned the back of my throat, but I refused to cry. I gave myself one moment to cradle the shimmering gold ribbons before shoving them in my pocket. On the streets of Inalgoth, capital of Alrenor, I couldn't be distracted or let down my guard.

I shuffled into the crowds milling through the wide street, taking in the sights and sounds of this city I both loved and hated. A city I'd lived in for all of my eighteen years. Everywhere haughty, gold-skinned Alrenians stared down their noses at me, still living under the delusion that they were somehow better than any other race. They were dressed in their usual finery: brightly dyed linen dresses and flashing jewelry for the women, and trousers, loose shirts, and vests for the men.

My dark skin and braided hair made me an easy target, fairly screaming my identity as a Forwyn—or, as they often preferred to call us, an infidel. A member of a race who worshipped Elhani rather than their god, the Giver of Life. And the simple clothes I wore in shades of grey, the ones that identified me as a Forwyn nun, only made me a greater object of their derision.

As I passed, one Alrenian man shoved me, hard, and I almost plowed into an Alrenian woman who stared at me like I was a molding pile of food on her plate. I staggered back to the sound of the man's cruel laughter.

Gritting my teeth, I lost myself among the strollers and shoppers, passing the rows of storefronts, all constructed from white stone and gleaming golden in the warm afternoon sunlight. I wound my way through the streets, pushing toward home. Occasionally a gurgling fountain fashioned in the shape of a dragon or an old imperial ruler interrupted the flow of the streets, and people lingered near, sitting or standing beside the water as they talked or tossed breadcrumbs to the gulls. Here and there, vendors with wares of fresh produce, fine clothes, freshly roasted meat, and pastries called out to the passersby from their tables set outside the shops. The mingling scents of food, saltwater from the two nearby seas, and horse manure from the horse-drawn carriages were chaotic, just like the capital of Alrenor often was in many other aspects.

I crossed a bridge spanning a channel of the Great Sea and breathed a sigh of relief as I left the crowded central streets and entered a quieter district of the capital. The Vayelta District, the one I called home. Though the sun was still high in the sky, my empty stomach growled at the thought of dinner back at the abbey. After braving the sticky heat of summer and the jostling city crowds most of the day, I was also eager to steal a few moments for myself in the cool solace of my bedroom.

Rounding a corner, I spotted home and increased my pace. The abbey that housed the Circle of Serenity was, shockingly, an old, abandoned Alrenian temple dedicated to worshipping their god and studying the war gift they admired so much. But generations ago, according to legend, the Forwyn god Elhani cursed Alrenor for enslaving the Forwyn people, and most of the old Alrenian gifts had disappeared. Temples once dedicated to learning about and practicing the various supernatural gifts were left to fall into disrepair, hollow shells of the glorious, shining buildings they'd once been.

To me, it served the Alrenians right for their greed and bloodshed, and I couldn't help the warm smugness that always perched in my chest whenever I swung open one of the heavy, carved double doors and stepped into the shadows of our abbey. It was fitting that a place once sacred to the race that had tormented my people was now a sacred place to Forwyn nuns.

The musical lilt of Naina's voice fluttered in the air, mingling with the tantalizing scent of baking bread. I scurried down the hall, the polished stone floor making every footstep echo. Even now, I couldn't ignore the faded paintings adorning the walls—all depicting bloody scenes of Alrenian conquests and victories supposedly granted by their god. Hungry as I was, my stomach still gave a nauseous lurch at the sight of bodies strewn before Alrenian warriors, clothed in shimmering dragon scale armor.

Leaving the entry passage behind, I flew through the spacious sanctuary, where broken windows let in a flood of balmy air and sunlight, and pressed on toward the stairwell leading down to the lower level. In the kitchen, Naina smiled and continued to sing a traditional Forwyn song as she lingered by the oven from which the scent of baking bread wafted.

Mother Naina was an older woman, her kindly face etched in wrinkles and her hair an elegant shade of silvery grey. Not a single one of her braids was unadorned with a colorful ribbon, because—as she liked to say—at her age, she'd seen and done everything. As our leader, I'd always admired her for her wisdom and knowledge, but as a fellow nun, I loved her for her gentleness and kindness. She insisted we all refer to her simply by her given name, Naina, rather than the formal title of Mother, but in my mind, she embodied everything a mother should be.

My mouth watered. Self-consciously, I pressed a hand to my aching jaw. The result of the only punch the man had managed to get past my defenses before I'd landed him on the ground. Once Naina turned around, there would be no hiding the injury, which I could tell from the touch was beginning to swell painfully. I thought again of my torn necklace of ribbons and blinked back the urge to tear up.

"Naina?" I asked, watching as she reached for some drying herbs hanging from the rafters overhead.

"Welcome back, Lo. I figured I could get an early start on dinner," she responded without turning around. "How did your rounds go?"

The poor family I'd brought food had been overjoyed to see me. But I'd lost the empty food basket on my way home when the Alrenian man had accosted me. Naina wouldn't be thrilled about that. We ourselves had little in the way of material possessions to spare in the abbey. Not many Forwyn people had much money to donate to us and our cause.

"The Ilyanii family is well," I said lamely as I plopped onto the table. It was huge, long enough to seat every woman in the abbey during the meals for which we all gathered together.

"Lo, how many times have I told you not to sit there?" Naina scolded, swatting me with a dishcloth as she turned around. But her gaze snagged on my jaw and her arm paused mid-swing. Eyes narrowing, she asked, "What happened?" as if she suspected I'd been the one to start the fight.

"A *filkni* Alrenian tried to destroy my ribbons," I spat, drawing the ruined necklace from my pocket to show her. "And then he punched me."

Naina set her hands on her hips. "What do you think you're doing, using language like that in my abbey? Do you think simply because you cursed in Alrenian, I will excuse it?"

My cheeks flushed with heat and I stared at my feet, where I swung them as I continued to sit on the table. "Forgive me, Naina," I murmured. "I'll do penance tonight."

Naina rolled her eyes. "Elhani help me," she sighed. "It's not about doing penance over and over. It's not even about the words you're using. It's about the anger simmering inside you." She stepped forward, and despite the harshness of her tone, her fingers were gentle as she tipped my face to inspect my injury.

Impatient, I brushed her hand away. It was a little disconcerting to have her this close to me when my ribbons weren't around my neck, hiding my scar.

No one at the abbey knew about my past—we didn't even share our last names with one another, claiming we were all part of one family now. But sometimes I wondered if my sisters had suspicions, if they knew I'd once been a slave in the palace, if they suspected I could be the one whose name the Alrenians cursed. *Amara'rekni,* the Alrenians called me in their language. Empress-Slayer.

Everyone knew of me, even if no one knew who the *amara'rekni* was. If my fellow sisters found out, would they look at me differently? See me as guilty and bloody, the way I saw myself?

"It's nothing," I said. "And—I know. It's just so hard not to be angry."

The corners of her mouth upturned, just a little. "I never said you couldn't be angry, did I?" she asked. "But I worry about you when you have no purpose for that anger."

I curled my fingers together in my lap. "I train and I run," I protested. "I fight better than most of the sisters here, and I've helped so many Forwyn in the city when the Alrenians have treated them poorly." I smiled slowly. "And I knocked that man to the ground for what he did to me."

Naina furrowed her brow at me and shook her head. "That wasn't what I meant, *ahnla,*" she said, her voice turning soft the way it did whenever she was spouting words of philosophical wisdom.

She held out her hand to me, and with another sigh, I dropped my broken braid of gold ribbons into her palm. No one else wore ribbons this frayed and old without replacing them, but Naina and the others had never pestered me. They could tell they were an important memento from my past, and they respected it. Especially given the color the ribbons were.

In Forwyn tradition, ribbons represented pieces of our lives.

Women preferred to wear their symbolic ribbons styled into their hair or around their necks. Men most often wore them on their wrists or necks—though some wore their hair long to show off their ribbons too. And gold ribbons were especially important to us, since they stood for lost loved ones. They were tokens to remind us that our loved ones had gone to Elhani's arms, to live in the Golden After.

My gold ribbons had been gifted to me the same night I'd slain Empress Karye. Then, foreigners from the kingdom of Misroth had been visiting, trying in vain to establish an alliance with the proud Alrenians. Instead, their negotiations had devolved into threats and secrecy. During that time I'd bonded with the Misrothian princess, who had taught me the first fighting skills I'd ever learned, and in return, I'd helped her tame one of the dragons.

When Karye had discovered our plans, I'd thought it was the end—of hope for my new Misrothian friends, and of my own life. And then…when the moment came, I'd saved my life, freed my people, and taken my revenge for all the atrocities Karye had committed.

I hadn't thought killing a monster would sear me with guilt, and yet, it had. In an attempt to comfort me, one of the Misrothian women had gifted me my gold ribbons. She'd taken ribbons from her own outfit, braiding them together and tying them around my neck, since my hair had been shorn to show my status as a slave. As a foreigner, the woman hadn't known what the gold represented to my people. Maybe it had been a happy coincidence, or maybe Elhani's hand had been in the gift.

For an instant, the memories tugged at my mind: my body coated in sweat and someone else's blood, my heart pulsing with relief and horror. The taste of my tears streaming into my mouth as I wept. The soothing humming of the Misrothian as she'd braided the ribbons together and tied them around my neck. Though that night—the night my people had finally wrested control of the palace and broken free of slavery—had only been three years ago, it often felt like a lifetime had passed since then. Other times, like now, it felt like only moments had gone by.

Naina scanned the frayed edges of the torn ribbons intently. "I think I could attach some string to each end so you can wear it again."

Suddenly overcome with emotion, I nodded, not trusting my voice.

Even though we discussed the topic often, I couldn't help the sigh and the weary words that tumbled from my lips. "Why do the Alrenians hate us?" I grumbled. The question was more rhetorical, borne of my frustration toward the man who'd torn my ribbons and assaulted me.

As always, Naina was calm and practical, immediately taking this moment as a chance to teach me. "First, they don't *all* hate us. I've met some kind Alrenians, *ahnla*, as rare as that may seem. Including my former master, may he rest in Elhani's embrace, who spent his final years freeing me and trying to teach his fellow Alrenians the way of truth and peace." She smiled gently. "And the others? They are a proud race, believing they are Chosen of their god. They resent that we are Elhani's Chosen People, that our god gives us powerful magic. That we can hear his voice, singing and speaking all around us and within us." She shrugged. "Many people all around the world hate others for being different from them. Whether they speak or act or look unlike them—it doesn't matter. Some people hate what they do not understand. But…in this case, I think the Alrenians hate what threatens them."

"They enslaved our people for over two hundred years," I said bitterly. "I don't feel like we threaten them enough. Even now, when we control the Alrenian government and the dragons, the Alrenians are still hurting us in the streets."

Naina studied me gravely. "They lash out because they're angry and afraid."

"Do you think the hatred will ever stop?" I pressed a hand to my jaw, thinking of how the Alrenian man had sprung on me, shoving me into an alley and attacking me. Simply because I was Forwyn.

"Maybe," Naina said softly. "But it must stop with us first. We who are dedicated to Elhani must be the stronger and braver people, the ones to work to make a difference." She shot me another grin. "Now get off my table so I can prepare this meal!"

She shooed me out the back door playfully, toward the abbey's walled-in yard. It was just as well she'd sent me outside—the multitude of feelings rushing through me had changed my mind about seeking the solace of my bedroom. Grinning, I rubbed my aching jaw.

I needed the familiar comfort of a sparring match.

CHAPTER TWO

Jaliana

WHEN I CAUGHT MY REFLECTION in the mirror, my smile was sharp as a knife's edge, my lips blood red from paint. Kohl darkened my eyes, which were the same shade as the Alrenian Sea. The same shade as my dead mother's.

"Empress Jaliana of the Alrenian Empire," I whispered as I took the pencil and extended the lines of kohl around my eyes, making them look narrower, harder. "Guardian of the Dragon Army. Captain of the Dragon Keepers. Leader of the Chosen People."

The words tasted sweet on my tongue, even if every one of them was a lie. I was only empress in name, not in practice. My smile collapsed and the commanding expression I'd tried to give myself transformed into sad uncertainty. With a trembling finger, I smeared some kohl away until it made me look younger, more innocent. Not the fierce empress my mother had been, or that I longed to be, but the demure seventeen-year-old the Forwyn wanted me to be.

Clutching the edge of the vanity, I drew a deep breath and stared at my fingers, adorned with the rings that, three years ago, the Forwyn had taken from my mother's corpse and given to me. My favorite was yellow gold with a fiery ruby set in its center. Sometimes, in a certain light, I could swear the ruby held tones of orange and yellow, like it was a flame caught in a gemstone. It reminded me of dragon fire and my mother's spirit. Tears threatened, but I blinked them away, knowing I'd ruin the kohl around my eyes.

When I looked up again, I saw a lost, scared girl, held captive in her own palace by her mother's killers. I saw the ghost of my mother in my all-too-familiar eyes, in the set of my jaw, in the freckles dotted across my cheeks and nose. In the gold flecks in my eyes and the gold skin that marked my proud Alrenian heritage.

As much as I longed to be Empress Jaliana to my people now, I also desperately ached for the days when I'd simply been Jalie, beloved daughter of Karye.

A knock at the door forced me to stand tall and push the sadness away. With careful practice, I'd crafted myself into the soft-spoken girl they wanted to see, never letting them know the raging pain burning inside me.

"*Amara*," a voice called gently, and I avoided grinding my teeth. It still hurt, three years later, to hear the Forwyn use my native tongue so casually. To use my official Alrenian title as if it meant something to them.

"Yes, Maila," I said, turning in time to greet the young woman as she entered my chambers. She passed through a small sitting room before stepping into my bedroom, where she paused in the doorway and tilted her head, assessing me.

I couldn't help but do the same to her. Normally, Maila clothed herself in unassuming, simple linen dresses that kept her cool in the Alrenian heat and didn't make her especially noticeable. For tonight, however, she wore a vivid green dress, the color of seaweed and siren's tails, and it set off her dark skin nicely. Her tight curls framed her face, which shone with rouge and makeup she'd brushed across her eyelids.

"You look lovely, *amara*," she said. Her Forwyn accent was thick—

all the Forwyn had clung to their native tongue even after generations of serving as slaves to us. While Alrenian was a language of contradictions—harsh consonants paired with long, musical vowels—Forwyn made it sound…different. Gentler.

It was grating to hear them speak *any* words from my native tongue.

Ignorant of my angry thoughts, Maila bowed her head and held out uplifted palms in an Alrenian gesture of respect. All for show. She had more power and influence over me than I'd ever had over her, and we both knew it.

Inwardly, I imagined myself stomping on my anger, like stomping out ashes escaping from a fire. *Don't pretend you care about me,* I thought.

Still, as I stepped forward, my dress rustling around my legs, I was pleased with the reaction I'd drawn from her. My dress was meant to give an impression, to make me be seen and heard like I hadn't been for years. Though the skirt was made of linen, dyed in shades of yellow and orange that faded to blood-red and black at the hem, the bodice was fashioned from dragon scales. It was sleeveless, the shoulders black and gleaming, the rest a fiery shade of red that reminded me of the ruby on my finger. The neckline dipped low enough to show off the matching ruby necklace I wore—another piece of my mother's jewelry.

Tonight, I was a living flame. And I hoped someday to set fire to the Forwyn Court of Elders and reclaim my empire.

Maila led the way from my quarters, sweeping down hallways still decorated with the relics of my ancestry. Paintings lined the walls, depicting our conquests and crucial moments in our political history, as well as instances in which the Giver of Life had blessed Alrenor and declared us his Chosen People. Statues of past emperors and empresses carved from marble stood glimmering in the torchlight flickering from sconces lining the walls. My footsteps echoed along a polished white floor that all my forefathers had walked.

Instead of encountering both Forwyn slaves and Alrenian nobles in the halls as I would have in my youth, I passed only other Forwyn, clothed in the fashions of my people except for the women's braided hair. Instead of walking with my mother, listening to her proud voice recalling a piece of our history or laughing along with me at one of my jokes, I walked with a woman whose brow pinched when she looked at me. Sometimes, her eyes gleamed with undisguised hatred, despite all the bowing and scraping she did for show. Sometimes, I half-expected to wake one night with a knife to my throat and her cold eyes staring at me.

I squeezed my hands into fists and lifted my chin higher, straightened my spine even further. Despite the act I gave the Forwyn, pretending not to care about being a pawn in their political maneuvers, I still refused to look beaten and humiliated before them. They would see I remained proud of the blood in my veins and the fire in my heart. Even if they'd stripped me of everything but my title.

They'd even tried to strip me of my respect and faith in my mother, staining my memory of her with words about her cruelty. "She slit her slaves' throats and laughed about it," Maila had once whispered to me hoarsely as she brushed my golden hair. She studied me carefully, clearly noting how much I looked like my mother. If Maila hated me, it was because of her.

But I refused to believe Mother had been cruel only for cruelty's sake. She'd been a strong empress, a leader determined to make the hard choices that were best for her people and her family. Perhaps at times she was brutal. That didn't mean she was a monster. After all, I remembered my mother's musical laughter, her warm smile as she curled up in bed beside me to tell me a story or talk about our days before we fell asleep. The woman I'd known didn't match the one the Forwyn claimed to have known.

Almost without thinking about it, my fingers slipped over the rubies inlaid in the necklace I wore.

It didn't trouble me that the Forwyn hated me. I hated them right back, for everything they'd stolen from me. My mother. My life. My dragons. My throne.

Soon Maila and I approached the swell of music and murmuring voices. Glasses clinked and silverware scraped against plates. Stepping outside into the palace gardens, where the afternoon was fading into evening, we followed a path to a pavilion where the Forwyn were already gathered for their feast.

Overhead, the royal dragons swooped through the air, their heavy wings thundering. Their Forwyn riders sent them circling in a beautiful, complicated pattern that looked almost like a dance. My throat tightened with longing I couldn't disguise from my face. I hadn't been on a dragon since my mother had taken me for a ride on Reyva, who had been stolen by the Misrothians.

Sighing, I dropped my gaze to the pavilion to scan the guests. My eyes immediately fell on the Court of Elders, clustered together as they spoke animatedly. As I approached, they turned toward me, their voices swiftly falling into silence.

"Jaliana," Elder Ettonou greeted me informally. Dressed in a loose-fitting, bright-colored outfit that an Alrenian noble would have once worn, he cut an eerie figure. An imposter stealing someone else's role. Only the braided ribbons of various colors hanging from his neck set his outfit apart as Forwyn.

Elder Ettonou's smile was warm as he dipped his head, but I wasn't fooled. Years ago, he'd been one of the Forwyn to suggest simply killing me. Every day since, he was quick to strike me in private, taking his hatred for my mother out on me. "You look..." His voice faltered, as if the golden braid trailing over my shoulder or my mother's outfit and jewelry reminded him too much of her. Or maybe it was my steady gaze.

His eyes widened ever so slightly, as if he'd seen a ghost. "You look radiant," he finished.

I stared at him, refusing to return his smile. Refusing to play his game.

Elder Mae'ona, a quiet, diminutive woman—older and more wrinkled than the other Elders—nodded and chuckled, as if at a private joke. I tried not to scowl.

Elder Ettonou cleared his throat, continuing. "While you are here, I want to introduce you to someone."

I pressed my lips into a thin line, never quite sure what sort of expressions to wear when the Forwyn pretended I was anything more than their political pawn.

"This is my son, Kovi," Elder Ettonou continued, gesturing to a young man standing beside him. My gaze raked over him, taking in the way he squared his broad shoulders and held his tall frame rigidly. Even his face was an unyielding mask, giving away nothing. "He recently graduated from Aerekni Academy," he added proudly, clapping his son on the shoulder. "We prepared this dinner in celebration of him."

My gaze shot to Kovi Ettonou once more, studying him more carefully. Beneath the red and gold uniform shirt he wore, I glimpsed defined muscles when he shifted his arms. His blank expression and impeccable posture made more sense to me now.

Aerekni Academy was an elite Alrenian fighting school. It accepted trainees around ages sixteen or seventeen, and pushed them through a relentless schedule, sending them off after merely three years to become soldiers, guards, or Dragon Keepers. Alrenor's finest warriors had once come from the academy, but now that the Forwyn held the empire hostage by claiming the palace and Dragon Keep, they also controlled the academy. It'd been three years since the Forwyn takeover, which meant there'd been time for an entire class of elite Forwyn soldiers to be trained.

My mouth tasted bitter, but I tried to hide it with an impassive expression.

Kovi dipped his head toward me in a silent greeting.

My eyes scanned the sword at his side. Forcing my lips to curve into a smile, I held out my hand. "It's good to meet you," I said.

Kovi blinked at my hand for a moment before recollecting himself. It was an Alrenian custom to greet someone new by clasping hands, not a Forwyn one. It irked me to think he'd lived his entire life in my empire and had forgotten *our* customs.

Since when did Forwyn customs take precedence in my land?

Before he reached out, he adjusted something on his left wrist. They were braided ribbons he wore like a bracelet: gold, black, red, and orange all woven together. Then his right hand was in mine, warm and calloused, his firm grip a clear indication that my assessment had been correct. This man was strong. And handsome.

To my unending embarrassment, heat flushed my cheeks, and I pulled away. How could I find the son of Elder Ettonou attractive? It disgusted me.

"It is good to meet you too, *amara*," he said, and when his warm brown eyes met mine, I saw the first hint of a personality behind his stoic expression.

His eyes were shining with amusement at my expense.

"He's the best soldier in the academy, graduating with the utmost distinction and highest honors," Elder Ettonou added proudly, his chest puffed out. He hadn't seemed to notice my discomfort. "He'll make a fine soldier, and a powerful Elder one day."

I swallowed back an insult, but to my surprise, it was Kovi who interjected. "We've spent a lifetime apart, Father. You hardly know me from any other soldier in the barracks. What made you think I wanted to follow in your footsteps?"

Tension swept through the Elder, who seemed at a loss for words. Did Kovi find his own father as abhorrent as I did?

I had to hold back my laughter. My eyes met Kovi's, and another jolt of awareness shot through me. His eyes were deep and dark, flecked with gold. His gaze didn't remind me of the Elder at all.

I tore my gaze away quickly and excused myself. Brushing past the Elders, I strode toward the opposite end of the pavilion, where food and drinks awaited on tables. A spread of endless delicacies and treats tempted me, from roasted duck and glazed salmon to sugared berries and cream-filled pastries. Paid servants rather than slaves now stood at attention beside the tables, cheerfully filling glasses to the brim with wine upon request.

I wanted a stronger drink, but right now, I needed something to cool myself down, to forget the humiliating blush staining my cheeks.

"Water, please," I said, holding out my hand until a man filled a glass with cold water and placed it in my grasp. I drank it in three long swallows and held out my glass for a refill.

When I finally stepped away, I started searching immediately for the Elders again. Pawn or not, I would find a way to make them share news with me. Tomorrow I was scheduled to sit in the throne room and meet with my people, and when both Alrenians and Forwyn came before me to make requests or list complaints, I wanted to be prepared. Even if I didn't truly have power to make decisions or answer the citizens' requests as I would wish, I wanted to be informed. Maybe if I could make myself persuasive enough, the Elders would give me more than the barest details about the state of my empire.

But as I crossed the floor, my slippers brushing along silently, a Forwyn woman intercepted my path. Her dark eyes were fiery, filled with unmasked rage. Since I didn't recognize her from the palace, I assumed she was a guest from the city.

"Excuse me," I began, forcing calmness into my voice.

"I'll never excuse you, you worthless murderer's daughter," she snarled. Her eyes dipped toward my mother's necklace and then the dragon scales adorning my dress, and her expression turned positively venomous. "Do you want to know what happened to my son?" she demanded. "My beautiful, kind-hearted, brilliant son?"

I swallowed. "No, I do not," I said, my tone still measured.

Ignoring me, she leaned forward. "Your mother murdered him," she hissed. "And you look and walk just like her. Like you think you still own Alrenor!" She scoffed. "What is it like now, to be *no one*, like we were? To know there is nothing you can do to reclaim your throne?" She stepped closer, her breath hot against my face.

I inched backward, only to find myself hemmed in by other Forwyn, looking equally murderous. My heart rate picked up, pounding a staccato rhythm that competed with the drumbeats of the party music.

"To know you are powerless to stop us?" she snapped. Like lightning, she extended her hand and ripped the ruby necklace from my neck.

Grunting in pain, I stumbled back into the arms of a Forwyn man. He caught me, his hands gripping my shoulders so tightly they ached. This time, my cry sounded pathetic in my ears. I was a scared mouse, not a roaring flame.

Shame seared through me. I was an embarrassment to my mother's memory.

A stern voice cut through the murmuring voices around me. "What's the problem here?"

My eyes shot over to the tall form hovering at the edge of the tight knot of Forwyn surrounding me. Kovi.

I concealed a grimace. I didn't need the Elders or their soldiers sending someone to rescue me all for show.

Lifting my chin, I met the woman's gaze with a glare of my own. Fury flooded through my veins, wild and intoxicating, and as swiftly as I'd fallen back, I sprang forward. The man's grip fell away, startled by my sudden movement. In an instant, I was nose-to-nose with the Forwyn woman.

"I am not no one," I hissed. "I am *Amara* Jaliana, daughter of Karye, and you will bow before me."

Before Kovi could wind through the crowd and intervene, I seized the woman's arms, and she gasped aloud, choking on a groan of agony. She pulled away from me as her knees hit the floor, her ivory dress pooling around her legs. I blinked in shock at the blackened skin and twin cuts, ugly and red, that marred her arms—arms that had only a moment before been whole. Unhurt. Around the discolored skin, her open wounds were deep and raw, bleeding mini scarlet pools on the pristine pavilion floor. Bright red against the white.

She lifted her head to gape at me with a mixture of horror and hatred in her tear-filled eyes.

All around the pavilion, gasps and terrified questions broke out. It was discord breaking the earlier harmony of polite conversation and light laughter mingling with the music. Now even the music came to a crashing halt as the musicians leaned forward to gape at the scene.

I stood petrified, blinking at the kneeling woman and then my own trembling hands. The woman's blood stained my fingers and palms, everywhere that my skin had met hers. Even if my fingernails hadn't been trimmed short, there was no way they could have cut that deeply. The woman's horror echoed my own.

One word was repeated over the others, until it rang in my ears, making me register the gravity of the situation. "Monster." If the Forwyn hadn't thought I was a monster before, for who I was and whose blood ran in my veins, they surely thought so now.

Vaguely, I was aware of the figures surrounding us, some drawing the woman to her feet, murmuring soothingly as they led her away to a healer. Others clustered closely around me, speaking stern words I couldn't hear over the pulsing of my blood and the echoing ring of "monster" crying out over and over in my mind.

I'd never seen or heard of something like this. And even though I was as shocked and confused as anyone else present, I knew it didn't matter.

Now that I'd proven to the Forwyn that I was dangerous, my life was forfeit.

CHAPTER THREE

Lo

PAUNI'A WAS THE ONLY OTHER sister not out on a round or inside the abbey completing chores. Instead, she was humming and weeding one of the gardens edging our yard. Her braids, adorned with ribbons in every imaginable color, were tied back in one large bow at the nape of her neck as she knelt in the dirt. Her hands were already crusted with earth, and a pile of weeds lay on the stone path beside her.

When she heard me, she glanced up and smiled in greeting. Her oval face amplified her cheerful, youthful appearance as her warm amber eyes met mine. "Did you come out to help, Lo?" she asked, but the smirk tugging at her lips gave her away. She knew me too well.

I shook my head, tossing my own braids over my shoulder. It was a relief to feel the weight of my hair, a luxury that I sometimes still marveled at.

As a slave, I'd been forced to leave my head shorn, forced to abandon the traditions of my people in adorning my hair with ribbons. It was why the braided necklace of ribbon had meant so much when it'd been gifted to me—why it was still a meaningful symbol.

"I was hoping someone would spar with me. I'm feeling—on edge," I admitted.

Pauni'a's eyes darted to my swelling jaw. "Would it have something to do with the fact that it looks like you've already been punched in the face?" she asked.

My smile was tight. "Maybe."

She nodded thoughtfully. Only a couple years older than me, Pauni'a was tall and lithe, one of the strongest and fastest members of the abbey. Though none of us considered ourselves warriors—certainly not like the Alrenians, that fierce race of unnaturally tall and strong men and women—we knew how to defend ourselves and our people. We kept ourselves fit and trained for moments like what I'd faced in the alley earlier today, when an Alrenian might decide to abuse their strength by cornering one of us. And for moments when we could help our own people, often ill-treated, even if we were the ones in control of Alrenor now.

"One match," Pauni'a said at last, setting down one final weed and standing to brush her hands on her tunic.

I couldn't conceal the excitement from my face. Pauni'a was my favorite sister to spar with. Matching up with her was always a challenge, always forcing me to think in creative ways and push myself to be faster, stronger, smarter. I was convinced that if anyone could train me to survive an attack from a burly Alrenian warrior, it was her.

Our space for sparring was a stretch of grass surrounded by our vegetable gardens and fruit trees, things we depended upon for food. Some things the Alrenians who'd abandoned the temple long ago had left behind: the stable in the far corner where we housed our dairy cow, the punching bags we'd refilled with fresh straw and re-stitched together, and the horizontal pole suspended in the air for pull-ups. Other items we'd added, such as the chicken coop or the benches under the trees where one could sit and listen for Elhani's voice.

Moving out to the open yard, I hopped on the balls of my feet and swung my arms, getting the blood pumping through my body. Pauni'a eyed my eager grin and shook her head at me as she stretched. I focused on my different muscle groups, warming up my legs and arms and rolling my neck. Then, as Pauni'a strode toward me, I fell into the familiar stance, legs shoulder-width apart, hands balled protectively in front of me. Ready to attack or defend.

Pauni'a's face gave away nothing as she moved, graceful and swift. One instant she was stepping toward me, and the next she lunged without warning. I lifted my arm to block her fist, the shock of her strike vibrating through my arm. But she was prepared for me to stop her, and my defense did nothing to slow her onslaught. Her foot slipped out to hook my knee.

But that was the same move I'd used on the Alrenian man who'd attacked me earlier, and I was expecting it. I hopped to the side, out of her range, before taking advantage of the time it took for her to turn and reorient herself. With quick steps, I moved in close and struck for her side.

Once again, she was faster. In one smooth motion, she captured my arm in a tight grip and pulled, using my momentum to yank me forward until I stumbled past her and fell, sprawled across the grass on my hands and knees. Gasping for breath, I rolled before she could leap onto my back and finish the fight.

Springing to my feet, I turned to face her just in time for us to clash again in a flurry of punches and kicks. Pauni'a broke through my defenses, striking my sore jaw. It throbbed, and I tasted blood from the jarring impact of my own teeth on my tongue. Just as I ducked low to avoid another strike, I heard Naina's voice echoing through the yard, bouncing off the high stone walls enclosing us.

"Girls! Haven't you heard a word I've said?"

Panting, Pauni'a and I broke apart and glanced at Naina, who stood with her wrinkled hands on her wide hips. Her eyes looked almost gold in the sunlight as she glared at us.

I cleared my throat.

"Forgive us, Naina," Pauni'a and I chorused.

"I called to you both to let you know the other sisters will be here soon. It's time to finish preparations for dinner, and I'd like your help."

"Of course." I dashed forward while Pauni'a hurried to clean up her mess from weeding.

As I slid past Naina to reenter the abbey, she reached out and slipped something into my hand. My heart leapt with relief when I opened my fist to see my necklace, the frayed edges of ribbon bound artfully with thick gold strings that could be tied together to form a necklace once again.

"I thought you were busy cooking dinner," I said, my eyes wide as I studied Naina's gently smiling face.

She shrugged. "I figured I could spare a few moments." She patted my arm. "Would you like me to help you put it on?"

Too overcome to speak, I nodded. She continued to hum the melody I'd caught her singing earlier in the kitchen as she wound the ribbon around my neck and tied it carefully in the back. When she finished, she stepped away, blinking a little more than usual.

For a moment, doubt crept through my mind. Did Naina know where I'd gotten this necklace? Or did she just suspect what it might mean, after the years of slavery so many of us had faced? Absentmindedly, my fingers slipped up to the braids cascading down my back, full of multicolored ribbons. Compared to the adornments in my hair, my necklace was shabby. Faded. Worn.

But before I could wonder more about what Naina or anyone else in the abbey might suspect about my past, the elderly woman shooed me gently toward the kitchen. "We'll have plenty of hungry mouths to feed soon enough!" she urged.

I tossed a smile over my shoulder at her. "Thank you, Naina," I murmured.

"Of course, *ahnla*. Anything for you."

❮❮❮❮❮

Seated on a stone bench in the sanctuary, I listened to the flames crackle on the altar at the front of the room. Early starlight pooled through the open windows onto the floor, making my sisters' and my shadows stretch into long, distorted shapes. We had a handful of visitors today, who sat quietly and respectfully in the back as they worshipped with us.

When Naina approached the front to stand before the altar, we all rose as one to join her. As she lifted her hands and raised her voice in a traditional Forwyn song of worship, we sang with her, clutching our individual candlesticks closely.

Beside me, Pauni'a swayed and smiled, as if listening to her own musical chorus. But I could never face our evening meetings with such a carefree heart. Every day, guilts old and new weighed on me.

Blood on my hands. Anger in my heart. And an unending emptiness that plagued me.

My free hand strayed to my neck, where my thin, jagged scar raised the skin of my throat. Concealed as it was by my braid of ribbons, most never saw it. But whenever I took off my ribbons in the privacy of my bedroom and looked into the mirror, my scar was often all I could see.

"Quiet your hearts," Naina directed us gently. "Listen to the voice of Elhani through the words in the Ihlu'i Text." At her mention of our Sacred Book, she lifted a bulky leather-bound tome, stored on a shelf near the altar, and read from it.

"I will not forget my Chosen Ones, so long as they do not forget me," Naina

intoned. *"Calm your minds and focus your hearts, and you will always be able to hear my voice."*

With a contented sigh, Naina shut the book and closed her eyes. "We can always hear Elhani, at any moment, because his voice is all around us," she said. "So often we are consumed in our own thoughts and worries, that we block it out. It is like music, coursing through the earth, sweet and strong and reassuring. From it, we hear his will and we have access to our magic." She smiled gently. "For we know, all magic comes from him."

I squeezed my own eyes closed, trying to concentrate on the lyrical sound of Elhani's voice. The soft, comforting tones were like a lullaby flowing through my brain—when I could hear them. It was something I was still practicing, how to hear his voice and know his will; how to concentrate well enough to tap into the magic he offered to us. Though the Ihlu'i Text explained that anyone could be granted Elhani's magic, only the Forwyn, his Chosen People who had dedicated themselves to him first, could hear his voice as we could.

At last, Naina called to all of us to take a few moments of silence to kneel before Elhani and pray, asking him to cleanse us and make us worthy before we approached the altar. I knelt on the cold floor and squeezed my eyes shut. *Forgive my anger. Forgive the part of me that still wants vengeance. I know now that it is empty.*

The familiar ache of grief and loneliness rose in my chest, but I squelched it. My life had a purpose now, and I would not wallow. I would make my dead family proud as they looked on, guiding me in my life choices alongside Elhani's immortal workers, the guidespirits.

Naina gestured, and we stood. I trailed Pauni'a down the aisle toward the altar, where one by one the sisters knelt and added their candlelight to the crackling altar. Each whispered their pleas and promises, their hopes and dreams, into the flames. *Health for my family.*

Justice for the Forwyn. Safety for our people.

As I knelt and lit one of the few pieces of tinder still untouched by the flame, I breathed my prayer under my breath. "Please, Elhani. If you don't take away my anger, guide me. Give my anger a purpose."

CHAPTER FOUR

Jalie

MY HEART POUNDED IN MY throat as I paced my room, the luxuries that had surrounded me all my life spinning meaninglessly before me. With my windows open to the muggy night, I felt like I was suffocating. But when I closed them, the lack of fresh air was even more stifling. Sweat beaded on my forehead, even when I stepped out onto my balcony to try to steady my breathing.

When I closed my eyes, I could see that Forwyn woman's gaze burning accusingly into mine, her blood trailing down her arms. The Elders would surely put me to death now. Any ways in which they could use me as a tool to gain Alrenian loyalty couldn't possibly be more important than keeping me from harming more of their people.

Armed guards had dragged me away quickly enough, shutting me up alone in my room for hours. When I'd tried the door earlier, I'd found it locked. Though my activities had always been closely monitored, I'd never been shut up like this before. The view from my balcony afforded me a glimpse into one of the numerous palace courtyards, and even more guards patrolled it than usual.

Drawing a deep breath, I reentered my room, seated myself on the edge of my bed, and moved to wipe my clammy palms on the skirt of my dress. But—wait. Fear froze in my chest and I halted with my hands hovering over my thighs.

I stared at those hands as if they belonged to someone else, studying each individual finger, each line running through my palm. They looked the same as ever. Nothing signaled to me that anything was different or inherently wrong with me.

But then—what *was* that? What had happened?

I stood to pace the length of my room again, my eyes darting toward the shelves lining the far end of my chamber. A few old books adorned the space, mostly for decoration. Many of them were works of fiction.

I'd grown up knowing about the old Alrenian gifts, said to be granted to my people by the Giver of Life. We were his Chosen People, my mother had always proclaimed proudly, and he had gifted us above all other peoples. Our proudest gifts were those that helped us in our conquests: war gifts, courage gifts, and protection gifts. But those, the best gifts of all, had also disappeared generations ago.

There were others, though. Healing gifts. Gifts for sensing others' feelings or intentions. Of all these supernatural gifts I'd learned about or witnessed, however, never had I seen or heard anything about a gift that could blacken skin and cut people like a knife at the mere touch of a hand.

A thought occurred to me, making me pause in my steps.

There was another gift that might help me find answers.

Some people could see the truth in visions of the past and present, discerning key pieces of information. Many truth-gifted men and women had served as imperial advisors for centuries. One of these men, Vionn, had aided my mother faithfully until the day the Forwyn had murdered her. Naturally he wasn't welcome to advise the Court of Elders, but if I could find him…

A knock on my door stilled my thoughts. Composing my face into what I hoped was a neutral expression, I squared my shoulders and approached my door. If this was the moment the Elders dragged me to the dungeons and condemned me to death, so be it. I wouldn't humiliate myself by looking afraid or uncertain.

With a fierce jolt of courage, I threw open the door.

Kovi Ettonou stood in the entryway, unaccompanied. When I glanced down the hallway, there were no guards in sight.

I frowned, hoping he couldn't see my growing terror. Had Elder Ettonou sent his soldier son to hurt me this time?

"Why are you here?" I demanded.

Without responding, Kovi shoved past me into my chambers. Anger flamed my cheeks, but he was as cool and unaffected as ever. His eyes scanned the sitting area, taking in every detail in moments before he passed on toward my bedchamber.

"What are you doing?" I asked, slamming the door and storming after him. If they'd sent him to drag me to a prison cell, I'd be halfway there by now. Which meant that I wasn't a prisoner—or at least, no more than I usually was.

Kovi didn't spare me a glance as he paused in my bedroom, continued his preemptory study, and moved on toward the washroom.

Following him, I repeated my question.

"Looking," he said as he stopped in front of my tub.

I crossed my arms and shot him a glare I hoped he could sense burning into his back. Privately, though, I was feeling relief. Kovi didn't seem like he wanted to hurt me. He didn't seem much like his father at all. "I didn't invite you to look," I said.

He turned to meet my stare, and I saw the same amusement that had flickered in his eyes at the party. Or maybe it was only my imagination.

I tapped my foot impatiently. "And why are you here, *looking*?"

Kovi tilted his head to the side, making the same scan of *me* that he'd just performed on my rooms. "Well, the view could be worse." He shrugged carelessly.

For an instant, I was at a loss for words. Part of me was righteously insulted. Another, smaller, shameful part of me was pleased. Most Forwyn men looked at me with fear or revulsion, so being appreciated was strange and not entirely unwelcome.

I crossed my arms. "You didn't answer my question."

This time I definitely didn't imagine the gleam in his eyes. Deep brown with flecks of warm gold that reminded me of Alrenian eyes, they shone in the candlelight bathing my bedroom. Why couldn't the Forwyn look as hideous on the outside as they were on the inside?

"The Elders assigned me to monitor you."

A twinge of unease crept through me, but rather than let him see it, I rolled my eyes and gestured toward the door. "I always have guards outside my chambers. Why would they replace them with you?"

The faintest flicker of a grin played about Kovi's lips as he stepped closer, exiting the washroom to enter my bedroom again. "The Elders believe it is a task best given to an Aerekni graduate."

Ignoring the loathsome arrogance seeping into his tone, I strode toward my vanity and lifted my brush. Instead of facing him, I stared into my mirror. *His presence doesn't trouble you,* I told myself.

Uncoiling my braid, I brushed through the length of my hair. Its long golden strands flashed brightly in the candlelight. "I assumed if the Elders made any changes tonight, they would involve me sitting in the dungeon with a death sentence hanging over me."

I watched the young man in the mirror. For a long moment, Kovi didn't move. Then he shifted, meeting my eyes in the reflection. Holding my gaze. I was the first to look away.

"You speak casually about your own death," Kovi said. He seated himself on my bed and leaned back against the plush velvet pillows, as if they were his. "Are you unafraid?"

My fingers tightened around my brush handle, but I forced myself to shrug and laugh lightly. "I'm no stranger to death," I said, dropping my tone meaningfully.

When Kovi's gaze darted up to meet mine again, I didn't look away. Instead, I hoped he knew exactly of whose death I spoke, and I longed for him to see the anger brimming beneath my cool exterior.

He didn't miss my implication. "Everyone tells me you are a lot like your mother," Kovi mused aloud. "They say you have her eyes, her arrogance, her temper. They whisper about how you are dangerous, how you should have been put to death the same night she was."

I swallowed back my anger. "You never met her?" It was surprising to me, considering Kovi's own father had served as a palace slave before Mother had died.

Kovi's stare in the mirror was so piercing, I had to drop my eyes again. "Your mother liked to split up families. I was sent away from both my mother and father as a young child. I have few memories of living here. I barely remember my mother, and I hardly know my father from a stranger. So yes, I met your mother, but no, I don't remember her."

When I dared to glance up again, I found the intense look on his face had fallen away. Catching my eyes, he gave me another infuriating grin. "But now I see it's you avoiding *my* questions. So…you *are* afraid of death."

"No one wants to die before their time," I said. I set my brush down and turned at last to face him. "And you saw what I did at the Elders' feast. I expected there would be consequences after a display like that."

Kovi smirked and pointed to himself. "Behold the consequences."

He hesitated, his expression turning more serious. "I've never seen any Alrenian gift or Forwyn magic that could do what you did."

I scoffed. "Forwyn don't have gifts. Or magic, as you call it."

Kovi's expression turned intense, like a challenge, daring me to continue arguing. A chill ran down my back, and I paused.

"Why have I never seen this Forwyn magic before?" I demanded. My memories scoured every moment I'd spent among the Elders and their people, and then around Forwyn slaves before that.

"Probably because most Forwyn haven't been trained in how to discipline themselves and wield it," Kovi responded calmly. "Few had time when we were your slaves, *amara*."

I hesitated a beat. "Were you trained?"

Kovi smirked. "All Aerekni graduates are. Why do you think the Elders appointed me to watch over you?" He leaned forward. "So where did you get your devilish powers?"

This time, I couldn't repress my laughter. Of course, this unbeliever with his fake god and his magic would claim *my* power came from something evil or unnatural. "If I had any clue what would happen tonight, or how to use my devilish power, as you call it, do you think I would have used it in front of everyone and risked being sentenced to death?" I lifted an eyebrow.

Resting back against my pillow, Kovi nodded. "Good point."

I started heading toward my door. "If you are to be my personal guard now, you can escort me to the library."

Kovi cleared his throat, not even bothering to sit up. "I don't think so."

"Why not?"

"You're not to leave your rooms tonight, *amara*."

I arched a brow at him, but my voice was low, trying to conceal the tremor building inside me. As much as Mother had raised me to be fearless, death terrified me. "The Elders are still discussing me, aren't they?"

Kovi inclined his head.

"You're here to watch me while they decide what to do with me." I grimaced. "Is that why you've barged into my rooms instead of stationing yourself outside my door?"

"After your display at the feast, *amara*, what else did you expect?"

"Stop using Alrenian words," I snapped.

Kovi's eyes widened almost imperceptibly. "I thought you would prefer to be addressed with your proper Alrenian title, rather than being forced to hear it in the common merchant tongue," he said, not bothering to conceal the sarcasm now dripping from his voice.

"If that were the case, I'd make you speak to me in Alrenian now, but you probably don't know my language," I tipped my chin up haughtily.

"Oh, serving your kind for years taught me plenty of Alrenian," Kovi said, a dangerous edge entering his tone. "But I prefer using the trade language when I can't speak Forwyn."

"Your people aren't worthy to speak Alrenian, to even think it," I ground out. "Who do you think you are, sitting and lounging in my bed, speaking my native tongue, graduating from an honorable school for my people? You're nothing but a thief, a usurper. Your people pretend to be righteous, but you have blood on your hands and greed in your hearts. You're lying, conniving, murderous *fakes*."

I stormed toward my washroom. "Enjoy my bed for now," I continued. "I'm taking a bath, and when I'm finished, I expect you to be sleeping on the floor."

This time, I heard the bed frame creak as Kovi stood. "I'll have to join you."

I froze before rounding on him. "What?"

Kovi shook his head, cringing in disgust. "Not in your bath or your bed—that would be vile."

I sneered at him. "Agreed. I'm glad you cleared that up."

"I mean, I will not leave you unsupervised while I'm here. I'll turn my back while you wash, but you're not to be left alone."

Pressing my lips into a thin line, I swallowed the bitter humiliation building in my throat and turned wordlessly. It was horrible enough to be monitored by this young man who stood for everything I despised, but to have no privacy… Now I truly was a prisoner in a gilded cage.

Gathering clean undergarments and a nightdress, I stared at the tub in my washroom. "Am I to have no maid to tend to me tonight either?" I asked quietly. But I already knew the answer.

"Did you think Maila would be subjected to that task after what you did to Lady Leanai?"

Realization struck me. My enemies wouldn't want to hurt me, or even lay a finger on me, if they finally saw me as a threat. Turning slowly, I studied his face, but the sharp lines of his jaw and his unyielding mouth gave away nothing. Even his eyes were dark, all mirth gone. "Are you afraid of me?" I asked, unable to stop the smile that spread across my face.

Kovi didn't rise to the bait. "You would like that, wouldn't you?" he responded calmly.

My smile faded.

"You'd like it if I quaked with fear whenever you threatened me," he went on, his own mouth twisting in amusement. "But do whatever you like with your monstrous power. I'm not afraid of pain. And I'm not afraid of death."

"Easy for you to say, as a graduate," I snarled. "Have you ever even seen real battle yet? Faced actual death?"

Kovi's eyes flickered with some dark emotion I couldn't place, there one instant and gone the next. "I've seen plenty of death."

The words made me conjure up images of him cutting down my people, ruthless and calm. I repressed a shudder and turned away.

Silently, I drew a bath, filling the luxuriously heated water that poured from the spout with scented soaps until the room smelled of vanilla and cinnamon. Inhaling a deep, calming breath, I glanced over my shoulder to be sure Kovi was facing away, stripped out of my clothes, and sank into the bath. I leaned back and closed my eyes. For one blissful moment, I pretended the Elders weren't debating whether they should let me live.

Scooping some bubbles into my hands, I looked back at Kovi. Spine straight, muscled shoulders squared, he stood like a perfect soldier with his eyes staring steadfastly out toward my bedroom. At least he was true to his word.

"When will they decide about me?" I asked after a long moment. "By morning?"

Kovi shifted almost imperceptibly, like he'd tensed his muscles a little at the sound of my voice. Annoyance? Guilt? Pity? Did any of the Forwyn have a heart buried deep inside?

"I believe so," he said at last.

I waited a long moment, hoping he would explain further, but of course he did not. Fear clenched my stomach as steam curled over my bathwater, turning the air thick and stifling. The bath failed to comfort or distract me any longer, so I hurriedly scrubbed myself clean and climbed out. As I drained the tub and dried off, I stared daggers at Kovi's back.

They send one man to guard me instead of keeping the usual host of guards posted in the hall, I mused. Despite what he'd said about not fearing me, or his pride in his illustrious Aerekni training, the temptation to replicate what had happened at the feast gripped me. With his back turned, Kovi would be far more vulnerable. All I needed to do was touch his skin, and maybe, hopefully, I could make him bleed.

But then what? I asked myself bitterly. I could try to run, but I would never get far. There were still guards posted throughout the palace and the grounds, not to mention the swarms of Forwyn nobility and servants who would happily capture me in an instant. I was hopelessly outnumbered, with nothing to do but await the fate the Court of Elders chose for me.

Still...

As soon as I'd finished dressing, I crept behind Kovi. His shirtsleeves were rolled up just enough to expose his forearms. Maybe it was curiosity, or maybe it was a petty longing to lash out at anyone with Forwyn blood before their people claimed my life, but I couldn't resist.

I reached out to seize his wrist, but before my fingers could brush his skin, Kovi was moving. He pivoted, both hands seizing me around the waist and drawing me toward him until I was hopelessly trapped. The muscles in his arms were as unforgiving as steel as I struggled, my arms pinned at my sides. My heart slammed painfully in my chest. Would he hurt me?

When I glared at him, his face was only inches from mine, the golden flecks in his eyes twinkling with silent laughter. His lips twisted into a grin.

"Not afraid, remember?" he murmured, his breath warm on my face.

He was too close. I recoiled, just in time for him to release me, letting me slip and fall onto the slick tile.

Frowning, he held out his hand. I stared at it in shock, wondering at this kind gesture, until I realized it probably came only out of pity. I sneered, mustering whatever dignity I had left to stand on my own.

I stormed back toward my bedchamber, inwardly groaning as I

listened to his footsteps following me. I tried to pretend he wasn't there as I threw myself onto my bed and buried myself under the covers.

"Not afraid? Oh, you will be," I whispered.

CHAPTER FIVE

Lo

MOONLIGHT FLOODED THE STREETS IN a silvery glow, but I hugged the shadowy edges, hoping to disappear into the night. My braids swung against my shoulders in a steady rhythm, matching the pounding of the supple boots I preferred for my running and training sessions. *One, two, one, two.* As sweat gathered on the back of my neck and my lungs ached with exertion, I forced myself to focus on counting out each step and keeping my breaths even. Anything to distract myself from the way the muscles in my legs burned when the street tilted in a gradual incline.

My sisters would be horrified if they knew about my nightly habit of sneaking out to run, even if the Alrenians were under a curfew imposed by the Court of Elders. They knew there were too many Alrenians and too few Forwyn guards to stop all curfew-breakers. Crimes against our people still happened all the time after dark.

But despite that fact, this was the time I felt the safest in the capital. When Inalgoth quieted, most of its residents retiring to their homes and its shopkeepers locking their doors, I could avoid the taunts and outright hostility from Alrenians. And with the Forwyn guards who did patrol the busier streets, I was in friendly company.

As long as I clung to the sleeping districts, far from the noisy inns, pubs, and other, less savory Forwyn businesses with bustling night life, I rarely encountered anyone but the occasional guard. The night was mine to enjoy, the cooler air a relief from the midday heat, the moon and drifting clouds my only friends. Tonight I could even see the dragons spiraling about the distant Keep in patterns, like the Dragon Keepers were competing with one another to see who could pull off the most complicated maneuvers while astride a dragon. They'd been out earlier, before the sun had set, but it wasn't unusual for the Keepers to push themselves, to go out multiple times a day for hours of rigorous training.

The sight always made my heart soar, even if I felt a pang of jealousy. Once, I'd tended to those dragons. Once, I'd dreamt of a day when I could be free and ride them myself. But that was before I'd learned that even freedom couldn't chase away my nightmares, and that some dreams were better left behind with the rest of my ugly past.

It was tempting to lose myself in watching the dragons, but mostly, I kept my eyes on my immediate surroundings, constantly scanning the nearby streets and alleys. Just because the night was quiet, the streets empty, didn't mean I couldn't run into danger. And despite the risk I took by being out here alone, I didn't want trouble. I only wanted to escape my twisting thoughts, my frequent nightmares.

Each time I closed my eyes, I could see it all so clearly. I could taste and smell and feel everything like it was happening all over again. I could see Ahko'edi, my younger brother, with his kind, intelligent eyes and the unwavering, reassuring presence he'd had about him. *The empress can't touch us. Not really,* he'd said when Karye had sent our mother out of the palace to serve as a slave elsewhere. When we'd realized we would probably never see our mother again. *No matter what she does, family can never be parted.*

Tonight, Edi's words echoed in my ears as clearly as his scream did, the same enraged scream he'd unleashed when he'd stepped between

Karye and me. When he'd taken her killing strike. For me.

I'd committed a minor crime, glancing up and looking too long in Karye's face, and her retaliation had been swift, brutal. Edi had recognized the bloodthirst in her eyes mere seconds before I had, and he'd stepped between us without hesitation. I'd never had the chance to reach out and shove him back, to take my rightful place in front of that killing blow.

The rest of the images always followed rapidly. Karye sneering and deciding it was a crueler fate to let me live and grieve. The months of pain I'd endured, reliving that horrible moment over and over. My desire for revenge, growing until it had consumed me.

And then…the night I'd finally had my vengeance, when Karye had nearly killed me—for the second time—and I hadn't frozen. I'd fought back.

The swipe of a dagger. A spray of hot blood against my face. The tang of copper filling my nose as my dreams of revenge collapsed with the body of Empress Karye. Her glazed eyes didn't fill me with relief or satisfaction or a sense of justice. They couldn't relieve the unending pain of losing my brother.

Instead, I felt…

Stop! I told myself, shoving all the memories away, forcing them into a dark corner of my mind where they could haunt me later. They would come back. They always did.

Now I frowned and pushed myself harder, lengthening my stride. I couldn't outrun my past, but I could distract myself. And I could do my best to atone for it.

A pebble rolled behind me, echoing in the silence. I slowed to a stop, catching my breath as I glanced over my shoulder. The street was empty, and nothing but my labored breathing broke the stillness. Maybe I'd dislodged the pebble?

No.

Despite the balmy air, the hairs on my arms rose with foreboding. Even if I couldn't see or hear anyone, I could sense something. Someone was watching me. And a guard wouldn't hide.

Heart slamming into my chest, I strained to catch Elhani's voice. To feel his magic running through the surrounding air. Through my veins.

But of course, my own troubled thoughts were too loud tonight, blocking out the notes of his endless song. I'd have to rely on the defensive techniques we'd trained in instead. *Breathe. Think.*

Though my breathing had steadied, my pulse continued to pound in my ears. My only question was whether I should run or face this invisible threat. Did I turn and keep going toward home, trusting in my speed? Did I dare turn my back on a possible enemy? Once I might have carried a weapon, even if they had been declared illegal, but that had been years ago, before the nightmares. Now, despite my training with the sisters at the abbey, I felt vulnerable. I *might* escape someone, but they were likely armed and stronger than me. I had nothing but my wits to defend myself, and at the moment, I couldn't even decide whether to stay.

That's when my anger flared to life again, and my senses seemed to heighten. Perhaps it was my imagination, but I was sure I could hear someone else breathing in the darkness of a nearby alley. Was that a pair of bright eyes studying me? I blinked, and they vanished.

"Who are you and what do you want?" I called out, my anger keeping my voice steady and strong.

A figure slipped out of the shadows, graceful and swift and silent. When it stepped onto the street, it stopped, maintaining several yards of distance between us. There, in the moonlight, I could see who was following me: a man around my age, dressed in fine clothing.

He didn't have the telltale golden skin tone of an Alrenian. Instead, his was a beautiful shade of bronze. His dark hair grew short and wavy, except where it curled more tightly around his ears. More than anything, though, it was his piercing blue eyes, so bright they seemed unnatural, that gave him away. He was Teramese.

For two centuries, Alrenor had been one of the lands cut off from the world by a mysterious barrier built by a Misrothian king. My understanding was that, after the Misrothians split from the Alrenian Empire, they'd wanted to ensure Alrenians could never enter their land and threaten them again. The barrier had locked Alrenians permanently within their own borders, barring them not only from the rest of their empire but also from the rest of the world. An isolated Alrenor was all generations of Alrenians and Forwyn slaves knew.

Then, three years ago, the barrier had broken. Trade with kingdoms across the Great Sea, such as Teramyl and Brevinn, had resumed. I believed the Court of Elders had even begun a relationship with Misroth. Foreign merchants and travelers had slowly begun making appearances on our soil, though not nearly as many as we'd hoped.

Unfortunately, the citizens of Forwyth, our homeland, had made themselves stubbornly scarce. Before I'd left the palace, we'd received word that Forwyth's Court of Elders refused to help by sending soldiers to secure our rule over Alrenor. They'd claimed their kingdom was dedicated to pursuing peace in Elhani's name, and that meant keeping themselves out of "Alrenian affairs." And their policy was clearly one other kingdoms had followed—for I'd seen few merchants in the capital over the years.

It was rare to see anyone in Inalgoth who wasn't Alrenian, Forwyn, or some unfortunate mixture of the two races.

And just because this strange young man wasn't Alrenian didn't make me trust him anymore. He shoved his hands in his pockets and smiled amiably at me. I frowned.

"*Amara'rekni*," he said, and my body went cold. "I've been waiting for the right moment to talk to you."

Empress Slayer.

"Who are you?" I whispered.

"So you don't deny it, Lo'laeni?" he asked, stepping closer. "Although it wouldn't matter what you said," he went on, "because I already know. It's why I'm here."

My muscles went taut. The only thing rooting me to the ground was a desperate need to understand how he knew who I was and ensure no one else ever found out.

"What do you want?" I bit out.

He held his hands up, palms facing me, as if in a gesture of surrender. "I'm not going to hurt you."

I rolled my eyes. "That's what all the stalkers and murderers always say."

A muscle in his cheek worked, like he was trying to hold back a smile. "Right. I wouldn't trust myself either, if I were you." He lowered his hands, sighing. "My name is Caesiem. This is my only weapon." He unbuckled a sheathed blade from his belt and tossed it on the cobblestones between us.

I studied him. "Are you one of *them*?"

A furrow appeared between Caesiem's brows. "What do you— Obviously I'm not an Alrenian, if that's what you mean…"

Crossing my arms, I set my mouth into a stubborn line.

Caesiem cleared his throat. "Yes. That's not good enough." He rubbed a weary hand across his forehead. "I came from Teramyl a year ago, and no, I don't support the way the Alrenians treat you, so I'm not 'one of them.'"

I scoffed. "Yes, I always believe everything a man who's been following me tells me. What do you want?"

He spanned the rest of the distance between us quickly, and I almost bolted. But his expression was earnest, and his knife still lay in the street. Setting my jaw, I waited.

Caesiem spoke low and fast. "I'm part of a…group. We're vigilantes, you could say. Many aren't satisfied with the Court of Elders' choice to keep Empress Jaliana alive. They sent me to find you, because we know there's much you could do to help us. To help your people."

I blinked at him. "How did you learn who I am?"

"*Amara'rekni*," he said again, the harsh yet musical Alrenian words sounding foreign in his Teramese accent. "You left the palace behind for an…abbey?" He frowned as if confused by my choice. "But it's clear. You're the right age. You wear that ribbon necklace like it means everything to you." He gestured to the newly mended ribbons tied around my throat. "And you have a scar on your neck."

I reached for my necklace self-consciously. Normally, it covered my scar, but while running it must have slipped down.

Perhaps the other sisters had guessed about my past before, but they never pressed me for details. All this time I'd lived with that *other* identity of mine concealed. To avoid undue attention from my people and vengeful retaliation from Alrenians. To block out the memories— memories that had haunted me anyway.

Now here it was, my past practically staring me in the face.

I studied the young man in front of me cautiously. He didn't seem especially threatening, but I knew that didn't really mean anything. He moved gracefully and energetically, like he thought his sheer magnetism and passion for his cause could reel me in. His Teramese eyes shone unnaturally bright in the moonlight, intimidatingly beautiful. All the tales I'd ever heard of the Teramese people had waxed poetic about their stunning features, especially their bright eyes contrasting with their bronze complexions.

His beauty made me trust him less. In Alrenor, everything beautiful was deadly.

"That doesn't explain why you were following me," I said. "If you wanted to talk to me, a visit to the abbey would have been the...normal way to go about it."

Caesiem flashed me a disarming smile, his teeth pure white. "Maybe I didn't want a normal conversation. Normal is boring...and possibly dangerous, depending on what you're discussing."

I cast him a sharp look. "If your group doesn't approve of the Court of Elders, it sounds very much like you agree with the Alrenians."

His face darkened. "We don't agree with a lot of things the Elders are doing—or rather, not doing. But that doesn't mean we agree with the Alrenians, either. We're our own cause."

With a laugh, I shook my head. "Who cares about the empress anyway? She's only a figurehead—something to appease the Alrenians and prevent civil war. It's the Alrenian citizens that trouble me more." I narrowed my eyes. "What does your group hope to accomplish? And what do you want with me?"

Caesiem's eyes widened eagerly. "Listen," he blurted, his eyes making a quick scan of the street to ensure we were still alone. "Figurehead or not, the empress is dangerous. My group sought you out because our numbers are still small, and we need all the help we can get. Jaliana needs to be executed."

CHAPTER SIX

Jalie

IT WAS IMPOSSIBLE TO SLEEP with the weight of my potential execution hanging over me like a storm cloud. Even worse was the constant presence of Kovi Ettonou. Sometimes he stood or paced on the opposite side of my room, like he was without need of rest or sleep. At last, he drew a book from a bag in the corner—one a servant had dropped off earlier—and settled onto my settee to read. Even though he rarely spared me a glance, I couldn't ignore him. Every once in a while he shifted, just barely, or drew a long breath that stirred quietly through the still room.

Sweet young Jalie. I startled at the gentle voice, drifting like a soft breeze kissing my brow. A lullaby lulling me into a dream. Sitting up, I scanned my room to find a woman standing before the doors leading to my balcony. I didn't recall them having been open earlier, but they were now, letting the night air brush across my face. It carried an unusual chill with it.

"Who are you?" I frowned, half-alarmed and half-entranced by the sight of the stranger in front of me. Her porcelain skin wasn't Forwyn or Alrenian, though it seemed to glow, as ethereal as the silver starlight outside. Fiery red curls tumbled past her shoulders while her blue eyes stared as if they could see straight into my soul.

A shiver of both fear and delight washed over me. It was like something within this woman called out to me, and something inside me answered.

My eyes shot to Kovi, who lounged on the settee, never lifting his gaze from his book.

The woman waved a careless hand toward the Forwyn soldier. "He can't see or hear us right now," she said in her breathtakingly beautiful voice. As she crossed the room to me, her silver gown whispered about her bare feet and glistened like it was made of the moon and stars themselves. "I think you've heard of me, young empress, though in only the worst sorts of ways. You know me as the Queen of Death, but from you, I prefer Nesrelle." Her red lips curved in a sweet smile.

I recoiled. "Nesrelle?" I breathed, my blood turning to ice. My earlier enchantment shifted into dread.

"Oh, my dear," Nesrelle sighed, as if I were a troublesome child. "I know you say you worship the Giver of Life, like the rest of your kind, so you think I'm evil. Made of shadows and blood and decay, most likely," she added with another smile, as if telling a joke. "But you know my story, don't you? How I was one of the Immortals created by the Life-Giver himself?"

Swallowing, I injected courage into my tone, the way I imagined my mother would. "Until you betrayed him."

Nesrelle shrugged, the motion slow and elegant. "Being assigned the task of escorting the dead to the afterlife was tedious," she said softly. A hint of sorrow shimmered in her eyes. She didn't elaborate, but I knew more about her story: how she'd fallen in love with a human destined to die. How she'd rebelled against the Life-Giver himself, and lost everything.

"Why are you here?" I asked, even though I suspected why. My hands tingled in her presence, as if the strange power I'd unleashed earlier was responding to her.

Her gaze pierced my own. "Do you want to know about the power you bear?"

"Not from you," I hissed through clenched teeth. "Never from you. Only the Life-Giver gives gifts. I want nothing to do with you." Drawing a breath, I gathered my courage. "I need you to leave."

Nesrelle merely shrugged again. "Very well. You'll change your mind soon enough."

She was gone in the blink of an eye. I found my balcony doors were closed after all. This time, when I sat up in bed and threw off my covers, Kovi reacted immediately. He cast me an unreadable glance before returning to his page.

Body trembling, I slipped out onto my balcony. I breathed deeply, relishing the way the garden's fragrance calmed me. The moon was full, draping the courtyard and its occupants in its glow. Now and then the silhouette of a dragon darted past the moon's luminescent surface in a flash of metallic color as its scales caught the light. The Keepers were often out late into the night or early in the morning, practicing at all sorts of different hours, in any type of weather.

Without glancing over my shoulder, I knew Kovi was behind me, standing in the doorway.

"I can't escape this way with all the guards outside," I said bitterly, my eyes tracking the Forwyn patrolling the courtyard in the dragons' shadows. "You needn't watch me so closely."

I heard him shift as he crossed his arms, but he didn't respond.

For a long while, I stood breathing in the scent of citrus trees, flowers, and saltwater, hoping Kovi would give up and watch me from inside.

So where did you get your devilish powers? Kovi had asked, and I'd scoffed at him. But why had Nesrelle visited me, wanting to discuss my gift? *Was* it even a gift? What if Kovi hadn't been wrong after all?

No. Nesrelle didn't empower people like this. She never had before, not in chronicled history. I refused to believe it was a possibility now.

"What sort of magic do the Forwyn possess?" I asked at last, my words sharp as daggers as I cut through the silence. I cast a glance over my shoulder to study Kovi.

His jaw was rigid, his shoulders squared as if prepared for a fight. I supposed it made sense after I'd tried to attack him earlier. "All sorts of magic. But unlike you Alrenians, we aren't limited to one gift. Once we learn to listen to Elhani's voice, to let his power work through us, we have access to all he offers."

For a moment I simply stared at him. "And you have no powers like mine?" I asked, lifting my hands, palms outward.

Kovi's bark of laughter was harsh, distrustful. "Nothing so...*obviously* dark."

I glared at him. "You only call it dark because you don't understand it. And because you hate everything about us and our gifts."

"I call it dark because it *is* dark, *and* because I hate Alrenians." I could hear the smile in his voice. "But don't play the victim here, Jaliana. You hate us too."

Huffing, I turned away again. Only one pure silver dragon remained, circling over the palace. Its steady wing beats rolled through the air like thunder. "What happened tonight...it's why I wanted to go to the library," I muttered into the darkness. "To try to understand what's happening. But I suppose it doesn't matter, since I'll likely be executed tomorrow anyway."

I considered mentioning Vionn's name as well, but it seemed unwise to speak the name of my dead mother's advisor. Not when my life's worth was being considered that very instant.

"The Elders don't want an all-out war," Kovi said, his voice gentler now. "I doubt that is what they'll decide." He hesitated. "Depending on the Elders' verdict… Perhaps tomorrow I can take you."

I turned back to him and studied the sharp lines of his face, but nothing in his expression gave away his thoughts. He wasn't doing me any favors. He was escorting me to a library that was rightfully mine, standing guard not as my friend or my protector, but as a defense against me. Nothing in him wanted to help me, only to understand my gift to better protect his people *from* me.

"I was supposed to sit the throne and meet with the people tomorrow," I murmured.

Kovi crossed his arms. "I'm sure it won't surprise you that that has been canceled."

Possibly to never be rescheduled. The next time the Forwyn and Alrenian people would see me might be for my execution instead.

Silently, I pushed past him, back to my bed to steal a few hours' sleep.

❮❮❮❮❮

I woke to the sound of murmuring voices. Someone was speaking in my sitting room with Kovi. My eyes flew open as the door to my chambers closed and Kovi reentered the bedchamber alone. The other person must have already left.

The settee across the room had a folded blanket resting atop it, alongside a pack someone must have delivered to Kovi during the night. I couldn't tell if that meant he'd ever slept or not. If he was the only one tasked with watching me, he had to sleep eventually.

I turned to glance at Kovi. His eyes met mine, the morning light making the golden embers in his irises flare to life. While I'd slept, he'd apparently left the chambers to exercise, because his white undershirt was damp and clung to his chest…his torso…his arms.

Heat rushing through me, I averted my gaze from his muscled body. Disgust, like a chill wind, followed swiftly afterward. It seemed fundamentally wrong to find my enemy attractive. I wanted to hate everything about him, from the way he spoke to the way he moved, from what he believed to how he looked and dressed. If everything about him was repulsive, it would be easier to remember the darkness lurking within him, to remember he and all his kind were beneath me.

To remember that even if he claimed to not really know his father, he still shared blood with the repulsive Elder Ettonou.

As my mind cleared, I focused on a more important matter. When Kovi had left my chambers while I slept, had I been unmonitored, even for a short while? Or had another guard relieved him? Would he make this a habit of his in the mornings to come?

"The Court of Elders has summoned you to a meeting one hour from now," Kovi said, interrupting my thoughts.

Of course, future mornings and chances of escape were irrelevant. It was already too late. *This* was the day when they would decree whether I lived or died. Fear writhed within my stomach like a snake, chased swiftly by shame. Alrenians were supposed to be fearless.

In a daze, I went about my morning routine. Before they had trapped me with Kovi watching my every movement, I would have dressed to spend time in one of the palace training rooms. My mother had always emphasized how important it was for an empress to know how to fight for her empire and herself. She'd taught me how to wield every sort of blade imaginable, how to shoot a bow, and how to use my body as a weapon. She'd also reminded me how often attempts on my life would be made when I reigned, and so she had educated me about the various poisonous plants that grew within Alrenor. Some I'd built up an immunity against under her tutelage.

But I couldn't dose myself with poison when a Forwyn was watching, not when I hoped he was ignorant about our Alrenian plants. And even if he agreed to escort me to the training rooms—unlikely—I didn't have time this morning.

Possibly my last morning.

Trying to ignore my fear, I strode toward my washroom. After scrubbing my face and cleaning my teeth, I gathered a simple ivory linen dress and blue sash. With the privacy of my changing screen between us, I dressed and Kovi bathed. He was so swift I could hardly believe it when he exited, dressed in his red and gold Aerekni uniform.

"Not much time left," he said impatiently.

Scowling, I stalked toward my vanity, where I brushed my hair and left it to cascade down my shoulders. Perhaps looking understated— even young and innocent—could help my cause.

But I knew, deep down, they had already made their decision. Nothing I could do or say would change the Elders' minds now.

I tried to pick at the breakfast already laid out on my side table by one of the palace servants, but my appetite was gone. I popped a berry in my mouth and gave up. Kovi merely made himself a cup of black coffee, the strong drink the Forwyn loved so much.

"Let's go," he said when he set down his empty mug.

Kovi was silent and solemn as he led me from the room and down the vast palace halls. All the intricate paintings that I would normally study with pride now rushed by in a blur. Despite my best attempts at maintaining a composed front, my palms grew damp and my breathing ragged the closer we drew to the throne room.

Or what had once been the throne room. Now, as the Forwyn guards—dressed in stolen Alrenian armor—pushed open the carved double doors, Kovi and I entered a magnificent room where the throne sat empty on the far wall. Numerous chairs were gathered in a large circle in the center of the room, each occupied with a Forwyn man or woman. Formally attired in vibrant colors, all wearing traditional Forwyn ribbons in their hair or around their necks or wrists, they sat quiet and still as I stepped forward.

The room itself was one spacious circle, adorned with immense columns near its walls. Instead of extending to an ornate ceiling, they stopped just below a smooth sheet of glass that gave the illusion that the space was open to the heavens. This morning, golden sunlight streamed from a cloudless blue sky.

"Empress Jaliana, daughter of Karye," said Elder Ilhoa, a stern-faced woman with greying roots and mostly silver and orange ribbons in her braided hair. Though all the Elders shared equal political power, she and Elder Ettonou were the most vocal members of the group. "Come forward."

Trying to ignore the pounding of my pulse in my ears, I slipped into the center of the circle. Kovi remained outside of it, standing at attention like a soldier awaiting further orders. Rather than meeting my quick glance, his eyes stared straight ahead, toward the empty throne.

Surrounded by the twelve Elders as they studied me intently, I lowered my eyes to the floor.

"We've called you before us today because of the crime you committed at our feast last night," Elder Ilhoa continued. Her steady tone betrayed no emotion. When I dared to look up through my lashes, keeping my chin tilted carefully and deferentially downward, I couldn't find a hint about their choice in any of the Elders' expressions either.

"Using currently unknown methods, you injured both of Lady Leanai's arms, blackening and cutting away skin. Since then, the wounds have spread, like a rotting, consuming infection devouring her flesh." Icy fear crawled up my throat and stole the breath from my lungs.

Kovi's voice echoed in my head. *Devilish.*

Gathering myself, I realized Elder Ilhoa was still speaking. "You attacked her unprovoked"—at this I had to resist a frown—"and caused an upsetting scene at a celebration meant to bring joy and unity to our people."

Your people, I thought darkly. None of my people had even been invited.

"Currently," Elder Ilhoa went on, "you may rule the Alrenian people as empress, as long as you work in agreement with the Court of Elders and treat both Forwyn and Alrenian peoples equally." Here, she lifted a brow as her piercing eyes searched my face. "Last night, you broke this agreement and forced the Court to reconsider our options."

My stomach tightened in anticipation. Here was the verdict.

After an unbearably long pause in which my blood continued to pound loudly in my ears, the Elder went on. "We have decided to spare your life and permit you to continue to rule as empress, but under stricter watch. From now until declared otherwise, Kovi Ettonou, soldier and graduate of Aerekni Academy, son of Elder Ettonou, will be your primary guardian, to be present with you at all times. This is in addition to the guards posted in the halls and on the palace grounds, for your protection as well as that of those around you. You will travel nowhere, within or without the palace, unaccompanied by your assigned soldier, or face a penalty of imprisonment and potential death."

Elder Ilhoa paused once more, her sharp gaze cutting into me. "Do you understand and accept these terms, Jaliana?"

I swallowed, but my throat remained dry. My voice was embarrassingly small when I responded. "Yes, Elders," I said, bowing my head even though my very bones ached in angry rebellion at the humiliating motion. Who was I, empress of Alrenor, to scrape and bow before these people? "I accept."

The Elders stood and dismissed me, like a naughty child being sent away. Kovi remained stationary by the doors until I drew near him. He shot one fleeting glance at me, his expression unreadable, before another set of guards pulled the doors open.

"To the library," I ordered as soon as we were in the hallway. Out of the corner of my eye, I saw Kovi's brow furrow. Likely he was thinking about how little authority I truly had, but he made no protests.

The palace library was an expansive space of glistening marble floors, deep mahogany shelves, and lush paintings in gilt frames. Golden light spilled through a single floor-to-ceiling window set in one wall, and towering statues frowned at us from the corners. A few Forwyn clustered at tables or chairs, speaking in low voices or poring over various texts. Guards lining the perimeter closely eyed the only Alrenians present, and I knew better than to approach any member of my people without express permission from the Elders.

Seeking the shelves dedicated to books on Alrenian gifts, I ran my fingers along the spines. There was everything here: large leather tomes with gold embossed titles claiming to contain all the information needed to master the war gift; collections dedicated to the mysteries and inner workings of the truth gift; and books containing endless knowledge about Alrenor's revered courage gift. Others gave insight into the rare protection gift, or the gifts of storytelling, wisdom, healing, discernment, and more. But nowhere did I see anything about the strange power I possessed.

I pulled books off the shelves, flipping through titles that claimed to list every Alrenian gift that had ever manifested.

Kovi hovered behind me, silent and motionless, except for when he needed to follow me down an aisle. I plopped book after book on a nearby table before settling into a chair to skim their contents. Pulling out the chair beside me, Kovi sat and plucked a book from my stack.

Opening it, he read through the pages, his forehead pinched in a mixture of curiosity and concentration.

For a moment, I caught myself wondering about the Forwyn and their magic again. Despite living among them for the last three years, I spent so much of my time in isolation in my own chambers that I knew little about their beliefs or lifestyle. I wanted to be skeptical about Kovi's claims, but I suspected they were true. Why else would the Elders assign him to me?

A pang of longing shot through me as I remembered the days when I'd lived in the company of my doting mother and her people. When loneliness and grief had been nothing but a stranger to me. *Why does it matter what the heartless fiends believe?* I reminded myself. *They think nothing of murdering an empress and holding her daughter hostage.*

I shifted in my seat to increase the distance between Kovi and me.

"What gift did your mother have?" Kovi asked, not bothering to lift his gaze from the book in front of him.

"Wisdom," I said softly, refusing to look at him. Grief made my throat tight and filled my brain with memories of her.

Kovi scoffed. "More like cunning," he muttered.

Anger simmered through me, and I pressed my lips together to keep myself from responding.

"What about your father?" Kovi went on.

"I don't know who he is."

This made Kovi pause and glance at me. "What?"

I waved carelessly. "He doesn't matter. Mother never married, so it's not as if my father would have been emperor or anyone important. She took many lovers over the years."

Kovi lifted his eyebrows but didn't comment further, instead turning back to his book.

After a moment, he continued, "You've really had nothing like what happened last night occur for you before?"

I shook my head, still scanning through my book. "Never."

Kovi turned to face me, his eyes assessing. Before either of us could say anything more, the quiet was shattered as the library doors burst open and a group of young Forwyn Dragon Keepers stormed in. They were all dressed in gleaming gold dragon scale armor, the same proud uniform once worn by Alrenians. On the battlefield, Keepers and soldiers adorned themselves in every shade of dragon scale armor imaginable, but in the palace, the Keepers and other elite guards and soldiers always wore gold. Each had a pair of swords sheathed ceremoniously across their backs and Alrenian daggers—long, curved, and golden—on their hips.

It was always jarring to see the Forwyn dressed the same as the Alrenians had once been.

The foremost, a young man around my age, scanned the library, his dark eyes burning with fury. As soon as his gaze settled on me, he strode straight in my direction, the other two Keepers flanking him.

"What do you..." I began, rising from my seat, but the man reached me before I could finish my sentence.

He seized me by the neck and slammed me into the shelves. Books tumbled to the floor, a few striking my head and shoulders on the way down. I clawed at his hands as they tightened around my throat, but to no avail. My lungs burned and my vision swam while the Keeper and his friends laughed.

"Yaelti," Kovi said calmly, but the Keeper didn't react, and Kovi didn't move to stop him.

"The Elders might have let you go this time, you worthless whore, but they'll see the wisdom in killing you soon enough," Yaelti snapped.

"Yaelti," Kovi repeated, and the Keeper sneered as he pulled back, releasing my neck.

I clutched my throat and gasped for breath, my chest heaving painfully. My eyes watered and my head spun.

Yaelti held his gloved hands out to me, still laughing. "Go ahead, see if your murderous power works on dragon armor."

Clenching my jaw, I forced myself to stand up straight and level a glare at him. He and his friends only laughed more before turning away, as if I were no longer worth their time. Fury smoldering inside me, I watched as they stalked out of the library, their grins arrogant and self-assured.

My gaze landed on Kovi, who stood motionless beside his chair, his expression unreadable. I rounded on him. "Some soldier you are!" Every word scraped against my aching throat like gravel, and my voice sounded raspy.

"I'm not here to protect *you*; I'm here to protect others *from* you," he said.

"Because clearly I'm the dangerous one here," I retorted, whirling on my heel and stomping toward the doors.

Kovi followed me out into the hall. "You're the daughter of a known killer, descended from a line of conquerors and killers," he said, his voice still infuriatingly measured. "You attacked an innocent woman at a party—"

"Innocent?" I repeated, stopping in the middle of the hall to face him. "She cornered me, and I've already told you several times that whatever happened last night has *never* happened before." I swallowed painfully. "And of course you would say my mother and ancestors are killers. You *hate* us. All your people want to do is use me and poison me against my own people!"

Kovi stared at me, the golden flecks in his dark eyes flashing with undisguised anger. "Yes, I hate Alrenians," he said, his tone dangerously low. "Your people enslaved mine for generations, murdered and abused us. Treated us like animals. Alrenians conquered whichever kingdom they set their eyes on and forced countless peoples into their bloody, greedy empire. And your mother?" He stepped closer, sneering. "The one you seem to think is so perfect and wonderful, gifted in wisdom? She murdered *my* mother."

I stepped back, shaking my head, even as a shivery feeling of unease washed over me. Something about Kovi's raw honesty jolted my conviction, making me doubt my memories and understanding of my mother in a way no other Forwyn had ever done.

"No," I insisted. "You're mistaken. Mother might have had to be cruel sometimes, because she was a powerful leader, and that meant making hard decisions. You didn't know her like I did. And it's clear the Forwyn are capable of great evil as well, actions *my* mother would have had to punish. *Your* mother must have done something—"

"My mother did nothing!" Kovi bit out. "She never harmed another soul in her life." He drew a deep, shuddering breath. "Do you know what her crime against your mother was?" Sorrow shimmered in his eyes, making my blood turn icy.

"She brought the empress tea that was too cold," he finished darkly. "So Empress Karye slashed her throat and left her to bleed out on her carpet before she called for other slaves to clean up the mess."

I swallowed back the feeling of gravel collecting in my mouth. "You said you were very young when you were sent from the palace. Were you even there when your mother died?" I demanded. "Or are you just reciting a story your manipulative father gave you?"

Kovi's eyes sparked dangerously. "How dare you."

"No," I said, "how dare *you* and *your* people pretend to be better than mine. You Forwyn have my mother's blood on your hands, and your rulers have used me as their pawn for three years!"

Turning away, I flew down the hallway in the direction I'd seen the

Dragon Keepers disappear. I choked back the wild emotions of disappointment and grief coursing through me, gladly trading them for my building rage.

I knew my memories of my mother were true. Maybe she hadn't been perfect—but who were the Forwyn to judge? They shed Alrenian blood as readily as they claimed we had shed theirs.

Kovi's story changed nothing. The Forwyn were still my enemies, and I hated them so deeply I could taste the bitterness of it on my tongue. They'd taken everything from me. The throne was still rightfully mine, and I needed to claim my title, to no longer be the puppet they wanted me to be.

I could almost feel my power tingling along my fingertips. I wasn't afraid anymore.

"What are you doing?" Kovi asked, trailing me.

Rounding a corner, I found Yaelti gathered with his friends, talking and laughing.

"You want me to test my power against your armor? Well, here you are," I snarled, seizing him by the arms.

Taken aback, Yaelti froze, his eyes widening in fear. Even his friends seemed at a loss. My power rushed through me, a burst of heat like dragon fire that coursed from my touch, snapping his armor until whole scales fell from his forearms, leaving his skin bare. His mouth opened in a scream as the flesh on his wrists blackened and a scent of rot and blood filled the air.

Before Kovi or the others could recover from their shock and grab for me, I released the Keeper. He stumbled back against the wall, groaning in pain.

I met his horrified gaze and flashed him a wide smile.

CHAPTER SEVEN

Lo

*J*ALIANA NEEDS TO BE EXECUTED.

At Caesiem's words, memories consumed me once again. *Family can never be parted.* Edi's glassy, empty eyes staring back at me. Dead. Gone. Karye's laughter: *I suppose having to live with the memory of this day will be punishment enough.*

Then the night I'd slain Karye. The scent of death filling the air as she murdered the other slaves around me. Her cold dagger to my throat. Then the moment I'd claimed the blade, slicing open her neck. The spurt of fresh blood against my face. The painful, lurching feeling of horror when I stared at Karye's body and her wide, vacant eyes, and all it did was remind me of losing my brother all over again.

She'd deserved to die, but that knowledge couldn't erase my guilt. Couldn't erase the agony of realizing all my hope for revenge had been in vain.

I couldn't face those feelings again. I wouldn't spend additional years of my life trying to atone for even more blood on my hands.

"You chose the wrong woman," I said, turning away from Caesiem before he could continue.

"Lo…" he started, picking up his blade from the street and jogging after me.

His use of my nickname startled me. How long had he been following me, watching me?

"No," I said, my voice harsh as I refused to look at him. "Stop following me. Return to your secret group. Leave me out of this."

At the sound of approaching footsteps, Caesiem fell into step beside me. My instinct was to melt into the shadows, but there wasn't time. I glanced over my shoulder, nearly sighing in relief when I spotted a Forwyn guard approaching. He was an older man, his eyes kind even as his bearded face set into a firm expression. He set me at ease at once.

As he drew near, the guard gave me a nod in greeting. "Are you all right?" he asked, his eyes darting to Caesiem suspiciously before returning to me. He'd probably heard my raised voice in the stillness of the night.

"Yes, sir," Caesiem said quickly, flashing him a dazzling smile.

The guard simply stared at him, his expression as unyielding as stone. "I'd like to hear from the lady," he replied shortly, the friendly glint in his eyes turning dark and threatening.

I relaxed the tension in my shoulders. "Yes, everything is fine," I said, and shot Caesiem a pointed look. "I was just returning home."

Studying me carefully, the guard asked, "Do you need me to walk you home?"

Not to be put off, Caesiem smiled again as he shoved his hands into his pockets. "That's unnecessary, right, Lo?" He turned his grinning face toward me. "I was escorting her home."

For an instant, I blinked at Caesiem, wondering at his sheer audacity. What made him think I'd trust him? He wasn't even one of *my* people, yet he insisted he wanted to help us? What made him think I wanted to even see him again? But before I could protest, I caught a flash of movement behind him, within the shadows at the edge of the street.

My breath caught in my chest when I saw the figure. All my life, I'd heard stories about the guidespirits, mysterious beings that seemed half-myth and only appeared every once in a great while to those of Forwyn blood. Some claimed they were the souls of those who'd gone before us, reappearing at important moments to guide or reassure us. Others said they were immortal beings apart from humans, sent by Elhani to ensure his Chosen People walked in his ways. In stories, they influenced fates and eased pain, ushered in miracles and granted peace in someone's final moments.

And here, now, I knew without a doubt I was being visited by a guidespirit. The figure glowed with an otherworldly aura, clothed in a shimmering, pure white gown like a Forwyn girl on her Celebration Day. She looked like a woman, black hair draped over her shoulders in waves as her gaze met mine. Though her expression was friendly, with her mouth set in a gentle smile, her deep eyes shone with a powerful light. She gestured toward Caesiem. Without speaking a word, I could sense what she wanted: I needed to listen to Caesiem and learn more about his cause.

When I blinked, the guidespirit was gone. I glanced back at Caesiem, who was still looking at me expectantly. Though in that magical moment when I'd met eyes with the guidespirit, it had felt like lifetimes had passed, in reality it had all happened in a heartbeat. I drew a breath, hoping the stories of guidespirits were true and this mysterious woman wasn't leading me astray. That this truly was Elhani's will for me, the path I was meant to follow.

"Yes," I agreed with Caesiem, my eyes meeting his unnaturally bright ones. "He's escorting me home."

Caesiem's eyes widened almost imperceptibly before his amiable smile slipped back into place. The guard nodded once more and bid us goodnight as he turned away.

"You changed your mind," Caesiem said casually, strolling alongside me down the street.

I glanced at the stars twinkling in the velvet sky, at the moon bathing us in its glowing silver rays. Everything seemed entirely normal again, without a sign of a guidespirit or anything else supernatural in sight, and yet—everything felt different. The hairs on my arms stood up, and I repressed a shiver, not of cold or fear but a rush of delight and assurance. Whatever was happening, it was Elhani-blessed. I was sure of it.

"Not entirely," I told Caesiem at last. "I'll meet with your group and see how I can ensure we keep my people safe. But I won't join any plots to murder the empress. I'm a member of the Circle of Serenity. It's against my vows to shed blood."

Caesiem looked askance at me. "Ah, I see." When he spoke, his Teramese accent made every sound seem richer, more beautiful than I'd ever thought the merchant tongue could be. As much as I distrusted the young man, I could have listened to him speak his musical words forever.

Despite his acknowledgment, he continued to shoot me skeptical glances as we wound our way toward the abbey. My annoyance grew until I could keep silent no longer.

"Why do you keep looking at me like that?" I ground out.

Caesiem shrugged and slipped his hands into his pockets again. As he strolled beside me, he settled into whistling a jaunty tune that must have been Teramese, because it was nothing I recognized. We passed a few more guards who greeted us warmly, reminding me that there was hope for Alrenor yet. When the natives slept, we Forwyn kept the land peaceful. Welcoming.

Finally, when we reached the abbey door, where there wasn't another soul in sight, Caesiem stopped whistling and turned to me, his earnest expression returning. "I'm not sure I see the point in vowing not to shed blood," he admitted, shrugging again, as if he could brush off my rising anger at this sentiment of his with a mere gesture.

"You don't see the *point* in choosing not to be like the bloodthirsty Alrenians and take other lives?" I said, unable to keep the shock from my voice. "Are the Teramese barbarians?"

Rather than look offended, Caesiem's mouth twitched, bringing out the dimples around his mouth. "No, we just don't think evil should keep living so it can keep killing the innocent." He leaned closer to me, tapping me on my shoulder like we were old friends.

I glared at him and slapped his hand away, and he laughed, as if he thought me the funniest person he'd ever met. "You're obnoxious," I blurted out.

The dimples around Caesiem's mouth flashed again. "I know you don't think I'm wrong," he said, his gaze steady as he watched my reaction. "You wouldn't have killed Empress Karye if you believed differently, *amara'rekni.*"

I lifted my chin and narrowed my eyes at him. "Stop. Calling. Me. That."

He bowed his head. "Forgive me, Lo."

"Only my friends call me Lo."

Caesiem offered me a crooked grin. "So I've heard. But if you're going to come with me to my…group…then I'll have to trust you as much as you'll have to trust me. So can we consider ourselves friends?"

I sucked in a deep breath. "I'll think about it. But I expect a full explanation about why a Teramese man has any interest in justice for the Forwyn."

He smiled warmly. "I'll come back to fetch you tomorrow night, and I'll explain everything." He lifted his hands where I could see them, palms facing me. "With no weapons. I'll take you to meet everyone and you can learn more about what we do. If you join us…well," he finished, "your people will thank you, I'm sure."

"All right," I said slowly.

He glanced toward the abbey. "Can you tie a ribbon outside your bedroom window, so I can find you?"

I frowned. "Didn't you just confess to spying on me?"

He merely cracked a smile. "Not *that* intently. Even spies have boundaries."

Rolling my eyes, I nodded. "I have a few extra for when they fray or break. I'll tie a red one outside—it'll be hard for you to miss."

"Goodnight, Lo," he whispered, and turned on his heel, taking up his tune again as he walked back down the empty street.

For a moment, I could only stare at his retreating back, wondering what I was getting myself into.

❮❮❮❮❮

Morning light filtering warm and golden into my room woke me from my restless dreams. I sat up, brushing the sleep from my eyes and recalling the events of the night before. Unease crept up my spine as I wondered what the sisters might think if they found out what I'd agreed to, even if I'd refused to break my vows.

My dreams had been bloody and violent, reminding me of everything I hated about my past. Nothing would make me change my mind. I would stay true to the path I'd chosen, no matter what Caesiem thought.

I rolled out of bed and went about my morning ritual, dressing in the grey linen tunic and leggings all the sisters at the abbey wore and entering the washroom to scrub my face, moisturize my hair, and clean my teeth. As I did, other uncomfortable memories surfaced: Caesiem's musical voice. His charming smile.

Heat flushed my face, and I cringed. Handsome as he was, he was infuriating. I would not be a silly girl and fall prey to his smiles. Especially because my vows also forbid it.

He wasn't worthy of trust, no matter his talk of friendship.

Had I truly seen a guidespirit last night? My arms tingled at the memory, and another shiver coursed down my spine. *Maybe it was another dream,* I thought.

But no, of course not. I would have never agreed to continue talking with Caesiem, much less agree to meet the other members of his group, unless I had seen something miraculous. I would simply have to trust that this guidespirit had a good reason for pushing me to make this choice. Something Caesiem and his group was doing *had* to be what my people needed.

I followed the scent of food toward the kitchen. It was O'emia's turn to prepare breakfast, so it was her I found pulling the freshly baked, golden *lini* from the oven. My mouth watered. A few of the other sisters had already gathered, picking up plates and helping themselves to heaping servings of scrambled eggs and sausage from the frying pan before O'emia turned and deposited a freshly sugar-dusted roll on each of their plates. I joined the line to gather my food, smiling and thanking O'emia as she offered me my own *lini*.

After we each finished filling our plates, we found our places at the long table. I seated myself between Pauni'a and Naina. When Naina stood, we followed her lead.

Just as we did in the sanctuary each evening, we sang a Forwyn song of gratitude to Elhani. Then we sat and ate as one. Naina passed a pot of coffee and dishes of cream and sugar around the table. Everyone chattered about their assigned rounds for the day, the atmosphere lighthearted and easy.

At my side, Naina nudged me gently. As usual, her eyes were sharp, discerning. Imagining she could see into my mind, my heart beat a little faster.

"You are quiet this morning," she murmured, keeping her voice lower than the surrounding conversations.

Shrugging, I lifted my coffee to my mouth and blew against the steam rising from it. In the buttery light spilling through the little kitchen window, the mysteries of the night before seemed distant. But the secrets weighed heavily on me.

"How is your jaw?" she asked, her gentle smile still in place.

"Still swollen," I said with a laugh, even though I knew that was obvious to her from a single glance.

She swallowed a bite of eggs. "You will be careful on your rounds today?"

I resisted the urge to roll my eyes. "Yes, Naina." Mimicking her, I elbowed her lightly in the ribs. "I won't punch any Alrenians today."

Naina frowned at her coffee. "That's not what I meant. Try to avoid a fight, but if they hurt you, make them feel it." When she lifted her chin to face me, her warm brown eyes twinkled with mischief. "If they start it, you finish it." She winked at me.

After breakfast, our group training passed in a blur: a quick hour of stretching and practicing our defense moves in a few rounds of one-on-one sparring matches on the lawn. Concealed from the city by the high stone walls surrounding the backyard, we practiced without fear of being noticed by the Alrenians. Though, in the skeleton of their abandoned temple, it was unlikely any Alrenian would ever trouble us. They avoided the building as if ghosts haunted it, either out of shame brought on by the loss of their prized war gift or fear of the curse that had caused the loss.

The morning air soon grew sticky, but the stifling heat of summer couldn't steal the peace I felt settling into my heart. This temple was our refuge, a place forever untouched by the cruelty and pride of our enemies. None of my sisters knew about my nightly forays or my encounter with Caesiem. Though I was uncertain and uneasy about tonight, I was more confident than I'd been earlier.

At last, sweaty and panting, we all stretched out across the grass to take a break. Naina, who always claimed her bones were too old and achy to spar with us younger women, distributed cool glasses of water to all of us. I downed an entire glass before accepting a refill, splashing some of it across my sweaty face.

"And now that you're all too exhausted to let your minds wander too much—I hope," Naina said as she grinned at us, "it's time to practice listening to Elhani's voice and channeling his power."

Stifling our groans, we pulled ourselves to our feet. At my side, Pauni'a shot me an encouraging smile and offered her hand to help me up.

"I'm terrible at this," I muttered, thinking about the night before and how, even when I'd felt the threatening presence of a stranger, I hadn't been able to concentrate on Elhani's voice to save myself.

Clearly overhearing me, Naina shook her head. "Some of us have louder minds than others," she said.

The other women giggled.

Louder indeed, I thought. The memory of Edi's voice, of his body bleeding out in front of me, was never more than a breath away. My past horrors were constantly roaring inside my head, refusing to be ignored.

"Concentrate," Naina said softly, closing her eyes. We all followed her example, breathing in and out gently as we shut out the world. "Listen for the music around you."

Don't be afraid, Lo, Edi whispered.

I suppose having to live with the memory of this day is punishment enough, Karye said, staring at me with dead eyes. The slit in her neck was a yawning void.

My eyes flew open. The chickens were pecking around their coop, fluttering and squawking irritably at one another as they fought over their remaining feed. Outside the abbey walls, the bustle of the city was at its height: pedestrians were calling to one another in Alrenian and Forwyn, carriages were rolling past, and a smithy's hammer pounded out a steady beat.

On my right, Pauni'a had already vanished. She must have channeled Elhani's magic to make herself disappear. Glancing around, I realized several other women had done the same.

My heart sank. It was one of the simplest aspects of our magic to master, and yet I had only managed it a handful of times in the past.

My mind was simply too loud.

Don't give up, ahnla, came Naina's voice inside my head.

I snapped my gaze to hers, meeting her gentle eyes. I could feel the power from Naina's magic flowing through me, making me feel electric. It hummed in the air, a soft echo of the constant song Elhani sang to us. Few Forwyn had mastered magic to the point of being able to communicate inside others' minds, so it always startled me when Naina did this.

Keep trying, Naina continued, her voice gentle. *I have had more years than you to practice listening to Elhani. While you were still enslaved, my kind master had freed me to live and serve within these walls. You are still new at this. Don't let that discourage you.*

Warmed by Naina's encouragement, I closed my eyes again, breathing deeply. It took countless more tries, but before we all stopped for the day, I'd finally made my entire body vanish once for several minutes.

Upstairs we had a washroom with a tub, but downstairs was a room that contained several showers. Today, I went there to wash. We didn't have a system that heated any of our running water, as the Alrenian palace did, but I was thankful we didn't have to draw from a well. I'd heard that there were still many cities throughout the empire that had to.

Afterward, I dressed in a fresh tunic and leggings. My sandal straps wound up to my calves and fastened securely with buckles. Lastly, I paused before one of the mirrors hung on the wall and gathered my braids into my hand, running my fingers over my ribbons. Grey to represent my vows to Elhani, my people, and the Circle of Serenity. Black to remember the pain in my past I'd overcome. Gold for lost loved ones who'd gone to the Golden After. Purple for acts of kindness and service. Scarlet to remember the need for daily sacrifice and penance to wash away my sins. White to symbolize the Celebration Day I'd never had—a tradition among Forwyn to recognize the day a girl became a woman, on her fifteenth birthday. Since I'd still been a slave back then, I'd never had a proper ceremony.

Today, I was thankful I hadn't had to wash my hair. With the ribbons, it was a long process of removing them and the braids, cleaning my hair, letting it dry, and then re-adding the ribbons. Soon, I'd have to remove my braids to let my hair rest. Usually during those weeks, I preferred to pull my hair into a bun and tie it with my ribbons, or wear it down and add all my other ribbons to the gold necklace I wore. But for now, I could enjoy my braids. I pulled them all back and secured them with a leather cord, tying it securely so it would hold my hair away from my face.

When I was finished, I found O'emia already waiting in the kitchen. We had a round to do together, visiting a few nearby families who needed food. Together, we gathered leftovers from our meal along with a loaf of bread and some dried meat and cheese, placed them in baskets, and set on our way through the already bustling streets of Inalgoth. The presence of Forwyn guards discouraged open hostility, but here in the city, the Alrenians outnumbered us and often openly stared.

"Naina told me what happened to you yesterday," O'emia said, casting a sidelong glance in my direction as we crossed into a poorer district of Inalgoth, one more heavily populated with our own people. Many of the ramshackle buildings had sheets rather than glass to cover the windows, but it didn't successfully block out the insects buzzing around their homes. Any Forwyn we passed in the broken cobblestone streets had an eerily familiar appearance about them: their thin frames, stooped shoulders, and constantly shifting, wide eyes brought back memories of slavery in bitter clarity.

In response to O'emia's comment, I shifted my basket on my arm and rubbed my jaw self-consciously. "He ambushed me, Emi," I confessed.

O'emia's eyes crinkled at the corners, filled with heavy sadness. Several years older than me, I'd rarely seen her do anything but smile cheerfully under all circumstances. She was a constant light in the abbey, and seeing her give way to sorrow was unnerving. Her gaze left my injured jaw to scan the decrepit homes around us.

"We don't deserve any of this," she said in a low voice. "We don't deserve their hatred of us, the way they cast off working men and women from jobs and leave them and their families to starve"–she gestured angrily at a home nearby, where we could hear a small child crying within–"the way their healers deny us and the way they refuse to see one of our healers." Her lips set into a thin line. "The way they verbally and physically attack us when our guards do not see, or refuse us service at their businesses." A muscle in her jaw twitched. "And what are we doing, having to train in self-defense each day, like warriors? We are nuns, Lo. Our ancestors in Forwyth dedicated their lives to Elhani and served those in need around them, but they didn't have to train each day in case they needed to protect themselves and their people. They lived in peace."

I swallowed back my own building anger and frustration. "I know."

O'emia shook her head. "There's so much still for us to do," she whispered, almost as if to herself. "We thought gaining our freedom and having some Forwyn in power would be the end of it—but it was only the beginning."

I'd spent the last few years believing the Court of Elders was slowly but surely changing Alrenor at its core. Now I wondered if it was all a beautiful, elaborate mask, concealing the putrid flesh that was the truth underneath it. A wonderful facade until one peered deeply enough at the empire to see the two races pitted against one another with hatred so strong it stretched across centuries. Generations of bloodshed. Generations of a quiet war waged in back alleys and on street corners and in basements, as both sides murdered and wronged and plotted.

When O'emia and I finished visiting our assigned families and distributing the extra food we had to offer, I turned to my sister.

"I'm going to check on the Ilyanii family again today," I said as we walked down the street, our empty baskets swinging from our arms.

O'emia frowned at the sky. "I promised Jo I'd help her collect donations and pray over visitors at the sanctuary this afternoon."

"That's all right," I said easily, handing O'emia my empty basket. "I'll go myself and come straight back."

"Lo, I'm not sure…" she began, taking my basket hesitantly.

Although it wasn't uncommon for some of us sisters to run errands and visit families on our own, I knew O'emia hated it when we separated. She considered Inalgoth too dangerous for Forwyn women to wander alone. But I wasn't afraid. My bruised jaw was my reminder that I could handle an encounter and escape, if a little injured.

"I promise, Emi, I'll be back no later than the fourteenth hour. Besides, we haven't had lunch yet today and I'm *starving*. You know I'll come home as soon as possible for food."

Smiling, O'emia relented. "All right. No later than fourteenth hour!"

As she turned to head back toward the Vayelta District and home, I circled toward the rundown neighborhood where the Ilyanii family lived. They were a young couple with two small children, one still an infant. Both were healers, but few Forwyn could afford to pay much for their services, and the wealthy Alrenians refused to associate with them.

I was happy to spend a half hour there, asking if their food supplies were lasting and if they needed anything else from us. I prayed with the husband and wife, and held their sweet, chubby-cheeked baby boy. It was in these brief moments that I felt the guilt and pain of my past slip away, and that Elhani seemed closer than ever. My mind would still, and his voice would ring clearly in my ears.

By the time I left, I was lighter and more confident than I'd been all day.

I'd almost reached the Vayelta District and had entered a less populated area of the city when I heard the frightened girl's cries. "Help! Help!" she shouted in Forwyn, her words ragged with her terror and desperation. I scanned the street—no one else was in sight, not even a guard. The sounds of the girl's shrieks and people scuffling came from an alley just ahead.

My stomach plummeted and rage took over. There was no room for fear or doubt in my mind as I sprinted for the alley. I didn't even stop to pray or reach for my magic—I just threw myself around the corner, ready to attack.

"Arrogant slaves, thinking you're worth more than you are," an Alrenian man spat in the merchant tongue. He clutched a coil of rope in one hand and a Forwyn girl's arm in the other. "All you were ever meant to be was a slave. *My* slave. And don't think this is enough punishment for your escaping and hiding from me all these years."

The Forwyn girl was younger than me, gagged and trapped between the first man and another, who gripped her other arm. Though she screamed and struggled, she was on her knees and clearly overpowered. Her face was already swollen, and blood trickled from her nose and a split lip. Tears streamed from her wide, horrified eyes. They were the eyes of a girl who'd suffered and would rather die than return to that suffering. Some of her braids had been shorn off, probably with a blade, and torn ribbons were strewn across the dank alley stones. My blood boiled at the sight.

Neither of the Alrenians had seen me yet. Dressed in the elegant clothes of gentlemen—something they would never truly be—they had their backs to me as they towered over the girl, laughing at her distress. Laughing at the way she thrashed and tried to fight back, even now.

"Let's go, you worthless *yirak*," the second man cursed.

The two men yanked on the girl's arms, dragging her through the alley. My heart slammed painfully against my chest. I could scarcely believe the gall of these Alrenians. They were seizing and forcing a girl into slavery *in daylight.*

I gritted my teeth. Part of me knew I would be mad to give chase, but the other part knew that if I retreated to find a guard, it would be too late. The girl would be lost.

With a feral cry, I launched myself toward the men. *Elhani, help me!*

In my anger, his voice was easy to tap into. I heard it coursing through the air, rushing around me like the very breath I breathed. And I felt his power—buzzing and thrumming through my veins.

"Let her go," I bit out. My words were a command that couldn't be ignored, roaring like the sea. They hummed with a power so strong I could taste it on my tongue, acrid and warm like smoke.

As one, the men froze, grimacing in pain and terror. "Please…" one pleaded, releasing the girl to hold up his hands. The other swallowed in fear and followed suit. The girl collapsed to the ground, gasping and squirming away. When she stumbled to her feet, she raced toward me.

Immediately, the men fled as if they were being pursued, the one dropping his coil of rope as he charged from the alley. I stared after them, waiting for them to turn down the next road and vanish from view. Waiting for the rush from the use of my magic to dissipate.

Stillness settled over the area. As the smoky taste melted off my tongue, I noticed the alley's stench, a disgusting mixture of human waste and rotting food from the trash piled along its edges.

What was that? I wondered, both thrilled and a little afraid of the power I'd wielded. I'd never used or witnessed anything like it. I'd heard of some being able to use Elhani's magic to control others, but I hadn't controlled those men. They'd released the girl of their own will—out of sheer terror. Of *me*.

I drew a breath and turned toward the girl, but she was gone. In her fear, she must have decided it was better to run than wait to thank her rescuer. I didn't blame her. If Karye were still alive and searching for *her* lost slaves, I would do everything I could to make sure she never caught me.

Adrenaline still pounded through my body as I exited the alley and continued toward home. It horrified me that there could be more incidents like this happening right then, all over Alrenor. The Forwyn were spread thin—though the Elders sent the Dragon Keepers on regular rounds throughout the empire to ensure the Alrenians fell in line everywhere, there was only so much they could do. If my people were mistreated in the capital, they were surely suffering even more throughout the rest of Alrenor.

Maybe the minor acts of kindness I did each day as a nun weren't enough. My thoughts flitted to Caesiem and his passion for the Forwyn cause. *I will do more*, I vowed.

CHAPTER EIGHT

Jalie

WHEN MY MOTHER FIRST LET me ride her dragon Reyva, I was six years old. She led me to the Dragon Keep first thing in the morning, with the early dawn's light only a blush on the horizon. A soft sea breeze tugged at my hair, filling my nose with the scent of brine and sand. She'd clothed me in armor that matched what the Dragon Keepers wore, except it was small enough to fit me. She said only royalty could wear armor like this and ride dragons at such a young age. My heart swelled with pride. Then, using gloves, she'd coated the armor in vylae, a liquid that was poisonous to humans but that emitted a scent a dragon's sensitive nose could detect. It calmed the beasts, making them submit to us and our commands.

When she was similarly dressed, we exited the Keep to wait at the arena, the flat expanse of rock outside, named for the games and executions carried out there. The arena ended in a cliff that overlooked the city and the glistening Alrenian and Great Sea beyond it—a view that never failed to steal my breath.

It was the Forwyn slaves who worked the Keep in those days, feeding and tending to the dragons in the Keepers' or my mother's absence. Two of those slaves, who had released Reyva from her den, now led her out into blossoming daylight.

The thrill of watching the great dragon emerge from the Keep, her muscles moving sinuously beneath her shimmering gold and ebony scales, was dwarfed by the adrenaline that coursed through my body when Mother lifted me into the saddle and helped strap me in securely. When I stretched out my fingers to brush Reyva's glistening scales, they were smooth and unyielding.

Mother climbed into the saddle before me, dismissing the Forwyn slaves. As she leaned forward, stroking Reyva's snout, she murmured a command and the dragon leapt straight off the cliff, plunging us into a freefall toward the city. Heart lurching into my throat, I opened my mouth to shout in terror, but the rush of air ripped the cry from my lips. My chest ached for oxygen I couldn't inhale, and the wind screamed in my ears.

Then Reyva unfurled her wings, taking control and soaring through the wispy clouds. When she reached an altitude that made the buildings below look like mere toys, she beat her wings in a steady rhythm that pounded through my entire body like thunder. A sense of freedom and joy like I'd never known before rushed through my veins.

This is what I was meant to be, I'd thought, over and over.

When we'd landed later, dismounting and pulling off our helmets, Mother had tossed me a fierce, carefree grin. "That is what it means to be Alrenian," she said. "We do not bow to fear. We do not flee a fight. We do not flinch away even if we must leap off a cliff, because we know we can fly."

Now, the memory fell away. Standing where I'd once stood with my mother, the wind still carried its familiar briny scent as it tugged at my dress and whipped my hair into my face. Dragons circled in the distance overhead, untouchable to me. I hadn't laid a hand on—much less ridden—a dragon in over three years.

"That Keeper attacked me first. You saw what he did to me in the library, though little did you care," I said without turning around when I heard Kovi's footsteps behind me. I'd fled here, to the arena outside the Keep, for reasons I couldn't quite explain. Had my mother's courage-inspiring words led me here, or the dragons themselves?

After all, I knew what awaited me now after my reckless display. And yet, I couldn't bring myself to regret it. Not yet.

"Are you crazy?" He asked it so matter-of-factly, that I gave in, turning to face him.

Kovi stood directly behind me, but I couldn't translate his expression. His lips were set, his shoulders squared, but his hands hung relaxed and open at his sides. His dark eyes didn't appear angry or afraid or anything else I would have expected. Every other reaction I'd anticipated, but for this.

He wore an expression filled with the same sort of calm that had settled in my heart. Despite my fear, I'd resigned myself toward what lay ahead. Under Forwyn leadership, any criminals sentenced to death were brought here, to the arena, just as they had been during the days of my mother's rule. But instead of being given weapons and a chance to fight, the Elders shackled them to a boulder set in the center of the arena. A dragon ridden by a Forwyn Keeper would release a single burst of fire toward the prisoner—and it was over, in a blaze of flame and light and smoke.

I gestured toward the rock, where the shackles fastened into it waited, glistening in the morning sun. "Maybe it's better to die than to live like this."

Kovi's gaze was level yet piercing, as if he could read my innermost secrets. "But you're afraid to die."

"Alrenians fear nothing," I said harshly, the lie tasting bitter on my tongue. Even if I couldn't face my death fearlessly, I wouldn't shame my blood by confessing my fear to anyone.

Kovi didn't reply. I stood staring at the dragons circling overhead until I couldn't bear the silence anymore.

"Well? Are you here to drag me to the dungeons?"

"I'm here to take you before the Court," he said steadily.

❦

The Elders hadn't condemned me to death. I sat still on my bed, staring at the wall, numb with shock and relief and confusion. Kovi hadn't moved from his station at the entrance to my bedchamber, keeping a respectful distance between us he hadn't bothered to show the first night.

"Since you didn't kill Keeper Yaelti, we will forgive this trespass," Elder Ettonou had proclaimed, his dark eyes flicking briefly toward his son. As the Elders had sat in their circle and conferred together in quiet tones, Kovi had joined them, approaching his father to lean forward and speak something into his ear. I longed to know what he'd said. What argument he'd presented to convince them to spare me, and what had possessed him to make such a request in the first place.

Now, I didn't bother to ask Kovi. I knew he hated all Alrenians, especially me, the daughter of the woman who had killed his mother. But the Forwyn were a self-righteous people, and I assumed it was likely he felt gratified by granting me mercy.

Kovi didn't give me long to process the declaration, however. For a short while, he let me stare and process. And then he released an impatient sigh. With a few measured strides, he crossed the distance between us. "Put on a cloak and cover your face," he ordered. "We're leaving."

Stubborn and furious, I sat motionless. "You will not order me around," I said, my voice low and threatening.

"Who do you think is in charge here?" Kovi met my gaze levelly, his dark eyes like bottomless, shimmering pools of water. Not a ripple of emotion disturbed their calm surface, even though I could tell from the very air around us that he was furious. His aura practically radiated heat, and I couldn't help but feel terrified. When he spoke again, his tone was quiet, but power shuddered through the air, slamming into me like a tangible thing. "You will put on a cloak, cover your face, and come with me."

Air seized in my lungs as my body moved, seemingly of its own volition, drawing me to my feet and moving my legs across the room to my wardrobe. In one smooth motion, I opened the door and drew out a deep brown cloak. My heart thundered in my ears as mingling fear and anger clutched me in a tightening grip. But I was powerless to resist. My muscles stirred like I was a prisoner in my own body. I tied the cloak around my neck and drew the hood up so that it concealed my face in shadow.

What is this unnatural power? my mind thought wildly.

I could sense the moment I regained control of my body. The tension in my muscles relaxed, and I drew a deep breath, finally able to breathe easily again.

When I turned to Kovi, he had the barest trace of a self-satisfied smile playing about his mouth. It was clear why the Elders had so confidently chosen him, and him alone, to guard me.

He has the power to control people.

I couldn't contain my fury, couldn't even stop to think.

Flying at him with a cry of pure rage, I reached out, only for him to catch both of my wrists effortlessly. His grip was powerful and unyielding, despite how I turned and twisted, desperate to free my fingers and slam my palms against his skin. He whirled me around, slamming my back against the nearest wall. With my hands trapped over my head, my body pinned between his and the wall, terror seized me in a raw way it never had before.

I was powerless. Even with my newfound curse, I was nothing. Kovi was larger and stronger, and even without his magic he could effortlessly parry my attacks. He could kill me in my sleep on a whim. Force me to do anything. Command me to press my own palms to my face and see if it made my flesh blacken and peel into a bloody ruin.

Hot, angry tears flared in my eyes, blurring my vision as I stared at him. My chest heaved with helpless fury and shame and despair. I was already a prisoner in my home. How dare he make me a prisoner in my own body, too?

"Don't. Ever. Do. That. Again," I choked out. It was humiliating to hear my gasping voice, to see the shimmer of tears swimming in my eyes.

Kovi's eyes widened a little, but with what emotion I couldn't tell. It was gone almost as soon as it had flickered to life. He leaned closer to me, his breath warm on my face. "I suppose that was uncalled for, this time," he admitted, in what was probably the closest to an apology I'd ever hear from Forwyn lips. "But I will not promise to never use my magic on you again, not unless you promise to never attack me."

Grinning, he studied me a long moment, still inches from my face. I glared back, wanting his golden-brown eyes and sharp jaw to be as hideous as his heart was. Hating myself for even noticing anything human about him when he was everything I despised.

Finally, he raised his eyebrows. "Well?"

I realized he'd been waiting for a response from me. I swallowed against the dryness in my mouth. My throat, swollen from the Keeper's attack, ached and burned. Ignoring the pain, I blinked back my tears.

"I thought you weren't afraid of me," I said slyly.

"Only a fool has no sense of self-preservation." Kovi leaned forward further, until our foreheads were nearly touching and his eyes burrowed into my soul. "So, are you going to attack me as soon as I release you?"

I stared back at him. "Do you trust my word?"

Kovi smiled. "No, but I want you to say it anyway."

"I will not attack you, so long as you never use your power against me again." I hesitated a moment and added, "And never let your people lay hands on me again."

His gaze flicked briefly to my neck, where I knew finger-shaped bruises were forming after the Keeper's attack.

"You're right," he said at last, releasing my hands and pulling back. "It was wrong of me to not intervene. Your mother's crimes are not yours. It's not the Forwyn way to let hatred guide our actions. Only justice."

My taut muscles uncoiled with relief at the distance between us, and my unsteady heartbeat slowed. I couldn't forgive Kovi for what he'd done to me or who he was, although I could admit to myself that in his stead, I would have done the same. I might have even laughed as I'd watched an Alrenian choke him.

Slowly, I drew my hood over my head again, hoping it concealed the teardrops on my eyelashes. "Where are we going?" I asked.

Kovi couldn't quite meet my gaze. Maybe I truly had shamed him. Maybe there was a bit of humanity in his cold, cruel heart. "The Elders shared some information with me about the injuries you've inflicted. Apparently, the healers are reporting that both Lady Leanai's and Keeper Yaelti's skin is festering, bleeding, and rotting away. Whatever you started in their skin is spreading further up their arms, like their flesh is rotting away from their bodies."

A chill of revulsion crept down my spine. Maybe I *was* a monster.

But when I pictured Yaelti's hardened expression as he squeezed my neck, prepared to snap it like a twig, I couldn't summon any remorse.

"The healers remember seeing something like it on one other person before," Kovi continued. "An Alrenian in your mother's court, who has been exiled from the palace and lives in the outskirts of the city."

My eyes widened in understanding. I remembered the cloaked figure always at my mother's side, the cloying scent if one stepped too near him. The same man I'd longed to see earlier: Vionn, truth-gifted and former advisor to my mother.

"Vionn," I said, cutting Kovi off.

He nodded.

"I'm allowed to leave the palace?" I continued. A sense of awe and anticipation swept over me. I'd never been permitted to leave the palace, not in the three years the Forwyn had been in control. And even before that, my mother had rarely let me leave its safety.

Kovi's lips pressed into a thin line. "You won't leave my side. If you do… I'll be forced to use my magic against you," he finished firmly.

"Do the Elders know?"

Kovi glanced away. "They do not need to."

Although I would have preferred nearly anyone's company to Kovi's that night, my joy over being able to leave overtook everything else. I couldn't hold back my grin, and I was thankful for the shadows enshrouding my face as Kovi led me from my chambers.

By now, evening had fallen, and torchlight cast long, flickering shadows throughout the palace. Fewer people walked the halls, but I could hear the distant mutters of conversations from behind various doors we passed. The Forwyn guards stationed at their posts said nothing when they saw Kovi and me passing them. I supposed as a son of an Elder, he would never be suspected of doing anything without the

Elders' approval.

We entered the gardens, where Kovi followed the winding paths so effortlessly I wondered when he'd learned the layout of the grounds. It made perfect sense that he'd be required to be familiar with them for his post, but I'd never seen him before the night of the party, and, other than this morning when he must have been exercising, he hadn't left my side since he'd been assigned to me.

The heat of the day was still at its height. Birds chittered and flitted from tree to tree. The sweet scents of citrus and warm earth mingled with the tang of the seas, whose distant waves I could always hear, even in the elevated palace grounds.

When we reached the main courtyard and the guards swung the gates wide for us without question, my pulse accelerated in my ears. I was really, truly leaving the palace and entering the capital for the first time in years. An invisible weight, so familiar I'd almost forgotten it existed, unknotted in my chest as I breathed deeply. Freely.

This is what freedom feels like, I thought, and for the first time since the Forwyn had murdered Mother and taken me captive, a new and wild idea took root. *I could run,* I realized. *Leave this land to rot, let the dirty Forwyn keep the throne.* With only Kovi to dodge, the possibility was realistic for the first time.

But, as Kovi strode through the streets of Inalgoth, so confident I'd follow he didn't bother to glance back at me, I knew that running from the throne was never an option. *Alrenians never bow to fear,* my mother's voice echoed in my mind. I could see her piercing gaze in my memories, both encouraging and challenging me. *We never run from conflict.*

But maybe I could escape and find fellow Alrenians who would help me take back the throne. I could amass the allies I so desperately needed.

With this hope buoying me, I focused on the sights of the vibrant city I'd missed so much. Everywhere buildings were gilt in gold by the setting sun, and palm trees waved their fronds in a gentle breeze. Water directed from the seas coursed through little man-made channels throughout the city. Artfully carved bridges spanned them, connecting the various roads and offering places for fishermen to cast their lines or giggling children to point at colorful fish darting through the water.

Along the streets, window displays gleamed with mannequins dressed in colorful attire, sparkling gemstones set in fine jewelry, or trays of sugar-dusted pastries. Outside, vendors hawked their wares to passersby, gesturing to bushels of fresh produce or handmade pendants, the new trendy fashion among Alrenians in honor of the pendants the Teramese wore. At the end of two hundred years of isolation due to a Misrothian barrier once placed around Alrenor, our land was starting to embrace other kingdoms' customs with relish.

At one street corner, a man strummed a lythra, a small bowl filled with coins at his feet. The song pricked at my memory, stirring something both joyful and painful in my heart. Snatches of words fluttered through my head, my mother's soft voice turning the melody both beautiful and haunting: *Silver starlight on the waves... Whisp'ring wind and moonlight's gaze...* The lullaby opened an ache in my chest, making me want to stop and listen to the words.

Even Kovi paused, mesmerized by the gentle, lulling rhythm. He must have heard my sigh, because he cast me a fleeting glance, surprise flickering across his face before he concealed it. Was he shocked to find I carried any semblance of humanity within my heart?

"My cruel, murderous mother sang me to sleep with this lullaby when I was a child," I explained, refusing to look at him.

He didn't rise to the bait, despite my tone. Ignoring my comment, he lingered a moment more to appreciate the music, but the Alrenian man noticed. Abruptly, his gold-toned fingers stumbled over the strings, the melody turning discordant and ugly before halting altogether. Around us, other Alrenian passersby turned sharp gazes toward Kovi.

It was then I realized there were no other Forwyn in sight in this corner of the city. I couldn't find a single guard posted nearby, either. Perhaps they didn't patrol this district as frequently. Whatever the reason, Kovi was now the only Forwyn in a sea of Alrenian natives.

"You," the musician said, his tone low and dangerous, his eyes narrowed. "Have your kind gained an appreciation for proper music now?" He tossed a challenging look in Kovi's direction.

Kovi's gaze remained level, unperturbed. "I would think it would serve your pride well to see an unworthy former slave enjoying your culture."

The musician's eyes were as sharp as daggers as they snapped toward Kovi's Aerekni uniform. "You swine," he growled. "You have already enjoyed our culture enough, blaspheming the halls of our academy and defiling our colors." He set down his lythra and took a threatening step forward.

Here, surrounded by fellow Alrenians, my decision was instantaneous. This was my chance to escape—possibly my *only* chance. I could find Alrenians who hated the Forwyn rulers as much as me, allies who could finally give me the opportunity to take back my empire.

With Kovi's attention on the musician, I ran. Behind me I could hear his calm yet commanding words to the Alrenian: "You don't want trouble. Return to your playing." I wondered if he was using the same controlling magic that he'd used on me.

As long as I could get out of his sight before he noticed my absence, I could avoid him ordering me to return. My hood flew back, letting my hair stream freely behind me. Dodging a couple loitering outside a bakery, I tore down a quiet side street.

Gasps and voices trailed me as I ran. "Empress?" someone called.

My heart thudded in my ears. As thankful as I'd be for help from my people later, now I needed them to be silent, not to shout out my location to Kovi.

I rounded a bend in the street and collided with a male figure, knocking us both to the ground. Before we hit, he caught me around the waist and twisted me around, so he landed on top. My back slammed against the cobblestones and the air rushed from my lungs as I stared up into a pair of gold-flecked dark eyes.

Kovi.

I opened my mouth in vain, chest burning and blood seething as I gasped for air. With his body over mine, I was far closer to him than I ever wanted to be. Every breath I inhaled smelled like him and the soap he used: coconut and a scent that reminded me of a sea breeze. He radiated heat, though he was barely sweating from exertion and he wasn't out of breath.

I had an overwhelming urge to wriggle free and slam my palms over the bare skin on his forearms, but I knew any attack from me would prompt his use of magic. And I *never* wanted to experience what it was like to be controlled by someone else again.

"Running away in this part of the city isn't the wisest idea," Kovi said calmly. Still hovering over me so I couldn't escape, he nodded over my shoulder toward a Forwyn guard posted on the corner. When I followed his gaze, I found the man studying us warily, but as soon as he recognized Kovi's uniform, the uncertainty in his expression settled and he offered him a salute with one hand on his temple.

Panting, I sat up as much as I dared with Kovi on top of me. I didn't want to bring my face any closer to his than I had to. "H-how did you get here so fast?" I gasped. I couldn't decide if I was more angry or fearful, wondering if he'd used some other mysterious, blasphemous Forwyn power on me.

Kovi's mouth twitched in amusement as his eyes flicked toward the mouth of an alley, intersecting the street we were on. He'd taken another route to intercept me without me ever seeing him in pursuit. "Have you trained recently to run five miles, day or night, in under thirty minutes? Did you think you could outrun an Aerekni graduate, empress?"

I sneered at him. "Arrogance doesn't suit a self-righteous Forwyn man," I snapped as I rose to my feet. He was a head taller than me and still entirely too close for comfort. With a sinking feeling, I realized I'd just ensured he'd give me even less space than before.

"Running doesn't suit a proud Alrenian empress," Kovi countered, this time openly smirking at me.

I refused to look at him as he stood and led me away, this time keeping his hand firmly on my arm.

<ᒡᒡᒡᒡᒡ

Vionn lived in a crumbling stone house on the outskirts of Inalgoth. It sat on a dark, half-abandoned street littered with trash and stray cats. The only sound was a distant baby wailing from another ramshackle home down the road. By now it was full dark, with swirling clouds blocking most of the starlight and stretching the shadows to unnatural lengths.

When Kovi pounded on the splintered front door, an elderly Alrenian woman answered. She was draped in a ragged, patched dress, one so faded that it was difficult to tell if its color had ever been something other than grey. Her watery gold and blue eyes studied us both warily.

"We need to speak to Vionn," Kovi said, his rigid soldier's stance an imposing sight in the doorway.

"Who are you and what do you want with a dying man?" she demanded, her voice strong despite how thin and frail her body appeared.

"This is your empress and I am her guard," Kovi said.

I took that as my cue to pull back my hood and reveal my face to the old woman.

Her eyes widened as she studied me. Abruptly, she dropped to her knees, holding her hands palm up in a traditional Alrenian gesture. "Empress Jaliana, Hope of Our People," she murmured reverently.

My heart leapt, joy and satisfaction filling me in a way a citizen's obeisance never had before. Before, though they'd bowed to me, the Elders had stood in my shadow, forever directing my actions. Many of the people who sought an audience with me knew it too, and some bowed to me only because I was a Forwyn pawn. But this woman was displaying her allegiance to me, and me alone.

For a reason I couldn't name, I couldn't resist darting a glance at Kovi. Though he kept his face impassive, his jaw seemed more rigid than before. I pressed my lips together to contain a smug smile.

"Rise," I told the woman, who dragged herself to her feet, her legs a little wobbly at first.

"My son was proud to serve your mother," the woman said, keeping her head lowered in my presence as she stepped back to let Kovi and me inside. "It is an honor for you to bless our humble home with your presence, and an honor for Vionn to see his new empress in his last hours."

"Is he contagious?" Kovi asked.

The woman sneered, tossing Kovi a spiteful glance like he was a rat that had entered her house. "Are you frightened, imposter soldier?"

Kovi merely shrugged. "I have to ensure you don't let your son infect your beloved empress as a parting gift."

The woman looked duly reprimanded. She blinked and nodded slowly. "No," she said softly, "his sickness isn't like that." She repressed a shudder. "He lives here after being banished from the palace," she continued, the hard edge returning to her voice, "and being unable to work anywhere else. But it isn't contagious." She held up her hands, clean and whole, as if in proof.

"Then lead us to him," I ordered, and the woman bowed and scraped some more, leading us deeper into the bowels of her dingy house.

The mingling stench of decay and blood struck our noses the deeper we went. We traveled through rooms nearly bare of furniture and down a narrow hall. Beneath our feet, each floorboard creaked and groaned. It was obvious when we paused outside Vionn's bedroom door, not only because the smell was so much stronger but also because the sound of his breaths rattling in his chest echoed off the walls within.

"Vionn, you have a guest I know will brighten your final hours," the woman proclaimed as she pushed open the door.

In the middle of a small, dim room sat a bed that looked more like a cot. It was covered with a rough, colorless blanket. Beneath it lay the former Imperial Advisor, or what was left of him. The entire space reeked of death and rot, so strong it was nearly unbearable. I choked back my urge to gag.

Vionn, the mysterious truth-gifted man who'd for many years shrouded himself in shadows using a thick cloak and hood, now lay with his diseased flesh bare to the world. It was a horrifying sight: he was scarcely recognizable as a living man, his face literally eaten away by whatever affected him, illness or curse. His skin was blackened and dead-looking, split in many places and oozing pus and blood. Some of his raw, open wounds were bound in bandages stained with seeping blood, but many were visible, perhaps too painful for him to bear covering.

Horror crawled down my spine. Was this what I had the power to do to people? Had someone like me once done this to Vionn?

As Kovi and I followed Vionn's mother into the room, Vionn's eyes fluttered open. He drew in a deep, gasping breath.

"M-my empress," he choked out, his voice raspy. He moved his head as if to bow it, but the motion was barely detectable. "I beg your forgiveness for my inability to kneel before you." He attempted to raise a trembling hand in my direction before it dropped back to the blanket. "You bestow an immeasurable honor on me with your visit. What may I do for you, *Amara* Jaliana?"

Kovi hovered by my side as I tentatively approached Vionn's bedside, his mother watching intently from the doorway. Everything within me wanted to flee the horror of this room, but I needed answers. I needed to know what gift—or abomination—was flowing through my veins.

"You are forgiven," I said, keeping my voice steady, hoping I sounded as royal and impressive as I recalled my mother being. "I remember and recognize the many years of loyal service you gave to my mother, and I thank you. But..." My eyes burned with the stink of the room; my throat was thick as I forced myself to choke down each breath. "I need to know the—cause of your affliction."

Vionn sighed deeply, closing his eyes in either shame or weariness. He held up a shaking hand, palm outward. It was one of the few patches of his skin not darkened with disease. "I have a little strength left," he murmured, opening his eyes, "to show you, *amara.*"

I blinked at his palm. It had been years since I'd been around a truth-gifted Alrenian, but I knew what he was speaking of: his ability to share a truth-vision with a mere touch. I reached out, but Kovi intercepted me, grasping my wrist gently but firmly.

A surge of electricity flooded up my arm. I told myself it had everything to do with surprise, and nothing to do with his touch—human contact was rare for me now, living among my enemies—or his apparent concern for my well-being.

"What are you doing?" he demanded, his tone low with suspicion.

The warmth in my chest, like the gradual thaw of ice, refroze in an instant. Kovi didn't care about my safety, and he never would. And I didn't want him to, either.

I rolled my eyes. "Unhand me. This isn't an Alrenian conspiracy. Vionn is using his truth gift to show me what happened to him."

Kovi's eyes flickered dangerously, but he released his hold on me. I placed my hand atop Vionn's cool, dry palm.

The vision pulled me in immediately. Vionn was kneeling in a private room that looked like it was a part of the palace staff chambers, his eyes closed as if he were focusing on calling a vision. Though he was alone, a commanding voice spoke through the room, echoing in the small space: *The truths you hold back from the empress will eat away at you. They will be your end.* The room quaked, shaking Vionn as he opened wide, terrified eyes, glancing around to study the shadows. He was alone.

Enraged, I yanked my hand back. "You kept secrets from my mother?" I demanded, glaring at the dying man.

Slowly, painfully, Vionn shook his head, rustling his pillow. "Never, *amara.* I only shared the truths she wanted to hear. I blocked others the Life-Giver sent, ones about the Forwyn. This affliction you see consuming me is a curse for the crime of misusing my gift. It is like a living death, one that stems from Nesrelle's power."

I felt a shudder run through me at the mention of the Queen of Death. It reminded me of her visit to me.

"The Life-Giver permitted Nesrelle to visit and punish me for my sins, and this is how she chose to make me suffer," Vionn continued.

"The Life-Giver expects all truth-gifted to share even difficult, unwelcome truths. I'm cursed for not speaking the truth he wanted me to: that Alrenor enslaving the Forwyn people grieved and enraged him." He closed his eyes wearily. "He has cursed all of Alrenor for our misdeeds."

My body burned with anger. "No," I said, shaking my head, refusing to believe despite what I knew about truth-gifted Alrenians. They couldn't lie, which meant that Vionn couldn't lie. "The Forwyn are unbelievers. Why would the Life-Giver curse his Chosen People for conquering a land of evil-doers? They are less than us. Defiled. Unworthy," I bit out, each word coming out harsher.

Out of the corner of my eye, I saw Kovi shoot me a glare, this time not bothering to hide his hatred with a soldier's impassive expression. I ignored him.

"Some Forwyn believe in the Life-Giver. They say he was a Forwyn man who came to fulfill their god Elhani's will. All I know for certain is that the Life-Giver took no joy in how we treated our slaves," Vionn whispered. "Forgive me, empress. It pains me because I do not want you to believe I think ill of your mother. I believe she wanted what was best for Alrenor. But what we did to the Forwyn… Our hands are red with their blood. No wonder the Life-Giver seems to be allowing Nesrelle to have her way with our empire. She must delight in all the despair and death we feed her every day with our crimes."

Ice shot down my spine. All the angry heat in my body disintegrated into a chill that made me numb. This was Vionn, speaking the truth, all but confirming Kovi's assertion that my mother was a murderer. A ringing started in my ears that blocked out whatever Vionn said next, his voice soft and rumbling until it ended in a harsh cough that racked his entire body.

I couldn't move. Couldn't think beyond one wild thought

screaming over and over in my mind:

No no no no no no no...

Or maybe I was screaming it aloud. I was vaguely aware of Kovi grasping my arm, pulling me to my feet. I must have dropped to my knees. He dragged me from the room, leading me out of the house in a blur.

Vionn's raspy voice replaced the ringing in my head. *Our hands are red with their blood.*

CHAPTER NINE

Lo

A S SOON AS WE FINISHED our nightly worship and prayers in the sanctuary, my sisters retired to their rooms. I approached Naina before she could do the same.

"Did you need something, child?" she asked as she shuffled away from the altar.

"I wanted to talk about something," I responded, brow scrunched in concentration. I wasn't sure how to explain my encounter with the Alrenians who'd tried to capture the Forwyn girl.

Rather than continue toward the stairs, Naina seated herself on a bench and patted the space beside it for me to join her.

Settling down, I sighed as Naina watched me patiently.

"I…witnessed some magic I've never seen before." I wasn't sure why I didn't admit that I'd been the one who'd wielded it. It felt so powerful—too powerful for me to believe I'd use it again. Though I knew it was a sin to lie, confessing I'd used such power would mean Naina would expect it of me again, and I knew I would only disappoint her.

Naina raised her eyebrows. "Go on."

I explained about the Alrenian men and the Forwyn girl, but this time replacing myself with a mysterious Forwyn woman I'd witnessed interfering. When I described the power of her voice, the way it had swept over the men like it had physically hurt them, Naina leaned back thoughtfully.

"There is much we've forgotten about Elhani's magic," she explained gently. "Much that used to be passed from one generation to the next in teachings and stories, that we lost in our years of slavery." A slow smile spread across her face. "But that sort of magic doesn't surprise me. For one, Elhani's power is limitless. And for his people? All we need to do is believe and focus on his voice, and we could be capable of nearly anything. For another, we know his voice to be powerful, so why wouldn't he lend that power to his own? If they believed."

I stared at my hands, awe rushing through me.

"This is why we have been feared and hated for so long," Naina went on calmly. "We Forwyn were the first people to dedicate ourselves entirely to Elhani, and that is why we are Chosen. Others have magic, but it isn't as potent as ours. Ours is a direct connection to our god. For others? Elhani's magic is there, but not to the same extent. The Alrenians didn't want to accept our strength, so they enslaved us. But now? Now, we are reclaiming our knowledge, our heritage, our power in our god."

I drew a deep breath. "It's...incredible."

Naina's smile tightened, just a little. Standing, she patted my arm before turning to leave. "Don't forget to do your penance for lying, *ahnla*," she added as she strode away.

I started, wondering how Naina had been so perceptive. Biting the inside of my cheek to restrain my grin, I knelt alone in the sanctuary to say a prayer.

A short while later, I sat on my bed, awake and fully clothed, wondering when Caesiem would arrive. I'd already tied an extra red ribbon to the trellis outside my window, signaling exactly where he could find me.

I didn't have to wonder long.

A pebble struck my windowpane, followed shortly by another. I crossed my room to peer outside. When I glanced through the glass, I glimpsed Caesiem's unruly dark hair and too-bright eyes tucked away in the abbey's shadow.

Meeting his gaze, I shot him a look that I hoped he interpreted as *Enough already,* and crept out of my room. The dim halls were always undisturbed at night, the other sisters all either soundly asleep or occupied with peaceful tasks like reading or praying in their rooms. I was the only one who dared to slip into the capital's streets after dark.

As soon as I stepped out of the abbey, blessedly cool air greeted me. Summer's heat was gradually giving way to milder autumn weather. I lingered near the door until Caesiem materialized like a living shadow, complete with a mischievous glint in his eyes and a crooked smile.

He was clothed in shades of grey and black, and his shirt had a hood, though he'd pushed it back. I'd changed out of my grey clothes, dressing in the one of the few outfits I owned that didn't identify me as a nun. Now, glancing at my blue tunic and brown leggings, I wondered if grey would have been an easier color to disappear in.

"You came," he murmured. "I wasn't sure. I thought maybe you'd change your mind overnight."

I rolled my eyes. "You practically broke my bedroom window. What else did you expect me to do?"

With a casual shrug, Caesiem started strolling down the street, clinging closely to the edges where the darkness was thickest. It annoyed me that he was so confident I'd follow, but of course, I did. "Perhaps I expected you to be out running through the streets again instead," he said with a single glance over his shoulder. "Do you ever sleep?"

I glared at his back. "Do you realize how disturbing it is to follow someone so closely you know all their habits?"

"Do you realize I'm a thief and a spy and it's in my job description?" he rejoined.

Misgiving shot through me, and I picked up my pace to match his stride. "Wait," I snapped. "You never mentioned being a thief."

Still staring forward, Caesiem raised his eyebrows in an exaggerated display of feigned shock. "Oh, didn't I?"

I curled my hands into fists, prepared to fight or run, whichever came first. Maybe the guidespirit really had been a dream. "Who are you exactly?"

"A Teramese thief who fled his country to make a life in Alrenor," he said, finally turning to look at me. He stopped and pressed a hand to his heart. "Now I spy for my group to help right the wrongs in your land, and I only steal when necessary. I swear on my parents' graves."

I narrowed my eyes at him. "I don't trust you."

Caesiem smiled, lifting a hand and wiggling his fingers to show off my necklace of braided ribbons, their gold tones glinting in the starlight. "You shouldn't."

Open-mouthed, I gaped at him. "You just swore on your parents' graves."

He shrugged, offering the necklace to me. "I never knew them."

I snatched my necklace back and glared at him. "You're an immoral scoundrel and the worst possible person an underground organization could send to recruit a nun," I fumed.

Caesiem grinned irreverently. "And yet here you are." His face sobered a little as he scanned the empty street. Had he heard something? "Come, we need to hurry."

Still scowling, I shoved my necklace in my pocket, hoping I'd have a moment to tie it around my throat again soon. My neck felt bare without it, and I was self-conscious of the scar it no longer concealed.

Caesiem led us out of the quiet Vayelta District surrounding the abbey and into Keldrik, the less savory district set along the shore of the Great Sea. It was filled with pubs and brothels and gambling houses, all leading toward the shipyards and docks, which were often filled with other dangerous and unwholesome nighttime activities. Plenty of abandoned buildings clustered near the coast, and I'd heard many stories about the crimes and atrocities committed within their walls.

Unease crept into my bones and I darted a furtive glance Caesiem's way. A thief might be at home here, but this was no place for a nun. For the first time in years, I almost longed for a weapon. Once again, I fretted that I'd misunderstood—maybe the guidespirit hadn't meant for me to follow Caesiem. Maybe this Teramese stranger was luring me to a quiet place where he could hide my body.

But when I closed my eyes, listening for the voice of Elhani, all I heard was calm reassurance. *Trust me,* his voice murmured.

Caesiem wound his way toward an abandoned brick building resting near the docks, where the moonlit waters of the Great Sea lapped deceptively gently. Almost as dark as the stories about this district of Inalgoth were the stories about the creatures that lived in the Great Sea. Most were said to only swarm the depths further out from the coast, but supposedly plenty others drew close enough to the shore at night to drown unsuspecting victims.

As if reading my thoughts, Caesiem gave me a pointed look. "Tread carefully," he warned, reaching toward a cord around his neck. From beneath his shirt he drew out a stone Teramese pendant fashioned in the shape of a water droplet. I knew little about their culture, but word among the Forwyn claimed the Teramese were a suspicious lot, relying on pendants to protect them. Other than the Alrenian replicas now popular to wear as fashion, I hadn't seen any before. I wondered what Caesiem's symbol represented, and how it was supposed to prevent a tentacled creature from reaching out of the water and pulling us in.

We tiptoed down a creaky bridge spanning a canal running parallel to the sea. It led toward the ramshackle building I'd seen. We paused for a moment outside its crooked door. With a glance over his shoulder, as if he still expected someone to leap out of the shadowed streets behind us, Caesiem rapped a precise pattern on the doorframe. *One, two. One, two, three. One, two. One.*

The door swung inward to reveal an Alrenian woman about my age. She had flame-red hair and amber eyes with the typical golden flecks of her race. Her expression was pinched, like she smelled something rotten.

I straightened in suspicion, my heart racing. "What sort of trick is this?" I demanded. I prepared every muscle in my body to run or fight, whichever it came down to.

The woman smirked and twirled a curved Alrenian dagger I hadn't noticed before. Her gold-tinted skin gleamed in the moonlight almost as intensely as her blade did, and a sick feeling consumed me.

Here it was, my final atoning for that night I'd slain the empress. The angry Alrenians had found me at last, the *amara'rekni* they so desperately wanted to kill in order to avenge their ruler. For the blood on my hands, I'd pay with my own. Perhaps they'd slit my throat in a wide, second smile like I'd done to Karye, and my blood would splatter across the abandoned floor and coat their hands in the same disgusting way Karye's had covered mine. But I doubted the Alrenians would feel guilt for my death or be haunted by it the way I was by hers.

"Eloreth," Caesiem said, pressing forward to step between the young woman and me, "this is *not* how we planned to greet the *amara'rekni*." He shot me an apologetic glance. "I swear, *not* on my parents' graves," he continued with a wary smile, holding up his hands just like he had the night we'd first met, "this is no trick."

Eloreth giggled, sheathed her dagger, and extended a hand. I blinked in surprise at the Alrenian gesture before I accepted it. "Forgive me," she said. "I'm a little paranoid opening the door here."

She shrugged and stepped back to let us in, but I hesitated in the doorway. I crossed my arms stubbornly. "You expect me to believe that a Teramese and an Alrenian want what's best for my people?"

Caesiem, already across the threshold, moved so that I could see further into the decrepit building. At a small, rickety table sat several Forwyn men and women, most as young as Caesiem, Eloreth, and me.

Slightly reassured, I stepped into the building, letting the musty air fill my nose. A young man seated on an overturned barrel at the end of the table stood and knelt before me reverently. Before I could even speak, the others followed suit, until only Caesiem and Eloreth stood beside me, eyes as wide as mine.

"*Amara'rekni*," the first man said quietly, peering at me with soft, kind grey eyes. Too kind for someone plotting to murder the young empress. The ribbons hanging from his neck were in just about every imaginable color, telling a tale of both great victories and great losses. "Elhani-sent. You've given our people hope, and for that, we are forever grateful."

I swallowed back my discomfort and forced a smile, even though all I really wanted to do was scrub myself until I finally removed the blood clinging to me, to claw off my filthy skin. To scream and weep until the ever-present weight of guilt lifted off my chest. "Please call me Lo," I said. I couldn't help tossing a glance over my shoulder toward Eloreth. "I prefer that my…other identity…stays a secret outside these walls."

Standing, the man nodded vehemently. "Of course. We know it's not safe for you." His grin widened, accentuating how young and innocent his face appeared. Dimples cornered his mouth, and his light grey eyes retained their soft appearance. When he stepped closer, I realized he was only a couple inches taller than me. "Thank you for agreeing to meet with us," he finished, gesturing toward a crate near the table as he and the others returned to their seats.

Caesiem and Eloreth sat with them, but I hesitated. "I haven't agreed to join you," I explained carefully. "Only to accompany Caesiem and see what you have to say."

Apparently the group's leader, the man nodded along as if he'd already expected me to say that. Perhaps Caesiem had explained my feelings better than I'd expected. "And that is just what we'll do tonight."

Appeased, I sank onto the vacant crate. To my discomfort, I realized that Caesiem's makeshift seat—another upside-down crate— was so close that his leg pressed against mine. Our proximity sent a jolt of warmth through me, making me angry. I shifted, but it failed to put any real distance between us, so I settled my face into a carefully neutral expression and concentrated on the leader across from me, who'd begun introductions. Aside from Caesiem and Eloreth, everyone else present was Forwyn, a fact which set my heart at ease.

"I'm Renni, and you've already met Caesiem and Eloreth. And this is Mio'e." He nodded toward a young woman with a hard expression on her face, framed by shorn hair that was painfully reminiscent of my days as a slave, when we'd all been forced to wear our hair that way and go without our ribbons. She had a few ribbons corded around her wrist, but I was sure she'd earned many more than she'd had the chance to acquire. Renni gestured toward another young man, who was toying with his own collection of ribbons, hanging from his neck—"Wilvhe."

Next Renni pointed to a quiet man who might have been in his early twenties—"Nu'or"—and a freckled woman with a bright smile that put me more at ease than anything else—"and A'elli."

I couldn't keep the questions from spilling out. "What brought you together? Why organize a Forwyn group to go *against* the Elders' decisions?"

Mio'e's eyes flashed with barely suppressed rage as she took me in. "Have you forgotten what it's like?" she asked in a rough tone. Her hand snaked through the short ends of her hair. "The degradation? The fear? The way they try to steal your culture, your faith, your very identity and name from you? You've spent too much time in your cozy abbey praying and feeling pious with your nun friends."

Tears burned my vision. "*No,*" I protested, my voice tremulous. "I could never forget. Serving the empress was an unending, waking nightmare of watching everyone I knew but could never dare befriend being ruthlessly maimed or murdered. I never knew my father, and Karye sent my mother away when I was still young. Later, she murdered my younger brother for protecting me." A stubborn tear escaped, spilling down my cheek. "The rage and fear and pain live on. And the nuns—we don't hide away in the abbey. We *help.*"

"It's not enough," Mio'e cut in sharply, echoing my own thoughts from earlier that day. "Do you know that there are *still* Alrenians keeping slaves?"

"Yes," I said. "What do you think we nuns have been doing these past few years? We do everything we can to rescue Forwyn when they're attacked or hunted down in the streets, to help with the work the Elders are doing—"

"The Elders don't have enough influence outside of Inalgoth," Mio'e interrupted, "or, truthfully, even within it. We may have control of the dragons to threaten the Alrenians for now, but that doesn't solve every problem." She gestured toward her hair. "I was hidden in an Alrenian family's basement, tucked away under the Elders' noses, right here in the capital. Kept to perform menial tasks, but mostly for them to feel superior, to cling to old traditions and defy the Elders as they abused me. They took all their rage over their lost empire out on me." She lifted her arms to display the tracings of white, spidery scars disfiguring her skin.

My breath caught painfully in my lungs as my gaze snapped to Renni.

"It's true," he said calmly. "The only reason she's here with us is because she escaped out the basement window and ran—quite literally—into me."

I folded my shaking fingers together and tucked them into my lap. It was hard to know which emotion was strongest in the whirlwind churning through my entire being—rage toward the disgusting, horrifying cruelty of the Alrenians, or hopelessness at how unending and insurmountable my people's problems were. And overall was the cloying, painful guilt for the enemy I'd killed. Had I shed blood for nothing? For so long I'd tried to appease my gnawing guilt by reminding myself that Karye's death had brought freedom to my people.

"And you've recruited a Teramese thief and this Alrenian?" I said doubtfully, once again turning to Renni for reassurance.

Eloreth interrupted. "Not all Alrenians agree with enslaving and hurting an entire race of people. Not all of us despise you for your faith and powerful magic. Some disagree quietly, but refuse to do anything. Some *are* working to help you. But I know change will only happen if Alrenians *and* Forwyn take a stand," she ended, jutting her chin out as if she expected me to argue with her.

A'elli reached out to grip Eloreth's arm. "She's been my friend for a long time—I was the one who brought her to these meetings."

Eloreth hesitated. "I wasn't always passionate about helping the Forwyn. But then I fell in love with a slave." She swallowed, expression hardening. "His masters beat him to death."

A heavy stillness followed as we all drank in her words. Even though I was sure her friends already knew the story, I could tell they bore the weight of its horror with her.

"I'm sorry," I whispered at last. I turned to Caesiem. "And you?"

"I met him when he saved my life," Renni said, breaking into a grin that eased the tension and sorrow in the room. "He helped me escape some Alrenian thugs."

Caesiem shot me an easy smile, his leg still warm against mine, his close presence maddeningly and infuriatingly difficult to ignore. "Even though I'm an immoral thief and liar, as you already pointed out, I do have a few standards. I hate what the Alrenians are doing to your people."

I frowned at the table, weighing my words. "I know circumstances are far from perfect for our people, and I want to change them," I said carefully. "But I also know the Elders are doing what they can. With their control over the dragons, the Alrenians are threatened enough that they haven't pulled together an outright rebellion."

"*Yet*," Renni interrupted. His innocent face looked a little sharper, a little crueler. "We have the dragons, yes, but the Alrenians have more trained citizens than we do. We might have claimed Aerekni Academy for ourselves, defeated other armies and taken other strongholds throughout the empire with our dragons…but there are still Alrenian soldiers opposing us. I know Hemlaen has a large resistance group, even now after Aerekni Academy graduates ended a rebellion there a few months ago. If we Forwyn let our guard down just a little, our control will be ripped away from us." He leaned closer to me. "Do you think we're the only secret organization meeting and planning? That only

Forwyn are plotting at night? Have you heard about the Forwyn bodies marked and skewered on the outskirts of the city for our guards to find?"

I swallowed thickly. "No," I said hoarsely, horror curdling in my stomach.

"Alrenians have been murdering our people, Lo," Renni said in a low voice, his eyes full of sadness. "They're beaten, strangled, murdered with stolen weapons. Sometimes the victims are guards, but plenty are average citizens like you or me. Their murderers have been leaving their bodies on pikes near the city gates. Every single one has a symbol painted across his or her chest: the Alrenian sigil, except the swirling sun is always in red instead of gold."

My stomach churned.

"The Alrenians are an unnaturally strong people, as you know," he continued, "and most have been taught since birth that they are superior, chosen, better. They are proud, and they are trained to be fearless and cruel." He darted a glance toward Eloreth and smiled. "Thankfully not *all* are like this…"

Eloreth waved the apology away before the words could leave his mouth.

Renni turned to me, his gaze intense as he leaned forward, pressing his elbows on the table. "How long do you think the Alrenians will sit by and allow themselves to be humiliated by losing control of their empire, despite the Court of Elders' advantage over them?"

"You think the Elders aren't doing enough," I said.

Renni exchanged a glance with Wilvhe.

Before either of them could say anything, I went on, unable to keep the heat from my voice. "You think the Court's decision to keep Empress Jaliana alive and on the throne as a figurehead to appease the Alrenians and avoid all-out war is wrong. You think the progress we've made peacefully isn't enough."

Renni tried to offer me an appeasing smile. "Peaceful progress is good—"

"Then why do you want to assassinate someone?" I ground out. "How will that stop the evils being inflicted on our people?"

"We're dealing with more than one problem, all as best as a small group such as ourselves can, *amar*—Lo," Renni explained softly. "But what we do know is that Jaliana offers the Alrenians who seek to start an uprising far too much hope. Especially now. She's a danger in more ways than one." He gestured toward Wilvhe. "Tell her, Wil."

Wilvhe spoke in a rumbling, rhythmic voice that I would have found soothing, but for the story he had to share. "I don't know how much Caesiem has already told you, but Empress Jaliana has become a threat. She's been…attacking Forwyn, using a strange, unheard-of gift to harm them." His eyes sparked with anger. "I'm a Dragon Keeper, and I've seen what she's done with my own eyes. First, she blackened the flesh of Lady Leanai's arms with a mere touch, right in front of the Court of Elders at a palace party. Lady Leanai's skin opened and bled, like someone had cut her, but for the blackness that spread over her, like rot. Then, my friend and fellow Dragon Keeper, Yaelti… Jaliana chased him down the palace halls, seized his wrists…and…" He shook his head, as if at a loss for words, and his expression settled into horror. "It was like nothing I've ever seen before. His skin blackened too, decayed and bled right before our eyes. Both victims are still in the palace infirmary, where the healers have been unable to stop the progression of this strange skin disease from eating up the flesh along their arms." He drew a deep, shaky breath. "Word of the empress's power is spreading. She's under constant watch by Elder Ettonou's own son, an Aerekni Academy graduate, but the Alrenians will hear news of her power and rejoice. She's harming Forwyn, and no one is stopping her. Not permanently, anyway," he finished, his eyes darkening with malice. "To let her live is foolish. Disastrous. She's outlived her usefulness, and if the Elders haven't admitted it yet, then it's time for us to stop her."

A chill shuddered through my body. The power they claimed Jaliana had was terrifying. I could see how it would help the Alrenians gain hope to revolt, despite the threat the Forwyn Dragon Keepers held over them. But what this ragtag band wanted me to do was unimaginable. Unforgivable. I'd already killed Karye, and her death haunted me daily. Why couldn't one dead empress be enough to save my people?

Did I have to further damn my soul by assassinating another?

"Revenge is an empty cause," I muttered, refusing to meet the others' eyes and instead staring at the tabletop. These broken, hurting men and women couldn't understand my guilt. Ironically, I even felt guilty for feeling guilt. Who made daily penance for slaying a monster?

"That's not what the Ihlu'i Text tells us," Mio'e said harshly. "Not when it's about avenging innocent blood. Surely as a nun you remember the story of Huro's murder and how his soul shouted to Elhani, begging for vengeance?"

I squeezed my eyes shut. "But it is for Elhani to judge and wreak vengeance, isn't it?" Helplessly, I reached into my pocket and fidgeted with my ribbons, letting their smooth texture slide over my fingertips and calm my racing heartbeat.

When I dared to open my eyes, Mio'e's gaze was murderous. "Are you claiming that fighting for justice for your people isn't a righteous cause?"

I sighed. "No. I just mean that…it isn't everything. Sometimes it's empty." I waved my hands vaguely through the air. "Look at all the injustice still happening, even after I slew Karye." Even the words tasted bitter on my tongue. I had never said them aloud. "I agree something must be done. We must stop Jaliana. I'm just not sure that killing her is the only way."

Renni raised an intervening hand before Mio'e could go on. "We'll give you time to consider, Lo," he said. "It's not just an assassination we want, anyway. We don't trust the Elders, but we believe in you and what you've done for our people. We need a powerful figure—someone as great as the *amara'rekni* herself—who could be part of a new leadership. Or even just a figurehead, if you prefer."

"No," I cut in, shaking my head adamantly. "I won't be a leader. I don't want to be."

"Would you consider being a spokesperson for a new government? You represent hope for our people," Renni said earnestly.

My throat felt tight, but I knew what he meant. Knew the value in what I could do, the difference I could make. "I'll consider it."

"Thank you." Renni paused a beat. "And can we count on you to help us, at least with some small missions? We need eyes scouting the city, ears listening. I know as a member of the Circle of Serenity you already travel into the city daily to help, but I want you to do more, for us too."

I nodded somberly. "Of course."

"You'll join Caesiem on his nighttime rounds," Renni declared. His lips stretched into a wide grin. "You can continue to be a nun by day, and our spy by night."

"Perhaps witnessing some of what we've seen on the outskirts of the city will change your mind about killing our enemy," Mio'e added, her gaze cutting into me like a knife.

"I'll help you," I said after a long moment. "But I'm not promising to kill anyone."

"Lo! Wait," Caesiem called out, trotting up beside me as I turned onto a street winding away from the docks. "I believe the tradition of a gentleman escorting a lady home isn't just restricted to Teramyl," he added with a smile.

"Good thing you're not a gentleman," I said without slowing my pace.

"True," Caesiem admitted with a shrug, "but I would feel better if I walked you home. It seems only right after dragging you out here."

I tossed him a withering look. "I still don't trust you."

Caesiem nodded, his expression turning solemn. "I know. That's why it makes sense for us to get to know one another a little better, since we'll be working together."

I spun to face him, forcing him to stop in the middle of the street. "Then know this: I don't need anyone to walk me home. I've survived on my own all this time. If you want me to trust you, let me walk *you* home."

Caesiem smirked. "How chivalrous of you," he said, shoving his hands into his pockets and throwing me a dimpled smile. "I love it when a beautiful woman worries about me."

"I'm serious. I want to know where you live. Why you're here, in Alrenor. Standards or not, your response wasn't satisfying. Why would a Teramese thief ever care about any Forwyn cause? Why give two demon tails about us?"

"Feisty," Caesiem muttered, and I resisted the suddenly overwhelming urge to punch him. "All right," he sighed. "I'll tell you the story, but can we please walk while I do it?" He scanned the dark street. "I don't like staying in one place too long."

It truly felt like everything in this city had eyes and ears. Perhaps it was my own heightened fear as a Forwyn woman walking Alrenian streets at night. I didn't argue with him. As Caesiem guided me down a quiet side street, his face settled into a somber expression.

"Why do you think someone becomes a thief?" he asked softly into the night, keeping his gaze focused on the shifting shadows the clouds cast upon the road ahead of us.

I didn't have to ponder that. "Greed."

Caesiem barely concealed his grimace. "Maybe it starts and ends that way for some, but not everyone. Do you know anything about Teramyl, now that your Alrenian barrier is down?"

"It was a Misrothian barrier," I corrected. "Their king placed it around Alrenor after the Misrothian rebellion from the empire, shutting Forwyn in with the Alrenians for two centuries." I frowned at the stars. "But no, I know little about Teramyl."

Caesiem nodded slowly, as if still musing over what he had to tell, reluctant to share it. "Teramyl is…struggling. Though not everyone would know it from the outside. It's the lower-class citizens who feel it every day, in their hollow stomachs and their illnesses."

He sighed, running his hand through his hair. "Maybe the gods or fate wants to punish us for some old, forgotten sin our ancestors committed. Our magic doesn't work like yours does, or like the Alrenian gifts. We draw it from the elements: earth, water, air, fire. But there are few mages, especially water mages, and most aren't powerful enough to wield their magic unless they're especially close to the element they draw from. And I'm sure it comes as no surprise that the water mages are the ones we need the most to stop the dragons destroying our cities and killing our people."

I studied the way Caesiem's face fell as he fidgeted with the teardrop pendant around his neck.

"They say that about a hundred years ago, the first plague struck Teramyl. It spread at an alarming rate. Thousands died in only a few months. There weren't enough healers to help the sick. Life nearly came to a standstill. The survivors were left with a broken world, with so many citizens lost it was hard to run the empire anymore.

"Then there was a second plague, one that, for some reason, didn't hurt children. Only the older generations grew sick. Many died. My parents might have been among them, although I'm not really sure. Like I said, I never knew them. There were so many of us plague orphans, that we had to band together to survive. My group and I lived in a condemned home. We stole food when we were hungry and medicine when we were sick. Theft wasn't about greed. Only survival."

I was struck silent, processing his words. Our footsteps echoed in the night's quiet. Ahead, a patrolling Forwyn guard encountered another, who paused to chat. Their whispered words drifted toward us.

"I'm not sorry, if you're wondering," Caesiem added, his voice harsh. "When the world is cruel to you, you're either cruel back or you lie down and die." He clenched his jaw. "I refuse to lie down and die."

The Ihlu'i Text called theft a sin. Naina vehemently taught generosity and condemned greed. As part of the Circle, we sisters were all encouraged to live simply. Our penance came in the form of sacrifices: food, drink, coin—whatever we were blessed with by Elhani. It was our way to admit our dependence on him and to purify the sins in our hearts by letting go of our selfish wants.

What would Naina think of Caesiem's story? Discomfort pressed on me like a storm cloud. I preferred my world of black and white, my haven from my past of murky grey. Caesiem's account made my thoughts spin and my head hurt.

"I'm sorry," I said at last, "but that doesn't explain why you're here, or why you supposedly care about what happens to my people."

"I've lived injustice," Caesiem said, finally turning to me, and his vivid blue eyes were full of an intense light I'd never seen in them before. Maybe he truly was passionate and sincere about this. "I've been spat on and cursed at and called every sort of name you can imagine, just for existing or fighting to survive. I know what it's like to be mistreated, to hurt, to feel despised and forgotten. I bought passage to Alrenor hoping to find the Land of the Sun, an empire of luxury. But I found a land as broken as mine, and I can't stand it. I can't stand to see innocent people being stomped on." He sighed. "Besides, if we don't resolve the wrongs committed against your people, who's to say I'll ever have any hope of being treated better? I'm not Alrenian either. They don't exactly love me being here."

"They mimic your pendants in their fashion," I grumbled.

Caesiem rolled his eyes and waved a hand through the air flippantly. "Who cares about fashion? They still call me vile names."

I frowned in surprise, though I couldn't say why the thought of the Alrenians scoffing at another race besides mine was surprising. "They do?"

"Why wouldn't they?" Caesiem said. "I'm not one of the Chosen People." He said the last phrase with an air of false awe, and, to my horror, I stifled a laugh. I couldn't *enjoy* this man's company.

Caesiem slowed to a stop, waving at the pub in front of us. The wood sign over its door read *The Broken Crown*. Golden light streamed from the building's windows, the scent of tobacco smoke, ale, and roasted meat heavy in the air. Even at the late hour, I could see that the place was full. Laughter and conversation in Forwyn tumbled toward us like music, cheerful and inviting. "This is it," he said.

"You live in a pub?" I asked.

"No, I live in a room above it. The owner lets me stay here if I play and sing for his patrons a few nights a week."

"Are you a thief, or an entertainer?"

Caesiem grinned. "Both. Come on in." He pushed the door open, holding it for me.

"I should get back to the abbey," I said uncertainly.

Caesiem crossed his arms. "I thought you wanted to get to know me before we start our first mission tomorrow night."

I frowned at him. "For a few minutes," I relented, and stepped inside after him.

The air was thick and hazy, but I could make out the faces of Forwyn men and women clustered together at tables, nursing drinks and feasting on plates full of food as they socialized. Serving girls in flowing skirts wound gracefully through the tables, never tipping their trays or spilling a drop of alcohol. Near the back stood the barkeep, a burly man with a thick beard and twinkling eyes. He noticed Caesiem and offered a friendly nod in greeting.

"Caesiem!" he cried. "I'd wondered where you'd gotten off to." Then his eyes landed on me. "Oh, you found a girl. Well, that explains everything."

For a moment, it startled me that this man would assume Caesiem and I were romantically involved. Couldn't the barkeep see I was a nun? Then I remembered I wasn't dressed in grey tonight. No one knew who or what I was.

"You called it, No'ahim." With a grin, Caesiem reached into his pocket for a coin and tossed a drae onto the counter. As he ordered a drink, I couldn't help but wonder if it was stolen money.

"Would you like anything?" he asked me.

I shot him a pointed look and lowered my voice so No'ahim wouldn't overhear. I didn't want the man looking at me askance for stepping into his pub—with a man, no less. But another customer had already approached the bar, pulling No'ahim's attention away from Caesiem and me.

"I'm a *nun*, Caesiem," I whispered. "I only drink when I'm sick."

The barkeep slid a mug of ale toward Caesiem, who lifted it and took a long sip, sighing with contentment. "Me too."

Skeptical, I burst into laughter, and then immediately regretted it when I saw the victorious dimples appear around Caesiem's mouth.

"Homesick, lovesick…any kind of sick," he clarified with a wink. "Which, since I'm so far from home, I'm pretty much at least one of those all the time."

No'ahim cleared his throat and leaned toward Caesiem. "I was wondering where you were because someone came in earlier, looking for you," he murmured, his expression somber. "I told them to come back later."

I didn't miss the tension in Caesiem's shoulders. Unease prickled down the back of my neck.

Caesiem nodded slowly. "Thank you," he said, turning back to me with a sheepish grin.

"Stealing?" I hissed.

Caesiem held up his hands with a careless shrug. "Old habits die hard, I guess. These still get me into trouble sometimes."

I leveled a glare at him. "I need to get home," I announced. I didn't like the fact that for a while there, I'd started to sympathize with Caesiem and relax in his company. Maybe even enjoy it.

Caesiem straightened, his light expression falling away. "Are you sure you don't want me to walk you home?" He studied me with his intense, beautiful eyes. I looked away first.

"No," I murmured. "I told you, I can manage on my own."

He stood and stepped closer, leaning in so he could whisper. I repressed a shiver when his warm breath touched my cheek. "We told you, the Alrenians are murdering Forwyn in the streets. You shouldn't keep up this habit of wandering alone."

I turned—a little too quickly, because I found my face entirely too close to his. Caesiem's eyes dropped to my mouth before dragging back up to my eyes. Heart pounding, I took a hasty step back. "I have magic," I whispered. "I'm not helpless."

Caesiem cringed, rubbing his temple. "I'm not saying you are. I know you're not. I just...want you to be safe."

The sincerity in his words took me aback. "Who will walk you home?" I teased.

Abandoning his drink, Caesiem stepped closer and looped my arm through his. "I'm a spy," he murmured, his eyes shining with mischief. "Anyone who wants to hurt me would have to catch me first."

As we exited The Broken Crown, I drew in a breath of fresh night air. The city was peaceful, its white stone buildings glistening silver in the starlight. But as I walked alongside Caesiem, letting him share stories about Teramyl and its beautiful rainforests, or about the ocean he'd grown up beside, I realized that maybe I was in a different sort of danger now than if I'd walked by myself. Something about his presence, aside from his charm and wit, put me far too at ease. Something in his passion for his people's suffering, as well as the Forwyn's troubles, that made him feel like a familiar friend.

Caesiem didn't seem offended when I pulled away, letting my arm drop. I kept myself at a comfortable distance, even as I tried to ignore the magnetic draw of his grin.

You're a nun, you idiot, I thought. *Maybe you were safer walking the streets alone.*

CHAPTER TEN

Jalie

ONCE AGAIN, I AWOKE TO find Nesrelle in my room. This time, she leaned against the wall beside my bed. Her gown was black, overlaid with gilded lace that caught the light with every movement. She looked almost bored as she sang the lyrics to the tune the street musician had played.

> *"Silver starlight on the waves*
> *Whisp'ring wind and moonlight's gaze*
> *Golden dreams all shim'ring bright*
> *Bring me hope on this dark night…"*

As I sat up, she caught my gaze and smiled. "Are you ready to learn more about your power now, little *amara?*"

Little amara. A reminder that I was not only an inexperienced empress, but also far shorter than most Alrenians. Including my mother. It was annoying, the way she crooned those words, like a term of endearment. Except that they cut deeply, reminding me of how inadequate I was compared to the leader my mother had been.

I drew a deep breath. "According to Vionn, it's not a gift. It's a curse. What you did to him—you're *tormenting* him."

Nesrelle stepped toward me, her blood-red grin almost gentle. "Yes, I did what your Life-Giver asked me to do. I am the Queen of Death, Jalie. It's my burden to deal in ugly things. The Life-Giver cursed Vionn. Your god was the judge; I am merely the executioner." She lifted her perfect, porcelain hands. "I am his hands."

"Blasphemy," I muttered. "You serve yourself."

Nesrelle cocked an eyebrow at me. "Believe what you want," she whispered. "You know, deep down, there must be at least a kernel of truth in what I say. And I'm the one who knows how your power works."

"If the Life-Giver cursed Alrenians for the blood on their hands, why would I have this—this *curse* to shed *more* blood?"

Nesrelle's lips twisted into a cruel smile. "You've seen the truth. The Forwyn aren't innocent either. They're cursed too. This time, *you* are the executioner, the weapon. *You* carry the curse."

I scowled. "How do I know you're not just saying all of this to get me to follow you? You want me to hurt and kill—death is your fuel. Every time I use this curse, it strengthens you. Doesn't it?"

"And it strengthens you," she breathed. "You've felt it."

I couldn't deny that. Even now, I could feel the power of the curse flowing through me, warm and intoxicating. I remembered Lady Leanai's cries as she'd knelt before me and Keeper Yaelti's wide, horrified eyes when I'd clapped my hands on him. Holding power like that over my enemies was…terrifying. And incredible. But at what price? What did Nesrelle really want with me? How could I believe a word she said?

Nesrelle sighed, as if she could hear my thoughts. "Honestly, Jalie. I know you were raised to believe you're one of the Chosen Ones, that the Life-Giver blesses your kind. But do you have a gift from him? No, he let me give you this gift instead. Did he save your mother? No, he asked me to carry her into the afterlife."

I swallowed back the bitter sense of betrayal that rose inside me with her words. *This* was true.

At last, I voiced my fear, confessing what I couldn't deny any longer. "Vionn said Mother was a monster. That she was cruel, and we are all being punished for it."

Nesrelle scoffed, her laughter like music. "Oh, little empress. You would trust the word of a dying, delusional old man over me?"

"He's truth-gifted. He cannot lie."

"But he *can* choose which truths he shares," she interrupted, stepping nearer to me. She leaned in close, so our faces were level, her eyes gentle yet piercing as she studied my face. "You knew your mother and her kindness, but you also knew her strength. The warrior and leader within. She told you what it was like to grow up as an empress, about the weight of difficult decisions it meant she had to carry. She was cruel when she had to be." She rocked back on her feet. "Just as you would be cruel, if you had to be, to escape the invisible chains these Forwyn have on you. To not let Elder Ettonou lay a hand on you one more time."

I couldn't resist flinching at her words.

"Is it so bad to be a monster," she whispered, "if it frees you from the demons who prey on you every day?"

I blinked back the tears burning my eyes, the rising fear that haunted me with each memory of Elder Ettonou hurting me, leaving bruises and marks that no one else ever saw.

"Think about it," Nesrelle continued gently. "I want you to understand how to use the curse, not to fear it. You've done well with it so far…but you can do so much more. You could be *free*."

And with that, she was gone.

❮❮❮❮❮

When I finally descended into sleep that night, I dreamt vividly. I saw my mother as I remembered her from my childhood, her golden hair cascading in perfect silken waterfalls over her shoulders. In the years I'd been young enough to be held and carried, I'd run my fingers through those strands to soothe myself into sleep during long meetings my mother had brought me to. She'd never been the type of royal mother to leave me for endless days, half-forgotten, with a nanny. She'd sung me to sleep, allowed me to curl up in her bed when I'd had nightmares, and permitted me to trail her throughout the palace. At least, she had when I was very young.

As I grew older, I had responsibilities: tutoring in academics and training in swordplay. I didn't have as much time to attend meetings with my mother, but she'd assured me I would again in the future, to prepare for a time when I'd replace her. I'd never imagined that day would come so soon.

My dreams were bright, an idyllic childhood that perhaps I'd crafted into something a little too perfect in these years of loneliness and mourning. But they changed quickly to nightmares. As my mother tucked me in, her gold-tinted skin shifted, turning to black, rotten flesh hanging off her bones. Her face transformed into the hideous, bleeding mass that Vionn's had been, and the stench filled my nostrils until I was gasping and choking in my sleep.

The nightmare shifted. My mother, dressed in dragon scales and armed with countless shimmering daggers, strode through the throne room. She was whole and healthy again, the picture of the courageous warrior empress I'd always hoped to be. She approached the opposite side of the vast space, where row upon row of Forwyn slaves knelt, heads bowed and bodies quaking. Men and women, boys and girls—all had shorn hair and thin, malnourished bodies. With a nasty smile, Mother drew two of her daggers and walked down the first row, cutting open throats as she went. Slice, slice, slice. The bodies thudded one after another in glistening pools of blood.

Vionn, his decaying skin so terrible I could see bone beneath it, stepped from the shadows. *Our hands are red with their blood...*

But Nesrelle was beside him. *The Forwyn aren't innocent either. Do not fear the curse.*

❮❮❮❮❮

Daylight was only just tinging the sky pink as Kovi woke me unceremoniously.

"Get ready," he said evenly, tugging the sheet off me. "We have an execution to attend."

I squinted at him and snatched for my sheet, hoping my growls were enough to shake him off.

Kovi wasn't swayed. He dangled the sheet out of my reach and watched me calmly, his voice level. Dressed in his impeccable uniform, he didn't look at all exhausted or uncomfortable after sleeping on my cramped settee. "Now, empress."

Huffing, I sat up and rubbed at the sand in my eyes. My entire body was leaden, my head ached, and my eyes burned. I could feel the effects of every tear, every toss and turn, and every nightmare I'd had. Unease coiled in my stomach, not only from yesterday's revelations but also from Kovi's news.

Forwyn executions were hideous affairs, and I hadn't had to endure one for a long time. Now I'd have to array myself in finery and stand beside the Elders, all in a disgusting display for the people. All to appease the men and women who controlled me.

Even worse, Kovi would be at my side to watch me for every moment of the torture.

He made a show of turning away as I readied myself, first stumbling to the side table to pick at the lemon pastries and fresh berries laid out for my breakfast. Pouring myself a cup of tea from the pot nearby, I added generous helpings of cream and sugar before taking the cup with me to my vanity. I took my time sipping it and brushing out my hair until it gleamed as golden as the sunlight streaming into my chambers.

Finally, I strode to the washroom, where I cleaned my teeth and face. Afterward, it took me a while to select an outfit from my wardrobe. I knew the Elders would expect me to look...well, imperial. Magnificent. But the thought of what I was about to witness made bile cling sourly to my tongue. I was tempted to wear mourning colors of black and grey to spite them, but I suspected Kovi wouldn't let me leave my rooms dressed so rebelliously. He'd probably use his magic and order me to wear something else.

Cringing, I chose a dress in Alrenian gold, its straps lined in shimmering ivory and gold dragon scales, its bodice embroidered with the swirling sun sigil of the empire. Though the bottom layer of the dress was ivory, the overskirt was made of layers of expensive, sparkling gold silk that cascaded in a short train behind me. I pulled on a pair of leather sandals painted gold, their endless braided straps winding patterns up my calves that I had to take time wrapping and tying together. Finally, I returned to my vanity to paint my face, tracing thick lines of kohl around my eyes, smearing gold across my eyelids, and adding rouge to my cheeks and lips. Finding a pair of dangling earrings crafted to match the sigil on my chest, I slipped those into my ears, and draped several layers of matching gold chains around my neck.

When I turned around, even Kovi couldn't hide the way his eyes widened when he saw me. I offered him an indulgent smirk.

Yes, I look like a proper empress, I thought. *Just as your father and his friends want me to look.*

Wordlessly, he led me through the halls toward a door leading onto the palace grounds. The sun was higher now, its brilliant light making my dress shimmer so brightly my eyes hurt. But when I remembered *why* I was clothed in finery, I gritted my teeth and forced myself to count out my breaths, trying to keep them steady and even.

I knew the Elders forced me to attend all of their executions to make a show of unity. To make me their figurehead. To help them keep up the falsehood that the Forwyn and Alrenians ruled alongside one another these days. I also knew that they wanted me to see what my fate would be if I ever stepped too far out of line.

The murmurings of the crowd reached my ears before we rounded the final bend in the garden path and saw the gathered people. The vast, flat expanse of the arena was the same as it had been the last time I was here, with the dazzling view of the city below especially breathtaking in the morning light. But this time, the rising rows of seats carved into the stone on one side of the arena were full of people—mostly Forwyn nobility from the palace. A smattering of Alrenians sat among them, likely forced to watch the horrid spectacle as I was.

The other difference was that today there was a figure chained to the boulder at the center of the arena. From this angle, I couldn't tell if the victim was male or female, but it was obvious by the way the light caught the golden sheen of the victim's skin that the person was Alrenian. My blood churned hot and fast through my veins.

The prisoner wasn't crying out curses upon the Forwyn Elders' heads or yanking on the chains drilled into the rock. Instead, the figure stood with shoulders slumped and head dipped low, staring at the ground. An Alrenian with the fight quenched from their soul was a painful sight.

Kovi grasped my arm in an oddly formal gesture, and I realized he was trying to appear like a respectful escort guiding me to my seat, instead of a captor leading me. My gaze snagged on Elder Ettonou's as Kovi drew me toward an empty space in the front row, mere yards from the chained prisoner. The Elder's lips twitched into a smile—not a friendly or respectful one by any means, but a smug one with a threat hidden underneath. *Play by the rules or else.*

As soon as Kovi and I sat down, Elder Ettonou strode forward, placing himself on the arena floor between the crowd and the prisoner. With upraised hands and a deceptively kind, patient smile, he waited for the people's chatter to die down.

"My dear people," Elder Ettonou called out into the stillness. Other than the soft breeze and distant rumble of waves along the coast, there wasn't a sound to compete with his commanding tone. Even the Alrenian captive was silent. "The Court of Elders and Empress Jaliana stand united in upholding peace and justice in our beloved empire." He gestured toward me, extending his hand pleasantly as if he and I were old friends. "Empress, come forward."

Heart hammering in my ears, I rose and swept forward until I stood at his side, facing the endless rows of people. A crowd full of my enemies. My back was to a fellow Alrenian, whose crimes may or may not have been horrible enough to deserve the fate Elder Ettonou was about to decree.

I held myself rigid, shoulders squared, and plastered a fierce smile on my lips. Just like Elder Ettonou, I knew how to put on a good show, even if everything inside me rebelled against it. At my sides, my fingers twitched, and I thought again of my hideous, intoxicating power. If I seized Elder Ettonou by the throat, would his skin rot with the curse as Vionn's had? As the skin of the other Forwyn people I'd touched had?

"Today we have a particularly unsettling crime to address, one that threatens our peaceful way of life and the coexistence of our two races, Forwyn and Alrenian."

What a liar. Heat threatened to rise up my neck and spread across my cheeks. I exhaled slowly and imagined my mother's lullaby. Listened for the distant sound of waves crashing on the shore and let the rhythm soothe my mind. I couldn't snap here, in front of a crowd of witnesses who would be all too happy to chain me to the rock with their other prisoner.

"The Alrenian woman you see behind us," Elder Ettonou went on, his tone growing firm as he pointed toward the chained prisoner, "is guilty of treason." I glanced over my shoulder to find the woman still hunched beside the boulder, long strands of stringy brown hair hanging in her face. She looked defeated. "She threatened the safety of our great Alrenian Empire by trespassing on palace grounds in the middle of the night and straying dangerously close to the chambers of our esteemed Elders and Empress."

I clenched my jaw. I highly doubted the woman had ever been a threat to me. Perhaps she'd risked her life to rescue me from my prison, though it seemed unlikely she'd have made such an effort alone. Either her companions were no-good cowards, or she'd been sent as a spy. My stomach sank and my heart pounded ever faster in my throat.

The Elders were executing all my allies, leaving me isolated and useless. My fingertips burned and my power itched to be used.

"When interrogated, the woman refused to give details of her plans, but she carried illegal weapons," Elder Ettonou snapped, drawing two curved Alrenian daggers from the sheaths at his sides and holding them up on display. "As you all well know, for your safety, only our highly trained soldiers, guards, and Dragon Keepers may carry arms. Breaking this law alone condemned this woman to a severe sentence—but all of her crimes at once? They are punishable by death!"

The people stirred, some shouting angrily.

"Kill the traitor!" a few Forwyn cried out, standing to stomp their feet.

Elder Ettonou sheathed the daggers and raised a hand until the crowd quieted. "We will deal with her according to the law," he reassured the people. He turned toward the Dragon Keep. "Keeper Wilvhe, come forth!"

As the ground rumbled beneath us, Elder Ettonou grasped my arm so tightly I could feel bruises forming. I bit my tongue to keep from crying out. Trapped in his vice-like grip, I let him lead me back toward the front row, where we each took our seats and he finally released me. A dragon whose named I remembered was Torla, with her scales shimmering in shades of burnt orange and crimson, lumbered forth from the cavernous mouth of the Keep. When she stepped into the light, her scales shone like she was catching fire, making my eyes burn. Upon a saddle strapped to her back sat a Forwyn Keeper dressed not in traditional Alrenian gold dragon scale armor—but black. Perhaps as an executioner, he'd been given a different color. Perhaps it was a new Forywn tradition. Though they were only for show, two crossed swords were strapped to the young man's back, and wickedly long daggers hung naked from his belt. His helmet concealed most of his face, but not his bloodthirsty smile.

I couldn't tell if Torla's footsteps were shaking the ground enough to make me feel off-kilter, or if the world really was spinning around me. Smoke curled from her nostrils, the acrid tang filling my nose until I could taste it on my tongue. Maybe it was my imagination—maybe I was losing my mind—but I thought I could already smell burnt flesh too. My stomach roiled. Sweat coated my back, making the fabric of my dress cling to me.

Curse this heat, I thought. It was like my blood was on fire. Every inch of skin beaded with sweat and I wanted to run, to scream, to tear at my clothes before they caught fire and I burned to death with this woman I'd never met.

I couldn't tear my eyes from the prisoner. Not simply because of the threat the Elders held over me—their gazes were so intent I could feel them on me even now—but also because I couldn't seem to move. My eyes were frozen on the living nightmare before me. I was trapped, helpless.

No one ever told me how my mother died. I hadn't been present the night she was murdered, because she didn't think it wise for the only two Alrenians with imperial blood to be in the same dangerous place at the same time. And with Misrothian prisoners staying in the palace during those days, any excursions outside of my chambers had been deemed dangerous. We'd never imagined it was the Forwyn slaves who'd been our greatest threat.

For long months, I'd refused to believe the Forwyn who'd taken control of the palace and claimed Mother was dead, half-expecting the empress to launch an attack and free me. But as the months bled into a quarter of a year, then half a year, despair had taken hold. If she'd been alive, my mother never would have left me among enemies for so long. I'd stopped looking for her, stopped hoping to hear her voice. No one was coming to save me. She truly was dead.

But that meant I'd been left to imagine all the terrible ways she could have died. Had one of the Elders done it? I often had nightmares of them overpowering her together, chaining her to the very boulder before me and slaughtering her with one of her own dragons.

Watching each execution was like watching my mother's last

moments brought to life before my eyes, just as my nightmares imagined them.

Torla launched into the air, her heavy wings thundering overhead and casting vast shadows over the crowd as the people gasped in awe and appreciation. Rather than drink in the beautiful, terrible sight of the dragon and its Keeper showing off in an unnecessary display, I stared at the prisoner. She'd lifted her head, showing a spark of life as she squared her shoulders and waited for death. For one instant, she seemed to notice my gaze and turned her head in my direction. Our eyes met, and I stared into dark pools of fury. The gold flecks in her eyes were fire. This Alrenian woman hadn't bowed to fear or despair after all.

"Avenge the empire!" she screamed, and I was sure it was a message for me.

Then Torla whipped around to face her, opening her maw. The prisoner vanished in a ball of fire, her screams mingling with the terrible stench that swirled through the air.

Maybe I was screaming too. I couldn't tell. My entire body shook and my breaths rattled in my chest like Vionn's had. I tried to heave air into my lungs, but they rebelled. Black spots danced across my vision.

Sweat drenched my whole body. I was drowning. I was burning.

One coherent thought coursed through the panic in my mind: *For this, Elder Ettonou, you will die.*

CHAPTER ELEVEN

Lo

NAINA HUMMED AS SHE WOUND my newest ribbon—a vivid orange one—around one of my braids. "This represents loyalty," she said gently, "for orange reminds us of the warmth and light of the sun, which faithfully rises and sets for us each day. Daily you've shown your sisters and me that your heart is sincere. You perform your duties unfailingly, and your devotion to Elhani and his ways is clear."

She tied the end of the ribbon and paused before me, a maternal grin on her face. In the morning light trickling through the kitchen window, her wrinkles stood out starkly on her skin, yet she looked as lively as a much younger woman. Maybe it was the sparkle in her eyes, or the freckles sprinkled across her nose and cheeks.

Despite my late night, I hadn't been able to sleep long after I'd returned to my room. When the sounds of Naina rising early to prepare breakfast had reached my ears, I'd crept down to join her. That was when she'd declared it was time for my next ribbon. Naina always liked to bestow them upon us in quiet moments like these, since traditionally, family members gifted ribbons. As our spiritual mother, she was the perfect person to choose when each of us sisters had earned a new one.

Loyalty. It made me queasy when I considered where I'd been last night. And with whom. Loyalty to Elhani's cause should mean obedience to the ones he'd given to rule over us…right? It certainly didn't mean enjoying a handsome man's attention when I'd vowed myself to the celibate life of a nun.

"Naina?" I asked quietly, lowering my eyes to where my hands were folded in my lap. The scents of coffee and bacon were already thick in the air, even if it was early enough that none of the other women had descended yet for breakfast. It was amazing the way Naina multitasked, moving from twisting a ribbon to flipping bacon with practiced ease.

"Yes, *ahnla?*"

I swallowed thickly. After last night, I'd been half-afraid that Naina would take one look at me and see my guilt written across my face like a brand. And yet…what exactly did I have to feel so guilty about? The sisters discouraged venturing outside at night, since no Forwyn person—especially a woman—felt entirely safe in Inalgoth after sunset. The nightly curfew on Alrenians made no difference. If an Alrenian wanted to break one law and harm a Forwyn, why would they hesitate to break another?

But meeting with a group of vigilantes seemed like walking a dangerous line. I hadn't agreed to defy the Elders or their laws, but giving the group an audience last night…that was close to considering treachery. I wasn't sure what Naina would think of that.

"Do you believe it was unwise for the Elders to let Empress Jaliana live and take her mother's title?" I asked. My voice sounded small in my ears. I was venturing toward an uncomfortable topic, because of how closely it tied in with Karye's death and the blood on my hands. I repressed a shudder as the memories threatened to flood my mind. What would Naina think if she knew I was the *amara'rekni?* Just bringing up the subject made me worry Naina would somehow see into my black heart.

"I don't think mercy is ever an unwise choice," Naina mused as she started scooping the bacon from the frying pan and piling it onto a plate. "Elhani always rewards acts of mercy, for he is its source."

"What if…the new empress is…" I drew in a slow, steady breath to temper my heartbeat. "As dangerous as her mother was?"

Naina turned. "Have you heard something?"

I nodded.

"That is for the Elders to concern themselves with, isn't it?"

"But what if—what if they decided they needed to execute her? What would happen?"

Naina paused, considering. I could tell she was taking my words seriously and deeply thinking of the consequences by the way she tilted her head to the side. "Many things could happen," she said at last. "It would anger the Alrenians, certainly. Some Forwyn as well. I think there are plenty of Forwyn who long for peace and unity. Or at least peace," she finished with a wry smile. "Unity might be a long way away yet."

"Would it start a war?" I asked, rising from my chair. "Would it be wrong of the Elders to kill her? Would Elhani bless us or curse us?"

Naina sighed, shuffling back toward the stove to fetch the coffeepot. "That is a question our ancestors have asked since time immemorial. Will Elhani bless our cause? Will we be victorious? Perhaps, though, we are always asking the wrong questions." She brought the coffeepot to the table and smiled at me. "Perhaps instead we should ask if our motives are right. If we choose causes that would please Elhani and his people, or not."

"Do you think the Elders follow Elhani's ways?"

Naina's lips pursed. "I pray every day that they do, now and as long as they rule, and you should too."

"If…" I hesitated. "If the Elders ever did what was wrong, or didn't do what needed to be done to protect the Forwyn people, what would be the right choice? To obey them anyway, or to work against them to help Elhani's people?"

Naina's gaze was piercing, as if she could see through my questions. As if she already understood my thoughts and fears, and knew my past and present secrets. But it wasn't frightening, not when she also bore such clear affection for all the sisters under her care. She was always patient and gentle, even when she challenged us. "What do you think?"

"I would listen for Elhani's voice and look for his guidespirits," I said at last.

"He will never lead you wrong," Naina agreed with a nod. "When the way is not clear, ask and he will show you, or send a guidespirit to lead you."

Her words made a chill shiver over my skin and the hairs rise along my arms. It seemed miraculous that I'd seen a guidespirit, even if the path she had shown me seemed complex and difficult. With my past, it was astonishing that Elhani spoke to me at all.

As Naina and I set out the dishes, my sisters entered the kitchen.

"Good morning, Lo," Pauni'a said, and I smiled brightly in return.

When I joined the line and seated myself with my sisters for breakfast, it felt like a weight had lifted from my shoulders. Naina shot me a knowing smile before the blessing. If Elhani had guided me to the vigilantes, then he had a purpose, and I would trust him. The Circle of Serenity couldn't fault me for doing exactly what they taught us nuns to do.

❦❦❦❦❦

Tonight, I was already outside waiting in the shadows for Caesiem before he could toss pebbles at my window. It was gratifying to see the way he started a little when I stepped into the street. It served him right after he'd been spying on me for Elhani-knew-how-long.

As usual, he was in motion, a figure radiating constant energy. He fidgeted with his pendant necklace while shifting lightly on his feet, graceful and soundless in an effortless sort of way. When I approached, his smile was brilliant as always, pure white against his bronze skin. "Good to see you again, Lo." Before he could turn and lead me down the street, I spoke.

"I have questions." My tone brooked no nonsense.

Caesiem's eyes glanced over my shoulder to the darkened abbey behind me. "More? Do you want to interrogate me here?" he asked skeptically, gesturing toward the darkened windows.

I crossed my arms. "I have nothing to hide from my sisters."

Caesiem's grin was slow, almost lazy. "You're a nun, meeting with a spy and a thief." He drew out the words in his musical accent. "Are you sure about that?"

"I can't believe you say *thief* that like you're proud of it."

Caesiem wiggled his fingers. "I mean, I'm pretty talented at what I do."

I scowled, and Caesiem chuckled in response.

"Fine, fine. You already know my story," he said, looking apologetic. "You know it didn't *start* as a hobby."

"Oh, for Elhani's sake."

"I swear I'm not trying to drive you mad…"

"Like *goehr* you're not," I interrupted.

Caesiem's eyes widened in surprise, or maybe he was impressed. "I didn't think nuns cursed."

"You're Teramese. What do you know about Forwyn nuns? Or our language?" I sighed in exasperation. "And you're avoiding my questions."

Caesiem scratched at his jaw uncomfortably. "I may not speak Forwyn, but I know a curse when I hear one. And I thought we'd already established that you don't approve of me, but you were going to help us anyway."

I shrugged. "I could always ask Renni to assign me to someone else. Or insist I only work alone."

Sighing, Caesiem shook his head, studying me with exaggerated sorrow. "Would you be more warm and welcoming if I was a…what do you call them?…a monk, come to talk with you about Elhani and prayer and sweep you off your feet?" He waved his hand dramatically through the air.

I stared at him. "You know *nothing* about nuns, do you?"

He blinked. "What do you mean?"

"Part of our vows include committing to a life of celibacy."

Caesiem cleared his throat. "You mean, you'll never…*be* with…anyone?"

"No." I held back my laughter at his disbelief. For the first time, I glanced back toward the abbey. Maybe our conversation *was* too loud, and we should be moving by now. But Caesiem was still studying me in surprise. It was almost comical to watch him process the information.

"Oh, come on," I said impatiently, grasping his arm and tugging him down the street. "We can walk and talk."

Caesiem glanced at my hand, where I held his wrist, as if shocked I'd touched him at all. I dropped it quickly.

"What do you want to know?" Caesiem asked. He was still subdued, as if his mind were elsewhere.

The streets were quiet as we walked, most of the windows dark. Occasionally we passed a friendly guard or a home flickering with the glow of candlelight spilling out into the darkness.

"I think you already answered my question earlier," I admitted. "I was going to ask if you still stole, now that you're in Alrenor and have a way to pay for food and shelter." My tone came out harsh and judgmental, but it was better that way.

Caesiem didn't meet my eye. "Sometimes."

I didn't bother to ask him why. Something in the way he carried himself reminded me of the guilt lurking in my own heart. Maybe I could allow him some secrets, just like my sisters allowed me to keep mine.

Picking up my pace, I asked gruffly, "Do you often make a habit of spying on other people?"

Caesiem shot me a sheepish smile. "All right, all right, I understand why that would be upsetting."

"Oh, do you? Good to know," I said sarcastically. "I'd still like an explanation."

He nodded. "Well, you know I've been spying for our cause. We monitor the Alrenians and the empress, as well as the Elders, when we can. Mostly we depend on Wilvhe for palace news, but occasionally I've poked around there as well."

I pictured Caesiem slinking amid the shadows of an expansive hallway lined with paintings and statues. It was strange to imagine him crouched in a corner, silent and still for hours as he studied members of the palace. Caesiem moved so much—speaking with his gestures or expressions, creeping swiftly and nimbly through streets, or using sleight of hand to sneak something off a person—that I couldn't imagine him being motionless for long.

"Anyway," Caesiem went on, "once we all agreed the *amara'rekni* herself would be an invaluable addition to our group, I set out to find you. Some Forwyn at the palace claimed you'd left to live in an abbey. Your Circle of Serenity is the only Forwyn abbey in Inalgoth, and I didn't think you'd stray far from the capital you'd grown up in. So I watched your abbey, listening to some of your meetings and prayers. Picking a different group each day to follow when you all split up to help families in need. Eventually I noticed things about you that set you apart from the others."

I cast him a sideways glance. "So then you decided to only follow me?"

Caesiem shrugged. "You made it easy, leaving every night to run. I'd noticed the ribbons around your neck. Everything about you matched descriptions I'd heard. You sparred with the other sisters in a way that...well, you seemed like maybe you were more experienced in an actual fight." He cleared his throat. "I never watched you in your room."

I rolled my eyes. "Oh, praise Elhani. You followed me and violated my sisters' and my privacy, but you didn't stoop so low as to watch me undress. How gentlemanly of you."

Caesiem's neck flushed red. "I didn't mean—I only hoped to—I'm..." He sighed. "I'm sorry, Lo."

Unsure how to respond, I let a heavy silence descend. Caesiem didn't try to speak again, but he cast me several apologetic glances. I gritted my teeth, refusing to let his sad, beautiful eyes sway me. It was too soon to decide if I forgave or trusted this man, so it was better to say nothing at all.

At last, we turned down a dark alley that stank of human waste and rotting fish. Caesiem paused before pressing himself against the stone wall of an empty shop, sinking into shadow. When I hesitated, he grasped my arm and pulled me beside him.

Uneasy, I glanced around, but the alleyway and the segments of the street I could see on either side were empty. Silent. I waited a beat before asking, "What are we doing?"

Caesiem nodded to the abandoned structure across from us. "Renni overheard a conversation yesterday. We expect some Alrenians plan to meet here tonight."

My pulse picked up speed. We might very well encounter some of the Alrenian revolutionaries Renni had spoken of last night.

It took a moment for my eyes to adjust to the darkness. The alley was narrow and crooked, shoved between two buildings of mismatched size. On our left, the street we'd come from practically glistened in the moonlight, its pristine cobblestones clearly swept regularly. To our right, the glimpse of road I could make out was a sharp contrast: dusty and covered in potholes and forgotten piles of manure. Connecting both was this wretched alley, heaping with refuse and discarded barrels and bins, pieces of furniture, and abandoned trinkets. It looked like a place where people went to toss away broken pieces of their lives and leave them to decay.

Across from us, the wall of the abandoned building—I couldn't tell what it had once housed—was littered with markings vandals had left over the years in various languages. Most were crude insults or individual's initials. There were no windows, save for a few small ones set too high for us to see into from our vantage point, but a door hung aslant on rusty hinges.

All the while, the alley's stink was heavy and oppressive.

I scrunched my nose and blinked, but my eyes wouldn't stop watering. "Thanks for taking me to a refuse dump," I muttered, and Caesiem bit back a smile.

"Only the best for a lady," he said. Then he leaned forward, body tense. "I meant to tell you the plan on the way here, but..." He shrugged. "You had questions."

I scowled at him.

"Anyway, we need to find out as much as we can about what the Alrenians are doing next," he began. "Sometimes, we've stopped them from killing Forwyn citizens, gathering enough details to intervene. Most of all, we want to know about the uprising. The Alrenians won't be satisfied with these petty acts of rebellion forever. We've heard talk of weapons being amassed and soldiers joining together, but we don't know where the weapons or the soldiers are hidden yet."

"Why don't you bring this information before the Court of Elders?" I asked. "Surely they can do more than we can."

"And let them find out about our plans to assassinate their empress?" Caesiem countered.

"It's the right thing to do," I snapped. "They can do far more to stop the Alrenians than you and your friends can. If you truly want to stop them and end all the wrongs committed against my people, you'll make sure the law is on your side."

Caesiem turned to me, his expression solemn and sad. "We've already tried that. Wilvhe is there every day, often holding court with them, but the Elders say they're stretched too thin to concern themselves with 'petty crimes.'"

I stared. "They said that?"

"Do you know what happened the last time the Court of Elders stopped a large Alrenian uprising?" he asked quietly.

I shook my head. Here, the Alrenians lived in the shadow of the dragons. They'd witnessed the Forwyn storm Aerekni Academy with the Dragon Keepers at the forefront, and the terrible slaughter that had ensued until a few Alrenians had at last fled or surrendered. There hadn't been a large uprising in Inalgoth in the three years since we Forwyn had taken the palace and academy. And I'd never strayed outside of the capital, to cities where the Alrenians still tried to fight back and rebel out in the open.

"It was in Aramith, last year," Caesiem murmured. "Wilvhe was present, as a Dragon Keeper, but he saw some of his fellow Keepers and soldiers commit unspeakable atrocities."

I blinked at him, repressing a sudden shiver.

Caesiem's gaze was sad. "Too many Forwyn got caught up in their bloodlust, their thirst for revenge. They set fire to portions of the city where innocent Alrenians—even children—were trapped. And far too many Forwyn died that day, too. The stories Wilvhe tells..." Caesiem's voice trailed off, shaking his head.

"What did the Elders do?" I whispered.

"Nothing. They didn't condemn or punish any of the Keepers."

I stared at Caesiem as he pressed his lips together. He seemed to be considering what else to say. But before he could continue, a noise made us both freeze. Caesiem peered into the distance as he tilted his head to listen.

Approaching footsteps echoed off the street we'd left only a few minutes earlier. I burrowed even deeper into the shadows, willing myself invisible, but my churning thoughts wouldn't let me focus on Elhani's voice. Breathing shallowly, I prayed the stranger couldn't hear us.

In the blackness, I could only make out some of the figure's features. It was a tall, slender man shrouded in a dark cloak and hood. A glint of starlight fell on his face when he stepped into the alley entrance, revealing his gold-tinted complexion. An Alrenian breaking curfew.

When Caesiem turned back to me, he mouthed, *I'm sorry.*

As the Alrenian approached, Caesiem seized me by the waist, pulling me back to his chest. I hadn't even noticed him drawing a weapon before the blade was pressed against my neck. The sensation was too familiar, too horrible, sending raw horror and flashes of bloody images racing through my head. Panic and instinct took over, and I cried out, thrashing and stomping on his foot.

Of course I couldn't trust Caesiem. He'd dragged me out to his Alrenian friends so they could kill the empress slayer. Fury shot through me, like liquid fire heating my skin. This was *not* how I would die.

When I gave into my anger, my mind cleared, and I could remember my years of training and all the ways I'd practiced with my sisters to get out of holds just like this one.

But I hesitated. Caesiem had apologized before he'd grabbed me. Maybe this was part of the plan? Did I dare wait to find out?

The Alrenian was speaking before I could decide.

"Who are you?" he demanded in a gruff voice, drawing a dagger from a belt at his side.

Out of breath as he struggled to hold me in place, Caesiem chuckled. "No one you need to be worried about, friend," he said. He spoke in perfect Alrenian, and my heart lurched, a chill trickling down my back.

He'd seemed so ignorant of Forwyn culture, yet he spoke Alrenian fluently?

As if he'd heard my thoughts, he leaned forward the slightest bit to whisper in my ear. "Shh." I wanted to slap him. How could he think that hushing me would have a calming effect?

The Alrenian man's footsteps squelched through mud and filth as he stepped nearer. "Friend? How can I be certain you're a friend, foreigner?"

"Because I'm not here to turn you in for breaking curfew. I'm here to collect *her* for a client of mine." At this, Caesiem swiveled, shoving me so I faced the Alrenian.

The man frowned at me. "Escaped slave?"

"Years ago. My client promised a hefty sum if I found and returned her to him." I could hear the smile in Caesiem's voice and resisted the urge to shiver.

It's all an act, I told myself, and prayed it was true.

As two more figures entered the alley, the first man broke into a slow smile. "Well, *friend*," he said, "perhaps we can offer you a heftier sum." He nodded toward the crooked door. "Come inside and talk to us."

Caesiem huffed out a laugh. "You think I'm just going to follow you into a dark, abandoned building? I'm quite comfortable here."

The man shot him a toothy grin, like a dog baring its teeth. "I wasn't offering you an option."

Quietly, the two other figures stepped closer, hands hovering over sword hilts.

With a whispered curse, Caesiem followed the man toward the door. A shiver coursed down my spine. I wasn't sure we'd ever walk out of this building.

Nodding briefly toward the other two forms, the man rapped a light rhthym on the door. Caesiem tugged on my arm, his dagger still pointed toward my neck as he led me forward.

When the door swung inward, a flickering beam of light poured into the darkness. Another Alrenian stood in the doorway, holding a candle aloft. I blinked until I made out the hulking, muscular figure of another man leering at me. Wordlessly, he stepped back to let the three Alrenians, Caesiem, and me inside.

The room was vast and mostly empty. Candles set on every available space—a few dusty, otherwise empty shelves, some boxes, and a long table—set shadows dancing along the dirt-stained walls. The ceiling stretched high overhead, too high to see beyond the inky darkness. All around the room, Alrenians sitting in rickety chairs or on overturned barrels turned their golden faces toward us.

In the safety of their meeting place, they had their hoods cast back. There was one man with a cruel, sneering smile that made me tense. A young woman with dark, curly ringlets and grey and gold eyes spent a lot of time smiling with her blood-red lips. Next my eyes fell on an older man with long white hair and a jagged scar down his forehead.

It was easier now to study the Alrenian we'd first encountered, who stood just ahead of us. He was young and handsome, with sinuous, muscled arms and a quick smile. With a nod toward Caesiem and me, he grinned around at the group.

"This foreigner has just the slave to help us," he announced.

Elhani, keep me safe… I tried reaching for his voice, but it was difficult when my heart pounded so loudly in my ears.

A bulky man clothed in a fisherman's jacket, his face weathered from his work, stood from his seat and stalked toward us. As his eyes roved over me, I gritted my teeth so tightly my jaw ached.

"She's young, looks fit," the fisherman muttered. He took a step nearer, as if to inspect me further, like I was a horse he wanted to purchase.

Caesiem cleared his throat. "What sort of job do you want her for?" he asked gruffly.

The fisherman snorted. "What's it to you, boy?"

There was the slightest pause before Caesiem spoke. Was he having doubts about this plan? For the first time, I noticed the way his own heart pounded against my back. His fear was strangely reassuring. It grounded me, reminded me that he was on my side. And somehow, it helped clear my mind. I always focused best when I was angry or when I knew someone needed me.

At last, I noticed a few musical notes drifting through the air, a few snatches of the beautiful strain always going on around me. I could make out two words: *Trust me…* My confidence soared.

"I don't want you using her for some crime that can be traced back to me," Caesiem said.

The man with the cruel smile barked out a laugh. "You're breaking curfew and trafficking slaves, and you're worried about our crimes?"

"Look," Caesiem said, a stubborn note in his voice. "I know how to keep my dealings quiet and away from the guards' notice. But I don't know any of you. I have my suspicions about what you're doing and why you would want a Forwyn slave. A man has to watch his own back."

"That's true," the young woman said, licking her teeth and laughing. The way she studied Caesiem, I couldn't tell if she was fantasizing about kissing him or cutting him into pieces. "But have a little faith in us. We've been committing crimes practically out in the open and we haven't been caught."

"Yet," Caesiem interjected. "And I was promised a great deal of money for this slave already, so unless you can offer more, I don't really appreciate you wasting my time. I explained to your friend here that I already have a client." He let an edge of weariness and frustration seep into his tone. "Unless you can give more than seventy ildrems, I'm not inclined to go back on my promise to him."

The fisherman's expression turned serious. "Is she strong? Can she carry a heavy weight for a few blocks?"

"She seemed feisty enough when he caught her," the first man interjected. I couldn't meet his leering gaze as he studied my frame, noting every muscle, every toned part of me. I wanted to scream, to attack, to flee this place.

"She's strong," Caesiem agreed, and I didn't bother to contain my growl of rage.

The Alrenians chuckled, and the red-lipped woman leaned forward, a nasty, eager glint in her eyes. "Does she have a strong stomach? Can she stand the sight of blood?"

I repressed a shudder as Caesiem reassured the woman that I could.

The fisherman stepped closer. "And she'll need to be a good little actress. She can be quite useful to us if she doesn't give us away to other

Forwyn. Otherwise, we'll kill her instead." He tossed me a nasty smile.

Caesiem's grip on me tightened, almost imperceptibly, but I prayed it was meant to be reassuring.

"We can offer thirty ildrems now and thirty-five more later, after she's completed some work for us," the fisherman continued.

"That's it? I have another idea," Caesiem snarled. "I'll leave, because your offer isn't tempting, and take her and my business elsewhere."

Several of the Alrenians drew daggers concealed in their belts, brandishing them threateningly.

"You really think we'd let you *refuse* our offer after seeing our faces?" one of the Alrenians scoffed, creeping closer.

Caesiem seized my shoulder and yanked the dagger away from my neck. "Magic?" he hissed frantically in my ear.

It didn't surprise me that he knew about Forwyn magic, considering most of his vigilante friends were Forywn. But it did surprise me that it was part of his plan. He trusted me to get us out of here?

I reached for Elhani's voice, and this time it came effortlessly. *Conceal me,* I prayed, and felt warmth flood my body. Power flowed around me, washed over me, rushed *through* me. My body and everything I touched—clothes, shoes, and Caesiem himself—disappeared.

Before the startled Alrenians could block our path, Caesiem slipped his hand through mine, and we charged toward the door. As we burst out into the dank alleyway, running and half-tripping over slimy rubbish, I listened for the pounding footsteps that would signal the Alrenians' pursuit. One heartbeat. Two. And then I heard them, crying out to one another as they split up, some running down the opposite end of the alley while others rushed toward us.

I leapt into the street and wound a circuitous route through intersecting roads and alleys, all the while praying so I wouldn't lose my focus on Elhani's voice. But my sprinting footsteps weren't quiet enough to keep the Alrenians from trailing us. My heart rammed painfully against my ribcage and sweat soaked my back.

As I swerved down another street, I realized we were nearing an outer district of the city, closer to the water. The scents of salt and fish permeated the air, and the tumult of crashing waves grew louder. We darted past a pub and what I thought might be a brothel, floods of warm light spilling from their windows and mingling laughter and talk echoing through the otherwise quiet road.

Caesiem's hand slipped in mine. I squeezed it more tightly before I could lose hold of it. "Don't let go!" I panted.

"Wouldn't dream of it," Caesiem muttered from somewhere right beside me.

If it weren't for the feel of his hand in mine, I might have forgotten he was with me. Even sprinting through the city, he was unnaturally quiet, his breaths and footsteps paced evenly with mine so as to be barely noticeable.

It was another jarring reminder that I was helping a *spy*. A thief. Running undetected through the capital at night was probably a regular occurrence for him.

We rounded another corner, and I came to a screeching halt. It was difficult to tell what registered first: the sickly stench of death, or the horrifying sight of Forwyn bodies, skewered and lined up in a row in the shadow of the city's outer wall. They were all in various stages of decay, each body wearing clothes that had been painted with the blood-red sun insignia Renni had mentioned. Each dead face proved that the Alrenians didn't discriminate by gender or age with their victims: there were both young and old, men and women. Words written in Alrenian were painted all over the wall behind them, words that blurred and swam before my eyes. One I made out clearly, however—a name. *Jaliana.*

Knees quaking, head spinning, I bent over and heaved the contents of my stomach onto the road. Tears burned my eyes.

All this time I'd thought I'd been making a *difference* with my sisters. I'd known about slave trafficking, known that the work we did and the influence we had was small, but it had felt like something. But now, seeing my brothers and sisters brutally murdered as a symbol for the Alrenian uprising, it felt like everything I did was nothing at all. Less than nothing, because I'd been ignorant of these heinous crimes.

"Lo…" Caesiem whispered, turning to me with matching pain and horror in his eyes. "I'm sorry I put you through all this tonight…" His voice trailed off.

It registered for both of us in the same instant. I'd released his hand, which would have disconnected him from my magic anyway, but it was clear from the way he studied my face that he could also see me. In my shock, I'd lost my grip on my invisibility. The warmth that had been bubbling through me was gone, replaced by a fearful chill.

"There you are," came a taunting voice in Alrenian.

CHAPTER TWELVE

Jalie

KOVI SCOOPED ME UP WITHOUT ceremony and carried me out of the arena, back into the palace. As he strode through the maze of hallways, I was barely conscious of what was happening. I didn't register the warmth of his arms around me. I didn't even feel humiliated at the thought of the entire Forwyn court seeing me like this.

Instead, my mind was consumed with the sight of the flames devouring the Alrenian woman. My nose burned with the acrid scent of smoke mingling with the sickly smell of charred flesh. My ears rang with the prisoner's screams.

And in her place, I kept seeing Mother. My beautiful, fierce mother with her adoring smile and her dragon stories. Her loud laughter that rang like music throughout the throne room as I sat beside her and we whispered about members of the court.

I couldn't feel anything but raw, all-encompassing grief and fear. I was losing my mother all over again, in an endless loop that my brain wouldn't stop showing, as if I were trapped in that terrible moment forever. A moment I'd never even witnessed.

The sound of running water splashing into a bathtub cut through the noises wreaking havoc inside my head. I opened my eyes to find my face pressed against Kovi's chest, which was unnervingly comforting. The rhythmic rise and fall of his breaths and the steady beat of his heart reminded me to slow my breathing and match it to his. My body was still soaked with sweat, but I wasn't on fire anymore. Now I was shaking with cold.

Without warning, Kovi dumped me into the tub, clothes and all. The water was the perfect temperature, steam curling up from the surface and around my face. I inhaled the familiar, soothing scents of vanilla and cinnamon. Something in my chest loosened, a knot unspooling. My shaking frame calmed as warmth coursed through my body.

I was in my washroom, away from the cruel shouts and cheers of the Forwyn. Away from the consuming fire. Away from the death.

For a moment, I forgot about my dress, even as the folds of my skirt swirled around my legs and the bodice clung to my skin. I forgot about the enemy soldier standing in my washroom, arms crossed over a broad, muscled chest I'd just had my face pressed against. I forgot about everything.

Then it all crashed over me. The humiliation of having been carried out of the arena. And in what state? Had I been screaming out loud? Had I been crying? I lifted a trembling hand to my face, but of course it was damp from the bathwater now.

Next came fear—what consequences would the Elders dish out because of my embarrassing display?

And finally, fury washed over me, hot and pure and life-giving.

The Forwyn said my mother had been a murderer. Even Vionn said the Alrenians had blood on their hands. But what I'd witnessed the Forwyn commit today—and plenty of other days before—was not an honorable execution. It was a spectacle of agony. It gave no room for the courage that Alrenians respected or the mercy the Forwyn supposedly revered.

When the Alrenians had ruled the empire, the arena had been the location of fights to the death for prisoners, but those prisoners were supplied with weapons. They were given a fighting chance. Those who were deemed unworthy to have a chance to live were executed quickly and efficiently with a public beheading. My people were known for their cruelty in battle, for even torturing prisoners when it was necessary, but when we sentenced someone to death, when we actually decided to take a life, we didn't draw it out. What the Forwyn did—this seemed infinitely more barbaric.

Tears pricked my eyes, and I hated myself for them. I didn't realize I was hyperventilating again until Kovi knelt beside the tub.

"Don't think," he whispered. "Take a deep breath through your nose—like that. Breathe out through your mouth."

His shoulders were rigid and his jaw was clenched, as if he hated himself in this moment—but his hands were shockingly gentle as he brushed wet strands of hair back from my face. My gaze snagged on the colorful ribbons he wore like a band around one wrist. But it wasn't enough to distract me.

I couldn't breathe, couldn't relax my coiled muscles, couldn't release the new knot building painfully in my chest. Kovi grasped my shoulders, his touch grounding me and forcing me to focus on his words as he told me to pay attention to the feel of the water around me and the sound of the birds twittering outside my chambers. I tried not to think about who it was that was touching me and closed my eyes. Focused on breathing. In. Out. Slowly, my breaths evened out and my heartbeat steadied.

As soon as my body relaxed, Kovi straightened. Something uncertain flitted through his eyes. Clearing his throat, he left the washroom without another word.

My heavy dress made exiting the tub difficult when I finally climbed out. Checking that he couldn't see me, I stripped out of my sopping clothes and wrapped a towel around myself. My legs were wobbly as I entered my bedchamber, removed my jewelry, and slipped behind my changing screen to dress in leggings and a fitted tunic. Normally I'd wear them for training, but today I wanted them only for comfort.

When I exited, Kovi was nowhere to be seen. I'd thought I just hadn't noticed him in a corner of the room earlier, but he'd vanished. In his place was an unfamiliar guard hovering in the entrance between my sitting room and bedchamber. The boy looked small, younger than Kovi or me. Inconsequential. I didn't have the energy to care. I swallowed thickly and turned away toward my settee. It wasn't until after I curled up there with the blanket Kovi had left that I noticed the mug of still-hot tea waiting for me on the table. Servants had left a tray with a teapot on the side table, but Kovi must have poured this mug for me.

A few minutes passed as I sipped the tea, calming my fear. The more it melted away, the more anger took its place. Hot and energizing.

"Where's Kovi?" I demanded of the stranger on the other side of my room.

I clutched my mug with white knuckles, staring blankly at my bedroom wall as the guard stepped forward.

I could sense his fear in his hesitation. The emotion poured off him, only stoking my anger further.

He was afraid of *me?*

He wasn't the one living with his mother's murderers.

He wasn't the one waiting to be condemned to death.

He wasn't the one watching his people be executed cruelly.

"He left—he said—he's in one of the training rooms," the boy spluttered.

I lifted my empty hand and stared at my palm. Nesrelle said she'd gifted me so I could inflict the Life-Giver's curse on the Forwyn people. Because they were as guilty as the Alrenians. I didn't doubt their guilt one iota. And maybe I didn't fear the curse I possessed as much as I had before, either.

And Kovi? His mercy was *hypocrisy*. I was certain his father had been the one to kill my mother. I knew Kovi himself hated me, hated all of my people. He might act like he was better than me by pitying me, but I knew he'd happily chain me up for my execution the moment the Elders ordered him to.

I gripped the mug handle tightly in my hand. "Take me to him."

"That's not…" the boy began.

"Now!" I shouted, hurling the cup against the wall. It shattered, splattering liquid across the floor. When I stood to face him, he must have noticed the murder in my eyes.

"Come with me," he said miserably.

He led me at a fast clip to another palace building, the one that housed our vast royal armory and numerous training rooms for guards, Keepers, and soldiers. In the private room once reserved only for Mother and me, the one lined with practice weapons and straw-filled dummies, the one with only two walls, its other sides open to the gardens—that was where I found Kovi, holding a practice weapon and speaking with his father.

The sight of Elder Ettonou made me stiffen, but my anger won out over my dread. I caught nothing from their conversation before both turned toward me.

"What was that earlier display of yours?" the Elder demanded, approaching me with the air of a predator.

"What display?" I asked, enunciating each word carefully, calmly. Relishing rather than fearing the anger emanating from him. The bruises he'd left on my arm earlier weren't the first marks he'd made on me. *But let him try to hurt me again now,* I thought. *I have the power to hurt him back.* Beside me, the young guard shifted uncomfortably.

Elder Ettonou stepped closer. My eyes met his dark ones, which churned with barely restrained malice. I was tempted to smile. Would he dare lay a hand on me when he knew what I could do?

"You know exactly of what I'm speaking." His eyes darted to his son before settling back on me. "What was that? What do you hope to accomplish with hysterics?"

My blood boiled. Hysterics? Did this man know what it was like to trip and fall into a pit of horror and pain so vast and so dark that it seemed bottomless? I wanted to charge him then and there, lay hands on him and see what curse Nesrelle had in store as retribution for the blood on his hands.

Instead I ignored him, stepping toward the wall where dozens of dull practice swords hung. I seized one and stalked toward the open center of the training room. No one moved to stop me, so I swung it easily, testing the weight of it in my hands.

"Answer me, you *filkni,* worthless *yirak,*" Elder Ettonou snapped, striding toward me. "Bow down and speak! You answer to me, *kowra!*"

That last word...that was too much. It was infuriating to hear him curse and insult me in his language or even the merchant tongue. But it was absolutely revolting to hear him curse at me in my own language.

"Father..." Kovi began, but I didn't need him to intervene for me.

Lowering my practice sword, I spun to face Elder Ettonou. "I didn't know you self-righteous Forwyn would ever use such language to address anyone, even an enemy," I said, forcing my voice to remain steady. I took a step toward him, closing the distance between us. "But I will not bow to you. And I can tell you're afraid." This time, I indulged in a smile. Slow, confident, predatory. I stalked nearer. "I can tell because you stooped to name-calling and gave into your anger. You, who have always played the game so well in public, maybe best out of all the Elders, pretending you didn't hate me and actually wanted unity and peace with my people."

Elder Ettonou's eyes widened as I stopped just in front of him. When I lifted my chin, he wasn't that much taller than me. His son remained on the other side of the room, but out of the corner of my eye, I saw him tense, watching me warily.

"Laying a finger on me would spell your death," Elder Ettonou said carefully.

"You're right," I said. "And I am outnumbered, for now." I met his eyes, hoping he could see the smoldering hate within mine. "But you know what I can do, and for now, that's enough. I can wait. One day, you won't have an army of dragons and Keepers to call upon, because they're mine. One day, you won't have a full Court of Elders at your beck and call. That's when I'll make you suffer."

Elder Ettonou glowered before shoving past me, his shoulder slamming into mine. "You'd better control her," he ordered, not bothering to turn around as he addressed his son.

Control me.

With his abominable magic.

I ground my teeth and turned toward Kovi, the practice sword's hilt biting into my sweaty palm.

Kovi was still holding his own practice weapon, a plain dagger. He'd removed his uniform jacket to reveal the clinging undershirt beneath, and he was already covered in sweat.

"You're dismissed, Marukio," he said without even looking at the other guard.

The boy retreated hastily.

Kovi strode toward me, his expression stony but his eyes intense. Fear slithered through my belly, but I didn't back down. I'd strike first, before he could command me with any magic again. Even without a curse to wield, I could attack him. I knew plenty of ways to kill an enemy. Mother and all my Alrenian trainers had been nothing if not skilled.

"Do you want to know what my father just told me?" Kovi spat out.

I was startled by the anger in his low, rumbling voice. His earlier gentleness seemed like a distant memory.

Good, I thought. *Show me who you truly are. Just like your father.*

Before waiting for me to respond, Kovi continued. "Your people are murdering mine. Slaughtering innocent citizens—in *your* name. Painting symbols on their bodies and leaving them, *impaled*, for our guards to find. They've written your name all over the walls near their victims, claiming it's your revenge."

He stopped right in front of me, glaring, one hand in a fist while the other squeezed his practice dagger.

I was full of venom. "And the Elders choosing to burn my people alive is somehow less horrible? More *humane*?"

"What do you know about humanity?" Kovi asked through gritted teeth. "You come from a bloodthirsty race. You Alrenians pride yourselves on how many kingdoms you can conquer. You enslave your victims and collect corpses like trophies. You might be in denial, but your mother *was* a monster—"

With a fierce cry, I swung my practice sword toward his face. "Monster?" I shouted.

Kovi stopped the blade effortlessly with his hand, its dull edge not even piercing skin. I slammed my knee up toward his groin, and he twisted away. This only enraged me more, and I unleashed a flurry of kicks, punches, and swings that he dodged and blocked.

"If you want to see a monster, look into your own father's eyes!" I panted.

"He's not a monster," Kovi snapped, just as I landed a solid kick to his side.

Grunting, he caught my foot, and I collapsed, head crashing against the floor. I rolled away and sprang to my feet before he could attack. He sliced his practice blade toward my face, and I ducked.

"You might call my mother a monster, but I've seen that the Forwyn are monsters too."

When I swung my sword again, Kovi lunged toward me instead of away. With one swift, fluid move, he knocked my weapon from my hand, sending it skittering across the floor. In two breaths he had me backed against the wall, his weapon pressed to my throat. I expected his dagger to be as dull as my own blade had been, but I didn't think it wise to test it.

I was trapped, with my hands locked at my sides. He pressed his body too closely against mine, making it impossible for me to lift my arms and free myself—or attack.

Drawing a shaking breath, I met his eyes. I refused to let him see the fear trickling through me. "Maybe we're all monsters," I whispered.

Kovi stared back at me, his face expressionless. Only his gaze hinted at the whirlwind inside. I stared into those beautiful, angry eyes, the fire within them uncannily reflecting my own. It was invigorating, the fury simmering almost tangibly between us. His gentle gestures had been confusing, but fury and hatred—I knew how to handle those.

The mere memory of him taking pity on me made my heart harden even more. My hatred sparked hotter. I swallowed against the dryness in my throat.

"And if we're all monsters, so be it," I continued. "If I am to be a monster, then I will be a monster in possession of the throne."

Kovi didn't move, didn't flinch. Unlike me, he was barely winded.

His blade was cold against my throat, but his breath was a warm whisper against my face. He didn't even bother to speak. His piercing gaze was threatening enough.

"I hate you, Kovi Ettonou, and all your kind. I'm going to take back my empire." I said it like a sacred vow, like a promise I would seal in blood. "And I'm going to destroy you, your father, and all the other Forwyn in this godforsaken palace."

Neither of us spoke again for a long time. Lunch awaited us when we returned to my rooms, but Kovi immediately went to the washroom to bathe and change. I took my plate of food out to my balcony.

When Kovi joined me with his own food and a book, I couldn't bear the silence any longer. I asked the question screaming inside my brain. "Why help me out of that arena?"

"Because I don't want to be a monster. I saw someone in need, and I helped."

My cheeks burned. "I'm not in *need*."

Kovi stared at me a moment longer before reopening his book, not bothering to answer me.

Gritting my teeth, I went to lean against the railing and stare out at the pure sky. Humid air made my hair cling to my neck. Insects chirred and birds sang, flitting from the branches of an orange tree growing so close to my balcony I could have reached out and brushed one of the creature's wingtips. The world smelled of briny sea air and rain somewhere out over the water, evident in the clouds brewing on the horizon. I studied the gardens, indulging in memories of happier times when I'd strolled through them with my mother or played with nobles' or Dragon Keepers' children, racing along the paths and hiding behind shrubbery.

Something caught my eye, and I blinked. A figure crouched behind a roedna bush, concealed by its verdant green leaves and large orange blossoms. With the stranger's hood pulled low despite the heat, I couldn't study his or her features. Until the figure glanced up and the sunlight flashed on the gold-toned skin of a woman with vibrant red hair. Her amber eyes met mine, her gaze intent and earnest. She blinked once, twice, three times, as if to communicate.

Avenge the empire, I thought, the dead Alrenian prisoner's words echoing through my head for the thousandth time. Maybe the prisoner had not been alone after all. But was this woman trustworthy, or a coward who'd abandoned her friend to a horrific death? And was she here now to help me?

Before I was done wondering, the woman vanished deeper into the grounds. I spared a glance back at Kovi, who continued to read his book. He hadn't noticed anything amiss.

No matter the risk, I had to find a way to meet with this Alrenian woman.

CHAPTER THIRTEEN

Lo

CAESIEM AND I TURNED AROUND to face a male figure, backlit by moonlight. As he stepped closer, I recognized the fisherman, brandishing a wickedly curved Alrenian dagger. Its sharp edge gleamed in the night.

Fear snaked down my back as I tried to listen for Elhani's voice again. This time, my lingering horror made my mind foggy. I couldn't hear the notes over the pounding of my furious heart.

Before I could move, Caesiem charged the man, taking him by surprise as he slammed his shoulder into his chest. The man recovered quickly, staggering forward and slashing his blade. But Caesiem had already drawn his own dagger, swiping the man's to the side before it made contact. As the two grappled, I raced toward them, my eyes scanning the street for anything I could use as a weapon. I didn't want to kill again—didn't even want to consider it—but I couldn't just stand by and watch someone be murdered. Maybe I could hurt the man enough to protect Caesiem.

I picked up a couple of rocks and turned back toward the men. My eyes snagged on the Alrenian's dagger, glittering on the cobblestones where he must have dropped it in their scuffle. There was no way I could dart between them to grab it without being crushed. But Caesiem still held his blade, which the two wrestled between them, each struggling to gain control.

I flung the first rock at the Alrenian, striking the side of his head. He grunted, but his grip on Caesiem didn't relent. In that moment, I could feel the same clear-headed adrenaline that had rushed through me the night I'd slain Karye. For survival, for justice, I would fight. Without overthinking it, I lifted a heavier rock and lunged at the man, slamming it against his temple. Occupied with Caesiem, he didn't even have a chance to turn toward me or fight back.

I didn't have time to panic or feel remorse as he slumped forward, collapsing on top of Caesiem. I knew he wasn't dead, only unconscious, but this act of violence still unnerved me.

Swallowing, I refused to let horror take over. Not this time.

I'd fought for what was right, and I couldn't regret that.

In the distance, more footsteps thundered toward us. I didn't want to wait to find out if they belonged to friendly guards or more Alrenians.

"Caesiem!" I tugged frantically on the Alrenians's prone body, but he was at least twice my size.

Grunting, Caesiem shoved the man off him and struggled to his feet.

"Run!" I cried out as Caesiem took a couple steps and teetered. I grasped his arm and pulled him along with me, flying down the street.

One, two, one, two, one, two. My feet pounded the cobblestones in my familiar rhythm. Everything was a blur around me, wind rushing in my ears. Somewhere behind us, echoing footsteps trailed, but they quickly died away. I prayed that meant we'd finally lost all the Alrenians for good.

I pushed myself faster, faster, until Caesiem gasped shallow, shuddering breaths as he stumbled behind me. Pausing at a street corner, I turned. He was hunched over, his face pale and pinched with pain. Blood blossomed across his shirt, a darker shade of black spreading along the charcoal fabric.

Questions whirled through my head, but there wasn't any time to ask Caesiem about his injury. I couldn't believe I hadn't noticed sooner.

"Stay with me," I grunted, grabbing hold of his arms when he looked ready to topple over. Without responding, he leaned heavily on my shoulder.

The amount of blood oozing from Caesiem's wound terrified me. He was so unsteady on his feet, I worried he'd faint. I couldn't carry him back to the abbey if he did. Scanning the street, I searched for a Forwyn guard, for anyone who could help, but it was empty.

"Hold on," I whispered. "We're almost there." That wasn't quite true, but the lie seemed better than confessing he still had several blocks left to go.

Caesiem was quiet, shuffling his feet doggedly, one in front of the other. I could feel his ragged breaths as he leaned into my side. He wasn't as warm as he should have been, his skin clammy and cold.

Walking in this way was far more taxing than running had been. My nerves stretched thin and taut, every sound shooting equal amounts of fear and hope through me. Fear we were being followed by someone who wanted to kill us. Hope it was a guard who could help me get Caesiem to the abbey.

"Naina is a healer," I murmured, hoping that if I kept talking, Caesiem would stay alert. "She knows how to use Elhani's magic to help people—and she can help you. Just keep going. One, two, one, two…" I felt a little ridiculous saying my running chant aloud, but the repetition was soothing. A simple pattern we could follow as we moved painstakingly forward.

We were nearly to the abbey's door when Caesiem stumbled and dropped to the street. "Caesiem!" I cried, trying in vain to rouse him. He lay unnervingly still on the dusty cobblestones, unresponsive no matter how hard I shook him or frantically called his name.

Casting a wary glance around to find the street still empty, I raced to the abbey door and threw it open. I tore through the halls and up the stairs, not caring how loudly my footsteps echoed or that my cries were waking all my sisters. Stopping outside a door at the end of the hall, I pounded on it wildly. "Naina, Naina!" I shouted.

Naina opened the door immediately, her eyes wide with concern. "*Ahnla?*" she asked.

"There's—someone is hurt outside. Badly. Hurry!"

Naina was already racing after me. Anyone who didn't know her would have been shocked at how spry she was for her age. Her strength and speed were exactly what I needed now.

Naina didn't waste time asking questions when I led her to the motionless man lying in the street. That conversation would come later. Now she was all business. Her clear head and steady voice grounded me.

"Help me bring him inside," she said.

Between the two of us, we hauled Caesiem into the abbey and carried him into the kitchen, the nearest useful room. We laid him on the table, and Naina checked his pulse as she rattled off orders. "Fetch my medical bag from my room," she ordered as she cut open Caesiem's shirt with a pair of kitchen scissors to assess his wound.

Having a straightforward task to focus on calmed my whirling brain. I didn't have to return to a night when a blade still wet and warm from others' blood had been pressed to my throat. I didn't have to wonder if the infuriating thief and spy who'd turned my understanding of Alrenor and its government on its head was dying—or already dead. All I had to do was run, jogging past sisters in the hall and stairwell who called out questions I ignored. I relished the familiar beat of my boots on the floor. Let the steady breaths pumping through my lungs soothe me.

When I returned to the kitchen with Naina's bag in hand, most of my sisters were clustered outside in the hall.

"I said, go to the sanctuary or back to your rooms!" Naina snapped at them, and the women fled.

I entered, setting the bag on the table beside Caesiem's prone form and staring at him. His face was still pale, but his chest was lightly rising and falling. Naina hovered over him, pressing wads of already bloodied bandages to his stomach with one hand while her other checked his pulse.

At one point, Caesiem stirred, eyes fluttering open as he emitted a groan.

"Fetch some broth," Naina said, her eyes trained on her work.

As soon as I'd spoonfed Caesiem some of the broth I'd heated, he slipped back into unconsciousness. Naina and I worked efficiently together, even though this was a dance we had performed only a few times before, and always in the infirmary. She remained posted by the table, reaching out for items as she requested them, always in time for me to set them into her palm. I stepped around her, moving about the kitchen to retrieve what she needed or perform various tasks under her instruction, always close enough to help her but never in her way.

I hoped and prayed all we'd done would be enough.

"He's lost enough blood to make me concerned," Naina told me at last, "but not enough that I think he's hopeless. Magic knit up the damage the blade made, but Elhani's power has more to do. Now we'll have to wait for the magic to work, and let this young man replenish his strength."

When she washed her hands and pulled up a chair, sinking into it with a sigh, I perched on the stool set by the fireplace, where flames were crackling despite the balmy night. Naina had told me earlier to build up a fire and fetch a blanket for Caesiem to keep him warm.

"We can move him to a proper bed after he's had some time to recover," she said. "His body has been through quite a shock and I don't want to disturb him any more tonight." Then she turned to me, and a new kind of unease settled low in my gut. "Can you explain to me what you were doing with this young man on the street?"

I shuffled uneasily in my seat and stared at my hands, folded tightly in my lap. "I'm not sure you would believe me."

"So it doesn't have to do with the fact that he's handsome, but something far more unusual and unbelievable?" Naina winked at me, dispelling a bit of my fear as I huffed out a nervous laugh.

"Actually, yes," I said. "He's…part of a group, mostly of Forwyn, who are trying to end the injustices done against our people. Or at least help."

Naina tilted her head thoughtfully. "Like us? Why did you feel the need to join another group?"

"It's…complicated."

"Because they're opposed to the Court of Elders and their laws?" Naina asked with a soft smile, referring to our earlier conversation. "But a guidespirit led you to them?"

Relieved, I returned her smile. "Yes." My gaze settled on Caesiem again. "But…I don't understand why. This man was a thief. I think maybe he still is. I'm not sure I agree with his or any of his friends' ideas, and I don't know what the guidespirit wants me to do exactly." I tugged on one of my braids and nervously began looping it around my finger. "There are some Alrenians committing crimes, and I tried to help him gather information from them tonight…when we were caught…" I trailed off, thinking of everything Caesiem had shared with me and shaking my head. "I'm confused."

Naina's lips were a taut line. "It sounds dangerous."

"But if the guidespirit led me there… I trust I'll be safe. Elhani protected me tonight," I protested.

Naina sighed softly. "I trust Elhani, and I trust you. Tell me more about what's confusing you."

I related some of what had happened over the past few days, omitting details about the vigilante group's desire to assassinate the empress.

"Sometimes the reasons a guidespirit leads us down a certain path or toward certain people aren't immediately clear," Naina explained once I'd finished. "All I can say is that you need to be careful." Her eyes darted again to Caesiem. "A pretty face often leads one astray."

My cheeks burned hot. "Naina, I wouldn't—" I protested.

She cut me off with a smile. "You've taken vows and I don't doubt your sincerity, Lo, but feelings are powerful and dangerous."

"I don't have feelings for him."

Instantly, guilt burned the back of my throat, sharp as bile. *Was that a lie?* I wondered, heart hammering. I tried to shove the emotion away, not wanting to examine it further.

"I'm not saying you do, but romantic feelings aren't the only kind that can lead someone off course. Friendship can create loyalties and ties that, if not founded in Elhani, can pull you away from his will as well. I simply want you to be aware…" She hesitated, glancing out the window where the night sky was brightening, shifting from velvet blue to a deep grey. The moon had already vanished. "The guidespirit may want you to help Caesiem and his friends, or maybe she wants you to stop them."

Sitting back, I mulled over her words. My eyes snagged on Caesiem, his chest rising and falling as he slept peacefully, as if he didn't have a care in the world. His muscled chest was exposed thanks to Naina's need to cut open his shirt, so I quickly shifted my gaze to his face. He could be so charming, but beneath that charm was someone who'd fought to survive. Who'd broken the law, left his home behind, and joined a ragtag band of vigilantes.

What did the guidespirit want me to do?

This time, Renni was the one to open the door of the abandoned building on the docks. His eyes widened when he saw me alone, shrouded in the last hours of dimness before dawn, but he stepped back wordlessly to let me inside. I scanned the shadowed room, finding the only other occupant to be Wilvhe, sitting with his hands propped on his chin as he studied papers scattered across the tabletop.

"We were just preparing to leave," Renni explained. "Where's Caesiem?"

"At the abbey. He was injured tonight."

Wilvhe's head snapped up. "What?"

Renni waved me over to the table, where I sat with them and explained everything that had happened.

When I'd finished, Renni drummed his fingers on the tabletop. "We always go out in pairs for safety," he explained. "Thank you for helping him."

Renni and Wilvhe exchanged a tense look.

"You'll keep us updated on how he does?" Renni asked me.

"Of course," I said.

Nodding, Renni leaned back, his face thoughtful.

"What is it?" I asked. I knew he was processing the conversation Caesiem had had with the Alrenians, and I wanted to know what Renni thought. Had we risked our lives for anything valuable?

"We already suspected the Alrenians were using Forwyn to…transport and display the bodies," he said, frowning. "To avoid the Alrenians being caught with them." He hesitated. "Most of the murders seem to be happening on the outskirts of the city, close to where the bodies are left. Caesiem's conversation with them seems to confirm that."

I leaned forward. "We need to take this information to the Elders! They could save some of these people. They could find and capture the Alrenians."

Wilvhe pursed his lips. "We've already tried to bring this issue before them, more than once," he said harshly. "They told us it wasn't an issue they could concern themselves with right now."

It was just as shocking to hear those words from Wilvhe's lips as from Caesiem's. "How could protecting our people not be important to them right now?" I blurted out.

Wilvhe shook his head. "They've been sending us Keepers on missions throughout Alrenor to quell uprisings, some small, but many growing increasingly larger and more threatening. I think they're more concerned about focusing their numbers on the possibility of war."

"Keeping Jaliana alive hasn't won the Alrenians to their side," I said quietly, sadly.

"No," Wilvhe said sharply. "And now that she's harming Forwyn in the palace, she's far too much of a threat. Not to mention the fact that any Alrenians who learn of her power might be further encouraged to rebel, claiming her as their 'rightful' leader."

I lowered my head to my hands. My body ached with exhaustion. The night was drawing to a close, and I hadn't had a wink of sleep. With my frequent nightmares and running excursions, I was used to functioning with only a few hours of sleep here and there, but this night was especially taxing.

"What do we do?" I asked quietly.

"Considering that the night is almost over? Nothing, for now," Renni said. "Go home. Get some rest. Make sure Caesiem is well tended to." He sighed. "Tomorrow it might be a good idea to let the owner of The Broken Crown know Caesiem will be out for a while, so he doesn't just throw out Caesiem's things and rent out his room to someone else." Renni smiled half-heartedly. "And in the meantime, we're going to plan and prepare."

Across the table, Wilvhe smirked and drew an envelope from his pocket, waving it dramatically before sliding it across to me. I picked it up, feeling how expensive and thick the paper was. It was already open, so I easily slid out the creamy invitation inside. An elegant script invited Wilvhe to the Forwyn-Alrenian Autumn Ball at the palace in honor of the empress and the Court of Elders.

I glanced at Wilvhe in confusion. "You're excited about dancing?"

"I can invite guests," he said eagerly. He swept a hand through his thick curls. "We could all attend."

"It will be a chance for us all to gather at the palace and…make our move," Renni explained. "We could work as a team and increase our chance of success."

"Your move to kill the empress?" I asked slowly.

"Yes. In all the time we've been watching and listening in on Alrenian meetings," Renni said, "the empress has been discussed in detail. The news of her new…gift…has spread, and it is strengthening the Alrenians' courage. All those murders? They've increased since Jaliana started attacking Forwyn."

"Jaliana is *murdering* Forwyn," Wilvhe cut in. "The Alrenians' crimes and terrorism in the capital are just signs of the larger problem the Elders have been trying to address, but they're not doing it correctly. Imagine Jaliana out of the equation. It would demoralize the Alrenians and sew division with a power struggle as they tried to choose a new would-be ruler. It could help us stop a brewing war. If we throw our enemies into chaos, we give our people a chance."

I frowned as my heart rate drummed faster. "You never told me the empress had killed anyone."

"Well, she very nearly has," Wilvhe said solemnly. "The first Forwyn the empress attacked, Lady Leanai, is doing poorly. When I went to visit Yaelti at the infirmary, the healers didn't expect she will last much longer." He swallowed hard. "Which doesn't give Yaelti much of a chance either, does it?"

"Surely the Elders will sentence her if she's a danger…" I trailed off.

Renni shook his head, his expression fierce. Frightening. Those warm eyes? That kind smile? A forgotten memory as he set his jaw and contemplated the young empress's death.

"Would you really want to leave that up to them, given their failure to take action in the past?"

"No," Wilvhe answered for me, in a voice as sharp as cut glass. "They will not do anything this time, either. They're choosing to announce Lady Leanai's death as an 'accident.' But we Keepers know the truth. And we cannot stand by this. It's time to do something."

CHAPTER FOURTEEN

Jalie

I WOKE WITH NESRELLE'S WORDS whispering in my ears, like the memory of a swiftly fading dream. *Don't fear the curse, little Jalie. Take back your life. Claim your throne. Make your enemies pay for their crimes.*

When I sat up, I found my breakfast tray had already been laid out, and Kovi was once again missing. In his place was the young, scared-looking guard, the boy Kovi had called Marukio. Stiff and silent, he looked ill-at-ease standing against the far wall. Completely at odds with the way Kovi had made himself comfortable in my room that first night.

Suppressing my smirk, I went about my morning routine, dressing in leggings and a tunic again. The sandals I chose were comfortable and sturdy. I braided my hair back carefully, pulling it away from my face.

As I chewed on a strawberry, I finally turned toward Marukio. "Today you'll take me to the Dragon Keep," I announced, as easily as if I really were empress and he were an attendant.

Marukio narrowed his eyes. "Kovi will be back shortly. You're not to leave these rooms."

Setting down my plate, I crept toward Marukio slowly, giving him time to rethink his decision. I didn't change my serene expression, but I didn't need to. With a movement of my fingers as I casually brushed back a strand of my hair, his eyes landed on my hands.

He was thinking of what I'd done to Lady Leanai and Keeper Yaelti. I could see the fear wash over him as his eyes widened. Tugging at the ribbons he wore around his neck, he swallowed, trying valiantly to conceal the uncertainty enveloping him.

"Don't be silly, Marukio," I murmured. "We're just going for a walk."

Marukio squeezed his eyes shut, as if he were praying. When he opened them, I was standing inches away.

"Fine," he ground out, shame tugging on his features. "But if you try anything…" He clutched his sword hilt threateningly.

Kovi wasn't at the training rooms today, or at least, he wasn't anymore once Marukio and I reached the Keep. Disappointment settled like a pit in my stomach when I noticed him at the mouth of the tunnel. Perhaps I didn't have nearly as much power and influence as I'd hoped. Fear wasn't the only reason Marukio had given in so easily. He must have also known that Kovi would be here.

Kovi was leaning against the wall as if expecting us. It was clear he had been training or exercising at some point this morning, because a sheen of sweat coated his face. He wore a black shirt, a damp one that hugged his muscles too closely. Though he wasn't in uniform, his sword and dagger both hung from his hips, and he stood with the rigid posture of a soldier prepared for a fight.

"How did you know I'd come here?" I snapped, hating that my voice cracked from my surprise.

Kovi nodded toward Marukio over my shoulder, and the boy

quickly left us. When Kovi turned back to me, his smile was lazy, yet something about it was threatening. "Because you and your kind are predictable." He gestured behind him, to the dim tunnel leading down toward dragon dens, training rooms, weapons rooms, and spaces for the hatchlings…all the rooms I hadn't been able to explore freely for years. "If you see what you perceive as weakness, you take advantage of it. And any opportunity to seize power or strength? You take." He settled his hand on his sword hilt, his grin vanishing into a stony mask. "Marukio may have not graduated the academy yet, but he's my cousin. We met and found we shared blood at the academy, and if you have any idea what it's like to grow up separated from family, to hardly know who you are connected to, you should know how important it is when you finally find family—any *family*. I asked for this assignment for him, to gain experience in the palace. The Elders granted it as a special favor to me. So if you ever lay a hand on him, if he ever comes to *any* harm here because of you, I'll execute you myself."

I wanted to be angry, to sneer at Kovi and shove past him, brushing his threats aside like they meant nothing. But I knew he could stop me with a single word. And instead of anger, I was pierced with an overwhelming sense of sadness and longing. I stared past him, toward where I knew the dragons awaited, and tears threatened.

It was impossible to describe the way being around the dragons made me feel, or the hope I'd felt mere moments ago when I'd imagined I could see one again. Just to look at them, to study their beauty and strength up close, would be comforting. They were part of my birthright, my heritage. They were in so many of the memories connecting me to my mother and my happy past. They meant so much to me, and to be parted from them all this time was a constant ache in my heart. To come this close and then be stopped…

It was almost unbearable.

It was enough for me to set aside my anger and my disgust, to look Kovi in the eye and try something different. Instead of trying to conceal my pain, I let him see it written across my face. I appealed to the softer side of him, the one that might have only pitied me, but at least saw me as human.

My words from yesterday still hung heavily between us. *If I am to be a monster, then I will be a monster in possession of the throne.* Perhaps he'd laugh in my face if I showed vulnerability now. But I had to try.

"Please," I said. "I just want to see the dragons."

Kovi's face softened almost imperceptibly, his stiff stance relaxing the slightest bit. He gestured behind him. "Then let's see the dragons."

Our footsteps echoed as we followed the descending path in silence. The air smelled of earth and stale smoke, and only the flickering torches ensconced on the walls lit our way. As we passed the weapons room and then the wide-open cavern that served as a training area, finding both empty, I realized that most of the Keepers were probably gone on patrol.

"The Keepers are off putting the rest of the empire in line, aren't they?" I said gruffly. As we neared the rows of dragon dens, their heavy doors shutting the beasts within, the silence confirmed my suspicion.

"Most of them are, yes," Kovi said. "Keeper Yaelti couldn't go, however." The note of anger was unmistakable in his voice. Setting his jaw, he didn't meet my sidelong glance.

"How is he?" I asked.

Kovi scoffed. "As if you care." He stopped in front of a den, staring at the dragon's name etched into the stone above the entrance. *Ryke.* "This is Yaelti's dragon."

But I couldn't tamp down my growing indignance. Yaelti had attacked *me* first. I had hurt him, yes, but I hadn't murdered him. And according to Nesrelle, I'd merely channeled a curse that Yaelti already deserved. In my mother's time, no one would have laid a threatening hand on her and lived. Only injuring his arms had been an act of mercy.

Unless it spreads and eats away at him, like Vionn's has.

I shoved the thought away and glared at Kovi. "It's not like I slit his throat," I said.

It was clearly the wrong thing to say. Slowly, Kovi turned to face me, his dark eyes blazing with anger. Torchlight bathed his face in an orange glow, accentuating the fierce set of his jaw.

"You think I deserve to die for what I did, don't you?" I said. "For the fact that my mother was a monster and now I must be too."

A dozen different emotions flitted through Kovi's eyes. "Maybe you do," he said at last, "but I will put what my empire needs over my desire for revenge. The Elders have decided you're to live, and I'm honoring that."

I couldn't keep the smirk off my face. Just like witnessing his anger in the training room, Kovi's admission was freeing, like a weight lifting from my shoulders. His hatred was infinitely better than his pity. Here he was on the same level as me, consumed with the same fiery emotions. "So you admit it," I breathed. "You aren't always perfect and self-righteous. You do want revenge."

"Vengeance is not for Elhani's children to execute," Kovi murmured, sounding like he was reciting something. Words from the Forwyn holy text? He swallowed as a muscle worked in his jaw.

"But you want to. You dream of seeing someone suffer the way you have. The way your mother did." My voice pitched higher; my emotions a whirlwind inside me. I was scarcely speaking to him anymore. It was myself I was addressing, and my mother's death I was thinking about. It was Nesrelle's voice in my mind, reminding me not to fear my curse.

"Fine!" The word exploded out of Kovi. He was leaning in so close to me, I could feel his hot breath on my cheeks. The careful control he always maintained was slipping, his arms shaking at his sides. "Sometimes, yes, I desperately want revenge. I close my eyes and I see my mother's body, over and over, even though I never actually got to see it—to say goodbye. I can imagine her death, bloody and violent and hideous, because I know what happened. It never stops haunting me. Every day I bury my anger deep inside, because I know the woman who murdered her is already dead. But I can't—I can't—I don't know how to cope with the anger when there is no one left alive to be angry at."

I blinked at the hot tears threatening my eyes. Every word he'd said reverberated in my chest, echoing my own thoughts and feelings so perfectly, I was speechless. Shocked.

This wasn't what I'd wanted. I'd wanted to see my enemy for what he was: angry, cruel, ready to slit my throat at a moment's notice. A monster like my mother and me. Like the Forwyn Elders. Instead, I felt…lost.

The silence settled heavily between us as Kovi composed himself, squeezing his eyes shut and catching his breath. The trembling in his body subsided. But I was breathless, the knife that seemed forever buried in my heart twisting itself deeper. As much as I wanted to pretend that Kovi was someone other, someone lesser, I couldn't ignore how similar we were. Or the pull of empathy that tugged on my heart.

Here he was, broken and human, and so utterly like me it was terrifying. Comforting. Horrible. Perfect. My heart pulsed in my ears, my blood hot and angry and…something else I didn't dare identify.

I hadn't expected mutual hatred and anger and hurt to connect us.

Kovi seemed to feel it too, because his face turned a little gentler as he spun away. "Do you want to visit the dragon or not?" he asked brusquely.

By way of an answer, I approached the pulley system that opened the door. Wordlessly, Kovi cut in front of me to lift the door himself, muscles straining as he worked the lever. I turned away to stare into the den, filled with natural light from the hole in the ceiling. It gave the dragon plenty of fresh air and sunlight without being large enough for him to escape.

I entered the den slowly, cautiously. Once, the Alrenians had tamed the dragons with vylae, a plant that was poisonous and unscented to humans, but that had a calming effect on the dragons. Our theory had been that the dragons must have been able to detect a scent that was unnoticeable to our human sense of smell. We'd coated our armor in vylae juice, encouraging the dragons to submit to us. Once a dragon knew and trusted its rider, they bonded and a Keeper rarely, if ever, needed to use vylae again.

But three years ago, a Misrothian princess who'd defied my mother had apparently found another way to tame the dragons, and she'd shared her knowledge with the Forwyn.

What if I, an Alrenian empress, couldn't do what a Misrothian or the Forwyn could do? What if Ryke didn't submit to me? Slowly, my confidence deflated, and a bitter taste slid across my tongue. Sweat collected along the back of my neck and under my armpits.

Before I entered too far into the den, Kovi stepped close, speaking low in my ear. His warm breath tickled. "I was told that the dragons respond to a display of confidence. They need to see us as equals. That's the key to earning a dragon's respect and trust."

First, I felt a prickle of irritation, that a Forwyn had to tell me how to tame one of *my* dragons. Then a rush of hope took over. My confidence returned, the embers in my heart warming to a flowing fire. *Alrenians are fearless. These dragons are* mine. *Ryke will know and submit to me.*

I lifted my chin, and a thrill rippled through me when I met Ryke's eye. His iris was as bright and pure as steel, and it gleamed with intelligence and curiosity—not malice. Though I'd mostly ridden my mother's dragon, Reyva, I recognized Ryke and his stunning emerald scales, accented with hints of turquoise. Perhaps he was assigned to Yaelti currently, but it hardly mattered. By birthright, every one of these dragons truly belonged to *me*.

When I crept further into the den, Kovi shuffled back into the tunnel, watching me. Carefully, I extended my hand, palm outward, toward the dragon's snout. A trickle of smoke swirled from Ryke's nostril as he turned toward my hand, sniffing it uncertainly. My heart pulsed in my throat.

I only needed to present myself to this dragon as an equal, strong and unyielding, rather than look like fearful, cowering prey. Squaring my shoulders, I stared straight at Ryke fearlessly.

"Do you remember me?" I whispered. Gently, I laid my palm against the scales beneath his eye, letting him study me as I trailed my fingertips toward his snout. I loved how warm and smooth his scales felt. I relished the scent of dragon smoke lingering in the air.

How could I be afraid when this was exactly where I was meant to be?

Comforting memories enveloped me as Ryke nuzzled my hand. "He's glorious!" A joyful laugh burbled from my lips, and I turned to glance over my shoulder, blinking back the happy tears threatening to make an appearance.

Leaning against the entryway, arms crossed, Kovi listed his head. His intense stare didn't unnerve me this time; he seemed more puzzled than threatening. I hadn't exactly meant to share this moment with him, but there had been no one else to look for. Unnerved, I turned back to Ryke, moving closer to his warmth. I would relish every moment with this beast until Kovi deemed it was time to go.

It was intoxicating to realize a dragon had remembered and submitted to me. Later, as Kovi and I wound our way out of the Keep,

Mother's words rang through my mind: *Whoever controls Alrenor's dragons, controls Alrenor.* I needed allies and a plan, but this was a start.

❮❮❮❮❮

"Do you know what this is?" I asked, plucking a vivid purple flower from a nearby stem and holding it under my nose to breathe in its light, fresh scent. Its velvet-soft petals tickled my face. Vaeletta were my favorite flowers, not only because of their rich coloring and aromatic fragrance, but also because of their hardy nature. They grew year-round, never troubled by the chill or lack of rain during the dry seasons of autumn and winter, nor by the occasional flooding that the rainy seasons of spring and summer always brought. And of course, they reminded me of my mother, who loved to gather them in bunches and place them in vases throughout the imperial chambers, until her rooms, her clothes, even her skin smelled like the flowers, and I'd started to associate their scent with her.

Currently, Kovi and I were walking through the gardens at my insistence. I'd told him the day was too beautiful to return to my chambers just yet, and even though I suspected Kovi was longing for a bath and fresh clothes, he didn't argue with me.

Here, in the scorching summer sun with the familiar smells of citrus, flowers, and fresh grass, I was at peace.

Maybe it was the fact that walking these paths brought back happy memories of Mother, of afternoons spent enjoying the trees' shade or picking blossoms for vases we placed in our rooms. It was why I plucked flowers now, gathering them into a colorful bouquet I planned to display near my bed, where the sight and smell would bring comfort.

But I also had other reasons for walking the palace grounds and asking Kovi about flowers. A plan was forming in my mind.

Kovi settled cool eyes on me, assessing my expression as if trying to read all my secrets. The gold flecks in his irises glinted in the sunlight.

"No," he said. "How do you know so much about flowers?"

"Clearly from growing up here."

"But you had gardeners to tend to the grounds," Kovi argued.

"That didn't mean I was ignorant," I scoffed. "A good ruler is knowledgeable about everything they own and care for."

"*Care* for," Kovi muttered under his breath, his expression darkening. "Whatever you say, Jaliana."

I swallowed my angry retort and spun around to stroll further down the path. The scent of roses wafted over me as I passed rows of bushes in nearly every color imaginable: darkest reds and brightest oranges, lemon yellow and blush pink, pale lilac and white as pure as sea foam. I gathered a couple, but that was all. I wanted variety in my bouquet—along with some specific plants.

"Don't call me Jaliana," I said after several long moments. "I prefer Jalie."

Kovi's lips twitched, as if he were amused. "I thought nicknames were what friends used to address one another."

I smirked. "Well, I prefer it if my enemies are less formal toward me, then. I'd rather hear my preferred name when you try to insult me."

This time, Kovi smiled outright. "Very well, *Jalie.*"

I halted to select some leaves whose veins looked like delicate, lacy patterns, and tossed Kovi a questioning look.

"No, I don't know those either," he said. "I'm a soldier, not a gardener." He crossed his arms over his chest, and I turned away to hide my smile as I arranged the leaves in my bouquet.

There was a pause.

"Why all the questions about plants?" he asked. He didn't sound annoyed, but genuinely curious. "Why carry on a conversation at all? I thought you hated me."

"I do," I replied steadily, flashing him a wicked smile. "But I also have no one else to talk to, and it's terribly boring. So you'll have to do."

Kovi snorted, and I almost laughed in response. He so rarely let any emotion show. For a moment our gazes snagged on one another and we caught each other in a mutual smile. I snapped my eyes away and continued down the path until we reached a patch of vylae, their golden buds swaying gently in the breeze.

"These I know," Kovi said, but I waved a dismissive hand.

"Everyone knows what vylae are." I smiled faintly and recited the children's rhyme my mother taught me, one all the imperial children learned: *"Vylae with your petals gold, make the Dragon Keepers bold. But vylae with your heart of black, steal breath and ne'er give back."*

I breathed in the flowers' aromatic scent, thinking how strange it was that when ingested, the plant was basically undetectable through taste or smell, even in water. With no known antidote for vylae, it would have been my easiest option, but trying to pick some with Kovi constantly at my side would be impossible. I could only choose the less obvious poisonous plants. Besides, it would be easier to work with ones that I'd built immunity against myself. Just in case. I glanced at my bouquet, where, along with my harmless collection, I'd also clustered poisonous varities, such as the lacy-veined leaves of nirimtha and red-budded corrilys.

When I turned away, I caught motion out of the corner of my eye. Kovi slammed into my back, knocking me to the ground so hard the breath rushed from my lungs.

As soon as I could take in a shuddering breath of oxygen, I protested. "Wha—"

Kovi clapped a hand over my mouth. I bit into his palm, but he didn't even react. "Stay silent," he hissed, his breath a tickle in my ear. "Someone just tried to shoot you."

I glanced up to see an arrow embedded in a tree trunk right above my head, its fletching quivering from its flight. My mind spun. It wasn't a new idea that there were people out there who wanted to kill me, but none had come close to accomplishing their goal before. The Forwyn in power guarded me carefully, their pretty pawn in a gilded cage.

The list of people who would want to harm me felt endless—and I knew it included both Forwyn and Alrenians. Most Alrenians wanted to help me regain my life and my throne—at least, I *hoped* most did. But some saw me as weak, a willing pawn to the Forwyn, and wanted me dead and replaced with a stronger imperial ruler. And while the Elders pretended all their people were of one mind, there were certainly Forwyn citizens who disagreed with the Elders' decision to let me live.

Despite all this, no one, Forwyn or Alrenian, had ever gotten this far in an assassination attempt before. The palace was heavily fortified with the Dragon Keep so near and armed Forwyn guards constantly patrolling the grounds. Who had gotten past their defenses?

Seconds stretched as I tempered my breathing. Kovi's body hovered over mine, uncomfortably close even when he sat up a little to survey the area. I could feel his heartbeat against my back, and every breath was full of his scent: sea salt and coconut. They were all little reminders that he was human. It was disconcerting.

I could almost hear Nesrelle's voice whisper in my ear. *Do not fear your curse.*

I drew a deep breath. The bouquet I'd so carefully collected was crushed beneath me, the mingling perfume of all its smashed petals tickling my nose. I concentrated on that scent as Kovi finally moved, yanking on my arm and gesturing back toward the palace.

"You aren't going to find the assassin?" I demanded.

Kovi only tugged on my arm harder. Giving in, I snatched the remnants of my bouquet in one hand and crawled after him.

This is humiliating, I fumed as we followed the path back the way we had come. Hiding from someone who wanted to kill me was beneath my Alrenian blood. If I'd been allowed a weapon, I could have dispatched the idiot myself.

Finally, Kovi rose to his feet, turning to pull me up beside him. Despite my attempt to shove him off, he didn't remove his grasp from my arm as he hurried us toward the palace. As soon as we were inside, he ordered the first guards we encountered to search the grounds for a would-be assassin.

"He—or she—fled as soon as they missed their mark, but they might not be too far away yet," he said as the two Forwyn men saluted and dashed away.

Kovi never let go of me, steering me back toward my rooms and slamming the door behind us. I stared at him.

"What was that?" I demanded.

He blinked at me. "I told you. An assassination attempt," he said simply, pushing past me to stride to my balcony doors and check that they were secure.

"No, I meant…" I hesitated, uncertain how to put my tangled thoughts into words. I glanced at my crumpled bouquet and, frowning, tossed it onto my vanity. Confused thoughts tumbled through my mind: Kovi carrying me from the arena, or immediately pushing me to the ground before the arrow could strike me. Each time, he could have easily stood back and let his enemy suffer or die.

He doesn't care, I told myself gruffly. *He's forced to keep you safe to keep up the Elders' appearances.* But that didn't explain away his kindness after the arena, and it made my head ache.

I *hated* him and everything he stood for, and he'd made no effort to hide the fact that he felt the same. Who showed compassion toward their enemy?

Of course, it changed nothing. If I wanted to escape, to save my people, then Kovi had to die.

Didn't he?

He's just playing mind games with you, trying to get you to trust him and think he's on your side, when really he will kill you without thinking twice, I told myself. Even if that didn't really make sense either. Nothing did, and it was driving me mad.

Without bothering to finish my sentence, I stalked over to my shelves to select a vase, fill it with water, and deposit the battered remnants of my bouquet inside. Satisfied, I turned back to the shelves and chose a book at random. I wasn't much of a reader, preferring to be out experiencing life rather than reading about it, but it wasn't as if I had many options at the moment. Settling onto my bed, I flipped the book open, but I found it impossible to concentrate.

"Was it a Forwyn assassin?" I asked carefully, lifting my head from the book I'd pulled into my lap and studying Kovi's features for any emotion.

He was still standing post by the balcony doors, gazing through the glass panes set within each one. "Were you expecting an Alrenian assassin?"

Rather than meet his inspecting gaze, I stared at my book. A rising flood of emotion was threatening me, and I didn't dare let Kovi see me vulnerable—not again. "I'm an empress," I said instead, keeping my tone careless. "I have a lot of enemies."

"I didn't see the assassin closely enough to tell," Kovi responded.

Time dragged. I flipped aimlessly through my book. The shock of the attack eventually wore off, transforming into boredom.

At last, a knock sounded on the door. Hand near his sword hilt,

Kovi went to open it, and I heard Elder Ettonou's voice. My chest tightened uncomfortably. I set my book aside and crept into my waiting room, where the two were speaking.

The Elder pointedly ignored me as I entered, keeping his sharp gaze trained on his son.

"You can handle the responsibility," Kovi's father was saying. "We wouldn't have given you this position if we doubted your ability."

"Did you find the assassin?" I cut in.

Elder Ettonou's eyes flicked coolly to me. "No, but that changes nothing. We've always known there is no shortage of people who want you dead." He paused a moment, letting his implication sink in: *he* was among those people. "Kovi can keep you alive, as long as you cooperate and harm no more Forwyn. We're opening the throne room to the people tonight, so they can come before their empress and the Elders, so your presence is required in two hours."

"Late notice," I observed, but the Elder ignored me and pressed on.

"This is your opportunity to remedy the damage you've done in your recent public displays." He studied me, his dark eyes unforgiving. "Make it count, or we'll be having another meeting to reconsider your worth." He turned to Kovi. "We also have the upcoming Autumn Ball, another chance for the empress to prove herself. You'll be expected to attend that as a guest and her bodyguard. Don't make it obvious you're there to do anything but escort her. People are talking."

He handed Kovi an envelope, and I wondered if it was merely a copy of the invitations the nobility had received, or if it contained specific instructions for his son. My fingers itched to snatch it from Kovi and read it myself.

Without another word, Elder Ettonou spun on his heel and left.

Unwittingly, I met Kovi's eyes, and we stared at one another. Now he was responsible for my safety at public events? Naturally the other guards would assist him, but that was a lot of weight to place on him.

I turned back toward my bedchamber, already mulling over the possibilities. It would be more difficult than ever to shake Kovi with at least one assassin on the loose, but the ball would give me opportunities I hadn't had before. If I could wait that long. I held back a smile as I determinedly ignored the bouquet on my vanity, pretending I had all but forgotten it. I threw open my wardrobe and pretended to lose myself in the excitement of preparing for a social event. It was easy to do, since I loved an opportunity to wear my finest outfits, perhaps even more so because I could show them off to my enemies and remind myself who I truly was.

Avenge the empire, I thought, the memory of the prisoner's cry stirring my constant anger back into a roaring flame. Knowing that I wasn't alone increased my confidence. I could do this. I could be patient, and I could be clever. No matter the risk, my throne, my people, and our revenge were all worth it.

CHAPTER FIFTEEN

Lo

HOW DO YOU KNOW HIM?" O'emia asked, her nose scrunched in that familiar way of hers whenever she was doubtful about something.

Naina, seated on my opposite side, laid a calming hand on my knee.

Since Caesiem was sprawled unconscious across our kitchen table with Ryhalla keeping watch over him, we'd all carried our breakfast outside to eat in the backyard. Despite my sleepless night, the warm sun on my back and the scents of coffee and oranges invigorated me. But they couldn't dispel my growing unease after my conversation with Renni and Wilvhe.

Naina spoke up for me. "Lo realized the boy was in trouble and sought my help," she said simply. "She performed her duty as a nun, and I performed mine as a healer."

"He's clearly a criminal," Eloiyah muttered darkly, stabbing into her egg with unnecessary aggression. "He broke curfew and dropped half-dead before our abbey, and we let him inside with us?" Her eyes strayed to the abbey, which was casting a slowly shrinking shadow as the sun rose higher. It was as if she expected Caesiem to jolt awake right then and begin attacking or robbing us.

"He nearly died." Pauni'a voiced my thought aloud, so I didn't have to. "What do you think he's going to do to us? You don't harm the people who save your life."

Eloiyah shrugged. "Maybe Teramese criminals do. What is he doing in Alrenor? Is he on *their* side?" It was clear from her tone that she spoke of the Alrenians.

"Maybe not," I said calmly, hoping my voice betrayed nothing as I peeled my second orange. "And it's not as if he's going to stay in the abbey." I tossed a glance Naina's way.

"He will for a short time, until he's fully recovered," Naina said, setting down her empty plate. "I trust you younger girls can keep level heads and pure hearts with a young man under the roof." She shot us mischievous grins to let us know she was joking. Mostly.

Even though she said it to all of us sisters near Caesiem's age— Pauni'a, O'emia, and me—I felt her gaze linger a moment longer on me. I glanced back down at my orange and nodded before devouring a section to keep myself busy.

"Nothing will ever shake our devotion," O'emia said steadily.

But as we reentered the abbey, each of us carrying loads of plates or leftover food, Pauni'a grasped my elbow and pulled me aside. "You're telling me everything about this later," she whispered. "His name, how you met, what *exactly* is going on…"

"*Nothing* is going on, Nia!" I protested, keeping my tone hushed.

"I didn't say you're breaking your vow," Pauni'a said quickly. "But that doesn't mean we can't *look* and appreciate a handsome young man." I glanced back in time to see the smirk flutter across her lips before it disappeared. "We just can't touch."

I sighed and shook my head, but she raised her eyebrows at me to emphasize her point. "*Later*," she repeated.

"Later," I agreed.

❮❮❮❮❮

Naina and I carried Caesiem to the infirmary and, leaving Jo'elli to look after him, retired to our rooms for some much-needed rest. By the time I returned hours later, Jo'elli had a bowl of beef broth sitting at the table beside Caesiem, who was stirring.

"I can give it to him," I offered.

In my concerned and exhausted state, I still hadn't changed my clothes from the night before, and Jo'elli's eyes strayed briefly to my rumpled shirt and leggings. Ignoring her, I pushed past her to pick up the bowl.

Jo'elli was over twenty years my senior, her dark curls already streaked with grey and her eyes flanked by wrinkles. She rarely spoke, often giving off a cold, arrogant aura, but Naina insisted Jo'elli was only shy. Whatever the case, she gave me a tight-lipped smile now and turned to go.

I seated myself in the chair beside Caesiem's cot, balanced the bowl of broth in my lap, and studied the man, who seemed barely coherent. Thankfully, he was clothed in a fresh linen shirt, so I didn't have to look at his bare chest again. But unfortunately, the shirt had been made to fit a nun, and although it was cut loose for us, it was anything but loose on his body. It hugged every muscle in his arms.

"I need you to eat," I said.

Caesiem only blinked at me drowsily, muttering something incomprehensible. He seemed worryingly weak and disoriented.

Carefully, I propped him up with a few pillows and fed him the broth, spoonful by spoonful, making sure he swallowed each bit. He slipped back into sleep soon after he'd finished the bowl, his chest rising and falling gently.

Did we meet so I could help you, or stop you? I wondered silently, resisting an urge to brush a strand of curling dark hair away from his ear. *Don't even think about touching him, not even as a friend.*

Pauni'a slipped into the infirmary not long after.

"He really is beautiful," she sighed, studying his burnished skin and wavy hair. She cast me an uncertain glance. "Is it wrong to think that? I know I said it's all right to look earlier, but I don't—"

"Do you think the Elders truly have our best interest at heart?" I interrupted. The question was so pressing I couldn't ignore it anymore, and it practically exploded out of me.

Pauni'a stared. "What?"

"Caesiem and his friends say they've told the Elders about Alrenians breaking curfew and murdering Forwyn, and the Elders have done nothing," I continued doubtfully.

Pauni'a pointed at the sleeping young man. "I take it that he is Caesiem?"

Nodding, I started my story from the beginning, confessing to my nightly running habit. I explained how I'd met Caesiem and seen the guidespirit that convinced me to meet Caesiem's friends. When I told her about what had happened the night before and what Caesiem and his friends claimed the Elders said about the recent Alrenian attacks, Pauni'a plopped down in another chair, her brow knitted in thought.

"It would be nice to speak with the Elders themselves," she mused. "I know we don't exactly live in seclusion, but we aren't truly immersed in the world either. I know little about the decisions the Elders make. Or much about palace life."

I picked furiously at a thread on my shirt. I wished I could tell her about my real dilemma, that Caesiem and his friends believed Jaliana needed to be killed to stop a war. That I felt compelled to help my people, but didn't want to risk my status here, in the Circle of Serenity, where I'd made a vow not to spill blood. Pauni'a didn't even know about my past and how I'd killed already.

"I don't know what to do, Nia," I said.

Pauni'a smiled softly, her eyes straying momentarily to Caesiem's face again. "Listen to the voice of Elhani, as you have been doing. The guidespirit already led you to save someone's life. I'm sure it will become clear in time."

"You sound like Naina," I complained.

Pauni'a shrugged. "Naina is wise and worth listening to." Then she sighed, lowering her gaze to the floor. "I don't regret my dedication to Elhani, but do you ever have doubts?"

"About what?"

"About whether you should have made your vows." Pauni'a jaw tensed. "We're so young still, Lo. What do we know about love? Did we make our decision too quickly, too carelessly? Sometimes I think this terrible ache of loneliness won't ever go away. So many of us former slaves were orphans without families. I thought coming here, dedicating my life to helping others and joining a family of sisters in Elhani, would erase that. And it helps. It really does. But do you ever think about falling in love? Wonder what it's like, or what it would be like to have your own family?" She blinked at tears glistening in her eyes, threatening to spill over. "I feel horrible even having these thoughts. To even imagine breaking my vows…" She cleared her throat. "I mean, *you* and the other sisters are my family. What more could I want? How could I covet more when I've committed myself to a simple life, to pushing away greed?"

"Elhani will forgive you, Nia. Do penance tonight. Give an offering. Spend extra time in prayer." I offered Pauni'a a tremulous smile. "I have doubts sometimes, too. And I understand your guilt. It's there for me too…all the time." I sighed and shook my head, fidgeting with some of my braids. My fingertips slipped over the satin texture of the orange ribbon Naina had added to my hair just a day ago. For loyalty. "I worry I'm not worthy all the time. But that's why I know I made the right choice to join the Circle of Serenity. I need to be here to serve him properly and do penance for all the ways I fail and sin."

Pauni'a sighed, as if a weight had lifted off her shoulders. "Thank you, Lo," she murmured.

Just then, Naina entered and suggested I take some time to wash up and change. Glancing at my old clothes, I smiled and thanked Naina as she took my place.

Pauni'a followed me from the infirmary. "You work so hard," she said softly, "and you're so faithful to confess and pray and do penance in offerings…I never imagined you struggled with guilt too."

More than you know, I thought as Pauni'a continued down the hallway, leaving me to turn back toward my room and find a change of clothes.

Tonight, I'd be spending extra time in prayer as well.

❮❮❮❮❮

Stepping inside The Broken Crown, I was enveloped in smoke and the stuffy warmth that came from too many bodies crammed together in one space. I paid no attention to the patrons crowded about the tables, smoking and drinking and laughing, but made straight for the bar. Once again, it was No'ahim on duty, and judging by his wide smile, he recognized me immediately.

I wasn't dressed in nun grey tonight, either, so I wasn't surprised when he leaned forward and greeted me with a "Caesiem's girl?" He hesitated, glancing around before lowering his voice. "Do you know what's happened to him? I scheduled him to play last night."

I hesitated. "Could I speak with the owner?"

No'ahim chortled. "I am the owner." He pointed toward the empty stool across the bar from him. "Why don't you have a seat? Would you like a drink?"

My hand strayed toward my empty pocket. Ordinarily I might have been tempted to order a coffee, but as part of my prayer and penance earlier tonight, I'd offered a large portion of my allowance. Mostly, the other sisters and I survived off the shared items we purchased from the rare donations we received from Forwyn citizens. We divvied up a small portion from the money we were given for allowances—money that was usually used to purchase our own clothes or other minor comforts. Tossing my coins in the offering basket beside our altar meant that my money would be given back to the Forwyn, used to buy the food and medicine we gifted the needy.

I didn't regret my choice, though I did long for the comfort of a warm drink. Stifling my sigh, I settled onto the stool and shook my head. Quietly, I made my excuses for Caesiem, explaining he'd been mugged and injured but was recovering at a nearby healer's.

"If there's a way for you to hold his room while he recovers, I'd be much obliged. Though I don't have any money to pay you for the favor," I added regretfully.

No'ahim waved me off. "His room serves me no other use anyway, so it's no loss to me. Though we'll miss his music. He'll be all right?" His expression was that of genuine concern.

"I think so."

Before I could protest, No'ahim slid a mug of coffee across the bar toward me. "You look exhausted," he said by way of explanation, "and I appreciate what you're doing to help Caesiem. I've become quite fond of him."

Thanking the man, I curled my hands around the warm mug and inhaled the rich, earthy scent rising from the steaming coffee. When I'd given it a bit to cool, I took a long, soothing sip. Nothing could calm my tumultuous thoughts or erase the horrific images I'd seen the night before, but the hot drink was undeniably comforting. As No'ahim served other customers, I nursed my mug.

I have to do something, I thought. Assassinating the empress couldn't be the only way to save my people and prevent a war.

Resolved, I drained my mug and set it on the counter. Thanking him again, I bid No'ahim goodnight and rose from my seat, winding my way around the full tables. But before I could reach the door, a hand reached out and seized my arm.

I stifled a cry as I struggled against the stranger's grip, flashbacks of cruel Alrenian hands in the palace racing through my mind.

"I only want to ask you a question," a man's voice said, his grasp on my arm loosening.

Scowling, I shook his hand off me. "Well, what is it?" When I turned to face the stranger, I found him shrouded in a hooded cloak. Suspicion prickled through me. Only someone with underhanded business would wear something that heavy in the stifling heat.

"I heard you mention Caesiem's name," he went on. I couldn't tell if he slurred his words because he was intoxicated, or if he was trying to conceal his terrible Alrenian accent. Was he Forwyn? A foreigner? "How do you know him?"

"What business is it of yours?" I demanded.

The man snorted. "*He's* my business," he said with a laugh, and I wondered uneasily if Caesiem had stolen from this man. Or perhaps he stole *for* him.

I gritted my teeth. "I really can't give you any information, and if you're a gentleman, you'll let me go home before the hour grows too late," I said pointedly, shoving past him.

He made no move to stop me, but I could feel his eyes boring into my back as I slipped out onto the street. Even after the door slammed shut behind me, I couldn't shake the anxious feeling that man had given me.

Drawing a deep breath, I tucked myself into the shadows and strode purposefully toward the palace.

The entire city seemed to hold its breath around me, the steady sound of my boots against the cobblestones like a heartbeat. Waves crashed against the shore, and water coursed gently through the channels I passed. A gentle breeze kissed my forehead, waving the fronds of palm trees overhead, and it tasted like salt.

It seemed surreal to be walking toward the palace again, toward the past I'd run from. When I passed the shadowy alleys, I could almost see my brother's form watching me. Almost hear his voice. *Family can never be parted.* I squeezed my eyes shut to block out the rising pain.

I realized too late how near to the city outskirts my path had taken me. Out of the corner of my eye, I saw the figure at the far end of the alley beside me and froze. When I turned to face it, I realized it was another Forwyn body, shoved gruesomely on a stake, clothes painted with the uprising's bloody symbol.

Horror and rage drew me closer, through the alleyway and toward the wall, where three new bodies were lined up in a row. A boy younger than me. Another whose face was unrecognizable. An older man. Their necks were all slit, three gory red smiles reminding me of other corpses, other nightmares. Painted on the wall behind them in Alrenian were two simple messages: *Avenge the empire!* and *For the empress!*

I choked on bile, on the scream threatening to tear from my throat.

It was almost like Edi was standing there in the shadows beside me, extending a hand. *She can't hurt us, not really. None of them can.*

Oh, but they could. Tears burned my eyes.

What *monsters* did this?

Black spots danced across my vision, and the world tilted. My fury was almost blinding. I drew several deep, calming breaths, but the air was tainted with the stench of blood and death.

I staggered back toward the street, and the next thing I knew, I was running. Sprinting. My feet devoured the distance to the palace, crossing bridges and following the winding, ascending routes of the streets as if they were nothing. Despite the pounding of my heart, the sweat soaking my back, and the fire in my chest, I felt no pain, no exhaustion. My anger fueled me.

The guards at the gate stiffened and reached for their sword hilts in alarm. Gasping for breath, sweat dripping in my eyes, I could barely speak. My words came out garbled.

"What did you say?" one of the guards demanded, a man with piercing amber eyes.

"I must…see…the Elders," I repeated.

His eyes raked over my body, taking in my simple tunic and leggings. They weren't the colors of a nun, but they weren't the clothes of a noble, either. To them, I was nobody—and I probably looked crazy.

"They don't see anyone at this hour," he said with a frown.

"It's an emergency," I said, injecting confidence into my tone. I straightened, reaching for the cord I'd used to tie my braids out of my face. Undoing it, I tugged on my braid wound with a grey ribbon, the one that declared my service as a nun.

Immediately, the guard's eyes widened. A nun was respected among the Forwyn. I could see instantly that my status as one of the sisters gave my words weight.

"An emergency?" the second guard asked.

"I need to see them as soon as possible."

The two stepped back, conferring with one another, before giving me a nod and swinging open the gates. The first guard approached me again. "I'll escort you to them right away."

Every step through the gardens and palace buildings was filled with a haunting memory. Karye's cruel laugh. Edi's comforting smile. Blood and slit throats and dead bodies.

The guard left me to wait in a private library, covered in dark shelves of old Alrenian books. An unlit fireplace was set in one wall, while another housed an enormous window with a view of the vast gardens. I sank into an armchair near the hearth and tried to let my adrenaline-filled body calm.

It wasn't long before the door opened and a tall, stern-faced woman entered, escorted by two guards.

"This is Elder Ilhoa," one of the guards announced.

Dressed in a long, embroidered robe that covered her nightgown, she cut an imposing figure even when she'd clearly just risen from bed. I stood and bowed before her, but she waved her hand.

"Let's not waste time with formalities, if there's an emergency," she said. "The hour is growing late. I don't want to see people bowing."

Her hair was pulled into a bun on her hair, wrapped with mostly silver and orange ribbons. The silver marked her status and the orange represented her loyalty and dedication to the Forwyn people. I prayed that was a good sign, since her frowning face didn't feel like one at all.

"So," Elder Ilhoa went on impatiently, "what is this emergency?"

"There is a group of Alrenians murdering Forwyn citizens in the empress's name," I said, every ounce of anger keeping my tone steady and strong as steel. "They leave their bodies on pikes, and they add more each night."

Elder Ilhoa heaved a sigh, striding further into the room to take a seat in the armchair next to mine. With a gesture, she encouraged me to sit down again.

"We're aware of this, of course," Elder Ilhoa said, her gaze cutting sharply into me. "Our patrol guards have found the bodies in the past and have properly and respectfully disposed of them."

I swallowed to quell my rising indignation, but my voice shook anyway. "Respect for the dead isn't enough. What about the living? Our people are being slaughtered, and we need help to stop this."

Elder Ilhoa hesitated, her expression never softening. "I cannot discuss matters of state with you, child, but I need you to understand. We are as appalled by these crimes as you are, and we hope we can execute justice soon. But removing our numbers from other assigned tasks right now is impossible. Our army is small, and most of our guards are stretched thin as it is. As for the Dragon Keepers, they have been patrolling the entire empire. We have to focus on the largest threats first."

I hesitated. "If the Alrenians are threatening us in Jaliana's name, is she really the sort of ally the Elders want on the throne?"

Elder Ilhoa's face darkened. "I understand your concerns, but you need to know there are many issues at play here. Trust us."

I stood, too furious to even think through my actions. "How can we trust you if you're letting us die in our own streets?"

Spinning away from the Elder's shocked expression, I stormed from the room without waiting for a response. The guard sprinted after me, calling out to me to stop as I strode down the hall. I slowed enough for him to fall into step beside me, wordlessly guiding me through the building.

Caesiem, Renni, and Wilvhe had all been right. The Elders were unwilling to do anything. Maybe this issue didn't seem large enough to them when they were worried about a potential war, but how could it *not?* How could they brush it aside and make excuses when these deaths were proof that the war had already started? Right under our noses?

I rounded a corner and came face-to-face with Wilvhe himself, dressed in his Keeper armor. "Lo," he said, eyes widening. "What are you doing here?"

Halting, I cast a sidelong glance toward the guard. "I came to see the Elders."

Wilvhe seemed to understand. "I can see her out," he offered to the guard, who bent his head gratefully and left without a word.

As we listened to the guard's retreating footsteps, Wilvhe studied my sweaty form and incensed expression. "Did you speak to them about the murders?" he asked in a hushed voice.

I nodded. "And I received the same unhelpful response you did, but I had to try." My entire body was trembling, probably from a mixture of exhaustion and adrenaline. "Why are you dressed in armor at this hour?"

Wilvhe's face was taut. "We were on a mission to quell an uprising in Vernae," he said. His eyes looked haunted. "They were chanting Jaliana's name and executing Forwyn in the streets. Thank Elhani we have the dragons, but..." He sighed. "It's bad, Lo."

I blinked, feeling tears burn my eyes. "How's Yaelti?"

Wilvhe's voice was hoarse. "They don't expect he'll make it through the week."

"I'm so sorry," I whispered.

At a loss for words, Wilvhe shrugged, and a heavy silence fell between us. Rousing himself, he asked, "Will you come to our next meeting tomorrow? We have a mission I think you could help us with." He scanned the hallway before adding in a lower voice, "It involves...doing what the Elders refuse to do. To try to save lives."

Anger still burning within me, I didn't hesitate this time. "Yes."

Wilvhe's smile was brief. "Thank you. Would you like a ride home on my dragon?"

As tempting as the offer was, I didn't want to be that obvious when I reentered the abbey. "No, I'd better walk."

"It's not safe to be in the streets alone," he said quietly. "I'll walk you back home."

I didn't object, because I knew he was right. Every time I shut my eyes, all I could see were those bodies all in a row and the message scrawled behind them. *For the empress.*

Had I slain one empress, only to let one just as wicked and cruel take her place?

CHAPTER SIXTEEN

Jalie

CLOTHED IN FLOWING BLACK AND ivory, with matching dragon scales that formed the gleaming straps of my gown, I settled onto the throne. *My* throne. With the imperial headdress of golden dragon scales weighing down my head, in the seat my forefathers and foremothers had occupied for generations, I truly felt like an empress.

My people waited to speak with me in a line that trailed all the way out the open doors. It was exhilarating. A small taste of what it would be to rule, one given to me every once in a while by the Court of Elders.

But not truly.

I glanced around, toward Kovi standing on my right and another guard on my left. The Elders encircled my throne, blocking my people's direct path to me—and mine to them. No one approached me without the Elders' permission. No one spoke to me without the Elders standing by, listening in and approving everything I said. If I made one wrong move—well, the Elders had already made their threats before we'd entered the throne room. I knew better than to step out of line if I wanted to live and maintain what little freedom I still had within the palace.

And I couldn't risk losing anything now, not when I knew Ryke would obey me and I had poisonous plants waiting in my room. Not when I knew my people were out there, crying out for our empire to be avenged.

An old Alrenian woman shuffled forward, bowing deeply to me when Elder Ettonou and Elder Ilhoa stepped aside.

"Your Imperial Highness," the woman said, tears in her pale grey eyes. Her voice was soft and tremulous, and she seemed thin and frail enough that just the act of bowing could topple her.

"Rise, please," I said. "What is your request?"

The woman kept her eyes on the floor as she spoke. "My husband worked for many years as a grocer in Inalgoth," she explained, "but six months ago he passed. Now I manage the business on my own as best as I can, but I have Forwyn"–her eyes darted uncomfortably to the Elders and then back to the floor–"who are refusing to do business with me. Those who do enter my store often berate and steal from me, or say I deserve to starve. I'm struggling to make a living. And I know I'm not the only Alrenian in this position. Please, *amara*, consider passing a law that would protect Alrenian businesses. There are families who cannot get work and are in danger of starv—"

A Forwyn man in line behind the woman cut her off with a sharp laugh. "Isn't this the same treatment your kind doled out to the Forwyn only years ago? The same treatment you *continue* to give our people? Many Forwyn are living in impoverished districts in the city, turned away from work by Alrenian businesses. There is still an underground slave trade. Any mistreatment the Alrenians receive is nothing compared to what the Forwyn face."

The elderly woman's eyes widened as she lifted her chin to stare at me.

I stood from my throne, my gown rustling. "This is abhorrent," I said, my words clipped. I glanced toward the two Elders at my sides, daring them to stop me or to disagree, but they said nothing. My gaze fastened on the man in line. "This new era is about unity and equality between our two races," I went on, even though I despised myself for saying those words so often drilled into me by the Elders. They were a lie, a poisoned sentence dipped in honey, and I could feel their bitter aftertaste on my tongue.

With a gentle hand, I reached out toward the elderly woman. A few of the surrounding guards stirred, and even the woman looked a little frightened. My insides froze, and I dropped my hand to my side. Of course word had spread about my strange power. Of course they were afraid.

"We will make changes," I declared, even though I suspected the Elders would ignore this wish of mine and never pass a law. It irked me, to speak like I had power when my hands were tied, but I smiled like the Elders wanted me to and pretended I could make a difference for my people. "Thank you for bringing this to our attention." I swept back to my throne, and the woman thanked me tearfully, bowing while she backed away.

I swallowed back the sour taste brewing in my mouth.

As the line continued to move forward and citizen after citizen made their requests, some clearly speaking to the Elders and others showing their respect toward me, weariness swept over me like a blanket. My brain grew fuzzy and my limbs became heavy. It was tiring to force my lips to curve into a smile for each Forwyn that stepped before me, paying lip service to me but clearly looking at the Elders for leadership. Some of them scarcely bowed to me at all, dipping their heads in the slightest appearance of respect.

Eventually, an Alrenian couple with their son, who appeared to be a little younger than me, approached. They dipped into low bows until I told them to rise, and the woman turned to me, her eyes meeting mine directly. She was walking the line between being brave and being disrespectful, but something in the hard set of her jaw commanded my respect rather than my anger.

"*Amara* Jaliana, are you aware that currently, only Forwyn are being admitted to Aerekni Academy? My son passes all physical qualifications, but he is turned away every time he applies. Are we truly equal and united if only Forwyn men and women are patrolling our streets or becoming soldiers? What does that mean for *our* people?" Her deep brown eyes bored into mine, the gold flecks in her irises bright and fiery.

I blinked at her. Black spots danced at the corners of my vision and I struggled to form a coherent thought. *Soldiers…Kovi…* My gaze darted to him, where he stood behind my throne, his face set as hard as stone.

The Alrenian woman was speaking again, but my heartbeat pulsed so loudly in my ears I couldn't hear her. My tongue tasted bitter, and my limbs were heavier than ever. Had I forgotten to drink? To eat? No, I'd been sipping from a cup the servants regularly refilled for me throughout the evening. I hadn't skipped a meal.

"I…" I started, but I wasn't sure what I was supposed to say. What had the woman requested again? The Elders turned to look at me, their expressions stern, silently reminding me not to do the wrong thing.

My ears rang as my knees gave way without warning. I collapsed toward the floor, a pair of strong hands catching me just before my head struck the glistening marble. Everything spun and whirled, and I couldn't tell if I was going to be sick or lose consciousness. My head throbbed as the ringing in my ears changed to a high-pitched squeal.

Voices murmured, but I couldn't discern a word they were saying. Sweat sprouted along my forehead and chills shivered down my back. My entire body shook as the hands that had caught me lifted me and carried me from the throne room.

By the time someone laid me in my bed, my dress was soaked through with sweat. I blinked up, my vision blurred and distorted, to see Kovi frowning and hovering over me. Others surrounded me too, but they were a little further away and harder to make out. Frantic voices echoed, but it felt like I was underwater, and their words were distant and muffled, indiscernible.

I caught one word in all the chaos: *Poison.*

How ironic, I thought distantly, nearly choking on the laughter that threatened to bubble up. *And I'd wanted to poison all of them first.*

I blacked out.

❮❮❮❮❮

When I opened my eyes, it could have been a few minutes or a few hours later. My stomach ached, only giving me enough warning to sit up before I emptied its contents into a bowl already waiting at my bedside. Again and again, sweat making my hair cling to my face, I shook and vomited.

The bed shifted as someone sat at my side, pulling my hair back when I became ill again. I was hot and cold, weak and trembling.

Poison, I thought again, remembering the word I'd heard before losing consciousness. My brain was too foggy to think clearly, to run through the symptoms and understand which poison had entered my system, or how it had happened. Was I dying? Had the Forwyn given me an antidote? *Was* there an antidote for this poison?

When I curled up in bed, moaning and throwing off the covers because my skin was burning with an inner fire, a hand pressed a cool cloth to my forehead. There was a voice. Quiet words, in a language I didn't understand. Kovi's voice, murmuring rhythmic words that might have been part of a chant, a song, or a prayer.

Elhani, I heard more than once. Was Kovi cursing me, or helping me?

I slipped into darkness.

❮❮❮❮❮

I opened my eyes to find the shadows staring back at me. A pair of gleaming blue eyes and a wicked red smile were shrouded in the blackness of my room.

"Nesrelle," I choked out, my voice echoing in the darkness. I couldn't see another living soul but the Queen of Death. Where were the Forwyn? Where was Kovi? Everything was dark and stifling, aching and empty. Was I already dead?

"Little empress," Nesrelle's musical voice responded. "You're growing braver, but so weak."

When I swallowed, it felt like coals were sliding down my throat. "Please don't let me die." I hated how the plea sounded in my ears. Would my mother have ever begged for her life like this?

"Oh, Jalie," Nesrelle murmured, reaching out with her cool hand to stroke the sweaty hair back from my forehead. "My curse lives with you. I couldn't allow that."

"Then don't take me," I rasped. "Please, go away. That's why you came, isn't it? Because I'm dying."

"It's true," she said, her beautiful eyes sad. "I thought you would plead to the Life-Giver to save you."

Fury lanced through me. "He didn't spare my mother."

"Indeed," Nesrelle said.

I extended my hand, and she clasped it in her cold one. "I'll use your curse. I know I can take back the throne. I know I'm brave enough."

Her red lips curved into a wide smile. "Oh, I know," she said.

"Then don't take me yet," I said, my voice gaining strength and conviction. "Don't let me die."

Then the world vanished into darkness once more.

❰❰❰❰❰❰

In and out of consciousness, I was vaguely aware of people entering and exiting my room, speaking in hushed tones, checking my pulse or forcing liquid into my mouth. It was too difficult to open my eyes, so I didn't bother. Everything ached, and it seemed as if a fire burned through my bones, devouring me from the inside out.

At some point, I was aware of Elder Ettonou and Kovi speaking somewhere nearby.

"You know your responsibility here," the Elder was saying. "We're counting on you because of your ability to wield such powerful magic."

"I remember enough about Mother to know she believed in mercy," Kovi said, an angry edge creeping into his tone.

"Your mother was murdered by a creature just like *her*. She doesn't deserve mercy."

"You want to be monsters just like them?" Kovi demanded. "I'm only offering basic human decency—"

"I want justice!" Elder Ettonou exclaimed. "Freedom! Hope! I want your children to grow up without fear that their mother will be murdered by one of those bloodthirsty Alrenian animals! How could you forget? How could you act like she's not an enemy?"

Kovi's words were low, hard. "I never forget," he said. "I think about Mother—what she said, what she believed, how she lived and how she died—every day. Maybe I've done terrible things with my magic, and maybe Elhani will never forgive me for them. But there are lines even I won't cross. I refuse to become like the ones out there who are impaling Forwyn and leaving them in our streets. I'm a soldier. I'll fight when it's right. But when I can show mercy, I'll show mercy."

"Are you sure you aren't just being softened by a pretty face?" There was a pause. "Don't fail your mother. Don't fail your people."

❮❮❮❮❮

The next time I woke, it was to someone hovering over me.

Dread froze my insides and my brain flew into a panic, certain I was in danger. Slick with sweat, I struggled, swinging my arms wildly.

It wasn't until a pair of hands seized me that I realized my throat was raw with my screams and I'd been thrashing against my bedcovers.

"Let me go! Let me go!" I shrieked, focusing my eyes to find Kovi above me, holding me down.

I glared at him. "I'll kill you," I snarled. "How dare you touch me!"

"I was trying to check if your fever had broken." His fingers were shockingly but comfortingly cool against my skin.

"Did you poison me?" My brain was foggy, and all I could remember clearly was that Kovi was my enemy. Yet even that didn't feel quite right.

"If I wanted to kill you, I'd do it cleaner and faster," Kovi murmured with a smile, but it didn't seem hostile. He leaned back, just a little, and searched my face. "How do you feel?"

"Horrified to have a Forwyn man leering at me right now," I snapped, and Kovi laughed outright.

"The antidote is working then," he said. "You're sounding like yourself again."

When he released me, he sat back on the other side of my bed, where the sheets were rumpled, the pillow indented. Snatches of memory flashed through my mind: someone pressing a cloth to my forehead, hands pulling my hair back, a warm presence at my side as I tossed and turned and shivered. Had he fallen asleep beside me while watching over me?

For a weak moment, warmth curled through my stomach, like the soothing sensation of a hot drink warming me from the inside out on a chilly day. Then disgust burned the back of my throat, because what sort of empress was I? Dependent upon my enemy as I hurled my guts into a bowl and screamed into the darkness?

Humiliating.

"*Get. Out. Of. My. Bed,*" I ordered.

Without a word, without even the slightest frown, he rose and settled himself on my settee.

I watched him closely as he lay down. With faint starlight filtering into my bedroom, he was only a shape in the darkness. The distance was relieving, but also a little disconcerting. I hadn't realized until now how comforting his presence had been.

He's your enemy, you idiot, I thought.

Everything he did was confusing. He spoke of anger and hatred, and I'd seen it shining clearly in his eyes, yet he was also gentle and kind. I thought of his hands brushing back my hair, of his comforting voice singing over me last night. Of how he'd talked me through my panic after the execution at the arena.

He said he did it because he wanted to help those in need, that he didn't want to be a monster like he claimed we Alrenians were. Vaguely, I recalled snatches of a conversation he must have had in this very room with his father, when I'd been half-awake. Kovi had spoken of mercy.

My head throbbed with confusion and pain. I was still feeling feverish and weak. My stomach ached from being ill, but not with the threat of being sick again. I'd probably emptied it completely.

Kovi had mentioned an antidote, but I didn't even remember anyone administering one to me.

"Do you know how and with what I was poisoned?" I asked finally, speaking into the blackness. My voice sounded gravelly.

A sudden thought made my eyes dart to my vanity, but my bouquet was untouched.

"Nethilys in your water cup you had in the throne room," Kovi said. "We have the Royal Guard investigating what happened."

I was quiet for a beat. "It was your father. He arranged it."

Kovi was silent for so long, I wondered if he'd fallen asleep. Then: "That would be treason."

"How so? He's made it clear from the beginning he wants me dead. The Court could sweep me aside, no longer a pesky pawn on their game board, and accuse an unknown assassin. They wouldn't have to concern themselves with me or my power, and they could claim me as a martyr for their 'unification' cause."

"The Court of Elders voted against executing you," Kovi said, his tone low and precise. Carefully measured, enough so that I was sure he was truly, deeply angry. "My father would never go against their decree and commit a crime like that."

"Maybe they agree with him too," I suggested. "Have you ever considered that they've met in secret? That they already decided I should die?"

I could see Kovi's form as he sat up. "They wouldn't assign me to you if they'd done that."

Perhaps not. Or perhaps all of Kovi's kindness and speeches about mercy were a way to get inside my head, to confuse me and gain my trust so they could destroy me in their own sick way.

One thing I knew for certain: I couldn't trust anyone. Especially not the man who was making the line between enemy and friend start to confusingly, dangerously blur.

CHAPTER SEVENTEEN

Lo

IT WAS MY TURN TO wake early and prepare breakfast. As I rose from bed, I moved as if in a trance, my thoughts sluggish, trapped in an endless cycle of repeating everything I'd learned the night before. When I'd washed my face and teeth, I dressed all in grey and slipped downstairs to find morning light flooding the kitchen. Selecting a basket, I trudged outside into the warmth.

Already I could catch the sounds of the city awakening beyond the walls. A carriage rumbled by, joining the voices of passersby. I tossed feed for the chickens and collected eggs almost in a blur. Instead of focusing on the chickens' excited clucks, I could hear Elder Ilhoa's voice once more, brushing aside my pleas. Instead of seeing the fresh eggs snug in my basket, I saw the row of dead Forwyn, their sightless eyes staring back at me.

By the time I'd milked our cow Tila and started preparing *lina* rolls, I'd lost my appetite. Dread coiled in my gut. My thoughts were too loud to reach for Elhani's voice, but I had a terrible feeling that I already knew what I would do. But was it the right thing?

The entire day passed in a daze, until I finally found myself kneeling in the sanctuary with my sisters. As always, Naina stood at the front, reading from the Ihlu'i Text and leading us in a communal prayer. When she invited us each up individually, I knelt in front of the altar, my heart pounding with anxiety.

I reached for Elhani's voice, but my stomach churned with my growing uncertainty.

Every time I thought of the dead Forwyn, of the Elder's dismissive words, my chest tightened painfully, and fire filled my veins. Every time I thought of those words—*For the empress*—and the description of the wounds Jaliana had inflicted, the embers of an angrier, more vengeful version of myself stirred to life again. Every time I thought of Wilvhe's and Renni's words about a coming war, I knew someone had to stop it.

Why couldn't that someone be me?

Is this why you led me to the vigilantes? Is this what I'm meant to do? Is this your will?

I lifted my head to glance around at my sisters, their heads bowed as they prayed on the benches, each having already come up to pray individually, or awaiting their own turn. They would never forgive me. A tear slipped down my cheek.

Shedding blood would break my vow to you and to them, Elhani. My sisters will cast me out. Will you damn me for going against my word to you?

I thought your will was supposed to be simple. I thought my vows were your purpose for me, and that they would let me serve you and my people.

My hands shook as I unfolded them, and my knees were jelly as I stood from the cold floor. I couldn't hear Elhani's voice because of the roaring of my thoughts in my ears, but I wasn't sure it mattered. It was like Mio'e had said when she'd referenced the old story of Huro's murder and his soul crying out for vengeance.

I could hear the cries of my people's souls.

As darkness enveloped the city, my usual restlessness came over me. I could feel my nightmares stalking ever closer, waiting to haunt my sleep. This time, I was thankful I had my meeting with the vigilantes to distract me. But first, I wanted to check on Caesiem. Exiting my room, I slipped into the infirmary, where O'emia was tending to the sleeping thief.

O'emia scanned me shrewdly. "You're fully dressed at this hour?"

I shrugged, not wanting to give away my secret but not wanting to lie either. Guilt always weighed me down, yet I never seemed to be able to stop doing the things that made me feel guilty. I didn't particularly want to add lying to the list.

O'emia crossed her arms and pursed her lips. "Fine, keep your secrets." She sighed. "If you plan to be here for a few minutes anyway, I'm going to make myself some coffee. It's going to be a long night."

That's for sure, I thought.

As soon as the other woman left, I settled into the seat beside Caesiem's cot, studying his measured breaths. The color had returned to his cheeks, but I didn't know what to think. What if he was too weak and never woke up again?

I'd feel guilty about that too, as if I'd failed this man I barely knew by not stopping his attacker soon enough.

I had to do something to work against the cruel Alrenians, and I hoped that would happen tonight. For a moment, I considered finding something I could use as a weapon before I left the abbey's safety. I didn't want to be among the dead Forwyn, left as a gruesome message to the Court of Elders. Yet the thought of holding a blade in my hand again still horrified me. Someday, I would have to for my people's sake, but not today.

When O'emia returned, cradling a steaming mug of black coffee, I rose and strode for the door, brushing past her. She halted me with one hand pressed to my shoulder.

"Lo," she whispered. "He's not worth it."

I squinted at her. "Excuse me?"

"You worry so much about this man. He's not worth breaking your vows. We're called to so much more than a normal, lowly human life." She said this in a voice full of awe, as if she expected to become an Immortal by devoting her life to Elhani. Something greater. "We're better than that."

"Better than men? Better than other people?" I asked. If anything, I'd always felt worse than other people. I served the Forwyn because of the blood staining my hands.

O'emia tossed her braids over one shoulder. "We're certainly called to more. He might have a pretty face, but that means nothing."

I rolled my eyes. "My only crime has been to have the decency to care about another human being," I retorted, forcing myself past her. And even though there were times Caesiem *did* give me butterflies with his charming smile, I knew I had the strength to resist. I had bigger things to worry about.

O'emia opened her mouth as if to say something, but I didn't wait. I slipped through the doorway and crept through the halls until I'd exited the abbey.

The fresh air was a welcome relief from my inner frustration. Maybe I was a fool. After all, I knew firsthand how dangerous it was to be outside alone. But I desperately needed to know what I could help the vigilantes do tonight.

If O'emia knew what was truly on my mind that night, she would have had something far greater to worry about. Perhaps I should have been grateful she didn't have a clue. I didn't need her telling me what I already knew—that I was damning my soul.

⟨⟨⟨⟨⟨

An unusually cool breeze off the sea whispered in my ear, making my skin prickle. As I crouched in the shadow of a house in the Keldrik District, I wondered what madness had possessed me to agree to this mission.

"You don't have to hurt anyone," Renni had assured me back at our meeting place. "But we want you to make sure the girl gets away safely."

"A girl?" I'd asked, throat tight.

"Well," Mio'e had interjected, her expression grim, "there are reports of a missing girl fitting this description." She'd slid a paper toward me across the table. I leaned forward and saw it was a missing poster bearing the sketch of a girl, probably no more than twelve, gazing back at me with large, inquisitive eyes. "And all our leads point to the Alrenians striking in the Keldrik District tonight. We think she'll be the Forwyn they use."

"And you think I can help her get away?" I'd asked nervously.

Renni tilted his head thoughtfully. "Well, you said you used your magic so you and Caesiem could escape the Alrenians unseen. You could do that again, right?"

Despite the doubt gnawing at me, I'd nodded. I couldn't tear my gaze away from the rendering of the too-young girl gazing up at me.

Now, I studied the quiet home across from me, every once and a while turning my head to scan the area and reassure myself that the other vigilantes were nearby. We were all stationed in different areas throughout the neighborhood, waiting for the Alrenians to make their move. From my position, I could catch sight of Renni crouched on a rooftop, only a shadow blotting out the stars, and A'elli tucked in the shadows beside a stone house on the opposite side of the one we were watching. Unlike me, they were armed with weapons—prepared to fight.

I was prepared to defend.

"You could still get hurt," A'elli had said just before we'd moved into our stations, scrunching her freckled nose with worry. "Are you sure you don't want a weapon?"

Just the thought of holding another dagger made nausea creep along my tongue and memories of that terrible night I'd slain Karye threaten to overwhelm me.

"I'm sure," I'd whispered.

The Alrenians didn't make us wait long.

Just as I turned my eyes away from where A'elli was hiding, I noticed movement in the street. A short, slight figure was tiptoeing along the cobblestones. As soon as she crept near enough for me to make out her features in the dimness, I recognized her as the girl from the missing poster. She was visibly shaking, her clothing torn and dirty, but otherwise, she appeared unharmed.

My gut churned, and I wanted to leap out then and there, to seize her in my arms and steal her away.

But my desire to see justice done against the Alrenians who had her this distraught made me hold back. I knew from Renni's instructions that I had to be patient.

For a long moment, the girl hesitated in the shadow of the grey stone building, staring at it like she was facing a mountain to climb. She tossed a worried glance over her shoulder. Whatever she saw, or whatever she knew waited behind her, gave her the final push to dart forward. She rapped on the door wildly, the sound echoing in the stillness of the night.

I grimaced as a young man answered, the sound of a baby wailing clearly emanating from further within the house.

The Alrenians were targeting a young family.

"Please," the girl whimpered, "I was attacked by Alrenian thugs and—and—I need help!" She burst into tears. In the light of the candle the man held aloft, I could see the girl's face more clearly. Blood glistened from a cut on her temple.

"Of course," the man said, face etched with worry. "Come inside."

"I—I have a s-sister." Sniffling, the girl wiped at her eyes with a shaking hand. "Please, she couldn't walk. We have to go back and fetch her. Will you help me?"

Within moments, the man was shuffling after the girl, armed only with a short dagger and his candle.

The vigilantes and I waited for the pair to disappear around the bend, winding through a narrow alley, before we sprang from our hiding spots to trail them.

Renni was like a shadow moving from rooftop to rooftop, and A'elli and the others all but disappeared. Heart pounding, I felt like I was creeping through the city alone again, clinging to shadows and listening for signs of danger.

Only the soft sighing of the sea filled my ears.

Until—it didn't.

A shout rent the night, coming from around the corner, just ahead of me. The Alrenians had struck.

As planned, I forced myself to cling to the corner and peer around into the next alley rather than leap into the fight. Other than Elhani's magic, I was unarmed and vulnerable.

The sight filled me with rage. A trio of Alrenians, armed with illegal weapons that glistened gold, had surrounded the young man. Off to the side, the girl cowered against the wall of a building, weeping. Too frozen to move.

Stumbling back, the Forwyn man tried to fend off his attackers, swinging his dagger wildly. As one of the Alrenians charged him with a sword, the Forwyn stepped back, dropping his candle. It sputtered out on the cobblestones.

The twang of a bowstring was the only warning before an arrow struck the Alrenian in the eye. He collapsed like a rock.

Gasping, the Forwyn man peered around. The two remaining Alrenians snarled in rage, turning toward their would-be victim, but that was when Nu'or sprang from the shadows. Wielding an axe, he met the Alrenians blow for blow until Mio'e rushed out to join him. More arrows rained down, and between one breath and the next, I watched each one of our enemies fall.

But…more footsteps approached. Alrenian reinforcements?

"Get them out of here!" Renni shouted from his position on the roof.

I sucked in a deep breath. *Elhani.* His song soared through the air, sweeping through my soul, until warmth tingled along my skin. I didn't waste time explaining myself to the Forwyn girl and man. Seizing them each by the wrist, I hissed, "Come with me to escape! Hurry!"

Terrified and confused, their instincts were, thankfully, to flee with me. Invisibility enveloped us all as I focused my magic.

We made the trip back to the man's house in safety, where I left the girl in his care. I didn't want to explain who I was, didn't want him to know even when he tried to thank me. The vigilantes wouldn't want their names known either—and they had made it clear they didn't want me to wait for them. We were all to escape the scene separately.

As planned, I raced back home to the abbey.

I'm one of them now, I thought as I crept back into my room, pulse still racing. *But even if the vigilantes are killing, they're killing murderers and saving lives. Surely this is why Elhani wanted me to meet them. Not to kill, but to save.*

Still, the thought of the vigilantes' ultimate goal haunted me. *Slay the empress.* The thought no longer filled me with horror, not when I'd witnessed the atrocities Alrenians were committing in the empress's name.

But to agree to help kill someone after the vows I'd made…what would that make me?

Amara'rekni. Nun. Vigilante.

What was I supposed to be?

CHAPTER EIGHTEEN

Jalie

"SHE'S DEAD!" ELDER ETTONOU'S VOICE pierced the morning quiet as he stormed into my chambers.

I jerked from sleep, my body weak and trembling but no longer feverish. My head pounded, likely more from lack of food and water than anything else.

I didn't have the chance to register much as I sat up and blinked at Elder Ettonou's figure stomping toward me.

Stirring from the settee, Kovi sprang to his feet, alert and stoic in an instant.

"She's dead," the Elder roared again, snatching a fistful of my hair and yanking me from bed.

I stifled a cry, biting my lip instead as my back slammed into the floor. Pain radiated down my spine. When he finally, mercifully released me, golden strands of hair fell from his fist. I stared at him, my eyes stinging with unshed tears of pain.

"You killed her," the Elder went on. "You killed—"

"*Father*," Kovi interrupted, setting a firm hand on his father's arm. "You can't avenge Mother by…"

"Don't talk to me about her!" the Elder snapped, not even sparing his son a glance. "Jaliana, you murderess, you will pay for slaying an innocent Forwyn noble."

"What?" I demanded. "I haven't killed anyone!"

"Lady Leanai died last night," the Elder snapped, his eyes so sharp they seemed to cut into my very flesh.

Horror washed over me in a violent flood, like a tumultuous wave in a stormy sea. *Don't fear the curse,* whispered Nesrelle's voice, but this—this was more than I'd asked for. I'd daydreamed about killing Elder Ettonou, of never letting him hurt me again, yet this…this was different. Actually knowing my own hands had killed someone stole the breath from my lungs.

"She's dead?" Kovi asked, his usual mask falling away to reveal his shock.

"Thanks to her and her witch's curse," Elder Ettonou said, stabbing a finger toward me. "The wounds on Lady Leanai's arms spread, rotting her flesh and weakening her. They eventually covered her entire body. We've never seen anything like it." He glared at me. "A cruel, horrifying abomination from an unbeliever. Do you work black magic with the aid of the Dark Immortal?"

But if the Forwyn are hurting my people, isn't this what they deserve? I wondered. Why didn't it feel satisfying then, to know I was getting vengeance?

I didn't have the strength to stand, not yet, but I tried to maintain some semblance of dignity as I met Elder Ettonou's gaze. "Never. I'm one of the Life-Giver's Chosen People. It's *his* curse that's killing your people. It's his judgment for the blood on your hands."

The Elder narrowed his eyes. "You have no right to speak about blood or guilt, you whose mother slaughtered us like animals!"

Heat spread through my chest. "And you do the same to my people now!" I shouted.

Kovi's father fisted his hands and stared at me for a long, silent moment. I couldn't read the expression in his stormy dark eyes. *This is it,*

I thought. *The moment he declares my sentence.*

He exhaled heavily and turned to his son. "She is not to exit these chambers unless the Court summons her," he said simply. "Do *not* leave her side." Without another word, he stalked back out.

Even Kovi seemed lost for a few silent moments, each of us staring after the Elder as thoughts tumbled through our heads.

When I tried to pull myself back into bed, Kovi rushed to my side. It was humiliating to need assistance, like I was a small child. As he grasped my arm, Kovi touched the lingering bruises his father had left on me at the execution and I flinched. Frowning, Kovi drew back my sleeve and stared at the still-dark marks, perfect impressions left behind from Elder Ettonou's fingers.

As I sank wearily onto my pillow, Kovi met my eyes. Something dark and intense lurked in his gaze, and I could tell it wasn't directed toward me. "Does he do this to you often?"

I looked away. "Not with you here to keep me in line."

Several long minutes passed while Kovi, who'd released my arm and stepped back, paced the floor restlessly. Shame burned through me, but the lingering weakness from the poison overtook all other feelings. My eyes drifted closed until I found Kovi sitting on my bedside, minutes or hours later, a cool cloth wiping gently at my stinging scalp. I wondered if it was bleeding.

I studied his face. His midnight eyes were both wary and gentle, which seemed like an impossible contradiction. My gaze traced his strong features, from his sharp cheekbones to his full lips and square jawline.

"Why are you helping me?" I whispered, even if I'd already asked the question before. It constantly nagged me. "We both hate each other and everything the other stands for."

Kovi didn't answer, merely studying my expression the same way I did his. The air was thick between us, filled with too many conflicting emotions—some easy and familiar and some new and terrifying. Maybe he was searching my eyes for something.

"My mother killed your mother," I went on harshly, needing to fill the silence. "And even if he won't admit it, I'm sure your father had a hand in killing mine. We are each other's best chance at revenge."

"Do you think hurting me will bring her back?" he asked, his face unreadable.

"It's not about bringing back the dead. It's about avenging blood. My *empire*. My *people*. And regaining my throne."

Kovi's lips curved into a rueful smile. "When I was first assigned to you, I thought watching you suffer would bring healing somehow. It hasn't."

"Nothing heals," I said bitterly, unable to meet his gaze a second longer.

"Maybe kindness can," Kovi murmured. "I'm not sure yet."

I didn't respond to that, instead changing the subject. "Why are you serving your cruel father?"

The gold flecks in his eyes sparked like a fire flaring higher. "He's requesting that I perform a task vital for this empire," Kovi said. His gaze flicked toward my arm again. "I don't approve of…everything he does." He swallowed. "I didn't know, Jalie."

I couldn't look at him, even though I believed him. What he didn't realize was that to me, his gentle spirit was more terrifying than his father's angry one. "He's not worried I'll kill you like Lady Leanai?" I asked.

Kovi watched me steadily. "He has faith in me and my abilities." He hesitated. "I know you won't kill me."

"Then you don't really know me," I mumbled.

Kovi smiled slowly. "I know you better than you realize."

I didn't bother responding, my body and mind weary. Instead, I closed my eyes. "It seems strange to think they saved me from being poisoned to death, when they'll probably kill me now," I whispered.

"They aren't going to kill you."

"How do you know?" I demanded, reopening my eyes.

A muscle in his jaw worked. "Because I won't let them."

Kovi's tone was so confident that I let it comfort me, soothing my fears and sending me into a dreamless sleep.

My eyes snapped open a short while later. It took me a moment to register that a sound had woken me: water running in my tub. I scanned my bedchamber to find my suspicion true: Kovi was gone. My heart leapt with a surge of hope.

Kovi couldn't leave me in the care of another guard anymore, so he'd retired to my washroom to bathe. For a few minutes, I was unsupervised. Free.

Light-headed but stronger than before, I pulled myself from bed and shuffled toward my end table, where a tray of breakfast food and pitchers of water, tea, and coffee sat. I didn't have an appetite yet, but I was tremendously thirsty. I drank three full glasses of water.

When I'd finished, Kovi hadn't returned from the washroom, so I crept toward my balcony doors. My head spun and my legs trembled from the exertion, yet I pushed through it. I didn't know when I'd have another chance like this. Holding my breath, I pulled one of the doors open slowly to ensure it didn't creak. The morning air washed over me, sweet and fresh from the sunbaked gardens mixed with the scent of sea brine. Ahead, the clouds hung heavy and low on the horizon, partially blocking the rising sun. I tiptoed out onto my balcony, breathing deeply and studying the grounds below.

One guard froze on her rounds to stare at me, but when I didn't move from my railing, she turned and continued winding her way along the garden path. I wasn't fool enough to try climbing down from my balcony in my condition, only to face dozens of armed guards all on my own. I spotted a few other Forwyn guards, along with a smattering of nobles—most were probably still lounging in bed, sipping their bitter coffee—clustered on shaded benches or strolling along the paths.

My pulse fluttered in my throat, equal parts anxiety and hope. Maybe the Alrenian woman wouldn't be out at this hour. What were the odds that I'd see her again so soon? But this was my chance to reach out to her, and I didn't know when I'd have another. Already, at any moment, Kovi could exit my washroom and discover me out here.

I'm not doing anything wrong, I thought stubbornly, but that didn't calm my worries. If he saw me trying to communicate with another Alrenian…well, any hope of receiving help from her would die immediately.

It would be just as dangerous if I were caught by one of the guards patrolling the grounds. Though they were tasked with keeping intruders from trespassing, they would notice if I did anything strange. And they would surely report back to the Elders.

I leaned heavily against the railing and drank it all in. Quilt-work patches of both sun and shade, gold and grey, spotted the vibrant gardens below. Citrus trees laden with their fruit stretched toward the sky, and thick bushes of flowers in nearly every imaginable color covered the ground like countless glittering gems. Fountains carved into dragons mid-flight or mid-snarl spouted sparkling water into clear pools. This sight never grew old for me.

My gaze snagged on a grouping of dragons taking flight from the

Keep. My breath caught in my chest. It always did when I saw them, beautiful and powerful creatures with their huge wings and glistening scales. Their armored riders were proud and fierce on their backs. The air thundered with dragon wing beats as they circled once and then, in a perfect formation, turned northward. Six dragons in total.

Were they on a mission? Part of a scouting party? Unease trickled down my spine. Were the Elders dispatching their Dragon Keepers to see to some sort of Alrenian threat or uprising elsewhere in the empire?

A flash of red hair beneath a lime tree across from my balcony drew my eyes from the sky. Crouched within the tree's shadow, beside a row of raevi with buttery yellow petals, was the Alrenian woman I'd seen earlier. As before, her hood was pulled low over her face, but a thick strand of her bright hair had escaped and hung over her shoulder, which was what had captured my attention. She was staring directly at me, her frowning face intent. Was she trying to tell me something?

Glancing around surreptitiously to check that the area was clear, the woman darted from beneath the tree to another, a little closer to my balcony. Each movement she made was all fluid grace and silent skill. Who was this woman? She clearly knew what she was doing. Where had she learned to conceal herself like that? To infiltrate the palace gardens themselves?

I leaned over the railing as far as I dared. The woman squatted behind a bush as a guard stalked past, sinking so low that even I lost sight of her. When she rose again, her eyes met mine immediately, and she lifted a hand, palm facing me, as if in greeting.

Hesitantly, I waved back. *Who are you?* I thought. *Are you here to help me? To help our people? Are there others with you?*

She started mouthing something, but I wasn't sure what she was trying to say. *I'm here to help?* My head spun with giddiness—and perhaps my lingering weakness. I almost didn't dare believe it. After these long years trapped within my own home, did I finally have some allies who could help me take back our empire?

A pair of hands seized me by the waist unexpectedly, startling the breath from my lungs. My heart hammered so hard against my chest it hurt. I stifled a cry as Kovi yanked me back into my room, turning to kick the door shut without releasing me. He pushed me against the wall, out of sight of the glass-paned doors. His narrowed eyes met mine. He was close—far too close.

"What are you doing?" he demanded, his voice a rumble so near I could feel it in my chest.

His close-cropped hair still damp, he wore his uniform pants but no jacket, only an undershirt that revealed too much of his muscular chest. He must have realized I'd disappeared before he'd finished getting ready for the day.

I set my jaw, refusing to step back or look away, because that would make me look weak. It would also give him an excuse to look back out at the grounds and see the Alrenian woman, who I prayed was escaping right this moment.

Kovi's eyes were sharp and suspicious, but I curled my lips into a smile, one I hoped he read as equal parts warm and vicious. If he was soft enough to pity me, to want to protect me, I wanted him to continue to do so. But I never wanted him to forget that I was a threat. I needed to use all of those elements to my advantage.

"Enjoying the fresh air, since I can't leave my rooms," I said.

"And making yourself an easy target for anyone who wants to finish the job they failed at twice now?" Kovi quirked an eyebrow at me. He frowned, as if noticing how much I'd begun to tremble, and led me back toward my bed. I didn't resist when he helped me sit down. My entire body was shaking from lingering weakness, and I hated it. Hated how pathetic and vulnerable I was.

When I looked at him, Kovi was still scowling. I couldn't tell if he was angry because I was threatening the success of his assigned mission, or if he was…concerned about me.

"What else do you want from me?" I bit out.

"You can't do anything like that again," Kovi said levelly. "I'm warning you now, before I'm forced to tie you up or use magic on you again." He smirked, as if hoping I'd give him an excuse to do either of those things.

A chill coursed through me at the eerie memory of my limbs moving without my permission. "I. Won't. Do. That. Again," I said slowly, firmly, glaring at Kovi all the while.

Nodding once, Kovi reached into his pocket and pulled out an envelope, dangling it before me.

"My father sent a message," he continued. "Two evenings from now, the court is assembling to honor the Dragon Keepers." His lips curved in a sardonic smile. "To display our Alrenian and Forwyn *unity*, you will ride one of the dragons, along with your bodyguard." He gestured to himself.

I couldn't help the joy that flooded my veins. "I'll ride a dragon?" I breathed.

Kovi's mouth twitched. "You Alrenians really love your dragons."

"Who wouldn't?" I exclaimed, unable to conceal my passion and excitement. "They're beautiful and powerful and fearless. They're everything we are or hope to be. Have you ever ridden one?"

Kovi shook his head.

"Then you can't understand."

A small smile tugged at his lips. "Then when I ride with you, you will have to show me and make me understand."

I knew better than to forget Kovi was my enemy, an obstacle in my path to regaining the throne, but I couldn't help the sense of comradery that warmed me, however briefly. Nothing could quell my joy. For the first time in far too long, I felt genuine hope.

CHAPTER NINETEEN

Lo

AFTERNOON LIGHT BOUNCED OFF THE gleaming marble buildings encircling me, slanting into my eyes until a headache formed. I squinted at the rush of citizens—mostly finely dressed Alrenians—shopping throughout the Akytha District marketplace, an open circular space with a huge fountain depicting Oreva, the first Alrenian empress. Vendors called out, listing wares and naming sale prices to tempt potential buyers. Children giggled and darted about the stone benches encircling the fountain, playing tag or reaching into the water to splash one another.

The beautiful buildings surrounding the marketplace were luxuries of the wealthy Alrenians: indoor shopping centers or infirmaries filled with healing-gifted workers. Aside from the palace itself, this district was the wealthy heart of the Alrenian capital. Though the threat of Forwyn guards kept the citizens mostly in line, this was a place I generally avoided at all costs. Alrenians didn't shy away from openly glaring or threatening me, as long as none of the guards were within hearing range. Any time I slipped into the crowd, it was impossible to blend in. I might try to cover up with a cloak and hood, but my plain clothes as a nun gave me away, and in the bright summer sun, it was too easy for Alrenians to see my dark complexion under my hood. Everything marked me as their hated enemy.

Today, however, I'd found paper announcements hung throughout the city, tacked to walls everywhere I'd looked, telling me that there would be an announcement from the Elders read in this marketplace. My curiosity won over my fear, and here I was, slinking along the outskirts of the circle, keeping my eyes downcast. Whenever I inadvertently stepped in an Alrenian's way, he or she shoved me and spat curses in my direction.

I kept my attention at the center of the marketplace, where I could see a Forwyn man striding toward the fountain. It was clear he was an important advisor or other member of the Elders' court based on his fine clothes, determined pace, and entourage of guards. In his hands, he clutched a large, thick envelope. He stood directly in front of the fountain and called out over the bustling chatter and hum of the marketplace. The vendors fell quiet, and the passersby went still, turning their heads to study the man. Other than the soft murmurings of people turning to each other, speculating about what the man would say, the market had gone abruptly silent.

"Citizens of our shining Alrenian Empire, part of our new age of peace, prosperity, unity, and equality!" he cried out.

The murmuring grew a little louder in the wake of this declaration. "Lies," someone snapped near me, while others complained about "enemy control" and "usurpers."

I pulled my hood a little lower over my face, desperately wishing it could conceal all of my Forwyn skin. The anger around me was a palpable thing, and I felt even less safe than ever, surrounded by this race of proud, cruel people.

"I have some somber announcements today from your Court of Elders." Again, I heard people speaking around me, incensed that their precious Alrenian empress hadn't been mentioned. I couldn't deny that it surprised me as well—were they not even bothering to *pretend* the empress shared rulership with them anymore?

"First," the messenger went on, "it is with great sorrow we announce the passing of one of our fine noblewomen at court, Lady Leanai, who was dedicated to our empire and to encouraging unity between our Forwyn and Alrenian peoples. She succumbed to a sudden and unexpected illness, and the Elders offer their sincere condolences to her family and all who knew and loved her. It is always a tremendous sorrow to lose a member of the court, but especially one influential in guiding our great empire into our new golden age."

Again, I heard people scoffing around me.

"Golden age?"

"Who does he think he's fooling?"

The messenger's face turned especially solemn, his brow crinkling as he looked out over the crowd. Even I thought it appeared rather theatrical.

"I have more terrible news," he continued. "To our horror, there has been more than one heinous attack on Empress Jaliana, though I am relieved to say that thanks to our loyal guards, none have succeeded. The clear intent has been to murder our beloved empress and weaken the Alrenian Empire's leadership. The would-be assassin or assassins have not yet been found."

My breath seized in my chest. *Assassins.* An uneasy chill ran over my body, chased by a cold sweat that collected under my arms and on my palms. I gritted my teeth and rubbed my hands on my pants.

But it wasn't us, I thought. The vigilantes were making careful plans for the Autumn Ball, and I'd been with them last night when we'd rescued the two Forwyn from the Alrenians. It had to be someone else attacking the empress.

"Let us be clear"—and here the messenger lifted his paper high, clutching it firmly in both hands as he read carefully, as if to be sure to get every word correct—"the Court of Elders and Empress Jaliana will not show any mercy to anyone who threatens the innocent lives of those dedicated to serve the Alrenian people. When the criminals are captured, they will face immediate public execution, and anyone who harbors or assists criminals of this sort will share their fate."

The man cleared his throat and raised his voice even louder, letting it echo off the surrounding buildings. "If anyone has any information at all about the assassination attempts, we demand you bring it before the Elders immediately. It is only by sharing your knowledge now that any guilt you have in this matter will be pardoned. To hold back will seal your fate." Pausing, the messenger glanced around at the crowd with sharp, accusing eyes. "Don't hesitate."

The empress killed an innocent person too, I thought, *and the Elders are lying about it. They want to keep a dangerous woman alive, and for what? Their political power?*

By the time I registered the messenger's voice again, he was finishing his speech. "May our gods bless us," he said, referring both to Elhani and the Alrenian Giver of Life, before bowing his head slightly and exiting the marketplace with his entourage of guards.

His speech, however, had fooled no one. Alrenian citizens all around me broke into heated discussions, their words a jumbled torrent of anger and hatred, horror and confusion.

"The empress has been under attack?" a woman repeated, her eyes wide as she held her little boy's hand.

"Who else would want to hurt her, but those damn Forwyn scum themselves?" a burly man rumbled.

"The Elders are power-thirsty—they claim unity, but this is the perfect solution to remove the empress and use her as a martyr for their cause!" someone unnervingly close to me shouted.

"Down with the Forwyn slaves!" someone else cried. "Down with the Forwyn!"

It became a chant, rising in volume and intensity as more and more people took up the cry.

Terror tightened every muscle in my body. I was smaller than most people in this crowd and horribly outnumbered. A Forwyn in a sea of hatred and growing chaos. It would be all too easy for them to shove me down and crush me, beat me, kill me.

I stepped backward, slipping toward the nearest wall, reaching for Elhani's voice and his magic flowing around and inside me. *Elhani, conceal me. Elhani, hide me in your arms. Make me like a spirit, as you are, as your guidespirits are. Hide me, save me.*

The instant warmth filled me, I knew Elhani's magic had concealed me. Reassurance coursed through my heart, but invisibility alone would not be enough to escape. I'd have to be cautious.

It was terrifying how quickly the anger escalated. Forwyn guards encircling the marketplace sensed the climbing tension and pushed forward, but that only incensed the Alrenians more. An especially daring—or especially foolish—man was the first to turn and punch one of the guards directly in the face. That one strike was all it took for a full riot to erupt. The guards drew weapons and shouted at citizens to stand down as the Alrenians roared and attacked with fists and anything else they could grab and turn into a weapon: rocks, barrels and crates from the vendors, or even produce.

Everything around me plunged into a deadly altercation. I ducked as another Alrenian swung his fist toward a nearby guard. Shouts of pain rang through the air, chased by the sounds of trampling feet and screams as families tried to rush their children to safety.

"For the empress!" someone in the crowd screamed, and others joined the cry.

"For the empress! Avenge the empire!"

"Avenge the empire!"

It chilled my blood. Those were the cries of the Alrenian resistance.

Despite the guards' elite training and weapons, they were severely outnumbered. Furious, red-faced men and women hurled anything they could at the guards, beating them down. A few guards incapacitated their attackers, who dropped bleeding to the cobblestones, where they were trampled by their own companions.

My heart throbbed in my throat when I heard a Forwyn guard's agonized cries as he collapsed in the street. An Alrenian man stomped on his head while a woman seized the guard's weapon. But before she had a chance to even lift the blade, the citizens surrounding the guard had already beaten his face into a bloody mess.

Turning away, I tried not to retch as I stumbled past an abandoned vendor's cart. I tripped over spilled produce, tomatoes bursting under my sandals. Someone slammed into me, throwing me to the ground in a slimy pile of smashed fruit, and shaking my concentration on Elhani's magic. My hood fell back and sunlight stabbed my eyes. When the comforting sensation of warmth that had enveloped my body slipped away, I knew my invisibility was gone.

"Forwyn *kowra*," a man spat, seizing me by the wrist.

Grunting, I rose to my knees and lunged for the man, startling him enough that he dropped my arm. I charged past him, dodging a panicked woman clutching a small child to her chest. Another Alrenian collided with me, but I caught myself before I went down.

Conceal me, I prayed frantically, sweat sprouting on the back of my neck. But I couldn't focus any longer. The soothing melody of Elhani's voice had melted away in the pandemonium.

Coming to listen to the speech was a fool's idea, I reprimanded myself, leaping to clear a prone body.

No sooner had my feet hit the ground than I felt a tug on my hood, wrenching me backward. I choked for air as my cloak ties cut into my throat.

"What's this?" a man sneered, tugging me so that I was facing him. Hideous as all their hearts were, few Alrenians could ever be described as plain, let alone ugly, but this man defied those odds. He was missing several teeth and his nose was too large for his face, bulbous and crooked. "A little Forwyn rat trying to escape."

As I fought against his grasp, the man laughed cruelly and slid his free hand around my neck. His eyes were cold and soulless as he squeezed. Sparks danced across my vision and I wrestled down the urge to clutch at his hand and try to pry it free. Instead, I collected every ounce of strength I had left and kneed him between the legs. Once, twice.

Crying out, the man dropped his hands and toppled forward. He launched curses at my back as I spun around and fled.

Just in time for the rumble of dragon wings to fill my ears and a gigantic shadow to blot the entire marketplace in darkness. I crouched behind another abandoned cart and stared at the sky, from which a single dragon was diving toward us. I studied the Dragon Keeper closely, but I could tell he wasn't Wilvhe as soon as he drew near enough for me to distinguish his features. Fresh shouts echoed throughout the space as the Alrenians realized their efforts were doomed.

I scanned the crowd, which had become as violent as a battlefield, but it was difficult to find the Forwyn guards among the people. Whether any had survived the onslaught was impossible to tell. But at least one of them had focused on Elhani's voice better than I had. *Better than a nun who has dedicated her life to the task,* I thought with shame. The only way a Keeper could have been dispatched this soon would have been due to one of Elhani's people using his magic to speak to another's mind.

It was shocking to realize someone else could wield Elhani's magic so well. The only person I'd ever known who could speak into others' minds was Naina herself, and she'd practiced listening to the voice of Elhani for years. Many more years than most of us former slaves had ever had the ability to study and practice.

Tearing me from my thoughts, the dragon snarled as it swooped low, smashing into the central fountain and cracking it. The empress's statue teetered and crashed to the ground in a plume of dust and debris. Alrenians dodged and fled, but they couldn't outrun the dragon. Extending its claws, the beast seized two people from the crowd and launched back into the air, their writhing bodies becoming mere spots in the sky as people everywhere froze and stared in horror. When the dragon released them, I could feel my heart plummet, as if it were making the deadly fall with those Alrenians. My enemies.

The Alrenians descended toward another street a few blocks over, their limbs flailing as they plunged to their deaths. Tears pricked my eyes. *Not everyone in this crowd was rioting,* I thought. *And the Keeper didn't even make sure there weren't innocent Forwyn in his path. What sort of justice is this?*

It sent a chill through me, the way the Elders had dispatched such a swift, violent response without concern over who could be harmed, guilty or innocent, Alrenian or Forwyn.

The crowd scattered as the dragon dove again, hunting for more prey. Not everyone could escape in time, and the beast seized two more Alrenians to repeat its deadly process over again. My body seemed frozen in place, but I knew I had to move. I didn't want to fall victim to this slaughter.

Swallowing back my terror, I threw all my willpower into hearing

Elhani. *Conceal me. Hide me. Protect me.*

This time, I could easily hear his voice singing back to me, clear and strong. Warmth washed over my body as the magic took over. Rising from my hiding place, I tore out of the marketplace and back toward the abbey.

As soon as I entered the building, I ran straight for the kitchen. The scents of stew and baking bread embraced me like a welcome, but despite not having eaten in hours, my stomach didn't respond. I was too horrified.

It was Pauni'a at the oven, flour dusting her face as she turned toward me. Her eyes widened when she saw me release the invisibility cloaking me and lean against the doorway, panting and sweating.

"Lo, is everything all right?" she demanded, wiping her hands on her apron as she rushed to me.

"The Alrenians are rioting," I gasped. "Attacking Forwyn guards. I think they might have killed them."

"*What?* Where?" Pauni'a's eyes darted past me into the hall, as if she expected Alrenians to break in our door and plow into the abbey.

"In the Akytha marketplace. I went to hear a Forwyn messenger deliver a speech," I added hurriedly when Pauni'a shot me a glare. "I know it was a risk, but..." I let my excuse trail off as I shook my head. "The speech angered the Alrenians, and they started turning on the guards."

"Did the Elders dispatch anyone to stop it?" Pauni'a asked.

"A Dragon Keeper," I said slowly.

Pauni'a's face settled into a satisfied smile. "Good. That will put those smug Alrenians back in their place."

For an instant, I nearly continued to explain the horrors I'd witnessed the Dragon Keeper committing, but I faltered. Would Pauni'a understand? I couldn't shake the sense that what the Keeper had done was wrong. A way to only risk Forwyn lives and anger the Alrenians further. And a way to harm innocent Alrenians…because there had been children in that crowd, along with adults who hadn't been rioting, only running for safety.

My mind whirled.

"If the Forwyn have it under control, we needn't worry about it," Pauni'a continued, her tone practical. She settled a gentle hand on my shoulder. "I'm sorry you had to witness it, though—those barbarians attacking our brave guards like that." She hesitated. "Was it awful?"

I squared my shoulders. *Yes, it was awful,* I wanted to say, *but I've seen nothing worse today than what I witnessed in the palace daily during our slave years.*

Instead, I simply said, "I'll be all right."

Pauni'a perked up, her eyes brightening. "I know something that will cheer you up. Your man's awake."

❰❰❰❰❰

When he saw me, Caesiem sat up and burst into a grin that made me feel unexpectedly warm inside. Then Naina's warning echoed through my head, and I turned my gaze away.

"You should drink and rest as much as possible," I said pointedly. "And not be sitting up."

Ignoring my statement, Caesiem toyed with the pendant around his neck. "I drank until I thought my stomach would burst," he said with a laugh, but he stopped short with a wince. His face turned serious. "Thank you for saving my life." He studied me, his eyes lingering on my rumpled clothes and the braids that had fallen loose out of the knot I'd pulled them into earlier. His gaze landed on my bare neck. Somehow, in the chaos of the past few days, I'd forgotten to put my ribbons back on after the night he'd stolen them off me. "Are you all right?" he asked.

Self-conscious, I tugged at my shirt to straighten it. "I just finished my rounds," I said, not wanting to go into detail about what I'd seen. "I'm glad you're all right," I added softly, and I realized that I truly was.

Caesiem glanced around, but we were the only ones in the infirmary. He leaned forward, lowering his voice. "I didn't get you in trouble with the other nuns, did I?"

I smiled a little at his concern. "No, Naina understands." I didn't add that she'd warned me about him and his motives as well.

Caesiem nodded thoughtfully. "I'm glad. I wouldn't want you to face any consequences because of me." He drew a deep breath. "I know how important your vows are to you. I want you to help us, but if working with me is an issue, I understand." He waved a hand through the air. "I'm a criminal—it doesn't make sense that you should spend any time around me, unless to convert me."

I cracked a smile at that.

"I'm sure Renni could find someone else for you to work with," he went on, "or that you could change your mind now and have nothing to do with any of us."

Rolling my eyes, I approached his cot. "Firstly, I can't avoid spending time with you for at least a little while longer because Naina will forbid you leaving too soon. You need to rest. And secondly, do you think I hate you? I saved your life."

He shrugged. "You're a nun. Isn't it your duty to save lives?"

"And I'm your friend," I said, a little surprised at the words coming out of my mouth. But it was true. Despite Caesiem's shortcomings, I liked him. He made mistakes, but he was genuine about his desire to help others. He'd risked his life in his pursuit of justice for my people.

Caesiem lifted his chin to stare at me, his eyes wide. "Really?" he asked, studying my face so intently, I felt heat threaten my cheeks. I wasn't used to a man staring at me. I wasn't used to having one that was my friend. It was all so different.

"Well, you said we needed to be friends since we work together, anyway," I said with my own shrug, but I smiled at him too.

His gaze flicked to my neck again, where I knew my scar shone like a pale crescent moon against my throat. "You're not wearing your ribbons."

The necklace was still in the pocket of my other leggings, where I'd shoved it after he'd returned it to me.

"Get them and I'll tie them on for you," he offered.

I went to my room to retrieve my ribbons from the leggings resting in my basket of dirty clothing, thankfully not yet carried down to our washing room. When I returned, I sat on the edge of Caesiem's cot and handed him my necklace. Before I could brush my hair off my neck, he swept the braids aside, his fingers lightly skimming across a patch of my bare skin. I suppressed a shiver.

Other than the occasional friendly pat from one of my sisters, I couldn't remember the last time someone had touched me. As much as we cared for one another, we nuns didn't embrace often. And as a slave in the imperial palace, I'd been especially isolated. My fellow slaves and I had been terrified to grow attached to one another, and my family had been ripped from me when I was young. Mother sent away. Edi killed.

This gentle touch was unexpectedly comforting. Pleasant. It was strange the way it made goosebumps rise on my skin even as I felt warmer inside.

Once, after we Forwyn became free, I'd found a young man at the palace attractive and interesting. I'd felt content when he held my hand or smiled at me. But it hadn't been enough to make me stay there, or to prevent me from taking my vows. Why did Caesiem's touch affect me differently?

Maybe when I'd chosen to become a nun, I hadn't realized the extent of what I was giving up.

Squeezing my eyes shut, I silently cursed myself for my weakness. I might have been considering breaking one vow, but that didn't mean I needed to break this one too. Killing might be necessary to save my people—having feelings for this man certainly wasn't.

Maybe I wanted to like and trust Caesiem, but if I had to stop him or work against him to follow Elhani and help my people, I would. And I certainly couldn't let my feelings grow deeper than friendship, no matter how nice it was to experience human contact or see his handsome face break into a smile.

As soon as he finished tying the knot at the nape of my neck, I jerked away. "I went to The Broken Crown while you were recovering, to tell No'ahim you still wanted your room. He agreed to hold it for you until you could return and play again."

"Thank you," Caesiem said earnestly.

I stood, turning to face him as I tugged my arms across my chest. "A cloaked man was there. He pulled me aside before I left and asked me about you." I frowned at Caesiem pointedly. "He talked about having business with you."

Caesiem shrugged almost sheepishly, pretending to wave it off as if it were nothing. "I told you," he said, "I'm not exactly…reformed."

I pursed my lips together, but didn't press the issue. Instead, I informed Caesiem of my trip to see the Elders, only to be turned away with Elder Ilhoa's dismissive words.

"How can they *not* care?" I whispered, tears pricking my eyes. "And it's all getting worse…" I described the rescue we'd made last night, along with what had happened in the marketplace, watching Caesiem's face grow darker and darker as I did so.

Caesiem stared off into the distance, frowning thoughtfully. "I'm not sure we can stop war from coming," he said.

"Renni and the others are trying to make plans to…stop the empress," I said significantly. "Wilvhe has an invitation to the Autumn Ball, and he plans to bring all of us as his guests."

Caesiem scrunched his face in thought. "You're coming with us?"

"I *can't* sit by and do nothing. I can't let my people keep dying. Everything is being done in the empress's name, and she's killing innocent people. I can't let this continue."

He nodded, leaning back against his pillow. His eyelids looked heavy with weariness. "What about your vow not to shed blood?" he asked, so softly I almost couldn't hear him. "It might not just be the empress we have to face. I don't think Renni would ever harm the Elders, but this is bigger than just slaying an Alrenian."

"I don't know," I murmured. "But I *also* made a vow to protect my people. And the empress is a threat to them, and the Elders…they're failing us too."

He paused, seeming to mull things over. "Could you tell me about the palace layout? Draw it out for me, perhaps?" he asked quietly. "Even Wilvhe isn't as familiar as you, and if we're to do this correctly, we will need a solid plan."

"In case we need to escape?" I asked. "If we don't succeed?"

"Among many things," he said, his gaze looking distant and exhausted.

"I'll bring it to you later, after you've had some rest," I promised.

Caesiem's eyes had already closed, and his breathing was rhythmic. For a moment, I lingered, watching his chest rise and fall. My fingers drifted to the frayed ribbons fastened around my neck, the ones that reminded me forever of both my strengths and shortcomings. My salvation and my damnation.

Was I truly willing to walk that road again? To give up everything I had here—my entire life in the abbey? My heart ached, but I felt a cold resolve building within my soul.

Elhani, if I do this, can you ever forgive me?

CHAPTER TWENTY

Jalie

TODAY, I WAS PERMITTED TO dress in full Alrenian dragon scale armor, from the helmet that slid over my carefully plaited hair to the boots that glistened on my feet. The suits Dragon Keepers wore were composed of multiple pieces, their inner layers crafted with comfortable, flexible fabric, while the outer layers were covered with the scales. Each piece was created to feel light and cool rather than hot and smothering.

The first was a long, sleeveless tunic made of pure ivory scales. Next I slipped into the bottom piece, which was fashioned like a pair of leggings, and then I slid on the long gloves that covered my hands and arms. While the leggings matched the tunic, the gloves and boots were covered in flashing gold scales. Finally, my helmet was also made with gold scales, with Alrenor's swirling sun insignia painted in ivory on either side.

When I stared at myself in the mirror, I couldn't help but admire the full effect of my empire's colors shimmering on my entire body. I'd even painted my eyes with glistening gold and ivory makeup to accent the armor. As I studied my reflection, I saw a warrior empress. Someone my mother could look on with pride.

Kovi, too, had been given armor to wear, his in Alrenian colors but opposite mine: his gold tunic and leg pieces were accented with ivory gloves and boots. When he slid his helmet on and met my gaze, his usual mask was gone. Or maybe I was becoming better at reading his expressions. Either way, I could see the discomfort and uncertainty flitting across his face, from the way his jaw worked and his eyebrows dipped for an instant. Then he glued on a smile.

"Come, Your Highness," he said, and I couldn't tell if his mocking tone was for me or for the ridiculous show we would have to put on. "Let's not keep your people waiting."

I brushed past him. "I take it we have to pretend we like one another's company today?" I asked over my shoulder.

Kovi scoffed. "You don't need to *pretend* to like my company."

"What?" I scowled, and he tossed me an infuriating smirk.

"I've seen how you look at me, so don't even pretend you'd rather have another bodyguard." He shrugged. "But it's not like we have to speak. I'll be busy scanning the crowds for threats to your life, and you'll be occupied with your imperial responsibilities. We can each pretend the other doesn't exist."

Except for when you have to ride on a dragon with me, I thought, but even that couldn't dampen my spirits.

Besides, Kovi wasn't exactly wrong. As much as it troubled me to admit it, his company was a lot less unwelcome than I'd expected it would be.

I turned my thoughts to a more pleasant topic. Today, I would ride a dragon again. My blood hummed in my veins, and my steps were buoyant. When we exited my chambers, Kovi had to increase his pace to match my stride.

"Empresses don't run," Kovi said, an edge of mirth in his voice.

I spun on my heel in the middle of the hall to shoot him a glare. "What did you say?" I demanded.

A slow smile spread across his face, like a dare. Insolent. Beautiful.

Maddening. "Empresses don't run," he repeated.

I sauntered toward him. "You know nothing about Alrenian empresses." Gesturing to my armor, I stared at him, planting a hand on my hip. "We're warriors. Dragon Tamers. We run whenever we please."

"For this event, I think the Elders expect you to maintain a dignified air," Kovi said, and this time I was sure I heard mockery in his tone.

"Are you deriding your father and the other Elders?"

Kovi glanced around, but the hallway was empty, for now. "I only find their desire to parade us before the people a little ridiculous." His eyes flicked to his own armor and back to my face.

I couldn't resist the smile that tugged on my mouth. "We've finally found something we agree on." I turned again, slowing my pace and putting on my most dignified expression. "Do you think the Elders would approve of this?" I said, holding back a laugh.

What was I doing? *Kovi is Forwyn,* I reminded myself. *You have nothing in common with him. His father is likely the one who murdered your mother.*

"Much better," he said, and I could tell Kovi was trying not to chuckle as well.

I fought to tune out the musical sound. It was easy to refocus, to think of Elder Ettonou's angry face or the dragon devouring the Alrenian captive in a ball of flames. Kovi was one of them. He was a soldier, prepared to *fight* for them, and he was tasked with following me everywhere to protect others from me just as much as to protect me from potential assassins.

I curled my hands into fists and set my jaw as we exited the palace, crossed the grounds, and set foot in the arena.

The arena seats were filled with Elders and Forwyn nobility, guards, and servants, but far below in the city, standing apart from the Forwyn citizens, I could see the gathering of Alrenians gazing toward the Keep.

Waiting to see our flight. Waiting to see me, their empress.

My heart nearly burst with the thrill of being close to the dragons again, and with the thought of my people seeing me as they were meant to view me: as their powerful empress. Not the pathetic pawn the Forwyn had created me to be.

As Kovi and I stepped closer, I noticed the Elders gathered near the front seats in the audience. Though they'd been standing and speaking amongst themselves, when I stepped into view they turned as one to stare at me. Some of them had measured looks that gave nothing away, but Elder Ettonou's eyes seethed with barely restrained rage. He hated me. He wanted me dead.

Like he wanted my mother dead, I thought, repressing a shiver. An image of him plunging a blade into my mother's chest flashed through my head. Then one of him laughing and snapping her shackles into place before dragon fire devoured her. Another of him shoving her from this arena, over the cliff edge into the city far below.

No, don't let him see your fear. Don't let him think he has any more power over you than he already does.

I squared my shoulders and stalked into the arena. A warm breeze kissed my temples, its scent filled with the sharp tang of seawater and dragon smoke. I relished it, inhaling deeper. These were the smells of home. My birthright.

The Dragon Keepers were scattered across the arena, each standing proudly beside his or her dragon. Every man and woman was arrayed in stunning dragon scales in shades of gold and ivory that flashed so brightly in the sunlight they made my eyes water. One Keeper stood apart from the rest, his confident stance and the swirling sun insignia painted on his shoulder declaring him the Captain of the Dragon Keepers.

The truly breathtaking sight, however, was the dragons: nostrils snorting smoke, feet shuffling, tails swishing, pupils dilating, and carefully tucked wings shuddering the tiniest bit in anticipation of their flight. I didn't know all of their names, but I recognized many, from Torla with her fiery scales, to Ziltha with her pure silver shimmer, to Ivez with his stunning tones of blue and white that, when the sunlight caught them just right, seemed to ripple like water.

I could tell by their numbers that some of the usual dragons were missing. Without Keeper Yaelti, the man I'd injured and whose dragon Kovi and I would ride today, there should have been eleven remaining Dragon Keepers and twelve dragons. Instead, only five Keepers and six dragons were present. The six I'd seen leave yesterday must have still been gone.

My eyes flitted back to where the Elders were gathered, weighing what I knew. They had executed an Alrenian rebel, with the war cry *"Avenge the empire!"* on her lips. Although I'd slain a Forwyn noble with my power, the Elders had brushed that fact aside in favor of continuing to flaunt the supposed unity between our peoples. First with this display of our dragons' power, and later with the festivities at the Autumn Ball—a tradition stolen, of course, from us Alrenians. And now there were Dragon Keepers missing, which would mean that they were elsewhere in the empire, probably "protecting the people" by quelling an Alrenian uprising.

As Kovi led me toward Ryke, the only dragon without a Keeper beside him, my stomach leapt with hope. The Elders must have been particularly concerned about Alrenian rebels. *Avenge the empire.* Were we finally headed toward war? Were my people rising against the Forwyn at last?

Maybe I wouldn't be alone, fighting a hopeless battle for my throne. Maybe there was an army out there, waiting for me.

My gaze settled on the Alrenians far below, like pebbles on the seashore. Were there rebels among them, at this very moment? The idea set fire through my veins.

When we paused beside Ryke, I prayed silently that he would submit to me today as he had before, in his den. My heart hammered in a mixture of fear and delight, hope and uncertainty, as I reached toward the dragon.

And then Ryke stretched his neck and nuzzled my hand, his scales comforting and familiar against my fingertips. This felt right. I couldn't hold back the laughter, strong and free, as it bubbled up.

Casting a glance toward Kovi, who hovered beside me, I caught his wide-eyed grin as undisguised awe filled his face.

"He'll let us ride," I said confidently, the old thrill of anticipation I'd always felt before climbing atop a dragon soaring through me.

As the Elders stepped forward to formally announce the Keepers and me to the waiting crowd, I circled around Ryke, trailing my fingers along his scales as I did so he could track my movements. My muscles remembered what to do before my mind even did. Ryke lowered his body slightly in anticipation, and I swung myself effortlessly into the waiting saddle strapped to his back. When I glanced toward Kovi, his expression had shuttered, returning to his usual blank look.

"Come," I said, gesturing for him to climb up behind me. "Ryke will let you on too."

As Kovi stepped forward, Ryke shifted and turned his head to stare at him. Kovi tensed, every muscle in his body stilling as he gazed back at the dragon. He forced his spine to remain rigid and lifted his shoulders, standing tall and proud. When the dragon snorted and turned away, I could hear Kovi exhale. He grasped the back of the huge leather saddle and swung up into the second seat built in behind mine.

As soon as we'd both secured ourselves in our seats with the leather straps and buckles attached to the saddle, Ryke pawed the ground impatiently. His wings twitched, unfurling slightly in his excitement. He longed for my command to fly, and I couldn't blame him. My body was thrumming with eagerness.

"Dragon Keepers." Elder Ettonou's booming voice echoed across the arena. His eyes flicked toward me. "Empress. Ride!"

I leaned forward in my seat, my breaths quickening and my palms clammy. I patted Ryke's side and murmured my command in Alrenian. "*Laeva.*"

Immediately, Ryke launched himself off the edge of the arena, dipping in a free fall toward the city streets laid out before us. My stomach shot into my mouth, adrenaline and the feeling of weightlessness encompassing me. There was nothing but the roar of the wind in my ears, rising above even the rolling cadence of the distant waves crashing on shore. That raging, humid wind stung my eyes and stole my breath. I was vaguely aware of the scents of brine and smoke, stone and earth, citrus and baked goods filling the air, the smells of the dragons and the seas and the city all enveloping me.

The details of the city seemed to rush up toward us, coming into better focus as we dove toward them. Each crack in the cobbled street. The flash of jewelry on Alrenian women. A snatch of applause echoing off the buildings. Closer, closer.

Ryke dove fearlessly, his wings tucked close to his body. Unafraid of the pull of gravity. Unafraid of danger.

He's magnificent, I thought, and a wild laugh escaped my lips, torn away by the wind. I was free. Elated. Fearless.

Hands seized my waist, so warm that I felt the heat even through my armor. Kovi clutched me tightly, as if it was all he could do to rein in his fear.

Composed, brave Kovi was afraid? The realization shocked me so much that for a moment I forgot the thrill of the flight and shifted in the saddle to glance back at him. Kovi clenched his jaw so tightly he could have broken teeth. His dark eyes betrayed no fear, but his face was taut, focused, as if he could not tear his gaze from the sight before him.

In the next instant, Ryke unfurled his wings in a beautiful display. Their span was huge, easily catching the wind and letting us soar low over the city rooftops. My heart was practically singing.

On either side, other dragons were swooping over the city and gliding alongside us, their Keepers as immersed in the thrill of flight as I was. Some whooped for joy or threw their arms into the air. But none of the other dragons had dared to dive as far as Ryke had. He was in a class apart from the others, a perfect beast.

I longed for him. I longed for this. Even in this moment, as every vein in my body pulsed with adrenaline and happiness, my heart ached with sorrow and loss. The Elders might have let me ride today, but this was the first time they had ever done so. There was no telling that they would ever let me ride again.

Below us, the city was vibrant and beautiful and rushing with life. Over Ryke's pulsing wing beats and the whistling wind in my ears, we sometimes dipped low enough to hear the rushing channels, diverted from the nearby seas. They glistened parallel to the cobbled streets, like silver serpents stretching and twisting through the capital. The buildings, bridges, and fountains shone in the sunlight, smooth and pure as the white sythrel blossoms in my garden. Against the stunning white of the city, the bright colors the citizens wore stood out starkly, a beautiful contrast. Guards in every possible color of dragon scale armor patrolled the streets, while Alrenians clothed in rich hues laughed or pointed in awe as Ryke flew overhead. Alrenians and Forwyn rushed from their homes and businesses to stand in the streets, clapping and cheering.

As their cries reached me, as tears streaked down my cheeks from the wind stinging my face, I couldn't deny that the Elders had been clever. Both Alrenians and Forwyn alike had at least one rider to applaud in this moment, and all had an appreciation and respect for the powerful dragons. For the first time in my life, I saw Alrenians and Forwyn standing amicably side by side, ignoring their problems and hatred for one another as they drank in the stunning sight before them.

Together, the Keepers and I commanded our dragons to swerve and spin and twist, executing a perfect aerial dance. Each time Ryke jerked sideways or spun upside down, Kovi grasped my waist.

"Show off," he shouted in my ear, and I smirked.

All too soon, the Dragon Keepers circled back toward the Keep. My stomach dropped in disappointment, in my longing to fly longer. I felt free and alive for the first time in years, powerful enough to command a dragon's respect. Able to see my own city and listen to my people cheer for me.

The order lodged in my throat, but Ryke didn't even need to hear my voice. Seeing his fellow dragons soaring back toward the Keep, he turned and followed. I gripped the saddle until my knuckles turned white and stared at the city, shrinking, shrinking, until the distance between it and me seemed endless. The buildings were children's toys again, the people and carriages and horses merely playthings. Once again, I was separated from my people by a gulf so vast I wasn't sure if I'd ever span it.

When Ryke landed beside the other dragons, the spectating Forwyn had already stood from their seats, shouting and applauding. They chanted the Keepers' names and cried words in their own language, a language my people had never deigned to learn. It was painful. Insulting.

I studied my white fingers, every inch of my body rebelling at the thought of releasing my grip on the saddlehorn and dismounting from the dragon. Blinking away threatening tears, I reached out to run my fingertips along Ryke's scales one last time, memorizing the way they flashed every shade of green in the sunlight. I wanted to drink in every second of this experience so I could return to this memory later, relishing the way it had felt to fly.

Kovi dismounted and extended a hand toward me. At last, I relented, swallowing back the bitter taste in my mouth. I unbuckled the straps from my waist and leapt from Ryke's back, ignoring Kovi's hand and pushing past him.

"Empress," Elder Ilhoa called, but I didn't stop. I strode from the arena, all but running toward the garden. Kovi's footsteps beat out a steady rhythm behind me, my shadow I could never shake.

Rage stirred inside me, rising until I thought I would burst. As soon as I reached a secluded path in the garden, where the crowd's applause was lost in the distant crashing of waves against the shore, I whirled on Kovi.

"Don't make me go back into the palace," I bit out. "It's just a fancy prison, until the Elders call on me again to be their pawn and try to help them stave off their war."

Surprise flitted across Kovi's face, so quickly I might have missed it before. But now that he was my constant companion, I was learning how to read his expressions, to see the things he couldn't quite hide behind his carefully constructed mask.

"They'll never let me ride again," I burst out, the overwhelming grief crushing my chest until I couldn't hold it back anymore. I choked on a sob. It was all too much. The perfect memories returning to me in the scent of dragon smoke and rushing wind, in the feeling of my stomach floating to my throat and my pulse pounding with adrenaline. I could hear my mother's laughter again, her voice low and soothing as she told me dragon stories. Her warmth when she wrapped her arms around me as we rode, until I could smell her soap—lime with a hint of floral.

In that moment, those memories were overwhelming in their closeness, as if I were recalling instants that had occurred only days ago. They were heartbreaking but comforting. Like my mother wasn't that far away after all. Yet when I remembered the Elders wouldn't let me ride a dragon again any time soon, it felt like those memories were being torn from me.

As if to further add to my pain, sunlight flashed on dragon scales as a solo beast took flight. I watched its form soar into the sky before diving back toward the city. Had one of the Keepers been sent alone to stop trouble brewing within the capital? Or was that the captain, going on extra rounds, savoring the wind and the sunlight and the thrill of flying a dragon simply because he could?

Pulling my focus away from the dragon, Kovi stepped forward. He reached out a hand before letting it drop back to his side. "You don't *know* that they'll never let you ride again," he said, but he seemed to understand as well as I did that those words were empty.

I sank onto the stone bench beside the path, relishing the cool shade of a nearby lemon tree. Slowly, my heart rate returned to normal as the sweat coating my face dried. Birds twittered, and a breeze rustled the surrounding leaves. A skink skittered up the trunk of an orange tree across from me.

From the corner of my eye, I studied Kovi warily. He looked almost uncomfortable standing in the middle of the path, frowning at a squirrel darting through some bushes. It was tempting to use what I knew about him to my benefit. He was compassionate enough to sympathize, and it seemed to be nearly habitual for him to comfort me. If I asked, he'd probably request that the Elders let me ride again.

But I didn't want to feel indebted to Kovi. It was already unsettling to remember the way he'd stayed beside me when I'd been sick with poison, curling up with me in bed and holding the sweaty strands of hair back from my face whenever I'd become ill. His gentle hands when he touched me. His tense expression when he'd thought I'd endangered myself by lingering alone on my balcony.

No, don't ask him for anything, I thought. *He's your enemy. His father wants you dead. His father killed your mother. He hates you. You hate him.*

And if everything went according to plan, I'd poison him myself for a chance to seize my throne. A chance for freedom.

Freedom. *Avenge the empire.* If it was true that the Elders had dispatched Dragon Keepers to deal with Alrenian rebels, then I had soldiers prepared to fight for me, to help me regain the throne, already waiting out there. Instead of struggling in a hopeless war alone, I could find help and a way to win.

My blood pulsed eagerly through my veins, renewed hope warming me. More pieces of my growing plan fell into place.

"I'm sorry," Kovi said after a long moment, as if he couldn't take the silence any longer.

As lost as I had been in my thoughts, I jerked my gaze to his in surprise. "What?" I asked.

"I'm sorry," Kovi repeated, his frown deepening as if the words were painful for him to say. "I could see how much you love flying."

I couldn't help the laugh that escaped my lips. "But you do not."

Instead of acting embarrassed, Kovi laughed with me. "You're right," he agreed. "I hate heights."

My mouth curved in the slightest smile as I cocked my head, studying him. "The man who doesn't fear death or pain is afraid of heights?"

"Everyone is afraid of something. If I have to face pain or death, I'd like to face it like a soldier and fight back, not as a helpless man careening toward his end." Kovi watched me steadily, openly, the sunlight glistening in his eyes and catching the gold within them. It added a warmth and gentleness to his gaze.

Stomach flipping, I glanced away. My own fears revolved around losing control—of my empire, of my life, of my choices. The utter unknown and chaos of losing my mother and my future to the Forwyn had forced me to face some of my greatest terrors, including my fear of death. And the Elders reminded me every day of just how much they were in control of me, filling me with rage. Kovi, too, had every ability to command me with his strange power.

Mysterious. Unknown. Out of my control and terrifying.

"How does your magic work?" I asked, and I could tell my change of subject surprised Kovi by the brief raise of his eyebrows. "Do other Forwyn have the ability to…control people?"

After a moment, Kovi settled himself beside me on the bench. "All Forwyn can use magic," he said. "If we listen to the voice of Elhani and focus on it, we can use some of his power."

I swallowed against the dry feeling building in my throat. "Anyone could control me like you did?"

Kovi shook his head as he watched a bee dart among some blue embyth. "Few know how to wield magic that powerful. Our magic is something many are only just now finding time to study in these past few years we've been free. But even if more knew how to use magic to control others—few would want to."

"Why not? Wouldn't people like your father love that sort of control over the Alrenian empress?" I didn't bother to conceal the bitterness in my tone.

Unfazed by my anger, Kovi shook his head again. "Magic as powerful as control comes at a cost," he said. He turned, meeting my gaze, his eyes searching my face as if weighing my reaction. "Every time someone controls another person, they become connected to them for a time. Actually…we're not quite sure for how long." He shifted, looking away. "Maybe forever."

Almost unconsciously, I leaned back, distancing myself from him. "Connected how?" I asked carefully.

Kovi shrugged. "I can feel your emotions." He hesitated. "It's unpleasant to feel the fear and pain someone else experiences when under your control," he went on, "and most people who want to control others would want to use them. Maybe even hurt them. Experiencing their victims' emotions tends to prevent the Forwyn from abusing any controlling magic."

I watched my feet as I kicked at pebbles in the path. No wonder Kovi had shown me compassion like no other Forwyn had before. He'd experienced my pain like it was his own. Perhaps, that night I'd been poisoned, he'd been suffering with fear and confusion right alongside me.

A soft part of me thought of his gentle hands again, his concern that night. But another side of me couldn't help but relish in this knowledge. It wasn't likely Kovi would ever try to use his magic to control me again, not at the price it required.

It would make my escape plans that much easier.

CHAPTER TWENTY-ONE

Lo

PAUNI'A'S EYES GLINTED AMBER IN the soft morning light as she laughed and offered me her hand. Taking it, I grunted as my muscles ached in protest. My side smarted where her foot had landed a perfect kick, one that had sent me sprawling on my back and gasping like a fish out of water.

"That was embarrassing," I said, cringing and wiping the sweat trickling down my forehead. "It's too early in the morning for this."

For some unfathomable reason, I'd agreed to Paunia's request to wake early and spar together before breakfast. Now I was blinking against bleary vision while my stomach growled angrily. Even in the golden light of dawn, with birds twittering in our ears, with the bustling sounds of the waking city enveloping us, all I could think about was my bed. Or some breakfast. Each breeze carried the scents of baking bread and frying bacon to my nose, making my mouth water.

"Why? Why is it too early?" Pauni'a asked, her gaze turning sharp. "Were you up late again? Leaving the abbey?"

"What?" I asked.

Pauni'a rolled her eyes, setting a hand on her hip. "Come on, Lo," she said. "You trusted me enough to tell me about how you sneak out at night, and how you've been helping the vigilantes. Don't feign stupidity now. You seemed so uncertain before. Are you still helping them?"

"Yes," I admitted. Last night, I'd snuck out to assist Renni and the others from stopping another murder attempt. But bodies were still being discovered near the city walls from attacks we couldn't stop with our small numbers and resources. It didn't feel like our efforts were enough, and I was understanding more and more why the vigilantes were so determined to assassinate Jaliana.

Pauni'a stared out into the distance, a crease between her brows. "I've been thinking about the things you shared with me. A lot. And after watching your friend Caesiem almost die, I can't pretend I'm not worried about you. I don't know what I'd do if I lost you." Her eyes were glistening, and she blinked hard before any tears could fall. "I know you want to help our people, but please be careful."

I swallowed, thinking of my growing resolution to help Renni and his friends stop the empress. Even if I survived that mission, I would be breaking my vows and possibly damning my soul. It would be easy for word to spread, and as soon as the other nuns found out, I'd never be welcomed into the abbey again. Pauni'a would just as surely lose me as if I'd died.

"I'll be careful," I whispered. "I don't want to lose you either; I don't want..." My voice floated away, and I sighed, blinking at the sun only just now peeking over the city rooftops.

Pauni'a leaned in unexpectedly, wrapping me in a hug. "In the meantime, I'm going to keep sparring with you as much as possible. I'll make sure you're so formidable, no one will ever dare stab you and leave you to bleed out in the streets."

I tried to chuckle in response, but my laughter caught in my throat as I squeezed her back.

A short while later, when we entered the abbey, the aroma of coffee, eggs, toast, and fresh fruit wafted toward us. My sisters were already grabbing plates and finding their seats at the table when we stepped into the kitchen. However, most of the women's attention wasn't on the food or even the mugs of coffee they poured, but on the young man seated at the head of the table.

Looking refreshed and content, Caesiem thanked Naina as she passed him the coffee pot. His eyes darted toward mine as soon as I approached, as if he'd sensed me the moment I'd walked into the room. He offered me a small, secretive smile before returning his focus to his beverage.

I bit back my grin and concentrated on piling generous helpings of food onto my plate. By the time Pauni'a and I reached the table, the only two seats left were one beside Naina and one beside Caesiem. With a side glance in my direction, Pauni'a claimed the chair next to Naina. I sighed inwardly as I slid into my chair, but Caesiem only murmured a quiet good morning before pointedly ignoring me.

I'm not going to be in trouble if you're friendly toward me, I thought at him, wishing I could blurt out the words, but I resisted.

Naina stood to lead us all in the blessing. As soon as she'd finished, I poured myself a large mug of coffee and took a sip. *At last. It tastes Elhani-blessed,* I thought happily. *Who in their right mind does anything before a cup of coffee?*

All around me, the women murmured quietly to one another as they ate. This wasn't our usual lively chatter. Though they tried to pretend everything was normal, I knew every other sister in the room was distracted by Caesiem's presence. It was unusual, disconcerting even, to have a stranger among our tight-knit group. An outsider who didn't believe in our god and didn't even look like us. I could almost hear my sisters' thoughts as they wondered if they *truly* could trust Caesiem. Others couldn't conceal their glances. It seemed some of the other nuns thought the same way Pauni'a did, that it didn't hurt to appreciate a handsome face.

At last, Naina tired of the way everyone else avoided speaking to Caesiem as a guest. Our hospitality, it seemed, was lacking. "I'm glad to see you're feeling well enough to join us for a meal," Naina told him warmly.

Caesiem swallowed a bite of egg and set down his fork. "I don't know how to thank you for everything you've done for me," he said in his musical accent. "But I promise I won't overstay my welcome. I can be out of here after breakfast."

"Oh no," Naina cut in, shaking her head vehemently. "There's no hurry for you to leave. Please don't mistake me. You're my patient and I'd like to keep an eye on you a little longer."

The surrounding women nodded in agreement, though I felt O'emia's heavy gaze directed toward me. As if she were expecting me to react in some way that would make me guilty. I pushed down my rising anger. As Naina always told us, we couldn't afford division among our own. We needed to stand strong and united when the empire itself was fractured and hateful.

"Well, thank you," Caesiem said with a graceful shrug, "but I still won't linger long. I have business to tend to."

Business. I knew he meant meeting with his friends and me again to prepare for the Autumn Ball. He would likely take the map I'd delivered to him late last night so we could all pore over it together. My heart pounded with anxiety and guilt at the thought of once again returning to the palace. Wiping a clammy hand on my leggings, I took a bite of my toast and tried to tamp down the memories threatening me.

They trickled in anyway: The iron tang of blood heavy in the air. The dull thuds of bodies hitting the earth. The former empress's merciless grip as her sharp voice filled my ears. The press of a dagger's edge against my neck...

My heart quickened and my body trembled.

Peace, ahnla. Naina's voice pierced through the disturbing images like a welcome ray of sunlight scattering the darkness. She must have noticed how troubled I'd looked. *Concentrate on Elhani's music. Block everything else out.*

Frowning, I focused until the strains of Elhani's song became audible again, a gentle caress as light as a feather, as quiet and peaceful as lapping waves. Immediately my body relaxed. Glancing up, I caught Naina's gaze and offered her a grateful smile.

Fortunately, my fellow nuns were still chattering and eating, oblivious to my inner turmoil. My chest loosened and I took a breath of air, finally relaxing fully.

I seized my coffee mug and took an extra-large gulp, burning my tongue. The familiar bitter taste was comforting, however, and the liquid seemed to fill my whole being with warmth to counteract the chill I felt.

"If you're well enough, you should join us on our rounds," Pauni'a was saying to Caesiem.

I had an urge to elbow her, hard, but she was sitting across the table. Just as I extended my foot to stomp on her toes instead, I caught Naina's gaze and decided against it.

Caesiem gestured with his free hand, his other grasping his fork. "Around the city to help families in need?"

Pauni'a nodded eagerly.

Caesiem's bright eyes shone. "I'd love to help."

❮❮❮❮❮

"I'm trying to pretend I hardly know you." Caesiem kept pace with me easily, his loping strides giving no hint about the grave injury he'd sustained. He carried his basket of food with ease too, like he felt no pain at all. Naina was practically a miracle worker, able to call on Elhani's voice so expertly when tending to the wounded and ill that some of my sisters boasted she could bring someone back from the dead. A few of the older ones claimed that she truly had before.

Caesiem turned, a grin on his face as he pointed at me. "Which, to be fair, is the truth. I *do* hardly know you."

Scrunching my nose in a frown, I swung my basket from my right arm to my left to shift the cumbersome weight. "You *followed me* for guidespirits-know-how-long," I retorted. "You certainly know more about me than I know about you."

"All right," Caesiem said, shrugging. He often communicated with his entire body, gesturing with his arms or utilizing animated expressions to share his meaning. It made him energetic and exciting, and a bit of a walking contradiction. How could someone who made himself appear so open be a thief and spy? Clearly, it was all part of the deception.

He turned to me, his blue eyes as pure as the sky and glinting with playfulness. "What would you like to know about me? Ask me anything."

I shot him a skeptical glance. "So you can lie?"

The corner of Caesiem's mouth twitched. "Only if I want to."

Huffing, I thought a moment. With the late morning sun beating down on us, my braids were already clinging to the back of my sweaty neck. All I wanted to do was seek one of the water channels or waterfalls in the center of the capital or rush toward the beaches. The stifling humidity was making me irritable.

"Did you have any close friends in Teramyl that you left behind?" I asked.

This time it was Caesiem's turn to be silent as he considered his answer.

As I waited, I studied our surroundings. The street we were on was wide and open, mostly empty of traffic since it was lined with homes. Everyone was either inside or at work for the day. We hadn't reached the most decrepit district in the capital yet, but this one wasn't one of the immaculate Alrenian neighborhoods either. Simple stone houses sat in neat rows, their lawns clean and trees well-tended. Some even had flowers blooming in their windows or ivy climbing the walls. Overall, this street spoke of successful Forwyn who valued practicality over Alrenian excess.

"Not so close that I'd choose staying with them rather than starting over here," Caesiem said at last. He shrugged. "In a band of thieves and orphans, do you think we could really trust one another?" He laughed airily, but I noticed the catch in his voice.

"How do you know how to read? Write?" I asked curiously. I hesitated, realizing I'd assumed he could because of his status as a spy for the vigilantes. But had I ever seen him read or write? "I mean, can you?" I added, inwardly cringing.

He flicked a sidelong glance at me. "Are you trying to imply that you think I'm an idiot?"

I rolled my eyes. "No, I just...I'm sorry. I just thought...you were an orphan, living with other orphans."

"It's fine," Caesiem muttered. "I did tell you to ask me anything." He smiled, thought it looked a little strained. "I know how to read and write."

"How?" I asked in surprise.

"The other orphans, mostly," Caesiem said, waving his hand carelessly. "Some who hadn't been orphaned as young as others. They taught the rest of us the basics of reading, writing, and mathematics. Things like that."

For a while, quiet descended again. My thoughts naturally returned to the subject that had haunted me ever since I'd seen the Dragon Keeper unleashing his fury on the rioting Alrenians in the marketplace. He'd been careless—careless enough for me to believe Forwyn had been hurt at the hands of Keepers and Forwyn guards before. Maybe even at the hands of our own soldiers. "Do you really think the palace is full of people who don't feel guilty for hurting other Forwyn when they put down Alrenian uprisings?" I asked in a low voice.

Caesiem's body tensed and his words came out low and quiet. "I trust Wilvhe, and he's there. He's seen what the Elders and other Dragon Keepers have done. He has every reason to want to believe in them and their cause, and he's turned against them."

I considered this information for a while, letting the silence stretch between us. We were drawing nearer to one of the more dilapidated neighborhoods, tiny homes growing even tinier and crushed closer together.

"You're wrong about me, you know," I said, shifting my basket once again to my opposite arm.

My abrupt subject change seemed to surprise Caesiem, who glanced toward me, his brow furrowed in confusion.

"How am I wrong about you?" he asked.

I almost stumbled over a cracked cobblestone in the road as I stared back at him. It was disconcerting the way his piercing eyes studied me. Maybe it was because I was so used to being an invisible slave or a member of a larger group of people. Or because I was so used to everyone watching me with expectation—even now as a nun, other Forwyn looked to me to provide for them, tend to them. They saw me for what I could do for them rather than who I was. With Caesiem, I was simply...myself. He looked at me like he wanted to understand me.

"You seem to think that as the *amara'rekni* I'm this talented killer. But I'm not some skilled warrior who carefully planned out the empress's assassination." I swallowed, tamping down the flood of guilt that prickled up my throat and along my spine. "I was just a girl trying to save my own life." With my free hand, I toyed with the ribbons around my neck, their smooth texture grounding me.

"But you slew the *empress*," Caesiem said, and this time he couldn't conceal the awe in his voice.

I averted my eyes, turning instead to scan the houses as we drew closer to the neighborhood we sought. There were fewer people here, and no Forwyn guards or Alrenians in sight. "Not because I was anything special," I protested. The words felt thick in my throat. Talking about that day made images flash across my mind again and my palms turn sweaty. "Did you hear about the Misrothians there that day? The princess and her friends? One of them had a powerful gift—one the Alrenians have always claimed as theirs alone. I wouldn't be alive if not for him. I wouldn't have had a chance to kill the empress." Slowly, I shrugged, trying to brush off the anxious feeling rising within me like a growing flood. "All I did was survive by a lucky chance so I could shed blood and feel guilty about it."

"But you want to help us now," Caesiem stated, his tone uncertain.

"I want to help my people." I hesitated. "And I don't really want to rule in a new government, as Renni suggested. Even if I need to be a figurehead..." I sighed. "I'm not sure about that either. But I want to do *something*. The Elders are failing. Or they just don't care."

Looking up, I saw our destination in front of us. It was one of the smallest, shabbiest homes on the street, its stonework crumbling and its windows covered in dirty, torn fabric that couldn't keep out the insects. I stepped forward to knock on the door.

Beside me, Caesiem fidgeted with his shirtsleeves before he dared to meet my eyes again. "Look," he said slowly, "I already told you, I respect your beliefs and vows as a nun. I was tired when we spoke earlier, but I think it's only right if I say something now. You don't have to join us at the ball. I don't want you to ruin your life here because I interfered."

His uncertainty took me aback.

Before I could answer, the door swung open. Eliho'an, a young widow, greeted us, looking frantic as she cradled a crying infant in her arms while two others—a small boy and girl—latched onto her legs. They looked dirty and thin, far too thin. As soon as she saw us, Eliho'an broke into a beaming smile that transformed her anxious face and eagerly invited us inside.

I could sense the weight of Caesiem's stare as he took in the meager surroundings: the scant furniture, the empty cupboards in the kitchen, and an underlying stench that often lingered in the impoverished households I visited. It was the sickly-sweet smell of rot and decay, from bad food and, sometimes, illness. But this was always one of the worst homes I visited, and it constantly weighed on my heart. Eliho'an was like most former slaves—with no known living family to help her care for her children and a meager income as a Forwyn healer, she relied on the generosity of neighbors and the Circle of Serenity to survive.

Caesiem and I set to work unpacking the food and medicine we'd carried in our baskets and then helped Eliho'an with a few cleaning chores around the house as she fed her children. I took a turn to cuddle her sick baby. Caesiem sat beside me on the too-small couch as I held the infant boy, who, despite his fever, watched me quietly, his gaze curious and open. I glanced up, meeting Caesiem's eyes, and something in my chest caught. Hurriedly, I looked back down, grasping the baby's hand and trying to ignore how self-conscious I felt. How close Caesiem was in this enclosed space. Or the fact that my other hand rested on the couch, a mere inch from his. If he wanted, he could shift, could brush his fingers over mine.

I cursed inwardly.

As we bid goodbye to Eliho'an and her family, even Caesiem received a warm hug from the children. He grinned and lifted them, whirling them until they giggled wildly.

In these moments, there wasn't a doubt in my mind that Caesiem cared about my people. His own life had taught him about want, about suffering, and his heart was full of compassion. Misguided as he was, he had good intentions.

When Caesiem and I stepped back out into the street, empty baskets on our arms, the sun hung low and blood-red in the sky. One of Eliho'an's neighbors waved to us from her open window before drawing the curtains closed. A mottled grey and black cat slunk out of a nearby alleyway, its ears flattened against its head as it hissed and darted past us. The distant sounds of the busier city districts had faded with the oncoming evening, transforming from bustling and chaotic to rhythmic and peaceful. Somewhere a bell tolled the hour.

Even Alrenor's usual stifling summer heat was melting into something mild, the briny sea breeze brushing through Inalgoth's cramped streets with all the comfort of a cool hand across a fevered brow. Autumn was coming.

We turned onto a busier street lined with finer residences. A carriage waited at the curb as an elegantly dressed Alrenian couple climbed inside. On the far corner, a Forwyn guard stood stiffly surveying the road as two other Alrenian couples strolled along, chatting and laughing. When they noticed Caesiem and me, they shot us ugly looks before turning away, as if we weren't even worth more than a passing glance. A half-hearted disgust. We were beneath them, little more than troublesome rats infesting their alleys and occasionally daring to make their presence known in their perfect streets.

It wasn't until we crossed to another road that Caesiem turned to me, a mischievous grin lighting up his face. He lifted a fist and opened it to reveal a necklace glittering against his palm.

I froze mid-step, staring dumbly at the necklace. "How did you…?"

He smirked. "That lady was too consumed with herself and her partner to notice us for long." He handed the necklace to me with a flourish. "It was easy."

Frowning, I shook my head. "You stole it," I hissed fiercely, eyes darting around to make sure no one was close enough to hear. "I can't wear stolen jewelry."

Caesiem scoffed. "The woman is clearly rich enough to buy another, but *you* need something convincing to wear to the Autumn Ball." He flashed me a crooked grin, his eyes bright in the gathering darkness. "Consider it my gift to you."

"Caesiem."

"Do you want me to turn around and give it back to her?" he asked, gesturing vaguely behind us.

My eyes widened in alarm. "No!"

He shrugged carelessly. "The way all those Alrenians looked at you, you know they mistreat your people and deserve far worse. This is just a minor inconvenience."

This time, I fought back a smile. "True."

"But *you*. You deserve all the finery in the world." This time, Caesiem's smile was all charm.

I rolled my eyes, even if his flattery still wormed its way into my heart.

"So," he went on, "there's nothing left to do but for you to put it on."

I lifted the necklace to scrutinize it. Composed of several fine chains of gold, it was the most expensive piece of jewelry I'd ever held in my life. Delicate pearls and diamonds hung from each chain, while a stunning pendant dangled from the lowest one. It was shaped like a simple flower with five petals, each set with a shimmering diamond.

"Do you need help?" Caesiem asked, but I'd already lifted the chain to my neck and fastened the clasp.

Pressing my lips into a firm line, I shoved the necklace under my shirt to conceal it and marched past Caesiem, my empty basket swinging from my arm.

"I never thought I'd see the day I owned stolen property," I muttered when he'd caught up. "I'm a nun, not some…thief."

Silence hung over us. Caesiem didn't seem troubled by my foul mood; instead, his expression turned thoughtful.

"I've been meaning to ask you… Why *did* you leave the palace?" Caesiem didn't pull his gaze away from the street or break his stride. "You could have been a leader there, an advisor to the Elders or some other influential figure. You could have helped your people politically. Why did you become a nun instead?"

I hesitated. His voice sounded genuinely curious, not judgmental, but the very fact that he'd asked those questions meant he didn't understand. I watched my empty basket swinging like a pendulum from my hand, moving in time with my steps.

As we crept deeper into the city, we passed inns with their windows aglow, and the scents of chimney smoke, roasted meat, and fresh bread lingered in the air. Nearby, a baker was locking his door, the aroma of sugar and pastry dough lingering around him, warm and inviting. I inhaled deeply, my stomach growling with the thought of dinner waiting for us back at the abbey.

"I couldn't stay there," I said at last, tossing my head to force the hair out of my face. My braids slid over my shoulders, tickling the back of my neck.

"Because of the guilt," Caesiem finished for me, glancing up to meet my gaze. In the gathering night, his eyes were startlingly blue, as if they caught every ounce of the dimming light and reflected it. "But didn't you think perhaps you could do more for your people there?"

I shrugged. "Maybe, maybe not. From what you tell me, it sounds as if the Elders are in love with their own power more than they're in love with their ability to help our people," I said bitterly. "All I know is living in that palace was living with my nightmares surrounding me every day." I repressed a shudder. "Every shadow held a horrible memory. I was young when I lost my mother, but she'd once served there before she was sent away. Slave families were often separated." I swallowed hard, trying to fight the tears stinging my eyes. I told myself it was pointless to mourn a family I'd barely had, just as it was ridiculous to grieve for a father I'd never met. But no matter what I told myself, the pain never faded. "When I tried to find her, I found out she'd already died."

Caesiem's eyes widened, and he opened his mouth as if to say something, but I cut him off. I didn't want his sympathy. I couldn't listen to it. If he said anything, I was positive I would crumble right there, dissolving into embarrassing sobs on the streets of Inalgoth.

"And the palace was where my brother was killed," I went on. For a moment, I squeezed my eyes shut. A tear leaked down my cheek, but I wiped it away quickly with my free hand. "I couldn't stay there with all that guilt, with all those memories," I whispered.

Caesiem stopped dead in the street, turning to face me. His bright eyes were filled with something that didn't look like pity—I couldn't tell what it was. Maybe because my own eyes were swimming with tears. His brow furrowed, and before I was fully conscious of what was happening, he was reaching for me.

A Forwyn guard marched down the road, scanning the darkened shops and locked doors carefully before passing us. Someone inside the nearby inn was singing and strumming a jiadro. Overhead, the Keepers were flying their nightly rounds, the dragons' wings beating like discordant pulses. *Thud. Thud. Thud thud thud. Thud.*

But beneath my ear, Caesiem's heartbeat was steady. My cheeks were hot and itchy from my tears, the wetness already making his shirt stick to my face. His arms held me closely but gently, warm and grounding. Everything else melted away as I let my grief wash over me; as the memories, cloudy with time and pain, flickered through my mind. My little brother Edi. His quiet laughter, his stubborn smile. His shy, reserved nature that concealed his strength and courage to anyone who didn't know him. Together, we'd kept our memories of Mother alive and our dreams for escape, for a better future, from collapsing into despair.

And then, one day, Edi had been ripped from me forever. By Empress Karye, cruel and arrogant and unfeeling. Empress Karye, whom I'd killed hoping revenge would fill the emptiness inside me, only to find that the void had opened wider. Now it was a yawning, gaping cavern. Endless. Full of shadows and guilt and grief and anger and eternal nothingness.

My heart was black with bloodshed, and full of holes.

"Lo," Caesiem murmured, and in that one word there lived a world of emotions.

That heart full of holes pounded in my ears. Heat swept through me, from my cheeks to my toes. Caesiem's fingers tightened around my arms and then slipped around my back, tugging me closer, and I leaned into him. He smelled like soap, filled with an aroma of zesty spices that tickled my nose, and something else. It reminded me of the brine of the sea, the foaming waves crashing along a rocky shore on a moonlit night. The creak of boats near the abandoned building in the docks. Secrets. Spying. Thievery and tricks.

Scowling, I pressed my hands against his chest and shoved him away. Caesiem stumbled back, muttering a curse, and I whirled away, running down the street.

Elhani, forgive me. Elhani, guide me.

"Lo!" Caesiem called out, chasing after me. "I'm sorry."

I couldn't stop, couldn't look back. To stop meant to analyze my feelings—to know, deep down, I'd already made my choice. So I kept running.

My footsteps beat out a steady rhythm to my endless prayer. *Guide me guide me guide me.*

CHAPTER TWENTY-TWO

Jalie

THERE HAD TO BE A careful art to my poisoning method. With Kovi and me trapped in my quarters together for the foreseeable future, it was difficult to have a moment of privacy. He was too alert, too dedicated to his assigned task. I couldn't let him suspect me.

When I seized a spoon from the breakfast tray the next morning, he watched me warily. I seated myself at my vanity and pulled apart the blood-red corrilys, tearing the blossoms from their stems and then picking off the petals, one by one. Selecting an empty jar from my collection of cosmetics, I laid the first petal within the jar and crushed it with the back of the spoon. Its musky scent permeated the air, filling my nose with an odor that was also faintly spicy. Strong and sweet. Alluring and deadly. I inhaled deeply, relishing the powerful feeling washing over me. Here at last was a tool to help me seize control of my life, and eventually, my empire.

Kovi's footsteps were almost silent as he shuffled up behind me and peered over my shoulder. My eyes caught his in my mirror's reflection, and I pursed my lips to conceal the smile threatening to overtake my face.

"What are you doing?" he asked. The curiosity in his eyes and the confused crease on his brow were maddening. How could he make my heart skip a beat with only a look? With only the sensation of his warm breath on my cheek when I turned my head toward him?

I ground my teeth together, willing my strange reactions away. It didn't matter how he looked or how compassionate he could be, he was my enemy. For an instant, I closed my eyes and imagined his father slaying my mother. I remembered Elder Ettonou's rough hands bruising me. I let those thoughts fuel my anger and direct my purpose.

Besides, I didn't have to *kill* Kovi. I only had to make sure he wasn't in my way.

"What's made you so interested in my cosmetics?" I asked demurely.

"I thought you'd gathered the flowers for a vase," Kovi mumbled, shaking his head and stepping back. He shrugged.

I couldn't help the disappointment that struck as soon as he moved away. The downside to being trapped within my own quarters was that he was the only person I had to talk to, the only one who could help distract me from boredom. It seemed a cruel twist of fate that I could want Kovi nearby just as much as I wanted him to turn around and leave.

Maybe I need to play nice for my plan to work, I decided. "The flowers were crushed. I've decided to use their perfume instead," I explained.

The sound of dragon wings outside pulled my eyes toward the windows in my balcony doors. My heart ached with longing to see the dragons again, to fly with Ryke over the capital. I knew the Dragon Keepers were out there now, circling overhead during their morning ride. The desire to step outside and drink in the sight was overwhelming.

I stood abruptly. The corrilys and my tangled feelings about using it on Kovi could wait. I set down the spoon beside my jar of smashed flower petals and spun around to face him. "I'm eating breakfast outside."

Without waiting for his response, I strode to the washroom to scrub the lingering corrilys stains from my hands. Mother had taught me all about the plants in our gardens, and though corrilys in small doses could help someone sleep, a large enough dose would ensure they never woke again.

"You need to know about poisons and how to protect yourself from them," she'd told me one day. "An empress will always be a target. This one is easy to build an immunity against, since little doses only make you sleepy. Others will be less pleasant."

It was the first poison we'd brewed together. I'd sipped the corrilys tea in small doses over weeks, then months, until at last, it barely affected me. Over the years since Mother had been murdered, I'd collected and brewed corrilys regularly to keep up my immunity. At least, I had until recent days, when I'd been confined to Kovi's watchful eye. But I knew a couple weeks wouldn't undo years of work.

It was the perfect poison for me to work with.

When I exited the washroom, Kovi was standing beside the breakfast tray, filling a plate with pastries and fruit. "You're not sitting out there alone," he reminded me.

I joined him, preparing my own plate and a mug of tea. As he poured his coffee, I studied him out of the corner of my eye. He added the smallest splash of cream to the bitter brown liquid.

Kovi went outside first, his eyes scanning the grounds before he pushed open the balcony doors and sank into one of the chairs overlooking the garden. Stepping out behind him, I drank in the warm scent from the orange trees nearby, their leaves gilded from the bright sun. The air was mild today, not as damp or stifling as it had been before, a reminder that autumn was near. Wispy clouds painted the sky, where several dragons soared and dipped low. The sound of their beating wings rumbled over the birdsong in the garden, making my heart swell until I thought it would burst with the ache to be one of those Dragon Keepers.

Smothering my sigh, I seated myself beside Kovi, laying my plate and mug on the table between us before leaning toward him.

His eyes flicked to me mid-sip, and he drew away the coffee mug from his mouth. A curl of steam rose from the liquid as he frowned. "What?" he asked.

In the morning light, the gold flecks in his eyes were warm, making even stoic, fearless Kovi seem softer. A tinge of regret about my plan to poison him fluttered in my stomach, only for a moment.

Don't give in to sentimental feelings, I thought, feeling cross with myself.

"What is it about coffee the Forwyn like so much?" I asked, hoping my tone was as airy and curious as I wanted it to sound. *Please just think I'm bored,* I thought anxiously.

With the smallest laugh, Kovi held out his cup toward me, his sleeve sliding up just enough to reveal the band of colorful ribbons he wore around his wrist. "Did you want to try some?"

I hesitated before reaching for his mug. My fingers brushed against his as I grasped it, sending a warm jolt all the way up my arm. Biting back my gasp of surprise, I plucked the mug from his grasp and lifted it. For one annoying instant, I remembered Kovi's lips pressed against it and my stomach fluttered a little. When I met his gaze, his dark eyes flicked to my mouth, and I realized, with a jolt, that he must have been thinking the same thing. Heat flushed across my cheeks.

I noted Kovi's bemused expression as he watched me take a sip. The hot liquid coated my tongue with its bitter flavor, rich and earthy. I swallowed and cringed, shoving the mug back toward Kovi while he laughed outright.

"Maybe it's an acquired taste," he said. His smile was broad and genuine. My stomach plummeted.

Is he playing mind games too? Why be so kind? Why smile and pretend we're friends?

Confusion and frustration boiled inside me. It was hard to scheme against an enemy when he *refused* to be my enemy. When he seemed to genuinely care.

All part of his trick to make me let my guard down, I thought. *Maybe he thinks he can convince me to side with his people and happily play the role of obedient, powerless empress.*

"It's disgusting," I proclaimed. Unfortunately, though, as strong as it was, I wasn't convinced the coffee could mask the taste of corrilys. The poison's spicy, slightly sweet taste would be too different and therefore too noticeable.

Kovi's smile turned teasing. "That's because you put enough cream and sugar in your tea for an army."

I scowled. "Why wouldn't I want it to taste sweet? Who wants to grimace and force down swallows of—dirt water?"

He laughed again, and I couldn't help myself—I drank it in. His voice was often a low rumble, and his laughter matched that timbre, but it was heartier. Full of life. It was strange to think this young man with this carefree laugh could be full of as much anger and grief as I was.

I shoved those thoughts away and embraced the moment. If he wanted to be obliging and kind, I could match the mood. If he wanted me to trust him, I could play his game just as well.

"Have you ever considered adding some sugar or cinnamon for flavor?" I asked. I sat forward in my chair, leaning across the table toward him. His eyes were still dancing with merriment, so I matched his grin.

"The coffee has plenty of flavor on its own. Why would I want to cover it up?"

"It's strong enough you wouldn't cover it. Just…complement it." I looked at him through lowered lashes. "What's not to love about something sweet?"

Kovi cocked his head to the side, studying me. "All right," he said slowly. "Sweeten the coffee. I'll try it."

My pulse pounded in my ears. Would he let me take his coffee inside and tamper with it? Was this my moment?

Not yet, I thought, scanning the garden and trying to be casual about it. There was no sign of the Alrenian woman with the red hair, the one I'd seen before. I didn't want to escape without contacting her. Maybe she could lead me to the other Alrenians who wanted to avenge the empire. My growing army.

Rising from my seat, I took Kovi's outstretched coffee and padded back inside. Unsurprisingly, Kovi followed me, and disappointment poked at my burgeoning hope. If he didn't trust me to be alone for a single moment now, when he seemed friendly, perhaps even flirtatious, then it was unlikely he'd leave me unsupervised later. Poisoning someone watching my every move was going to be difficult.

Pouring more cream into his coffee until it was the color of caramel, I spooned some sugar into the mixture and then selected one of the spice jars resting on the tray. I often had a habit of sprinkling cinnamon and sugar onto my toast. Adding the cinnamon, I stirred the coffee until I was sure it was mixed perfectly and then lifted the mug to inhale its scent. I took a long sip and closed my eyes in delight.

"Delicious," I murmured. Even better than its taste was the fact that I was sure it could conceal the corrilys' flavor. If I could convince Kovi to let me make his coffee for him again this way—and *if* I could slip in the one additional ingredient when he wasn't looking.

Before I could even reopen my eyes, Kovi was beside me, gently prying my fingers off his mug. He sniffed at it uncertainly before lifting his gaze to mine. My heart skipped a beat—just one pathetic moment of weakness—when he gave me a crooked smile. He drank slowly and then lowered the cup, his face contemplative.

"Well?" I asked.

"Not bad. A little sweet for my preference."

I pretended to pout, crossing my arms and sticking out my bottom lip. "You won't want me to make it again?"

Kovi laughed, and this time, I couldn't read him. Was he truly amused, or was that laughter forced? His eyes were as warm as ever, his smile gentle, but something seemed off. Did he suspect me?

"You want to make me coffee?"

My heart lurched. I was being *too* kind, too quickly. Wanting to make friendly conversation when he was my only companion might make sense, but wanting to do something kind for him…that was a little unbelievable.

I shrugged, forcing a smile. "I suppose what I really meant is that I want to make coffee like that for myself every day. Would you share your coffee pot?"

Kovi's shoulders relaxed slightly, and it was only then I realized he'd ever tensed in the first place. "Now that sounds familiar. I didn't think you would ever stoop to make anyone coffee—certainly not an enemy," he said lightly, his grin still in place. "I haven't forgotten how much you hate me and want to destroy me."

It was strange for him to mention our animosity so casually. As strange as the fact that he didn't act like my enemy anymore, not at all. Suddenly, I remembered what he'd told me yesterday about his magic building a connection with the person he used it on. Did he still feel that with me? Is that what made him compassionate?

No, this is just proof he's playing a game with you, I thought darkly.

But…did he *still* sense my emotions, even now? He'd mentioned he didn't know how long the connection would last, that it might never vanish. If he could feel everything I felt, that could make my plan much more challenging.

"Let's go back outside," I said abruptly, longing to change the subject. I wanted to see him drop his guard again so I could refine my plan, and I hoped I'd find the Alrenian woman, too. The difficulty, of course, would be communicating with her when Kovi was present.

This time, I strode past Kovi and set foot on the balcony first. There—a flash of red behind a tree just below. My heart leapt to my throat in anticipation. She was here. The next instant, she was darting, swift and silent, toward the palace wall until she was almost directly beneath my balcony, beside the orange tree that grew close enough for me to touch. She was out of sight, as long as Kovi didn't crane his neck to the left and peer over the railing…

I twirled back toward Kovi, praying he didn't detect anything amiss from my expression, praying he didn't see the Alrenian woman lurking in the palace's shadow. He had a book tucked under his arm, an inkwell and pen in his hands.

"It's incredibly boring to watch the dragons when you're not astride one," I declared with a dramatic sigh.

"Are you saying you've already changed your mind about being out here? We just stepped outside," Kovi said slowly, lifting a cool eyebrow. "And you haven't even touched your breakfast."

"I'm not hungry," I lied. "It makes me feel sick to watch your people fly *my* dragons." *That* wasn't a lie.

Kovi rolled his eyes.

Hesitating, I tipped my chin toward his book, still resting near his chair. "What are you reading?"

Shooting me a pointed look, he pushed past me to return to his seat. He set everything down and picked up a strawberry, eating it slowly, deliberately, as he stared at me with a stoic expression. "It's believable when you say you want to talk to me because you have no one else to talk to. But it's not nearly as believable when you're trying to ask me so many questions, before you've even touched your breakfast. You can't be *that* interested in me," he said. "Not beyond the clear physical attraction, anyway."

My cheeks flushed scarlet. "Wh-what?"

"I love how you keep feigning ignorance, even when I can *sense* your emotions. I know what desire feels like." Kovi grinned and chose an orange, peeling it carefully. "But we're not friends," he added bluntly.

"I know," I bit out, and I did—but something in my chest ached to hear him say it aloud. To remind me that the only person I had to talk to, the only soul who bothered to comfort me these days, didn't care the slightest bit about who I was or what happened to me. Even if it had been a farce, I longed for his earlier friendly manner.

"So you don't really care about my interests. Maybe you like the way coffee tastes when you add all of that sugar to it"—he gestured toward my bedroom, where I realized he'd left his half-full mug on the tray—"and maybe you *are* bored. But there's no way you want to know what I'm reading."

I set my hands on my hips. "What are you saying?"

A loud cry echoed throughout the arena near the Dragon Keep— one of the Keepers had landed his dragon and was shouting and punching his fists in the air. My heart lurched with envy as I stared at his distant form leaping off an ocean blue dragon and running his fingertips along its scales.

"What are you planning, Jalie?" he asked in a low voice.

It wasn't the first time he'd used my name, but it still startled me every time, making me snap my gaze back to his face. It was oddly comforting to hear my name come from his lips, the way his Forywn accent softened it and stretched it out, like a name to be savored. He studied me carefully, his eyes never leaving mine. My mouth went dry, so I swallowed.

"You want something from me," he continued. His gaze flicked toward the Keep and back to me.

I pressed my mouth into a thin line and hazarded a quick glance into the garden. I didn't see the Alrenian woman. Disappointment fluttered in my belly. Had I missed my opportunity? I strode toward the balcony and leaned against the railing.

Tied carefully to the opposite side was a roll of paper. The woman must have scaled the nearby orange tree when Kovi and I were talking. My fingers tingled to reach out and untie the string immediately, but I couldn't let Kovi see. I turned to face him again.

"Fine," I said, crossing my arms over my chest and glaring at him. "I want you to let me see the dragons again. To fly again. If you speak to the Elders, you could convince them."

Kovi popped an orange slice into his mouth and stared at the Keep thoughtfully as another dragon landed.

With his attention elsewhere, I turned again, pretending to watch the dragons too. I loosened the string and curled the paper in my fist.

"I could send a message to my father," Kovi said at last.

Spinning around, I grinned. "Soon?"

The corner of his mouth twitched. "Tomorrow."

"You know," I said, lifting my skirts to settle into my chair, "I think my appetite has returned."

"Oh, has it?" Kovi asked, shaking his head and opening his book. He dipped his pen into the inkwell and began skimming over the pages, occasionally writing in the book's margins.

My breath caught in my throat as I lifted a pastry with the hand holding the paper. Cautiously, I worked to unroll it quickly. I took a bite, keeping the paper pressed firmly in my hand, and then, preparing to take another, stopped long enough to stare at the tiny message scrawled across the wrinkled, torn sheet resting in my palm. *Before the Autumn Ball—fourteenth hour. By Ilahnna's fountain.*

CHAPTER TWENTY-THREE

Lo

CAESIEM WAS NOTHING BUT A whisper and a shadow in the hall when I cracked open my door. If not for the fact that he was directly opposite my entryway, I likely wouldn't have ever noticed him at all.

As it was, my eyes locked with his immediately. It was almost eerie to see Caesiem standing so still and quiet. So unlike the version of him I normally witnessed.

"Where are you going?" I hissed, suspicion prickling up my spine. For a moment, I wondered how Caesiem had left the infirmary unnoticed until I remembered that we'd moved him to an unoccupied bedroom this evening.

"I have business, remember?" Caesiem murmured. There was a tautness around his mouth, a stiff set to his shoulders. Maybe he was ashamed of himself. He should be.

I crossed my arms and leaned back against the doorframe. "You're supposed to be resting and recovering."

The corner of his mouth quirked, just a little. "If you let me walk around half of Inalgoth, I think I can handle walking down to the pub." He hesitated. "It's urgent."

"If you didn't steal, you wouldn't have these problems," I said, more harshly than I'd meant.

A flash of pain flickered across Caesiem's face, so swiftly I wondered if I'd imagined it. "It's more complicated than that."

I rolled my eyes. "What, are you a compulsive thief?"

He grinned half-heartedly, and I knew he was dodging the truth. "Something like that," he lied.

After a beat, Caesiem spoke again, studying me carefully. "Speaking of people not doing what they're supposed to, you're supposed to be staying within the abbey walls. Where are you off to?"

I glowered at him. "I can't sleep."

"You're going out again?" Caesiem hesitated. "It isn't safe."

"I'll stay in the backyard. Run the perimeter a few times or something." I shrugged.

His gaze was piercing, trying to determine if I'd lie to him the way he so easily lied to me. In a breath, he was right in front of me, far away enough to still be considered respectful, but near enough that I could sense his body heat. Or maybe that was my imagination. Surely I wouldn't notice from two feet away.

"Why can't you sleep?" he asked.

I loved and hated that he cared enough to ask. "I thought your business was urgent."

Caesiem ignored my attempt to avoid the topic. "Is it because of…" He swallowed, averting his eyes. "The reasons you left the palace?" Ever since I'd run from him earlier this evening, I'd done my best to evade him. I'd seated myself far away at dinner, and when he'd sat beside me during evening worship, pleading with me to forgive him, I'd muttered that I did. And then I'd ignored him.

Or I'd tried to. His presence had been incredibly distracting, from the intent, respectful way he'd attended to everything Naina had said, to the tiny smile he'd tossed my way when I'd lifted my voice to sing with my sisters.

Even now, in the dark hallway, Caesiem's eyes were bright and intent. Once again, I recalled how I'd fancied the attention of a Forwyn boy at the palace. He'd been handsome and friendly, and I'd thought I felt something in his presence. But Caesiem? He wasn't even touching me, and yet I could feel the heat of his gaze scanning my face, down to my lips. It made my heart pound and my stomach flutter. No one had ever made me feel like this, just with one look.

Maybe that was why I confessed what no one else knew. The things that kept me running at night, forever haunting my waking and sleeping moments. "Yes," I whispered. "I can't sleep at night because of…memories from my time at the palace."

Caesiem extended his hand, letting it hover in the air. So close. Just a few inches more, and he'd be cupping my cheek in his hand, or brushing a braid back behind my ear. He'd be grasping my hand in his or tracing my jawline. There were infinite possibilities in those few inches of air between us.

He wanted to touch me. He knew he shouldn't touch me.

My heart hammered against my ribcage. I *wanted* him to touch me.

Caesiem let his hand drop back to his side. "Business," he repeated, jolting our thoughts away from the forbidden. He stepped away, light and graceful as air. "I'll be back before morning, so Naina doesn't fret." He offered me a half-smile, and then he vanished into the darkness.

I sucked in a breath the moment he left, thinking it would cool me, but the hall was still stifling. I needed the fresh air waiting outside.

Slipping through the abbey and out into the yard, I threw myself into some of my usual routines—push-ups, curls, and sparring matches with imaginary partners. I punched and kicked the dummies until straw flew out of them. Until I disturbed one of the chickens roosting in their coop.

Tossing thoughts of Caesiem aside, I naturally returned to the other topics worrying me. I couldn't stop thinking about the Alrenian resistance members, and how even now, they could be murdering another one of my people and forcing a Forwyn slave to set up the body for part of their hideous display. Nausea danced along my tongue.

There was no way I could determine their target, but a part of me longed to leave the safety of these walls and scour the city. Despite what I'd told Caesiem. Despite the fact that I had no idea how I'd stop the Alrenians if I ever found them.

For the empress.

I balled my hands into fists. The best way I could serve my people was to be the *amara'rekni* again. I needed to survive to make it to the Autumn Ball and help Renni and his vigilantes stop Jaliana and her followers.

Dread curled in my stomach, but I forced it down. No matter the cost, I had to save my people.

Elhani, forgive me, I prayed for the thousandth time.

Naina's voice startled me from my thoughts. I spun around—but she wasn't behind me. She was using her magic, speaking into my mind. My noise out in the yard must have woken her.

You need to sleep, ahnla. Her tone was gentle yet firm, coaxing a smile to my lips. *Give whatever troubles you to Elhani, and get to bed.*

⟨⟨⟨⟨⟨

True to his word, Caesiem was back the next morning. He met me on the stairs as he exited the washroom, dark hair damp and slightly curling. Naina had sent Pauni'a to purchase some new clothes for our guest earlier, meaning he now wore a loose-fitting shirt and pants in the same plain grey the sisters and I wore. The outfit of a monk.

I couldn't help grinning at his expense, but he just laughed with me.

"Me? Dressed as a monk?" he whispered as we descended the stairs. He leaned in close enough for me to hear, close enough I had to repress a shiver. "That's laughable."

Caesiem followed me as I fed the chickens and gathered their eggs. Naina had already gone into the stable to milk Tila, but she was far enough away that I knew she'd be out of earshot.

"Will we meet with Renni and the others tonight?" I asked Caesiem quietly as I added an egg to my basket.

Caesiem paused, swinging his basket and rocking back on his heels. "Not tonight. I have other…business." He made a face.

"The Autumn Ball is only a few days away," I said, trying to keep my tone measured even as my frustration mounted.

"I know," Caesiem said apologetically, reaching for an egg. "I just…if you really want to, we'll talk with them again before the ball. But I don't…" He studied the dirt, not meeting my eyes. "I don't want you to give up your life for this cause. I've seen you with the sisters, with your people. You have purpose and peace and happiness here."

I squeezed the basket handle tighter. "And nightmares and helplessness," I whispered. "I won't ever be able to get the images of those…" I swallowed. "Those murdered Forwyn out of my head."

"I know," Caesiem repeated. He finally met my eyes, his own full of grief. "I shouldn't have ever dragged you into this. You're not…what I expected." Setting the last egg in his basket, he straightened.

I listed my head. "What do you mean?"

"Like you said, you're not a fierce warrior." As soon as the words were out of his mouth, he lifted his hands, almost defensively. "But don't take that the wrong way. You *are* fierce. You're strong and kind and passionate and loyal and *good*." His neck reddened as he spoke, and I jerked my gaze away, suddenly overwhelmed. "I guess I figured I'd find an empress slayer already prepared to assassinate whoever she needed to, not a nun who was fighting for peace."

I'm not good, I thought, imagining the countless times I had to do penance and beg forgiveness, to give offerings and wipe away tears in Naina's presence. But I shrugged and said, "Sometimes fighting for peace means you actually have to fight.

Caesiem nodded, tight-lipped. "If you're sure, we'll go the night before the ball. Just know, you probably won't be able to change your mind once you learn their plans." He shifted on his feet uncomfortably.

I met his gaze unflinchingly. "I understand."

❮❮❮❮❮

Starlight turned the sea to liquid silver as it swirled and foamed beneath the rickety bridge. With each groan and creak of the wooden boards under my feet, my stomach lurched. Heat rushed through my veins and my palms grew clammy when I imagined fanged monstrosities circling in the deep or a tentacle emerging from below.

Mist kissed my nose, and I drew a deep breath, inhaling the scent of rotting fish and brine. Though the air was still cool, the breeze had died as the mist settled over the water. I longed for a gust of wind to dry the sweat gathering along the back of my neck.

Just before me, Caesiem walked cautiously, his hand once again clutching the pendant hanging from his neck.

"Did you encounter sea creatures on your trip over from Teramyl?" I asked in a hushed voice.

Caesiem shot me a questioning glance. "Do you really want to hear about that now?"

I swallowed, trying to relax the tightness in my throat. "I thought they didn't swim this close to shore."

Caesiem shrugged, one hand still on his pendant. "Better to be careful, right?"

Earlier that night—after days of helping with abbey chores and tasks, of participating in training sessions and prayer time, and after nights of vanishing for his mysterious "business"—Caesiem had sought me out.

"The Autumn Ball is tomorrow," he'd said, reminding me of what I already knew while he watched me jump for one of the bars placed in the yard. I pulled myself up until my chin hovered above it. Sweat stung my eyes as I met his gaze. "If you still want to, we meet tonight to finalize plans."

"All right," I huffed out, dropping and then pulling myself up again. "I want to go."

Caesiem looked tense and unusually still, but he hadn't argued.

A few hours later, evening worship over and my sisters fast asleep, Caesiem had crept from his guest room to mine. Together, we'd slipped from the abbey and walked the now familiar path toward the abandoned shed out on the docks.

Along with my ribbons, I wore the necklace Caesiem had stolen for me, tucked carefully beneath my shirt. It was likely worth more than the entire abbey. As much as I hated the Alrenians, guilt clung to me like a cloak, and I wondered if I should have thrown the necklace back at Caesiem when I'd had the chance.

As we neared the doorway, Caesiem hesitated, pausing on the creaking boards to glance over his shoulder at me.

"Are you trying to talk me out of this again?" I asked with a half-hearted laugh. I didn't want him to give me another chance to turn away, not when my mind felt like a battlefield. *But the guidespirit wanted you here,* I reminded myself. *Maybe Elhani will excuse you from breaking your vows, since you followed this call. Don't be a coward.*

Brow furrowed, Caesiem shook his head and turned away. "No," he muttered. "I know your mind is made up."

At that instant, the door swung open.

"Get in here," Eloreth snapped, waving frantically. "You're both making enough noise for the entire city to hear."

Caesiem and I swept forward, and I released an audible sigh of relief once we crossed the threshold and Eloreth shut the door.

"So what's the plan?" Caesiem asked immediately, his grin wide and carefree. Nothing like the uncertain, weighted expression he'd worn only moments ago. He turned toward Renni and the others, who were already clustered around the table.

Renni leaned forward eagerly. "Come, sit down and find out." He declared it with an air of mystery, and I had the distinct impression he enjoyed the idea of leading a secret organization as much as he loved its cause.

As Caesiem, Eloreth, and I settled into our rickety seats, Renni beamed at us. "We've been collecting suitable clothing for tomorrow's ball."

With a flourish, Wilvhe and Mio'e drew vests, trousers, shirts, and dresses from a crate sitting behind them. All were in typical Alrenian fashion, the vivid colors and styles all adopted by the Forwyn nobility once they'd claimed control of the capital. Most were made from linen, the cuts flowing and loose to keep the clothing light and airy in the humid Alrenian weather.

"Try this one," Eloreth said, tossing me a long ivory gown.

I held it against myself, studying the intricate gold and blue beading on the bodice and the knotted gold and blue cords forming the straps of the dress. A matching sash hung from its narrow waist, from which the skirts draped so loosely I wondered how I'd move with all that extra fabric swishing around my feet.

My breath caught in my chest. It was the most beautiful piece of clothing I would ever wear. And I'd feel like an imposter in it. I loved it for its beauty and despised it for what it symbolized: the Alrenian court and its gruesome memories. Seeing that the Elders expected attendants of their Autumn Ball to dress in the Alrenian style was another disappointing reminder of all the ways the leadership had failed my people. Had failed me.

They were supposed to differ from Alrenian leadership, but sending Dragon Keepers to terrorize citizens and throwing lavish balls were all eerily familiar acts. My chest tightened just at the thought. When I'd left the palace, I'd thought my people had their freedom at last, but now I was wondering if we'd merely traded one tyrannical leadership for a new one.

There was no privacy in the small room we occupied, so we all slipped on the fine outfits over our clothes.

Renni finished tugging his blue vest over his shoulders and whistled. "You all look like fine members of the court," he said, winking at Mio'e. I was a little surprised to see a shy expression creep over her usually hardened face.

Beside me, Caesiem fidgeted restlessly with his shirt collar, alternatively tugging and straightening it until I could no longer restrain my urge to reach out and still his hands.

"Stop," I whispered.

We realized how close we stood in the same instant. Heat shot through me, but I didn't back away. We stood frozen, staring at one another, for a too-long breath. My hands were still clasping his, and I couldn't seem to bring myself to let go.

And then Caesiem shattered the haze in my mind, clearing his throat and pulling away with a sheepish laugh. "Sorry about that. I can never stay still." He gave me a half-grin. "It drives…" He paused. "Well, it drives everyone crazy, I think."

A'elli shot us a curious look, making me back up. Embarrassment radiated through me. What was I doing, losing my head around this young man?

As usual, my fingers strayed to the ribbons knotted around my throat. This time, though, I touched cold metal first. The reminder of the stolen necklace I wore only made me sweat. Impatiently, I strode to the corner and tugged the dress off.

"Well, our clothes fit," I said as I returned to the center of the room. My voice came out like a bark, demanding and annoyed. At least it was better than giving away my fear or shame. "Wilvhe invited us all. What time do we show up? What are we doing when we get there?"

"We'll all arrive together ten minutes before seventeenth hour so Wilvhe can confirm we're his invited guests," Renni explained, reluctantly pulling off his vest and laying it back in the crate. "Naturally, the goal is to ensure we all spread out, pretend to be there only to enjoy the party, behave like wealthy members of society…"

"Are you planning to assassinate the empress right in front of the Elders?" I cut in. "How exactly do you plan for this to work without being killed before you ever step near her?"

Tension fell over the room. Everyone's eyes turned to me, weighing my worth in this venture. I could almost read their thoughts: *Is she a liability? Will she back us up or betray us? Will she cause us to fail?*

Renni shrugged, but I could tell he was feigning carelessness. "We have plans in place for various circumstances."

Mio'e shot me a dark look. "Are you truly with us?"

I spoke through clenched teeth. "Just remember, if we fail, the

Elders will make Jaliana out to be a martyr for their cause, and we'll all be executed. We won't save any lives."

"If you're truly loyal to Elhani and his cause, nun, you'll understand our willingness to die for our people," Mio'e spat.

Eloreth's eyes bored into me like daggers. "We've been preparing and planning for a long time." Her eyes flicked briefly to Caesiem. "You either trust our cause or you don't. Are you with us, or not?"

I glanced at Renni. "If you tell me *every* piece of your plan," I demanded. "I refuse to walk in blindly. If you don't tell me everything, my ignorance could ruin us. By being a part of this, I'm risking my life too."

Caesiem shifted uncomfortably. His hands were in motion again, one at his side where his fingers drummed against his leg and the other toying with the pendant around his neck. "You don't have to be a part of this," he spoke up, and this time, everyone's eyes turned to him. His tapping fingers stilled, his gaze tearing away from me to study his friend's faces. "I'm only saying, I dragged her into this. She can still back out."

"Hardly," Eloreth said. "She knows too much. And she's supposed to be a leader or a figurehead, remember? Otherwise she's useless. Either she's helping us, or we're ensuring her silence."

Unease swam through me. Suddenly the air was stifling. The perpetual scents of brine, mildew, and rotting fish were overwhelming. I was going to be sick.

"Are you threatening her?" Caesiem demanded, his tone turning low and deep like the rumble of a slumbering beast awakening. Something dark flashed in his eyes.

I shoved myself between Caesiem and Eloreth before the tension could heighten any further. "All of that is beside the point," I said, shooting Caesiem a glare over my shoulder. He looked wounded. "I'm going with you. No need for threats." But when I glanced back at Eloreth, I kept my eyes narrowed. Just because I was willing to join them didn't mean I would pretend I trusted them.

"All right," Renni said, eagerly rubbing his hands together as if the last few minutes had never happened. He reminded me vaguely of an excitable puppy, always grinning, always ready for the next adventure. Always prepared to offer friendliness toward anyone. He seemed to think his bright manners could smooth over the brewing unease in the room. He was wrong.

As we discarded our fine attire, laying it back in the waiting crate, Caesiem pulled out the map of the palace I'd drawn, rolling it out over the table. We leaned forward, studying it, as Renni described everything their group had planned in Caesiem's and my absence.

CHAPTER TWENTY-FOUR

Jalie

NESRELLE'S VOICE JERKED ME AWAKE. "Why would you feel guilty that the curse took a Forwyn life?"

I sat up in bed, surrounded by a quiet night. Kovi was still asleep on my settee. Long shadows cast strange shapes along my walls. Perhaps this was only a dream.

Nesrelle's piercing eyes studied me shrewdly. "You begged for your life, and here you are. You longed for vengeance after the Forwyn slew your mother, and here it is. You want your throne, and you have the power that will help you reclaim it. Why feel guilty about any of that? I have given you everything you've wanted." Her red lips curled into an almost feral smile.

My heart pounded a staccato beat in my chest. "I didn't think the curse would kill," I said, my voice raspy, still thick with sleep. "I expected them to suffer. I didn't plan for them to die. It took me by surprise." Everything I said sounded weak, even in my own ears. It terrified me to admit my uncertainty to the Queen of Death.

"And what about your fears over this boy? He's a soldier of the enemy. He hates you. Stop hesitating, stop flirting, and poison him."

I blinked. "But…"

"Would your mother have wavered in her purpose, if anyone dared stand between her and her throne? Between her and her ability to save her people?"

My throat ached. "No," I whispered.

Nesrelle sneered. "Then don't waste the curse you carry. Don't waste this chance I've given you."

Nesrelle was gone in the blink of an eye, leaving my mind whirling.

As I rose from my bed, blood pumping wildly through my veins, I was enveloped in the lingering scent of corrilys. Over the past few days I'd continued to crush and boil petals, filling my rooms with its warm, drowsy odor. Now and then, I'd sensed Kovi's eyes on me as I worked or paged through books or found other ways to pass the time. I'd feared that maybe he suspected something. But mostly, we'd ignored each other. Kovi had alternated between reading and making notes in his book, writing in a journal, and pushing himself through rounds of exercises. Sometimes we sparred, because it was something we could do to pass the time, and occasionally we spoke, but it always felt like we were treading carefully. Trying to avoid the connection that we both wanted to ignore.

Now, with Nesrelle's words pounding through my brain, there were some things I couldn't ignore any longer. I strode purposefully toward Kovi, where he was sleeping on my settee, and tugged the blanket off his form. Immediately, he sat up, seizing me by both wrists with one hand while pressing a blade against my throat with the other. I didn't even have time to process the fact that he slept with a dagger beneath his pillow before he was standing and pulling me against him, only my trapped hands leaving space between us.

Kovi's breath was hot on my face, his heartbeat as erratic as mine. "What are you doing?" he asked in a low voice.

I didn't miss a beat. "You said you knew I wouldn't kill you."

Kovi's mouth twitched with suppressed amusement. "I'm confident, yes. But would I bet my life on it? No. I'm not a fool." His dark eyes searched my face. "Let me ask you again, what are you doing?"

It was as if my head were filled with honey. *Enemy,* I tried to remind myself. *Enemy.* But I was painfully conscious of the warmth of his body, of every one of his solid muscles as he held me close. My treacherous eyes lingered on his lips.

"I need to know," I said after my too-long pause. "How many…" *How many of my people have you killed?* I swallowed back the words, not sure I wanted to know the answer. As a Forwyn soldier, even a recent graduate, he had to have killed some. And wouldn't that knowledge remind me that he was my enemy? Wouldn't it help me to stop hesitating and make my move?

Slowly, Kovi lowered his dagger and uncurled his fingers from around my wrist, freeing my hands. He stepped back, creating space between us. I noticed the absence of his warmth almost as keenly as I'd felt it earlier.

He smirked. "You woke me in the middle of the night to ask me a question you can't finish?"

I dropped my gaze, overwhelmed by his piercing one. "I couldn't sleep."

Kovi settled back onto the settee, and after a moment, I sat beside him, still avoiding the way he studied me.

I changed tactics, switching to a new subject. "Can you still sense my emotions?" I asked hesitantly, terrified of the answer.

This time Kovi smiled fully. "Have you stayed up thinking of every question you've ever wanted to ask me?"

I tapped my fingers on my thigh impatiently, then fidgeted with the hem of my nightgown until I'd tugged it down farther.

Kovi sighed. "What do you think?" he asked, his lips taut and eyes averted.

My entire body was tense. "You feel them," I said uncomfortably.

"Some." His tone was soft, evasive.

The guilt over the horrible death Lady Leanai had suffered tugged on me again, even as Nesrelle's words seemed to whisper to me on the breeze. It hadn't been an honorable death, and it hadn't been an honorable kill. Lady Leanai and I hadn't faced one another as equals, allowing me to defeat my enemy fairly. Killing someone hadn't been at all like I'd imagined it would be, back when I'd trained under Alrenians. Back when I'd thought all my kills as a future empress would only ever be necessary and just.

According to Nesrelle, all I'd done was give a curse to Lady Leanai that she'd deserved to suffer. But the woman hadn't been a direct obstacle to my throne, and she wasn't one of the Elders who so ruthlessly slew my people. Had it been right for her to suffer and die, simply because she was Forwyn? Once, I wouldn't have hesitated over my answer. All Forwyn had seemed as evil to me as the Elders did. Now, knowing Kovi, I wasn't so sure.

I repressed a shudder as my eyes settled on my bed and I considered the long night looming before me. Nesrelle had woken me from nightmares only to leave me with my waking ones.

With the tumult in my mind, I didn't even bother to continue my conversation with Kovi. I shuffled across the room and curled up in my bed, wordlessly processing what Nesrelle had said. What Kovi had said.

As if Kovi sensed my reluctance to lie awake alone—likely feeling my anxious emotions—he followed me.

"I can't sleep," I repeated. "Can you…stay? Sleep here. I don't want to…be alone." Immediately, I hated myself for my weakness. But I didn't take back the question. I simply waited, trying to study his impassive face in the darkness.

Without a word, he nodded, lying down on the opposite side of my bed. It was so large that it maintained plenty of space between us, space neither of us crossed. But I could feel his presence like it was something tangible, a warm reassurance in the dark. It was a jolt of confusion and remorse and anger and fear. An electricity thrumming gently and painfully—welcome and unwelcome—all at once.

There was a long pause before Kovi spoke into the night.

"We have a choice, Jalie," he said, as if he could read my mind. As if he knew about the conversation I'd had earlier with Nesrelle. Or perhaps he was simply reminding himself. Maybe he was as confused as I was. "You and I? We might be angry, and we might have darkness inside. But maybe we don't have to be monsters."

❮❮❮❮❮

Without bothering to knock, Elder Ettonou stormed into my rooms as the golden rays of late morning kissed the sky on the day of the Autumn Ball. "Wake up, empress!" the Elder barked. "Kovi."

Sensing the figure looming over me, I jolted awake, heart racing. The first thing I registered was how close Kovi was, his arm draped loosely over my waist. I didn't have time to experience disgust or comfort or any other contradictory emotions, because Kovi was already wrenching away, leaping from my bed to stand at attention.

When I sat up, I saw the Elder's fierce glare and the two guards behind him. Between the guards, trapped in their relentless grips, was a steel-faced Alrenian man about my age. Two more guards trailed them, as if my chambers were to be flooded with angry Forwyn today. What was happening?

Before I could even stand, Elder Ettonou's gaze darted back and forth between Kovi and me. "Are you defiling my son, you whore?" he hissed. But I didn't have a chance to answer. He seized my wrist and dragged me from the bed, slamming me against the nearest wall.

"Father!" Kovi exclaimed. He lunged for us, but the two guards who'd entered the room last were faster. They darted forward, grasping Kovi's shoulders and holding him back as he struggled to reach me.

Elder Ettonou's eyes were like two dark pits as he slid his fingers from my wrist to my index finger. Disgust burned in his gaze. He sneered at me, like I was a piece of dirt staining his perfect life in *my* palace.

"How dare you beguile my son?" His voice was low and terrifying, bringing back dozens of memories of bruises and cuts and unending shame. "How dare you lay your filthy fingers on him!"

"Stop!" Kovi tugged against the guards, but despite his strength, the effort against two men was futile.

In one cruel, smooth motion, Elder Ettonou twisted my index finger until it popped out of socket. I bit my tongue to silence my cry as pain shot through my entire hand. Nausea twisted through my stomach, and my eyes stung with tears I refused to shed in front of this man. Not again.

"Bring him forward," the Elder ordered the guards holding the Alrenian.

They shoved the prisoner toward me and forced him to kneel on my carpet, one covered in the swirling sun insignia that decorated our flag. One that reminded me daily of my people and my heritage. Though I wished to fight back, to intercede, the Elder's grasp on me was fierce.

"I want you to see what fate awaits the spies and criminals who work in your name," the Elder continued in a crisp voice. "This is what happens when one of your kind trespasses on palace grounds."

The prisoner lifted his face to reveal deep brown and gold eyes. His jaw was set, his mouth an unflinching line. "*O j'eh y'vonu*," he said. It was the old motto of the Alrenian Dragon Keepers: *I will not bow to fear.*

"Wait—" I bit out, struggling against the Elder, but it was too late.

One of the guards drew a dagger from her belt and slit the prisoner's throat. Crimson sprayed, and warmth splattered across my face. The man's eyes stared straight into mine as more blood poured from his wound, spilling across my carpet. He fell, face down in his own gore, with a dull thud that echoed endlessly in my ears.

Without ceremony, the Elder released me, nodding to the guards to free Kovi as well. As two men carried out the body, the other guards marched out silently. Before the Elder left, he cast one more dark look over his shoulder.

I wanted to leap after him, slam my hands against his face, and watch my curse—or my gift—eat away at his flesh. Watch him suffer the way he made so many others suffer. But I was frozen in place, trembling with rage and horror.

"Make sure you're on your best behavior for the ball tonight. If you don't do what's expected of you…well, I think you know."

My pulse pounded in my ears as the Elder disappeared, leaving behind the stench of blood and a throbbing pain in my finger. Those senses fell to the back of my mind, though, in the onslaught of emotions. The fiery fury coursing through me made my skin feel hot. I could hardly catch my breath, as if I were already chasing after the Elder and avenging that young man's death.

One of my people, murdered before my eyes, I thought. Another wave of anger screamed through me.

"Jalie," Kovi said, at my side in an instant.

Tears streamed freely down my cheeks, blurring my vision. The world spun, and for an instant I nearly whirled on Kovi to strangle *him*, wanting to take my rage out on anyone, anything.

Instead, Kovi led me to my washroom, gently pushing me until I was seated on the bench beside my tub. I was scarcely aware as he cradled my finger tenderly in his hands, before quickly and efficiently yanking it back into place. Then he was wiping the blood from my face with a cool, wet cloth, all the while murmuring words in Forwyn.

A tolling bell above the palace sanctuary, the sanctuary I'd stopped visiting not long after Mother's death, rang eleven times. I had three hours left to find the Alrenian woman and escape—hopefully with her help. I couldn't be weak. I couldn't waver. Today couldn't have served as a better illustration to prove that my people's lives depended on my success.

Impatient, I waved Kovi away. He stepped back slowly, watching me a moment before leaving me alone as I started my morning rituals: washing my face, cleaning my teeth, and brushing my hair. I strode out to my bedroom to select a simple ivory and blue dress I'd wear until it was time to pretend to prepare for tonight's ball, and then I stood behind my changing screen to pull it on. At last, I approached my vanity as if to apply color to my face, having to skirt around the fresh blood staining my carpet.

Meanwhile, Kovi went about his own routine silently, neatly folding his blanket and resting it on the settee, slipping into my washroom when I'd exited, and changing into a fresh uniform.

I'd left some of my corrilys mixture in the same jar I'd first crushed the petals inside. It waited on my vanity table, the red faded to a faint blush color, one that wouldn't be noticeable in Kovi's dark coffee.

My mind whirled. *It doesn't have to be a strong enough dose for him to die,* I thought. Nesrelle's voice echoed in my ears, reminding me that this was my only chance. It was as if she was right there, leaning over my shoulder, breathing into my ear: *Don't let him get between you and the throne.*

Determination solidified within me. I could do this. I tried to move quickly, to snatch up the jar, but it was too late—I already heard Kovi's footsteps. My hesitation had cost me valuable time. Half-panicked, I lifted the jar to my lips and took two large gulps of the mixture.

Time for a new plan, I thought, pulse racing in my throat. But could it work?

As Kovi stepped out from behind my changing screen, I dabbed a bit of the liquid on my wrists and neck for show before replacing the stopper.

Everything is normal. Don't suspect anything.

Kovi ran a hand over his jaw, a furrow between his brows as his eyes landed on the bloodstain and then on me. "Jalie..." He began, my name sounding, as always, musical in his Forwyn accent.

"Don't start," I interrupted.

He frowned but remained silent as I strode into my sitting room, where a servant had left our breakfast tray. Blissfully distant from the gory scene in my bedroom. Carefully, I slipped the half-full jar of my corrilys mixture into my pocket, just in case. My hands shook when I picked up a plate and filled it with pastries. Lastly, I mixed an extra-sweet mug of tea. Entering the room wordlessly, Kovi stood entirely too close as he chose his own food.

My blood roared in my ears. One mistake could ruin everything. What if, in my panic, I'd miscalculated the amount I needed? I wasn't sure I'd have another chance like this, and in my desperate anger and fear, I could almost feel it slipping away, rushing through my fingertips like sand.

"No coffee with cinnamon today?" His smile was crooked, as if he'd realized I wanted to pretend the earlier events of this morning hadn't happened. My heart skipped a beat. Were we playing the same game we'd played before? It was what I wanted—needed—but it was also terrifying. Uncomfortable. Standing this close to him, gazing at him through my eyelashes and breathing in the scent of his soap, felt like a betrayal. Of my mother. My people. Myself.

Because I didn't need to feign my attraction or the strange connection I was beginning to feel. It was painful and wrong and strangely exhilarating in its wrongness.

"I decided I wanted something sweeter." I took a step closer to him. I'd already left my plate and cup forgotten on the table.

Don't waver, I reminded myself.

Kovi set down his plate, and though he didn't step back, he didn't move closer to me either. "Changed your mind about poisoning me?"

I paused, failing to conceal my horror while my insides turned to ice. "What?"

He gestured over my shoulder, toward my vanity. "Your perfume is corrilys, a poisonous plant. Don't tell me you know so much about how to prepare it for a perfume and don't know what it does if ingested?" His smile was hard.

"You told me you knew nothing about the plants," I said, feeling stupid even as I spoke the words.

"You expected everything I said to be the truth?" This time, Kovi did step nearer, looming over me. For the first time in days, I was truly frightened of him. He was tall and muscular, and I was trapped in his shadow, his dark eyes cutting into mine. He made an imposing figure. Memories of how it felt to be forced to obey him by his magic fluttered through my mind.

When had I let myself forget he was a soldier? An *enemy* soldier?

He was close enough that I could feel his breath on my face, warm and scented with mint from cleaning his teeth.

My fingers twitched at my sides. *Forget mercy. Grab him and let him suffer the consequences. Leave him. Think of what will happen to your people if you don't.*

But he'd still be able to cry out and alert the guards posted in the hall. If I attacked him, there wouldn't be any escaping. I'd seal my fate as much as his.

"I changed my mind," I whispered, widening my eyes. "You've shown me kindness when I didn't deserve it. You and I—we aren't that different. You understand me. I can't—it's not you I hate. I know that now. You're not like other Forwyn…" It was a little disconcerting, saying those words, because they weren't entirely lies. There was a kernel of truth within them, that growing strangeness that frightened me.

Unexpectedly, Kovi softened. Maybe he believed me. Maybe he could still feel the horror and pain pulsing through me as the young Alrenian's death flashed through my mind, the memory like an endless loop I couldn't ignore even when I tried to pretend all was normal. He reached out tentatively, framing my face with both his hands. His palms were warm and rough against my cheeks. And then he said the last words I'd ever expected him to say. "I'm sorry, Jalie," he whispered. "For what you had to witness today. For what the Elders—especially my father—have done to you."

My surprise shifted into shock as he leaned forward and kissed me, his lips soft yet insistent. Distracting. He dropped one of his hands to my waist while the other tangled in my hair, holding me close. My head whirled with confusion and pleasure, because the feel of his warm mouth on mine was even more exhilarating than I'd imagined. And because, impossibly, I'd pulled off my plan without even trying. I didn't want him to pull away, so I kept my hands loose at my sides and deepened the kiss. If Kovi tasted the corrilys on my lips, my tongue, I prayed he didn't recognize what it was.

Kovi pulled back, just a little, his mouth still against mine as his lips curved into a smile. It was only then that I noticed his hand wasn't on my waist anymore. He'd slipped it into my pocket and withdrawn the jar

I'd hidden there.

"I don't expect everything you say to be truthful either," he murmured against my lips. "I can see through your games."

He stepped away, but stumbled, blinking as his eyelids grew heavier. His head jolted toward me, his eyes wide with shock and a gratifying hint of fear.

I smirked when he sank to the floor, too weary to stand. As he slipped into the swift wave of unconsciousness the corrilys enacted, I knelt over him and plucked the jar from his weakening grasp. His eyes were already fluttering, desperate to fight against the corrilys' effects.

"You played this game well, Kovi," I said, "but you lost."

CHAPTER TWENTY-FIVE

Lo

"YOU'RE GOING TO THE PALACE?" Pauni'a whispered, her eyes large and shining with her eagerness. "But why didn't you tell me before?" A crease formed between her brows. "Are you sure it's appropriate?"

I shifted on my feet. "Caesiem's friend invited us. We want to address the empress's injustices."

The Autumn Ball was only a few hours away, and Caesiem had already left the abbey the night before. After we'd met with Renni and the others, Caesiem had been unusually quiet as he'd walked me back home. Finally, he'd said he would meet me at the abbey the next evening, bid me goodnight, and slunk away toward The Broken Crown.

I'd brought Pauni'a to my room to help me prepare, but I couldn't help the sinking feeling in my stomach as I explained what I was doing. I was sure I'd never again be welcome at the abbey after tonight. If Renni's plan was successful, news of the empress's death would spread swiftly, and it wouldn't take long for Naina and the other sisters to put the pieces together.

And that was only one problem, an issue I wouldn't even face if I didn't escape from the ball.

Trust the guidespirit, I told myself. *Trust Elhani.* I'd repeated this in my head constantly since last night, when doubt had threatened my resolve. I had to believe there was a reason I was needed tonight. A reason I was led here.

Oblivious to the lump building in my throat, Pauni'a nodded thoughtfully. "What are you going to wear?"

"They're letting me borrow some things," I said evasively, not wanting to reveal that I knew at least one item I'd be wearing tonight was stolen. Opening my wardrobe, I pulled out my ivory dress.

Pauni'a clapped a hand over her mouth to stifle her gasp. She hadn't been a slave in the palace like I'd been, so she wasn't nearly as familiar with their finery as I was. She touched the material gingerly, marveling at the beadwork, before staring at me, mouth hanging open.

"I shouldn't be admiring a dress like this," she murmured. "It's only temporary…not of true value." Her eyes flicked back to it. "But it's the most beautiful thing I've ever seen," she breathed. "You'll look stunning in it." Her eyes shone.

"Will you help me prepare, Nia?" I asked.

"Of course!" Pauni'a clapped her hands with delight. "When will I ever have the chance to touch a dress like this again?"

I sat on the floor while Pauni'a perched on the edge of my bed. "I suppose we should leave out your grey ribbon tonight," she said, quietly undoing its twists and setting the ribbon aside. She added, "No one needs to know you're a nun. Then they'd be suspicious about why you are there." She laughed lightly, but my muscles tensed.

I couldn't tell her she might never see me again. I couldn't say goodbye. Not exactly. My eyes burned, and I stared straight ahead as she tugged at my braids, pulling half up and out of my face, and securing them with a leather cord.

"Do you think the Elders will listen to you?" Pauni'a asked quietly.

It relieved me to know that she assumed the vigilantes and I planned only to speak with the Elders about Jaliana…not try to assassinate her.

The lie tasted bitter on my tongue, but the idea of sharing my actual plans with her for the night made me feel even worse. "I don't know." I repressed a sigh as I recalled the way the Elder had dismissed the murdered Forwyn citizens, despite my pleas. At the memory of the speech and ensuing chaos in the Akytha District days ago. "During the speech at the Akytha District," I went on, "they made Jaliana seem like a suffering martyr for their cause, but then when the riots began, they didn't hesitate to send a dragon to kill Alrenian citizens. For all their talk of unity, they seem eager to shed blood."

"It seems like they're more interested in power," Pauni'a said, her voice low and disapproving. "And they're making the Alrenians hate us more. After all the hope we've placed in them to protect our people…" Her voice drifted off.

"I feel the same," I whispered, tone wavering. "I thought they were on our side. Trustworthy. Now I feel like we're lonely and powerless in our cause. Like we sisters are some of the only few taking a real stand for our people. For a better life than this."

"Then take a mighty stand tonight, Lo," Pauni'a said fiercely. "Show them your strength. Make them listen to your cause and let them see you won't bend. Let them know their people are worth more than their greed."

CHAPTER TWENTY-SIX

Jalie

DROWSINESS MUDDLED MY SENSES AS I stared at Kovi's prone form, but the feeling was a mere nuisance that would wear off soon enough. It was difficult to calculate how long Kovi would be unconscious given the unorthodox way I'd administered the corrilys, but based on how quickly it had taken effect and how much I'd consumed, I expected I had at least ten hours. Corrilys was normally taken in much smaller doses. By the time the Autumn Ball commenced in six hours and the Elders noticed his and my absence, I would be miles away. Hopefully with the Alrenian woman to lead me toward the resistance.

With the guards' shift change and my meeting hours away, I had plenty of time. I ate my fill from the breakfast tray before carefully wrapping some remaining pastries. I paced my rooms regretfully, avoiding the bloodstained carpet. I hated to leave my treasured belongings behind, even temporarily. I had led my entire life within these walls, and it was terrifying to imagine leaving them now.

Assuming I might have to go without simple luxuries for a while, I decided to enjoy them one more time. I took my time combing and braiding my hair before applying some cosmetics. I twisted my braids into a crown encircling my head and secured them. It would do until I could wear the real thing—without owing any allegiance to the Forwyn Elders. Without being told by them when I should and shouldn't wear it. Outside, the bell tolled the twelfth hour. Two hours until the shift change and my meeting in the garden.

Even though I knew it would be more practical to change out of my dress into a tunic and leggings, I wanted to appear somewhat like an empress when I finally met with an Alrenian subject alone. If the Forwyn hadn't already taken the dragon scale armor I'd worn to fly Ryke, I would have changed into that. The only jewelry I permitted myself to wear was my mother's ruby ring, because I couldn't bear being parted with it.

Approaching Kovi, I watched his chest rise and fall evenly. His face appeared relaxed and peaceful. Gentle. Kneeling over him, I undid his belt and fastened it around my hips, where it hung a little loosely, but securely enough to work. I attached his sword and dagger to my sides and smirked at him before crossing my room.

Seizing Kovi's bag from my settee, I dumped out its contents and sorted through them. Extra clothes. Several bulky books. A journal. A pocketknife, tinderbox, some rope, and a water canteen. Apparently graduates of the Aerekni Academy packed like they were about to be sent off into the wilderness at any given moment.

I filled the empty bag with spare outfits, Kovi's tools, my wrapped pastries, and several oranges. Then I filled the canteen and added it to the pack. If the Alrenian woman couldn't lead me to the resistance, I might have to travel for a while before I found them myself. Considering, I stared out past my balcony toward the grounds, where two guards crossed paths and disappeared deeper within the garden.

This was the missing piece in my plan that made me the most nervous. I was depending on a stranger. If the woman couldn't or wouldn't help me, I was on my own. Again.

But I refused to let doubt stop me. I would find a way. And I could be patient—I'd proven that fact to myself over these past several years.

Hesitating, I returned to the settee for Kovi's journal. Maybe he'd written notes about his meetings with the Elders that would give me information about their plans, or about the resistance they were trying to quell. If they trusted him enough to assign him to me, surely they trusted him enough to share other information with him. If Alrenor was facing an all-out war, he'd be one of the soldiers the Elders would depend upon to save their precious leadership. I shoved the journal into the pack as well.

A small pit formed in my stomach, almost like guilt. Like…regret. Though Kovi had played a game similar to mine, I knew deep down it couldn't have all been a farce. I could still feel his hands as he'd brushed back my hair after I'd panicked during the execution of the Alrenian woman. His comforting presence when he'd lain in bed beside me, curled close to my body. His warm lips, firm yet gentle, as he'd kissed me.

But most shocking of all were his words, echoing in my head even now. *I'm sorry, Jalie.*

Was he truly sorry? Had he meant that, or had it been part of the game? A way to soften me, allow him to embrace and kiss me so he could steal the corrilys?

If it hadn't been part of his trick, there were still hundreds of other questions. What made him feel the need to apologize on behalf of his people's rulers? Did he only feel pity for me, or did he empathize with me over our shared grief and pain? Was it because of his connection to my emotions?

I strode out to the balcony to wait out the remaining time, inhaling the floral and citrus scents thick in the air. A briny whiff from the seas mixed with the sweet aromas. A lizard darted from its sunning spot on my balcony when I stepped near. Birds twittered and hopped from tree branches. The distant sound of sea waves thrummed like a steady heartbeat over it all.

I tried to block out the tenderness and regret I'd felt moments earlier—no matter the kindness Kovi had shown me, we were on different sides of a brewing war. Perhaps he deserved better than to wake up hours later to the wrath of his father and the other Elders, but at least I'd spared his life. We belonged to different peoples with different beliefs. My mother's words came back to me: *They aren't the Chosen People of the Giver of Life, not like we are. They're unbelievers, unworthy. They choose not to follow him. They are tricksters, blasphemers. We rule over them because we deserve to. We are the children of the Land of the Sun, and we walk in the light while they choose darkness.*

In every way, Kovi and I were still opposed. He would never permit me to rule my empire, even if it was my birthright. When war came, he would side with his people, and if we met in battle, I couldn't count on his compassionate heart to choose mercy. After all, if given the chance, Kovi would have gladly killed my mother—I was sure of it. And I'd gladly kill his father when I had the opportunity.

At last, the fourteenth hour drew near. Heaving the pack over my shoulders, I waited until all guards were out of sight, preparing to speak with the new guards at their shift change. Then I swung over my balcony railing. The index finger Elder Ettonou had injured protested, sore and awkward, but the pain was manageable. I'd endured worse. Holding on securely with one hand, I extended my other arm toward the orange tree that grew close enough for me to touch, stretching for the thickest branch within arm's reach. I grasped it and released my hold on the railing.

For one heart-stopping moment, I dangled precariously from one arm, my fingernails digging into crevices in the tree bark. The tree swayed precariously, a little small to support my weight. I exhaled, forcing my pulse to steady, and swung my body forward. Again and again. On my fourth swing, I drew near enough to seize the branch with my free hand. I shimmied down the branch until I could set my feet on the one below it. Constantly, I scanned the grounds for guards. If all went according to their usual routine, I had a few more minutes before any would come this way.

At last my feet hit the ground. I darted toward the nearest garden path, clinging to tree shadows and sinking behind shrubbery whenever a leaf rustled or a branch creaked. Each time it was only a breeze brushing through the trees or a squirrel fleeing from my approach. I'd memorized the guards' patterns correctly. I'd climbed from my balcony swiftly, without mishap. Elation fluttered through my chest and my confidence expanded, swallowing all my previous doubts. My plan was coming together perfectly.

Ilahnna's fountain was tucked in a quiet corner of the gardens, far from the pavilions and sprawling palace buildings. Nearer to the walls encircling the grounds, it was likely one of the last places the guard assigned to this area would patrol. The fountain rested in the center of a small courtyard and featured the statue of a famed warrior and captain of the Dragon Keepers, who'd won the Alrenians several battles during the Misrothian Rebellion. Towering over the flowers growing along the courtyard's edges, she frowned toward the north—toward Misroth. One hand on the dragon curled against her body, her other extended a curved Alrenian blade toward her unseen enemies.

I paused in Ilahnna's shadow, hope and anticipation tingling through my veins. I didn't have to wait long. Striding soundlessly from an intersecting path, the Alrenian woman stepped into the courtyard and pushed her hood back from her face. Her fiery red hair shimmered in the afternoon sunlight while she assessed me. Her face was stony, unreadable.

"Jaliana," she said, her gaze lingering on my pack and my weapons before it latched onto my face. Her eyes were a striking shade of amber, accentuated by the gold flecks gleaming in her irises.

"*Amara* Jaliana," I corrected, my tone turning sharp. She should know better than to approach me so informally, without bothering to use my title. We might be short on time, so I could excuse the fact that she hadn't tried to kneel, but addressing me in such a familiar manner was inexcusable.

"Right." She continued to stare at me, until my insides squirmed. Adoration and awe I would gladly accept, but her hardened expression gave me no indication of her intentions.

Doubt seized me. Was she one of the Alrenians who despised me, who thought me weak for living in the shadow of the Forwyn for years? Did she think me beneath her and her fellow resistance members?

Narrowing my eyes, I strode toward her. "I know the Alrenians have formed a resistance, and that the Elders are trying to stop a war. I'm prepared to escape and join you, to lead the war and restore true Alrenian leadership to the empire. We don't have time to waste, so you can explain details about the resistance and who you are on the way." I waved toward the Keep impatiently, spinning on my heel. "Follow me."

My ears registered her whisper before I felt a cool blade pressed against my neck. "*Va kowra*," she snarled, her voice thick with venom. *Kowra.* It was a curse, a vile condemnation with roots from a blend of words meaning *monstrosity* and *plague*.

Shock and bitter betrayal slammed through me, but my years of training were swift to kick in. My mother's words thrummed through me, comforting and familiar. *Clear your mind of fear. Trust your instincts. Believe in your strength.*

This commoner, this *nobody* dared to demean and threaten me? I twisted closer toward the woman while simultaneously slapping my hand against her wrist, squeezing until my fingernails drew blood. My gift washed through me like lightning, intoxicating and powerful. A gasp of pain hissed through her lips, quickly morphing into a strangled cry as she dropped her dagger and crumpled to her knees. I turned to face her, watching her stony expression melt into agony and terror. Blood streamed from her wrist, where the flesh was already blackening and peeling away, exposing muscle, tendon, and bone.

I didn't even think about the blade behind me or the weapons at my waist. Hovering over her, I grinned, all teeth and threat. *"Amara kowra,"* I snapped.

Empress Monstrosity. Empress Plague. For her, a disgusting, lowly traitor, I could be all those things and more.

I clapped my hands on either side of her face, and her cheeks blackened instantly. It was horrifying and fascinating, and I could not tear my gaze away. The woman screamed as flesh and features vanished in rot and blood. Her body shook and her hands pounded against my chest in vain. I didn't feel her strikes. I didn't feel anything but my gift, my curse, flowing through me. Nothing but the simultaneous wonder and horror pulsing in my heart, in my head, in my soul.

It took a mere instant and an eternity for the woman to collapse and her body to still, her face unidentifiable. Drawing my hands away, bile filled my mouth. Terror quickened my heart. What had I done?

My hands shook. Mother's voice was in my head again. *Never let anyone stand in your way. You are the next Chosen Empress. No person on earth is more important than you, and nothing is more important than your sacred duty to protect your throne and your people.*

But never had I imagined it would involve killing in such a brutal, horrible way.

The memory of Nesrelle's words came to me next. *Don't fear the curse, little Jalie.*

Tears burned my eyes. Despite the voices in my head, guilt and fear chilled my entire body, shuddering through me violently. This time, I'd struck intending to kill, and even though it had been to save my own life, it had been gruesome and violent.

And the power inside me burned brighter. I had sated a small piece of my anger and thirst for vengeance. A part of me had *relished* it.

My plan was falling apart. The woman hadn't been here to help at all, but to assassinate me. I was at a loss how to find the Alrenian resistance, and a little terrified that it didn't exist at all. Not on the large scale I'd imagined.

Worst of all, I knew someone must have heard the woman's screams. I had to get out of here—fast. And if I didn't want to raise suspicions, I needed to hide the body that had clearly died at my hands, from the curse I carried.

Panicked, I worked to drag the woman's corpse into the shrubbery, concealing it as best as I could. Noticing the blood slicking my hands, I wiped them on the woman's shirt. Then I dug up fistfuls of dirt and tossed them over the blood staining the courtyard, scattering it so it looked like an animal might have caused the mess.

As footsteps approached, I raced away, heart hammering in my throat.

Get to the Keep. Threaten whoever you must. Find Ryke.

Mentally, I repeated the words like a chant, stumbling over my own feet as I ran. Sweat dribbled into my eyes. My lungs burned. Despite the heat and the sweat slicking my body, I shivered. There wasn't enough air in the world to fill my chest. Everything around me appeared hazy, distant.

The footsteps didn't fade away, only drawing nearer. Pounding against the earth. Chasing me.

I had made the final turn leading to the arena when I noticed a figure blocking my path. Shock, horror, and disappointment roared within me—all of that, and I'd failed. Just before I slammed into him, I drew up short, gasping for breath, staring in disbelief at who stood before me.

Kovi.

CHAPTER TWENTY-SEVEN

Lo

THE WESTERING SUN CAST THE abbey and surrounding buildings in shades of orange and red as I descended the steps to meet Caesiem. Leaning against the abbey, hands shoved in his pockets, he stood unusually still as he stared at the sky. The Dragon Keepers were running through their evening flight, twisting into formation and then splitting apart to soar and dive over the various capital districts.

I reached Caesiem just as the blue dragon coasting overhead—whose name I remembered was Ivez—threw our street into shadow. A moment of darkness before evening light bathed us once more.

As if stirring from a dream, Caesiem straightened and shook his head before turning to me. His mouth twisted into a half-hearted grin, and he fidgeted with his shirt collar. Even now, his smile was charming enough that I couldn't look directly at him. His ocean blue vest set off his bright eyes, making them even more intense than usual. "You look like you belong at court," he said.

It was the wrong compliment, and as soon as the words left his mouth, he seemed to realize it.

"That's not what I meant…" His voice drifted away. Just like the night before, everything about him seemed tightly wound. The way he wore his fine clothes—stiff and uncomfortable and slightly rumpled—

made him appear like the imposter he was. His eyes looked darker than usual as he worked a muscle in his jaw. The familiar magnetic energy surrounding him had faded away. He stuffed his hands into his pockets again and stilled himself, like he wanted to become a part of the abbey wall. To disappear into another dragon shadow. To vanish into the earth.

"Are you all right?" I asked, shooting him a pointed look before turning down the street. He had no choice but to push off the wall and follow.

For a long while, Caesiem didn't answer. He strode by my side, hands still shoved deep in his pockets, his gaze faraway. Forwyn passed us in the street, smiling and greeting us cheerily, their eyes lingering appreciatively on our beautiful attire. The Alrenians we encountered scowled, probably remembering times in the past when they would have been the ones invited to the palace's Autumn Ball.

The evening was quiet around us as the sun descended toward the horizon, staining the sky shades of orange and red. The air tasted of sea salt and the mingling aromas of wood smoke and food when we passed homes, pubs, and inns. As the bustle of the day faded with the shops closing and citizens returning home, a deceptive peacefulness hung over the city. To me, it felt like the calm before a raging storm.

We were crossing a stone bridge spanning a channel when Caesiem finally spoke. In the evening light, the water sparkled red, like surging fire or gushing blood.

"Lo," he said, his tone so low and hushed, almost desperate, that it immediately yanked my attention from the channel.

I lifted my eyes and met his gaze, intense and troubled. Beneath his furrowed brow, his eyes reminded me of a darkening sky, tinged grey with gathering storm clouds.

"I know what you said, and that Eloreth made threats, but you still don't have to do this." Caesiem's voice turned pleading as he stepped closer to me, bridging the gap between us. "You don't have to go. *We* don't have to do this. We could turn around right now and find somewhere to wait everything out, somewhere where no one would find us, and we'd have time to decide what to do. There's still this last chance to change your mind. Before…"

He hesitated, shaking his head. His eyes searched my face, his hands hesitant as he reached out and took mine. My heart rammed into my ribs in response, but I didn't pull away. His skin was too warm.

"No," I insisted. "I *do* have to go. You know that." My voice shook. "I can't change my mind." I swallowed, gathering my courage. Reminding myself of the reasons I had not to turn and flee tonight. "Whatever the consequences."

Caesiem pressed his lips together, as if holding back from saying something. He looked agonized, his body tense as his hands squeezed mine, like I was a lifeline. "Are you certain? I'm not sure I can forgive myself if I'm the reason you lose the life you have at the abbey."

But I shook my head. "You aren't the reason. This is my choice."

Caesiem studied me for a long moment, his eyes studying mine. "Whatever happens, I only want you to be happy."

The fact that he cared enough about what I wanted made me pause. I stepped closer. In that moment, I wondered how it would feel to drag my fingers through his hair or press my mouth to his. The intensity of his gaze trapped my breath in my throat and made me dizzy. He was magnetic, and the fact that he was forbidden only made him more so.

But…I was already breaking my vows. I had nothing left to lose. There was no reason not to give into the pull growing between us. I swallowed down my lingering guilt. The anger already thrumming through me twisted together with desire, until my entire body felt warm, and I threw myself into the moment without care for the future. I leaned forward, curling my fingers around the back of his neck, tugging his face toward mine. Inhaling sharply, Caesiem responded immediately, cupping my face and closing the final breath of air between us. His lips were as hot as mine, as if he were burning with the same consuming emotions. Anger. Desperation. Fear. Longing. Confusion. Our kiss was right and wrong, exhilarating and terrifying, gentle and fervent.

But guilt screamed through me anyway. *Thief. Spy. You barely know him. Your vows vows vows...*

Gasping, I yanked away and took a step back. I was too close to the bridge, and my back slammed into stone. Biting back my grimace, I dragged my eyes from his. "Let's go," I said gruffly.

Caesiem couldn't hide the hurt in his expression, but he nodded and stepped away from me, giving me the space I desperately needed. He slid his hands back into his pockets, as if that was the only way he knew how to keep them still.

The walk to the ball took too long and not enough time all at once. As the streets rose, winding toward the looming palace, memories overtook me. Rare moments stolen with my family. My mother's laughter or my brother's smile, his reassuring presence. Over time, their faces had grown fuzzy in my mind and the exact timbre of their voices had faded, but I remembered the way I'd felt around them perfectly. Safe and loved, like I had my own personal refuge, a place to flee from the cruelties of the world, a place that no one could ever touch. Karye had proven that idea to be wrong—so wrong. She'd stolen everything from me.

The raw grief of losing my family was like a punch to the gut every time it washed over me. The void never shrank, never became any less shocking or horrifying with the passage of time.

My limbs grew leaden as we approached the palace gates, where other guests gathered, waiting in line as the guards checked that each person had been invited. It was all surreal, the sight of so many Forwyn clustered together in attire the Alrenian nobility had once worn. Waiting in line for an immaculate ball that Karye would have once hosted.

It was like both everything and nothing had changed. Discomfort squirmed through my chest, alongside a growing horror that someone might recognize me. Being lauded as the *amara'rekni* tonight would be more than I could bear.

That's absurd anyway, I thought. *Dressed like this, you look nothing like you would have back then.*

"Renni has the invitation with our names on it," Caesiem muttered to me, tugging a watch from his pocket to check the time. "But they still have a few minutes." We stood close, giving those around us the impression that we were a couple, but we might as well have been miles apart. Avoiding eye contact, keeping our shoulders and arms carefully withdrawn to prevent any accidental touching, a chilly awkwardness had descended between us.

We didn't even have to wait long. A short while later, Renni strode toward us, joining us in line. Though he tried to conceal it, it was clear he was worried from the way his eyes darted around, studying each of the other waiting guests. "Something's wrong," he murmured, leaning toward us to avoid being overheard. "Everyone is here"–he nodded toward where his friends stood, near the gates where I hadn't spotted them before–"except Eloreth."

"There's still time," I murmured.

Renni's jaw was tight. "No," he said. "Mio'e had her dress. Eloreth was supposed to meet her beforehand to get ready. She never showed."

CHAPTER TWENTY-EIGHT

Jalie

BLOOD ROARED SO LOUDLY IN my ears I couldn't think clearly as I stared into my vanity mirror. My makeup was flawless, everything I'd smeared in my encounter with the traitorous Alrenian woman carefully corrected. I wasn't sure how I'd applied it with my shaking hands. I didn't remember selecting the dress I wore, a flowing gown of blue so deep it was nearly black. Its halter collar was secured around my throat with a thick gold band, from which hung dozens of glittering dragon scales of both gold and silver. They clinked together across the entire bodice of the dress when I moved. My back was bare but for delicate chains strung with more dragon scales to match the front.

I wore a matching headpiece of dragon scales shaped like a crown. They caught the fading daylight with every turn of my head, flashing and demanding attention. Once I might have relished a chance to look the part of empress, to show the Forwyn Elders and nobility that they were beneath me. That I was someone to fear.

Now it all felt empty. A hollow show. I was still a prisoner at their mercy. I was still a woman who carried a curse. Who'd killed someone intentionally this time.

My body trembled with guilt. I couldn't stop seeing the woman's ruined face, couldn't stop hearing her agonized screams. I could argue that I'd only reacted to save myself before she could kill me, but I couldn't argue that the curse I'd inflicted on her wasn't brutal.

Mother would have told me an empress had every right to defend herself. Perhaps even more of a right than anyone else, because an empress was the chosen leader of the Chosen People. I had a responsibility to survive so that I could claim my throne and rule my people. But none of those facts erased my lingering horror.

Don't fear the curse, little Jalie.

I truly was a monster. A *kowra*.

My guilt abated a little when I saw the bloodstain left on my bedroom carpet. The young man's death flashed vividly through my mind, and I imagined unleashing my curse on Elder Ettonou. That would be justice.

The past few hours had sped by in a blur. My calculations had failed. There would be no surprising Kovi now, no second chance to catch him unawares and run. I'd planned and waited and killed for nothing.

Kovi lingered by the door as he waited for me, arms crossed and jaw set. Instead of his usual uniform, he was clothed in traditional Alrenian formal clothes, though they were still in shades of red and gold. While his shirt sleeves flowed loosely off his arms, his vest was fitted, drawing far too much attention to his muscled chest and torso.

I scowled at his reflection in my mirror. We'd hardly spoken since he'd stopped me in the arena and dragged me back to my rooms.

When he'd seized my arm, I'd almost been too shocked to fight back. "How did you get here?" I demanded.

"Let's see," he said, tugging me effortlessly back toward the palace. Any traces of the kindness or gentleness he'd shown earlier were a distant memory. His dark eyes were pools of anger, the gold flecks within them sparking dangerously. "When I woke up on your floor to find you gone and my weapons stolen, I came to the one place I knew you'd have to go if you wanted to escape."

"But…you should have been asleep for hours," I spluttered.

"I suppose your dosage was off when you chose such an unusual method for administering the corrilys," Kovi said dryly. "Not to mention, as an Aerekni student, I was trained to build up a tolerance to various poisons too. I'm surprised you hadn't thought of that."

To my dismay, heat flared across my face. For an instant, Kovi's eyes flicked toward me and I knew he could see how red I was. I hoped he thought the reason for my burning cheeks was my fury. And I *was* furious, along with being embarrassed by my miscalculations and the memory of his lips on mine.

"You played the game well," Kovi murmured, his breath warm against my ear as he leaned in, never slowing his stride, "but you lost."

When we'd stormed back into my rooms, he'd dropped my arms and seized my waist, unfastening his belt and weapons from my hips. I didn't resist, only glowered at him as he strapped his sword and dagger to his sides. Kovi matched the intensity of my stare, but in his reserved, soldierly way. His anger wasn't as obvious. He didn't need it to be. The steadiness in his movements as he handled his weapons and the stoniness of his expression were threatening enough.

Next, he removed his bag from my back and tossed it carelessly to the floor. He didn't bother to search through or empty it, not yet. "You have a ball to prepare for," he said, voice low, and with that, he'd left me to my devices.

While I'd sat at my vanity applying cosmetics and unbraiding my wild hair, a Forwyn servant had arrived to deliver Kovi's clothes. He'd left my sight only long enough to dress behind my changing screen, and then he'd taken up his position leaning against my door.

Now, he finally broke our silence as I met his gaze in the mirror. "It's time to go."

Striding across the room, I paused in front of him, waiting. He didn't quite meet my eyes as he offered an arm and turned to open the door wide for us both. I laid my hand carefully against his forearm, hating myself for the jolt of warmth that coursed through my body.

It was ridiculous to exit my chambers this way, arm-in-arm with Kovi. My bodyguard. My enemy. But tonight would be all about formalities and the show the Elders loved for us to put on.

As we slipped down the hallway, guards saluted us in the Forwyn style. Torchlight danced along the walls, distorting the painted expressions of Alrenian emperors and warriors. The scales and chains on my dress clinked with each step, a gentle rhythm in the quiet that had settled over this part of the palace. Most of its occupants would be outside already, at the pavilion where the Autumn Ball was being hosted.

At last, I couldn't take the heavy silence between Kovi and me any longer. It was irking, though I refused to consider why I found it so. I lifted my chin stubbornly and glanced toward him.

"You can't tell me you wouldn't have done the same as me, if you were in my position," I said.

Kovi didn't answer, only stared straight ahead as we exited a set of doors and descended stairs to the grounds. The sun was setting, casting long shadows across our path. Though the pavilion wasn't yet in sight, the sounds of musicians tuning their instruments and people chatting and laughing together drifted toward us.

"If you were a captive in your own home," I continued stubbornly, determined to make him talk, "forced to obey the whims of your enemies—the ones who'd murdered your mother—you would do everything you could to escape."

Kovi halted, dropping my arm and stepping in front of me to block my path. Mouth set in a tight line, his expressionless mask vanished, revealing the anger and pain beneath it. "You're right," he said in a tone that made it clear he didn't think I was right at all. "Your circumstances are so much more difficult than mine. All I had to do was be secluded with the daughter of the woman who murdered *my* mother. To watch you behave as if the entire world should be laid out at your feet, and everyone should stop and stare in awe of you, because you're *chosen*. I have to feel your emotions, and to know that sometimes, we're all too much alike in the ways we're grieving. I had to spend every waking moment with you, hating you until I couldn't anymore because I knew your hurts and your fears…and you became *human* to me. So instead I have to hate myself, because Elhani help me, how can you *not* have compassion on your enemy when you see yourself in her?"

I was frozen, unable to move, unable to tear my eyes from his face. *I'm sorry, Jalie.* It hadn't been part of the game. He'd meant it. He still did.

Kovi's voice turned gentler. There was something else in his eyes now, mingling with the anger and the pain. "How can you not be fascinated by her, when she is fierce and clever and stunning?"

My tongue cleaved to the roof of my mouth and my lungs seized. The world was spinning, tilting. I didn't know what was up and what was down anymore. I had an urge to break the distance between us, to run my fingers through his hair and taste his kiss again, and it horrified me.

Those feelings were a betrayal of my mother, my people, and everything I was and believed in. Kovi was nothing but an obstacle in my path. A handsome, intriguing one, but still a problem that I needed to solve. I couldn't afford to let him distract me. Mother would have been ashamed to see me with him now, ogling him like an airheaded girl.

Before I could respond, my eyes fell upon movement over Kovi's shoulder to see Elder Ettonou approaching us. Clothed in green and silver, he struck an imposing figure as he paused behind his son.

"Kovi. Empress. It's good to see you both so punctual," he said smoothly. "Come, there's no time to waste. The festivities will begin in a few minutes. You wouldn't want to be late when your guests are waiting."

Kovi and I followed silently, despite the angry words burning within my chest. *How dare you order me about. How dare you pretend you're better than me.*

Torches lined the garden path, their flickering glow blending with the dying daylight, splashing the leaves and flower petals in warm shades of red and gold. We rounded a bend, and the pavilion came into view. The aroma of food hit me first: roasted meats and fish, sugared fruit and fresh vegetables, slices of cheese and golden loaves of bread, chocolate pastries and candies and cakes. I eyed the tables laden with food at the far end of the pavilion as my stomach growled.

The Forwyn Elders and a few other members of court stood at the other side, laughing and conversing. The center was open and empty, its marble floor pristine and glistening, ready for the guests to pair up and begin dancing. Throughout the surrounding garden, tables and chairs rested in the shade, waiting for occupants who wanted to sit and eat or have a moment for a more intimate conversation away from the crowd. Still tuning their instruments, the musicians were seated outside of the pavilion on one of the pathways, surrounded by blue embyth and palm trees.

For an instant, I nearly forgot the tangle of emotions rioting in my head and heart. Excitement and nostalgia claimed me instead. Everything was so similar to the way Mother had held her feasts and parties, and I couldn't help the longing overflowing inside me. For the night, I wanted to be carefree, to pretend she was alive, and that this was an Alrenian Autumn Ball. I wanted to dance with partners who couldn't conceal the admiration they felt for me, and I wanted to eat every delicacy laid out for the feast. I wanted to watch the twilight fade and the stars peek out over the grounds, to inhale the perfume of the gardens and live in a moment of pure bliss.

But the illusion fell away almost as soon as I'd dreamt it.

When Elder Ettonou led us up the steps and into the pavilion, the other Elders shot me tight-lipped smiles and deceptively polite nods. No one saluted or bowed or knelt. No one stared at me in awe. To them, I was a pawn, and an inconvenient one at that.

Two of the Elders stepped forward to address Kovi and me, and I exchanged formal nothings with them. All the while, I was overly conscious of Kovi's presence, his every movement. If he so much as glanced my way for an instant or shifted on his feet, I could sense it. I couldn't focus on his words as the Elders spoke with him, but I noticed the quiet rumble of his voice, the way it washed over me.

My thoughts wouldn't stop racing. I couldn't do this. I couldn't play pretend and smile and dance and flirt and laugh around these people. I couldn't stand beside Kovi and listen to my pulse hammer along to the beat of the drums coming from the garden.

As the guests trickled in, winding through various garden paths toward the pavilion, bowing and curtseying too precisely—too carefully, before the Elders and me, I scanned the grounds for an escape. There had to be a way to run. I had to have a second chance.

Fierce. Clever. Stunning. How could Kovi say those things to me? How could he look at me like he meant them? He knew as well as I that those sorts of feelings were wrong. I'd seen the pain in his eyes as he'd spoken the words.

There had to be other Alrenians out there who would welcome me to their cause. I refused to believe that every member of the resistance hated me and wanted me dead like that treacherous woman had.

Avenge the empire, the captive woman had said before the Forwyn executed her—and I knew she'd seen me in the crowd. I knew that message was for me. She'd wanted me to act and avenge her, to seize my crown and my rightful leadership.

I will not bow to fear, the Alrenian man had said after he'd met my eyes. Resigning himself to a dignified death for his empire, witnessed by his empress. Embracing his end fearlessly. I was sure he'd wanted me to know that I had other brave soldiers like him.

I could still feel my curse coursing through me, electric and warm. It was almost like a living thing, buzzing and thrumming through my veins. I had the power to do what needed to be done.

Kovi's quiet words and molten eyes wouldn't sway me.

Tonight, no matter who else stood in my way, I was escaping.

CHAPTER TWENTY-NINE

Lo

A S MUCH AS I'D DREADED this night, I still wasn't fully prepared for the searing rage and betrayal that coursed through me at the scene. The pavilion where the Elders were hosting the Autumn Ball was the same one that Empress Karye had once used to hold most of her parties. The same sweet scents of flowers and greenery and citrus permeated the air, mingling with the tantalizing aromas of food. As darkness descended, the torchlight danced throughout the gardens in an eerie manner, reminding me vividly of that night. The blood. The thuds of bodies as other Forwyn had been murdered around me. The feel of the blade in my hand, slicing across Karye's throat…

I repressed a shudder as Caesiem and I neared the party. Ahead of us, Renni escorted A'elli, both chatting and leaning into one another while they walked, as if they were a carefree couple. Behind us, Nu'or and Mio'e were quieter, wearing plastered smiles I hoped no one would see through. Wilvhe had met us at the gates when the guards had checked for our names. He'd greeted us cheerfully, though his face fell with concern when he noted Eloreth's absence.

"I'm heading to my room to prepare. I'll see you back at the pavilion," he told us, pulling away from the long line.

Now, Caesiem tapped his fingertips against his thigh and scanned our surroundings constantly, as if expecting one of the other guests to step out and reveal us as assassins at any moment. The nervous energy radiating off him only made me feel worse. Sighing softly, he extended his hand toward mine.

He shot me an apologetic glance. "We should probably keep up the appearance," he explained.

I let him take my hand and thread his fingers through mine. This time the anxious aura hovering between us felt different—electric and giddy. Caesiem squeezed my hand and ran his thumb along mine until I felt shivers roll down my spine. He tried to smile reassuringly, but it was tight-lipped and uncertain. I grinned back, hoping we looked convincing to everyone around us. Hoping he took it as a sign that everything was all right.

Even if it wasn't, not really. My chest was tight, and my breath felt shallow. I tried to concentrate on the distracting sensation of Caesiem's hand in mine, but as we climbed the steps toward the Forwyn nobility and Elders, I recognized faces of former slaves who'd served in the palace alongside me. The past I'd spent so much time running from was now startlingly close, staring back at me as if no time had passed at all.

A young woman in a pale pink dress stared at me a little too long as she raised her wineglass to her lips. My heart climbed into my throat and I turned away, praying she didn't recognize me.

Ahead of us, the Elders stood grouped together, joined by a blonde Alrenian woman clothed in gold and blue, and shimmering with gold and silver dragon scales. A matching headpiece glistened in the torchlight each time she moved. She turned her head and her eyes met mine, narrowing when she noticed how openly I stared. Bright blonde hair, freckles sprinkled across her nose and cheeks, and a fierce, sharp jaw—she looked so much like a younger version of Karye that my stomach clenched. Empress Jaliana, daughter of the woman I'd killed. The woman who'd slain my brother and almost murdered me.

As the guests ahead of us bowed before her and the Elders, I tried not to let my panic show. *You're happy to be at this ball with Caesiem,* I told myself, forcing my mouth into a grin and leaning toward him. I pretended to laugh at something. For a moment, bewilderment flickered across his face before he realized what I was doing and chuckled along with me. His laughter sounded as strained as mine felt, and I hoped no one noticed.

When it was our turn, we knelt before the Elders first before turning toward the empress and doing the same. Though I tried not to meet her gaze again, I could feel Jaliana's eyes on me, sharp and intense. Guilt slithered down my back and sweat beaded under my arms, even though I knew there was no way she knew who I was. It wasn't possible that she could look at me now and see the *amara'rekni*, the girl who'd killed her mother. And yet, it felt like the title was burned into my forehead for all to see. As if Karye's blood dripped from my fingers. As if at any moment Jaliana would point toward me and cry out for my execution, and the Forwyn Elders, desperate to appease her so they could continue to use her as their pawn, would hasten to obey.

It was all my guilt and paranoia, though. As Caesiem and I stood in unison, I spotted a young Forwyn man at Jaliana's side. With his well-muscled arms, stiff stance, and stoic expression, I assumed he was a guard, perhaps her personal one. A flash of curiosity lit and died in his eyes, and for a moment I wondered if *he* somehow knew who I was. Was he a former palace slave too?

Stop it, stop it, I told myself, following Caesiem as he grasped my hand again and led me toward the food tables.

When we were a safe distance away, apart from the crowded line, he pressed his mouth close to my ear. His breath tickled as he asked,

"Are you all right? My offer still stands, you know. We could leave right now."

I spun toward him, and for a moment our faces were dangerously close. He pulled back first. I swallowed.

"No, I'm not backing out, Caesiem," I said. "And I could ask the same of you—if you're all right."

Caesiem was as restless as ever, his gaze constantly scanning the party. His bronze complexion looked pale in the evening light. His eyes snapped back to me, and he smiled feebly.

"It's just the usual jitters before…" He shrugged. *A mission,* he mouthed. Forcing cheerfulness into his voice, he tugged on my hand. "Let's eat."

Renni and A'elli were already at the food tables, though none of us acknowledged each other as Caesiem and I joined the line of guests taking plates and filling them. Nu'or and Mio'e joined the line soon afterward, pretending they didn't know us as well. All part of the plan. We'd agreed that this was the best way to ensure most of us could survive. If one of us were caught, we weren't to implicate the others.

I couldn't help thinking that if Eloreth was somehow captured, she would have no problem outing me. Once again, I wondered nervously what had become of her. Renni had insisted that she'd never betray our group, but I had my doubts. Perhaps she'd raced to the Elders or the empress herself to share our plans, and even now she and some palace guards were closing in. Concealed within the garden, she'd point each of us out to the guards and then they'd arrest us all before we could execute our plan.

More paranoia. I tried to shake it away. To focus on what I needed to do tonight to save my people.

The tables were covered with a tempting array of foods: crab, roasted duck, lobster legs, and glazed salmon; an assortment of cheeses;

sliced oranges, sugared coconut squares, and berries in cream; and loaves of every sort of bread imaginable. Desserts had their own table: an enormous layered cake took up the center, while pastries, cookies, chocolates, and pies surrounded it. Despite my anxieties, my mouth watered as I filled my plate and followed Caesiem to one of the round tables set out in the garden. He chose one close enough to the pavilion to offer an unobstructed view of the activities. As soon as the first dance was announced, Caesiem and I would need to be up there.

We ate slowly, silently. Caesiem scanned the party often, noting where our friends were positioned, where the empress and her guard stood, and where the Elders lingered—usually close to Jaliana. Shoulders hunched and brow furrowed, Caesiem poked at his food, barely eating anything. His tension only made my stomach clench more.

Elhani, guide me, I prayed out of habit, before I remembered with a jolt that he'd probably turn a deaf ear toward me now. His guidespirit may have led me to the vigilantes, but that didn't mean Elhani would want me to break my vows to him. Every muscle in my body was tight. As delicious as the dinner was, my appetite faded fast. Two bites of food and my stomach felt full and sick.

At last, one of the Elders stepped forward to make an announcement. Caesiem and I sat up in our chairs, alert and prepared in an instant.

Voice low, gaze locked on the Elders, Caesiem spoke at last. "It's time."

CHAPTER THIRTY

Jalie

"THE FIRST DANCE OF THE night," Elder Ilhoa began, "will honor our Empress Jaliana. We are forever grateful for Elhani's blessing on her life and our empire."

"Forever grateful," I sneered under my breath. "Forever grateful they can use me to strengthen their own power over *my* empire."

As the musicians started a slow song, Kovi slipped his hand into mine and whispered in my ear. "This is our cue, empress. Let's dance and show them how it's done."

His voice calmed my seething blood, helping me to focus. For now, it was wise to behave as if everything were normal. That would provide my best opportunity to escape later, I hoped.

Kovi led me to the center of the pavilion, where we were surrounded by our audience of Forwyn nobility and Keepers. Dressed in their finest Alrenian styled clothes and jewels, clutching glasses filled with the wine my mother and her court used to sip, they ogled me like I was a strange animal performing for them. A few frowned and muttered to one another when Kovi drew me closer, setting one hand on my hip as he led me in the first steps of the dance. Others gasped outright. In my earlier anger, it hadn't fully registered to me how casually Kovi had touched my skin. He didn't fear what I could do to him.

I let the music fill my ears and the other sights melt away. With the last of the daylight fading, the surrounding garden was merely a pool of shadows; my audience's faces were but a blur. I concentrated on the rhythm of the song and the warmth of Kovi's body so close to mine. Torchlight flashed across the glossy white floor as my slippers whispered across it. Twisting, turning, Kovi and I took up the entire floor, moving as fluidly and effortlessly as water. The chains and scales on my dress jangled together like their own music.

Gazes locked, Kovi and I ignored the rest of the world. I couldn't quite read his expression. Lips a straight line, his face was impenetrable. But his dark eyes shone in the torchlight, reflecting flame and the glistening scales crowning my head. His gaze was deep and endless, and I was certain if I let myself fall into it, I'd never unravel all its mysteries. It filled me with too many contradicting emotions—anger and longing, fear and comfort—yet I couldn't tear my eyes away.

"Are you thinking of ways to poison me again?" he asked, allowing the barest trace of amusement to dart across his face.

I shrugged, my skirts swishing around my legs as Kovi released me and I twirled for the dance. When we came together again, I spoke. "It wasn't enough to kill you." Why was I defending myself? It was better if he thought I wanted him dead. After all, he'd called me his enemy in the same breath he'd called me stunning. That was the most important part of his declaration—the only thing worth holding on to or remembering.

We would always be enemies.

"I know," Kovi said, and I remembered how he'd said that he knew I wouldn't kill him. Maybe that was why he'd taken my hand tonight without a second thought.

He wasn't afraid of me.

I wasn't exactly afraid of him, either. Only the way he was

confusing me. It'd been easier when I could hate all the Forwyn equally, when I could condemn them all as cruel and beneath me.

"You're awfully confident around the daughter of a monster," I said coldly, pressing my fingers harder against his for emphasis, letting my nails bite the slightest bit into his skin. He didn't even flinch.

Without me even noticing the change, the song had switched, and other couples were whirling about the dance floor, surrounding us. Kovi stiffened as one of the male Dragon Keepers approached us. Clothed in perfectly polished gold dragon scale armor, he extended a gloved hand and smiled warmly.

"May I cut in, Kovi?" he asked. Something about his face was familiar… My stomach lurched unpleasantly as my body reacted before my brain caught up. And then I knew. He'd been one of the Dragon Keepers with Yaelti the day the man had attacked me.

"Wilvhe," Kovi said, his expression hard and his voice deepening to a threatening rumble. "You know that you may not. Elders' orders."

Wilvhe laughed and waved away Kovi's sternness. "You're taking it too far. They didn't want her dancing with any strange guests. *I'm* not a stranger; I'm a Dragon Keeper."

Kovi shook his head firmly. "I need you to step away, Wilvhe—"

That's when commotion erupted on the other side of the pavilion, jerking our heads in the opposite direction.

CHAPTER THIRTY-ONE

Lo

AS SOON AS THE DANCE floor was opened to all the guests, Caesiem and I wound our way toward it. I was grateful that there was so little attention on me, with everyone else either concentrating on their own partners or continuing to stare outright at Jaliana and her guard. There'd been an intensity in the way they'd danced, eyes fastened on one another as they'd flowed across the floor in perfect unison. It was startling to see the connection between the empress and a Forwyn soldier, enough to make a pit of doubt form in my stomach. Was assassinating Jaliana truly the way to cripple the brewing resistance?

It didn't take us long to set our plans into motion. Wilvhe, attired in traditional gold dragon scales, strode confidently toward Jaliana and her partner, as if he interrupted dances or approached the empress all the time. The guard tensed and stared blank-faced at Wilvhe, who didn't give up.

That was when Mio'e cried out. Standing at the edge of the pavilion with a wineglass poised in one hand, she let out a wild shout and pointed accusingly toward Nu'or. "Scoundrel! You *boerl*!" She sloshed her wine into his face and then hurled the glass at the floor, where shattered pieces and crimson droplets scattered across some of the dancers' paths. Lifting her heel, she stomped on the glass for added emphasis, crushing it into smaller pieces.

"P-please," Nu'or slurred, playing the perfectly distraught yet drunken lover as he reached his arms pleadingly toward her. Wine coursed down his face, giving me the urge to laugh despite my racing heart. "I didn't mean…please listen to me…"

Renni was already pushing through the crowd, his expression so heated I could practically feel the anger pulsing off him. "Is this man causing you trouble?" he asked, pointing firmly toward Nu'or while shooting Mio'e a compassionate look. The gallant hero.

"Are you trying to steal her from me?" Nu'or shouted, swinging a fist at Renni's face.

Guards jogged toward the two as they broke into a fight, slamming fists and wrestling one another to the glass-strewn floor.

This is it, I thought. My eyes darted toward Wilvhe, who stood stock-still beside the empress, feigning as much shock as the other guests. He was within arm's reach. All he had to do was stretch out his hand…

Did I run forward and intervene? Could I reach them in time? Did I dare? Or did I follow along with Renni's plan?

That's when I realized Caesiem was no longer standing beside me. We'd been meant to approach the Elders together, to speak with them and draw their attention away from what Wilvhe was doing on the dance floor.

Why was Caesiem diverting from the plan?

My head spun as I searched the crowd desperately. Most guests were frozen as they took in the drama unfolding before them. My gaze fell on the Elders, still standing together at one end of the pavilion, as if they were above dancing. As if they were far too important to engage much with the other guests. A few were whispering and chuckling amongst themselves as they tipped back their glasses and rolled their eyes at the fighting men interrupting their party.

Beside them, numerous Dragon Keepers stood in a perfect line, dressed head to toe in their dragon scale armor, their helmets concealing all but their eyes. In the dancing torchlight, their gazes were dark and unfathomable, almost unnatural looking. A fearsome presence meant to keep the guests distanced from the Elders. On the Elders' other side, servants held trays of food and drinks for them.

But…Caesiem was there too, stepping over shattered glass to pause in front of the Elders. His face was focused, intense. The earlier restlessness and anxiety had melted away, as if his doubts and fears had never existed at all. In its place was raw determination. One hand balled into a fist, and the other clutched the knife he'd concealed in his boot.

"Bow down to your new rulers," he said, his voice echoing throughout the pavilion. I hadn't realized before then how still it had become, how even Renni and Nu'or had stopped fighting and the musicians had stopped playing.

I gaped at Caesiem, my mind unable to understand what was happening.

One of the Elders—a short yet proud-looking woman with grey hair—threw back her head elegantly and laughed. "Who do you think you are, boy?"

Whatever else she'd been about to say died on her lips as the Dragon Keepers launched into motion. Swift as a heartbeat, they drew daggers from their belts and seized the Elders, pressing blades to Forwyn throats.

My head spun. The scent of blood hung in the air—no, it was there, in my memory… Karye's maniacal face and gleaming eyes. The slick sound of her blade slicing through skin. The spray of blood. The thud of a body.

Around me, guests were screaming. Some tore out of the pavilion, self-preservation overcoming every other instinct. Some stared blankly, too dumbfounded to move or react at all.

With their free hands, the Dragon Keepers yanked off their helmets and tossed them to the floor, clanking dully. The sound snapped me back to the present. I drank in the sight of the Keepers beneath their helmets. *Teramese.* Not Forwyn. Their faces were painted with a stripe of rich brown around their eyes to hide their bronze complexions beneath their helmets. More war paint in shades of white and red was spattered across their faces in varying patterns, giving them an imposing appearance. Their eyes, which should have been as bright as Caesiem's, shone an unnatural, muted black.

Disgust and horror shuddered through me.

The guards who had been restraining Renni and Nu'or dropped their charges and lunged for the Elders, but shadowy figures broke from their hiding places within the garden. Blades clanged together and Forwyn blood splashed across the ivory floor.

"Kovi!" one of the male Elders cried out, and the guard near the empress raced forward, sword drawn.

Wilvhe took his chance and reached for Jaliana, but she was already running. Blue skirt billowing around her, she slipped out of the pavilion, away from the Elders and the screams and the blood.

I couldn't process much besides how livid I was. White spots flashed across my vision as I watched Wilvhe tear after Jaliana. As if the empress posed any threat to our empire now. As if any of our old worries or plans mattered anymore.

Caesiem, I thought, enraged. Body quaking, I thought about hurling myself at him, screaming and smacking my fists into his face. *Thief. Liar. Traitor.* I'd saved his life. I'd trusted him. I'd believed him when he said he wanted to help my people. I'd risked everything to join him in this horrible plan.

He'd just betrayed us all.

But I didn't run toward Caesiem and the Elders. Instead, a different compulsion seized me. I raced after Wilvhe and Jaliana, something desperate and heated coursing through me. Was it Elhani guiding me at last?

Ahead, Wilvhe seized a handful of Jaliana's dress and tried to yank her back. With a ferocious cry, she tugged free, the fabric tearing. Wilvhe growled and lunged, tackling the empress to the earth. I knew he'd poisoned his gloves with vylae juice, knew that it wouldn't take much for him to smear it across her mouth or wipe it into her eyes. All it took was a small amount to enter the body. It was a certain death sentence when there was no known antidote for vylae.

Panting, I thought of Jaliana's face, the moment she'd seemed to soften when looking into her guard's eyes. *Don't let her die tonight.* And that, I was sure, was the voice of Elhani, finally sounding out in my mind, strong and clear.

"Get off her," I demanded, stealing the dagger from Wilvhe's belt, which he'd left unguarded. "Don't do this." My hand shook.

Wilvhe twisted off the empress, his eyes widening when he saw me hovering over him, clutching his weapon. "Lo," he ground out, face twisting with betrayal and rage. "What are you going to do, stab me? I should have known not to trust you..."

"No, I took it so *you* won't use it!" I protested. "She's not the one to attack tonight. We could stop the Teramese—"

"Drop it!" Wilvhe commanded, his hands lifted in a threat.

Behind him, the empress had staggered to her feet, but she seemed too shocked to flee. Or maybe I was terribly wrong, and she was preparing to attack us both.

But as I met Wilvhe's eyes again, I refused to back down, my hand clutching the dagger more tightly. "Don't poison the empress," I insisted. "Let her go."

"Drop. The. Weapon," Wilvhe said.

I didn't move. His gloved hands whipped out quickly, shooting toward my bare arms. My body moved instinctually, a hundred defense lessons and sparring matches guiding my muscles. With a flick of my wrist, I flung the dagger at Wilvhe. I threw all my strength into it, and my aim was precise.

Blood gushed down his armor as the blade pierced his throat. I stepped back as his corpse collapsed, face first, in front of me, arms still extended in his attempt to take my life.

Jaliana's wide eyes and pale face stared at me for one second. Two. Then she vanished deeper into the garden, her slippers gliding and dress rustling softly as she wound her way toward the Dragon Keep.

CHAPTER THIRTY-TWO

Jalie

THERE WAS NO TIME TO wonder why a Forwyn woman had just saved my life. No time to wonder why or how the Teramese had infiltrated our ball, betraying an age-old alliance to seize control of Alrenor. Perhaps their government had grown greedy and had seen an opportunity with the Alrenian Empire torn almost in two. And there was definitely no time to wonder if Kovi or anyone other than the Forwyn woman had seen me escape.

All I could do was follow my original plan. If I could escape the Forwyn and Teramese, if I could steal back one of my dragons, I could find the Alrenian resistance. Together, we could form a plan and take back our empire.

The tang of blood filled my nostrils before I'd even entered the Keep. There I collided with the first of the Teramese kills. It was enough to horrify and sicken me, even if they were Forwyn bodies. Enemy bodies. The true Dragon Keepers lay in tangled, gruesome piles, stripped of their armor, their limbs mangled. Soaking in pools of their own blood, the corpses stared back at me with wide and unseeing eyes.

I gagged and covered my nose, dragging my gaze away. Nausea danced along my tongue as I pressed forward, plunging past the nightmarish sight, forcing myself deeper into the Keep. Shadows swallowed me whole, the darkness like a living thing. Distant shuffles reached my ears. I prayed those noises were from the dragons, not more Teramese waiting to ambush me. My slippers scuffled on the pebbles underfoot, sending them skittering into the descending tunnel. As the metallic scent of blood faded behind me, the acrid odors of smoke and ash rose to take its place. Most of the torches ensconced along the uneven stone walls had gone out, but a few lit my path. The steady rhythm of my breaths rushed loudly in my ears, competing with the rapid beating of my heart.

The air was heavy and still as I entered one of the first rooms off the main tunnel—the armory. Alrenian weapons and dragon scale armor hung on the walls, a treasury laid out for my escape. I tore off my dress and kicked off my slippers, stepping into a comfortable, flexible pair of armored leggings. They fit nearly perfectly. In the dim light, they shone emerald green, shot through with veins of gold. I found the matching tunic, mantle, gloves, helmet, and boots, and hurriedly tugged them on. Last, I secured a belt around my waist and fastened a dagger and sword at my sides.

I met no one as I slipped deeper into the Keep, past the training room and the spaces where some of the other dragons resided, their names marked over the massive doors enclosing them. Somewhere in the distance I heard a few hatchlings playing, claws scraping along the floor and small wings fluttering as they chased one another.

I stopped before the den marked as Ryke's. Drawing a breath as anticipation flooded my veins, I reached out to crank the lever that raised the door. My muscles were unused to the strain after weeks without training, and my body was still weaker than usual after being poisoned. The door groaned and creaked as it lifted, revealing the beautiful green creature waiting within.

Ryke recognized me instantly, and without hesitation, shuffled forward. His eyes gleamed in the starlight flooding through the opening in the ceiling.

Heart leaping, I extended my palm, placing it gently on Ryke's snout. His scales were warm and welcoming. He leaned into my touch, almost knocking me backward with his weight. I laughed, and it echoed through the chamber, startling me after the stillness that had surrounded me all this time.

"Let's get out of here," I murmured to him in Alrenian. Striding to one wall, I retrieved the leather saddle hanging from a hook and brought it toward Ryke. He unfolded his wings a bit and wriggled with excitement. "You're ready for another ride, aren't you?" I asked with a grin.

I could taste my freedom on my tongue, delicious. Intoxicating.

Though it had been years since I'd saddled a dragon, my hands remembered how to fasten and tighten the buckles like I'd just done it yesterday. My fingers were quick and dexterous. Heart light, I inspected my work to ensure it was secure, and then I leaned back to pat Ryke's side.

"We're as ready as we'll ever be."

Movement in the entryway made me freeze. Even my heart stopped for a moment. Before I turned my head, I already knew, deep in my bones, who would be there. Maybe I'd been expecting him all along, knowing that somehow he would break free of the chaos at the Autumn Ball to find and stop me.

The dagger scraped sharply against its sheath as I drew it, pointing its curved edge toward Kovi. His own blade was steady in his hands, darkened with blood as he held it outward. Slowly, carefully, he stepped forward, edging his way into the den.

Ryke snuffled sharply, the scent of blood reaching his nostrils. I felt no fear. He'd bowed to *me* and listened to my orders when Kovi and I had flown. Ryke's loyalty was toward me, and it was Kovi who had reason to be wary of the dragon.

"Come back with me, Jalie," he said, his words steady and quiet, as if he were trying to calm an angry beast. I could hear the unspoken words finishing his statement: *Come willingly, so I don't have to force you to.*

I unleashed a short laugh, squeezing the dagger hilt tighter. "So I can be a prisoner of the Teramese now too? Or another corpse they can add to their pile out there? Tell me, they've already killed some Elders, haven't they?"

"I won't let them touch you," Kovi said, but his expression was tense. Doubtful. He couldn't guarantee anything now that even his people's hold on our empire was crumbling.

Still, all he needed to do was use his magic and command me, and I would be at his mercy. My chest tightened. "You already know how this will end if you keep stepping forward," I said, voice cold. I kept my expression hard, refusing to let him see any hesitation, hoping he couldn't hear the way my blood raced through my veins. "You've been a fool not to fear me before."

Kovi stopped moving but smiled, meeting my gaze unflinchingly. "I already told you," he explained calmly, "I'm not afraid of death."

"But I know you fear for your people," I said, eyes lingering on the blood dripping off his sword. Droplets splattered on the floor, staining the stone a rusty shade. "You'll do anything for them. Just as I'll do anything for mine." I paused, then asked the question that had been churning through my head since the first night I'd met him. The one I'd been too afraid to ask the night before. But now I had to know, had to remind myself in the best way I could that Kovi, gentle as he could be, was my enemy. "How many of my people have you killed?"

I knew the answer could not be zero. Though the Forwyn clung to their own language, religion, and traditions, they'd adopted many Alrenian customs over their generations living among us. There was no doubt in my mind they would have called upon Aerekni Academy graduates at the first sign of an Alrenian uprising or resistance. The newest soldiers were always sent before anyone else. It was a way to test them, to see if they were truly prepared to fight for their people. Kovi would have had to prove himself before he was assigned to me.

There was a pause, a breath as we stared at each other. "Four," he said at last. "Directly. Indirectly…many more."

I spoke through clenched teeth. "Then you understand. My people always come first. I didn't kill you before, but if you force me to, I will now." Every word grated out of my aching throat, but I refused to back down. "Just like your people will always come first for you. There is no room for mercy in war. There *is* no choice for us, Kovi. We have to be monsters, or our people die. Or we die."

Maybe it was my imagination, but for a moment I thought I saw hurt flash across his face. Then it was gone. Jaw set, grip tight on his blade, his eyes flicked from me to the dragon. My heart pounded. If he commanded me with his magic, this was all over.

"Stand down," I ordered, voice quavering. "Your magic might be able to control me, but it's no match for a dragon." It was a guess, one I prayed was true. "If I command him to, Ryke will kill you in an instant."

To my shock, Kovi obeyed. Stone-faced, eyes cold, he stepped back against the wall, leaving the entrance wide open for Ryke and me to leave.

Sheathing my dagger, I sprang into the saddle and strapped myself in. Just before Ryke leapt out into the tunnel, I met Kovi's eyes.

"I'll find you," he said, and I couldn't tell if it was a threat or a promise.

Then Ryke and I were tearing through the wide tunnels of the

Keep, winding upward until we burst out into the night air. A cool breeze tasting of the sea brushed against my face. *"Laeva!"* I commanded, and Ryke plunged off the cliffside, soaring over the city. My heart surged into my throat as Ryke's wings thundered through the air and the wind stung my eyes. *Freedom.*

I didn't spare a glance back at the palace as we swerved northward, leaving the capital behind. There was no time for regret or fear or doubt. No time to waste wondering how my people would defeat both the Forwyn and Teramese. I had an army to find, and a throne to claim.

CHAPTER THIRTY-THREE

Lo

MY MIND REELED, REFUSING TO process what had just happened. The world spun, twisted, giving out beneath me. Spots danced across my vision and my pulse screamed in my ears.

"Elhani spare me," I breathed, but how could he spare me from myself?

All I'd wanted to do was save the empress, to follow his will by attending to his guidespirit and listening to his voice. But now blood was splattered across the front of this fine gown that belonged to someone else. I wore a stolen necklace. I'd trusted a liar who'd just hurled my entire empire into danger—who'd helped foreign warriors invade the palace and seize control, all in a few frenzied moments.

My sisters would never accept me back into the abbey. I'd lost everything. The empire I thought I'd been trying to save was crashing all around me, and everyone I'd wanted to believe in was guilty. Renni and his friends for trying to assassinate the empress. Caesiem for betraying us all. The Elders for craving power more than mercy or our people's safety.

Rage gripped me. I hated them all for what they'd done to my people. For what they'd stolen from me tonight, upending my peaceful, hopeful life. There was nothing left.

Curse Alrenor, I thought darkly. Perhaps we Forwyn had never been meant to try to make this land our home. Maybe we'd always been meant to return to Forwyth, to leave this familiar empire and its cruel, bloody memories behind.

Tears burning trails down my cheeks, I stumbled half-blindly through the garden, desperate to flee this nightmarish place.

In the middle of the Teramese rise to power, I was no one. Just a shadow slipping through the grounds and darting for the gates. Steel on steel rang out behind me; angered and agonized cries pierced the air. But it was all distant, faraway. Disconnected from me.

I'd given years of my life to the false idea that I could make Alrenor my home, that I could help bring my people a better life. Now all I wanted was to watch this palace burn to the ground. To leave the Elders to their wretched fates.

As I wound my way around the last turn in the path, entering the outer wall's shadow, a stunning view of the city lay before me. It flickered with a warm yellow light from countless candles burning in windows. Chimney smoke curled toward the stars. The night had turned cool, the breeze feeling a bit more like autumn's kiss than the earlier humid air. Beyond, the seas glistened silver.

My gut churned when I glimpsed the foreign ships already flooding the harbor, all flying the red flag of Teramyl. They weren't even trying to hide their presence, or the fact that they had an entire fleet here, prepared to overrun us completely.

"Lo!" Caesiem's voice shattered through my thoughts, bringing me back sharply to the present. To the warm blood staining my bodice and the sweat trickling down my back. To the livid feeling coiling and straining within me like a snake, poised and ready to strike.

I hadn't felt this angry in years, since I'd longed for vengeance against Karye for my brother's death. I'd buried it so deeply that I'd fooled myself. All this time I'd thought I was full of indignation, a righteous passion to rescue my people and redeem my empire. But after all these years, it was plain, ugly fury that drove me. A need to push the nightmares back and fight against the world.

Maybe I'd never wanted to see the empire unified and healed. Maybe I'd always wanted to watch it burn.

"Lo," Caesiem gasped, closer now. I refused to look back at him. I couldn't stand to see his face.

"I should have let you die," I said, letting every ounce of my hatred pour into my words. "I should have left you to bleed to death in the streets that night."

"Lo, I had to—there was no other way …"

"I don't want to hear your excuses, and I don't want to hear you say my name ever again!" I cried, stepping forward. His hand on my shoulder stopped me.

"Please, just listen to me, just this once, and then I'll never try to explain again," Caesiem begged.

"Let me go!" I whirled on him and slammed a fist into his face. He reeled back as blood streamed from his nose.

For a second, we stared at each other, Caesiem wiping his sleeve across his face. I panted, shaking out my fingers, knuckles already aching from the impact.

"I deserved that," he mumbled.

And then I was running, sprinting like I never had before in my life. I pounded down the pathway that spilled into the city streets. My steps echoed along the cobblestones, passing closed shops and deserted squares, darkened alleys and stray animals lurking in the shadows. Everything rushed by in a frenzied blur. I couldn't think straight. I was numb, hollow, lost.

All too soon the abbey loomed before me, and what once had been my refuge, my home, made me feel tense and sick. Darkened windows and stonework towered over me, foreboding. It was as if the building itself were shutting me out, demanding I go elsewhere.

The door flung open with a pitiful groan. It wasn't as late as I thought it was, for the sisters' voices, raised in song, echoed from within the sanctuary. Every shadow in the hallway seemed darker, deeper. I prayed I could slip into my room and gather my things without being noticed. I longed to be a wraith, unseen and unheard as I took everything that still belonged to me in this world and ran from the life I knew.

I couldn't focus on Elhani's voice to make myself invisible. I could only cling to the shadows as I darted up the steps. When I entered my room, it already felt cold and unlived in. Every inch was achingly familiar and comforting, but foreign. No longer mine.

Gathering a bag, I began packing. I collected the few coins I had, enough to buy a few nights' board at a cheap inn while I determined what to do next. I tore my dress and necklace off and slipped into a shirt and pants, adding spare outfits and a pair of sandals to my bag. The outfits were in nun grey, but they'd have to do for now. Then I kicked off my slippers and tugged on my boots. Considering the necklace I'd tossed to the floor, I picked it back up and slipped it inside with the clothes. Maybe I could sell it. Finally, I gathered my gold ribbons from where I'd left them on my dresser and tied them around my neck.

"Lo?" Pauni'a was quiet, uncertain. "I didn't feel well, so I stayed in my room tonight… I didn't expect you back already. What are you doing…?"

She hovered in my doorway, a woven purple and green blanket draped over her shoulders. Her glassy-looking eyes fastened on my bag and then the bloodied dress I'd discarded on the floor. Her mouth dropped open. "What happened?" she breathed.

I blinked back my gathering tears. "No time to explain," I said, hating myself for the sharpness in my tone. If I didn't speak harshly, I'd break down into sobs. I'd cling to Pauni'a until Naina came and found what I'd done, and my sisters all threw me out of the abbey themselves. I couldn't bear to see their looks of horror, disappointment, and shame. I couldn't let that happen. I had to leave—now.

Pauni'a didn't argue with me. "Where will you go?" she whispered, shivering and gathering her blanket more closely about herself. She must have caught an illness from one of the sick families we'd been tending to recently.

"I'll figure it out," I murmured. "Don't worry about me, Nia." I finally dared to look her in the eyes, to see the tears shining in her gaze. I bit back my grief. "Goodbye. Take care of yourself." I swallowed. "War is coming to Alrenor. The palace was invaded tonight. Don't get involved. Don't let our sisters get involved. Care for the poor and sick, and stay here, where you're safe."

Pauni'a kissed her fingertips and pressed them to her heart in an old Forwyn gesture. A goodbye. "May Elhani hold you in his hands," she whispered, her eyes glittering with tears, "and the guidespirits lead you home." Her voice cracked on that last word—home. The place I was leaving behind.

"You too," I whispered, and then, before I could give into tears, I shoved past her and darted down the steps.

Drawing a steadying breath, I pulled open the front door and sprinted out into the night. The shadowy streets stretched before me like foreign roads, my familiar routes feeling strange and foreboding. Everything looked different now that I was an outsider, belonging nowhere. The city I'd called home all my life melted into a streaky mess from my tears. I settled my bag on my shoulders and ran into the night.

This. This was normal for me. The steady echo of my footsteps. The rhythm of my breathing. The drumming of my heart. The pulsing adrenaline that steadied my emotions and cleared my head.

I was always running from something.

TO BE CONTINUED

NOTE FROM THE AUTHOR

Thank you for reading *Empire of Dragons*! If you have a moment, please leave an HONEST review on Amazon.

The empire has fallen. A new one will rise.

Guilty...

Lo abandoned everything—her friends, her way of life, and perhaps even her soul—to save her people. But a shocking betrayal left her reeling...and the Alrenian Empire in enemy hands. Against all odds, she's determined to continue fighting for her people's freedom. Playing the role of spy and deceiver, Lo plots among her enemies by day and dodges her would-be killers by night. Unfortunately that means staying close to the thief who stole her heart—and her empire.

Haunted...

Caesiem has spent his life fighting to survive. Life has always forced him to make the hard decisions—kill or be killed, take or be left to die. Even after being adopted into the imperial family, his every decision has hinged on keeping the struggling Teramese people alive. But as he and his army establish a new empire and prepare for a looming war, he begins to question everything he ever thought he knew about his allegiances— and his own identity.

Dedicated...

Kovi promised nothing would get in the way of his decision to serve and protect his people. He has always been the perfect soldier—no matter the price, or the pain. So when the Teramese make an offer that could spare Forwyn lives, he knows his loyalty is to his people...not his heart.

Afraid...

In the fight to regain her throne, Jalie thought winning her freedom would be the hardest step. But now she faces threats from all sides—even from fellow Alrenians who label her as weak and unworthy. Desperation leads her once again to Nesrelle, Queen of Death, who offers a bargain…at an uncertain price.

All have fought for their people. But will their sacrifices be worth the cost?

EMPIRE OF TRAITORS

Book Two of the CURSED EMPIRE series

ACKNOWLEDGMENTS

There's always this fear when I begin a list like this that I'll leave someone out. I think that's because so many people contribute to a book, even if it's in some small, less definable way from years ago. It could be the fact that my parents read to me as a child, or introduced me to *The Lord of the Rings*. Or the influence of my brothers when they let me read drafts of my earliest fantasy novel aloud and offered feedback. Or suggestions made by an English professor in a class I took longer ago than I care to mention.

But there are also tangible ways many people have assisted me with the writing and publishing process of this book. First and foremost, Julienne Calhoun and Sheree Whitelock have been by my side from the beginning as alpha readers and editors, as well as cheerleaders, idea soundboards, encouragers, and so much more. I can't thank you enough for believing in me!

Sheree, thank you for also being my social media/marketing brainstormer and helper throughout all of this. So many times I was floundering, and you got me through the overwhelm.

I'd also love to give a special thank you to my friend Malcolm Carter, who has offered so much encouragement throughout this process. It's hard to let imposter syndrome defeat you when you have someone sending you inspirational messages and telling you that your dream isn't too big!

Also thank you to my husband, for tolerating and helping me with all the weird things marketing a book entails, like stacking books and cosplaying characters. You knew I was a nerd when you married me...

There's also my incredible beta reader team: Lianne Anta, Tricia Ghent, Monica Khan, Maura Klotz, Lorraine Larson, Maren Bivar Letemple, and Sara Smith! Words can't express how much you have helped me along this journey and shaped this story. Your feedback and excitement has been invaluable and contagious!

I also have had an incredible street team, consisting of Angela Cronin, Tricia Ghent, Julie Janis, Maura Klotz, Maren Bivar Letemple, Anya Phillips, Vanessa Rasanen, Sara Smith, and DK Suaidah. You've been so enthusiastic and supportive, and I can't tell you how much it means to me! You've done so much to spread the word about this book, and it's been an incredible experience and a privilege to work with you.

Of course, I can't go without acknowledging how grateful I am to God for the blessing to be able to write and share my stories with the world.

And last but not least, I have to give a tremendous thank you to my readers. Whether this is the first book you've ever read from me or you've been on this journey with me from the beginning, I appreciate you so much. Thank you!

ABOUT THE AUTHOR

Rachel L. Schade was born on the first day of summer in a small town in Michigan. She attended The Ohio State University to learn how to write obnoxiously long papers, cite people who use big words, and discuss her passion: books. She has a great love for the color blue, sunshine, chocolate, and not folding her laundry. Currently she lives with her husband and fur babies, and surrounds herself with books and coffee on a regular basis.

You can email Rachel at rachelschade@gmail.com, or find her on Facebook and Goodreads: Rachel L. Schade, and on Instagram: @rachelschadeauthor.

www.rachelschadeauthor.com